MIST

Lark has been wandering the country for many years, with no real place to call home. Then she meets Matthew Williams, a Canadian who has inherited a run-down hill farm in North Wales. Young and enthusiastic, Matthew has no knowledge of farming and no experience of living in the countryside. Entranced by the beauty and wildness of the place, Lark agrees to help, and together they throw themselves into getting the farm onto its feet. Until a terrible accident brings Matthew's father over from Canada, and suddenly none of their lives will be the same.

MIST

MIST

by

Mary Fitzgerald

Magna Large Print Books
Long Preston, North Yorkshire,
BD23 4ND, England.

British Library Cataloguing in Publication Data.

Fitzgerald, Mary
    Mist.

    A catalogue record of this book is
    available from the British Library

    ISBN   978-0-7505-4192-3

First published in Great Britain in 2015 by Arrow Books

Cover illustration by arrangement with Arcangel Images

Published in Large Print 2016 by arrangement with
Arrow Books, an imprint of The Random House Group Ltd.

Magna Large Print is an imprint of Library Magna Books Ltd.

Printed and bound in Great Britain by
T.J. (International) Ltd., Cornwall, PL28 8RW

Prologue

Biting, sleety rain blew across the mountainside, dousing the already soaked fields and refilling the half-frozen puddles in the muddy farmyard. In the lower fields the sheep huddled miserably against the stone walls, half-grown lambs pressed against their mothers, silently enduring the familiar climatic conditions. No other animal or bird stirred on this Snowdonian afternoon. The rabbits had gone to ground and the plovers and seagulls who usually whistled and cried across the high moorland were sheltering in their nests.

Above the fields, the hill was shrouded in mist. It was March and a cold spring was following a cold winter. There had been unusually high winds this year which had brought snow, not only to the tops but throughout the valley. On several occasions the old man had awoken to a still and blanketed yard. He had seen it all before, of course, but this year it had seemed worse somehow, and he was very tired.

Now, in the rain, he was struggling to rebuild a dry-stone wall next to the dilapidated gate. He heaved and grunted as he pulled the heavy stones on top of each other, carefully positioning them so that they would fit properly and stay upright and steady without mortar. He needed the wall, otherwise the sheep would stray out and be all over the county.

'*Duw,*' he gasped, calling on his God more in anger than in prayer. His head was swimming and the rain, driving into his face, confused him. The old dog, who had reluctantly followed his master into the field, lay close by. He heard the imprecations but ignored them. They meant nothing to him. These were not orders and certainly not the terms of affection which he occasionally received. He kept his one good eye on the sheep but otherwise made himself into a small ball, fast against the boulders, better sheltered than the man.

There was a sudden choking noise and the dog looked up. The man had stopped working and was leaning against the wall, trying to catch his breath. As the dog watched, the farmer began to slide down until he came to rest in a sitting position, back to the stones and face looking upward towards the misty hilltop. The dog got up and walked cautiously towards his old master.

Oh, it was hard to see up through the mist, but he knew his eyes were fixed on the right place. He could feel his breathing getting shallower but the pain had gone, and anyway, it didn't matter now. He didn't notice the sheep shuffling towards the gap in the wall but felt the dog's freezing nose as it pushed into his palm. 'Good dog,' he muttered soundlessly, and weakly made a cup with his hand for the dog to push against.

The rain had stopped and the mist was lifting when the battered Land Rover splashed through the puddles in the yard.

'Geraint!' called the young man who jumped

out of the cab. 'Where are you, man? Your sheep are all over the road!'

The dog barked and the man looked up to the hillside. 'Jesus,' he breathed and ran across the yard and up to the field.

'Oh God,' he said angrily, as he knelt beside the sitting figure on the wet grass. He took off his jacket and wrapped it closely around the stiff, cold shoulders. 'Geraint, man, wait while I call the ambulance.'

The old man licked his crusted lips slowly and gazed past the youngster's concerned face towards the hilltop.

'She's coming, can't you see? There, where the mist is clearing.'

The younger man frowned but glanced briefly over his shoulder to the empty hillside where shredded cloud swirled in the wind. 'Hush now, man, I'm just going to the house to phone. I'll be back straight away.'

But the old eyes were not focusing. 'Oh, *cariad*,' he whispered. 'Oh, *cariad anwyl*, I can see you.'

The dog began to howl as the young neighbour came running out of the farmhouse. He slowed his steps, the blankets he'd hastily pulled off the bed drooping from his arms. There was no need to hurry now, nor to try to provide warmth. Just decency.

Chapter One

The June heat was bouncing off the pavements this Friday afternoon. Usually a cooling breeze blew off the water, providing some respite from the brief, intense Canadian summer. But not today. The lake was still and glittering, its brightness emphasised by the black clouds rolling up far to the south. There would be a storm tonight.

Downtown, the city was quiet, the shops half-empty and the streets clearing. People were leaving work early in order to spend a long weekend at the shore, or perhaps inland at one of the woodland campsites. There was so much to do, and such a short summertime to do it in.

John Williams stood at the vast window of his office suite, ten floors up on the corner of Yonge and Bloor. He watched the scene below without interest. Behind him, a conversation was taking place and he was giving its participants time to discuss the project in relative privacy. Privacy was afforded anyway because they were speaking in another language, but he was also giving them a chance to use gestures to express their approval. He didn't imagine that there would be disapproval. His design was faultless. This would be the seventh shopping mall he'd designed, and the scale model, laid out on a table in the middle of the room, was undoubtedly the best he'd done.

He leant forward slightly. There was activity in

the street below. A cab had shunted into the back of a saloon car at the traffic lights. *Inattention,* he thought, watching as the cabbie slowly emerged from his vehicle and moved forward to survey the damage. Even from this far up, John could see the taxi driver raise his arms in exasperation and stare fiercely at the car in front. The car door opened slowly and a large, blue-overalled leg appeared.

John felt the first frisson of excitement. *Shit! This should be fun.*

'We wondered if parking would be a problem.' The voice behind him was momentarily confusing. Of course, that was it. The cabbie had been looking for a parking space and hadn't noticed the lights changing.

'Got to have been that.' He spoke out loud and leant further forward to watch the unfolding scene below. The saloon driver was enormous and was even now grabbing the cabbie by his lapels.

'Mr Williams, did you understand me?' Mr Li stood up abruptly and pointed at the model. 'We are concerned about the parking. There should be spaces for at least two thousand vehicles. This will be a very large complex.' Mr Li and his colleagues had come all the way from Hong Kong, representing a consortium of Chinese entrepreneurs.

A police car was cruising down the street now. John waited for it to stop. A small crowd had gathered, watching as the two men squared up to each other. The saloon driver was jabbing his finger at the cabbie's face and as John gazed, the finger was folded into a fist and a punch was thrown.

11

'Christl!' John waited excitedly for the retaliation.

'Mr Williams!' This time the voice was accompanied by a hand which discreetly patted John's sleeve. It could have been an electric shock. Startled, John turned round to face his visitors, his confusion still showing.

'Sorry, Mr Li. I was miles away,' he lied, a flush coming to his face. He gave himself a slight shake and walked into the centre of the beautifully furnished office to where the other two men were standing.

The model dominated the room, exquisitely constructed by a craftsman who had followed the design perfectly. John accepted that other firms now presented their work in the form of a computer-generated movie, and he suspected that was probably the way to go, but he liked the models, and so far, none of his clients had found them less than satisfactory.

'Yes, parking, gentlemen.' John, now back on track, lifted away a section of the model and demonstrated a capacious underground car park which would run the length of the building. He showed how the egress would be obtained over a mile away, close to the railway station so that potential customers could take their cars all the way to the complex or park and ride.

The Chinese became interested again, forgetting, John hoped, his earlier lapse. He took the opportunity to stroll once more to the window and quickly glance out. The street was clear: the damaged cars had been moved and the protagonists had disappeared. He sighed and turned back to his guests to find them standing in a line watching him. Mr Li was frowning slightly and one of the others said something in Cantonese which deepened the frown.

'Is there anything else I can tell you about?' John strove to keep the desperation out of his voice. He wasn't on top of his game today. He knew it and could see that they were uneasy.

'We would have to consult with...'

The shrill ring of the telephone on John's desk broke into Mr Li's quietly voiced note of caution.

John gestured an apology. 'Excuse me for a moment, gentlemen,' he said, moving to the phone deck on his desk. He pressed the answer button and picked up the receiver. 'Yes, Annette, what is it? I did say that I wasn't to be disturbed.'

In the outer office, the middle-aged secretary sighed and dabbed a paper tissue at the open neck of her blouse. A sheen of menopausal perspiration was gathering again and she knew that any slight argument would make it worse.

'Mr Williams, I'm very sorry, but there's an important call for you. It's your son.'

John held the phone close to his ear and lowered his voice. 'Matt? Oh for Christ's sake, tell him to call back later. I can't talk now.' He looked up and smiled confidently at the clients. 'Be right with you, Mr Li.'

Annette screwed the tissue into a little ball before continuing. The urgency in her voice was unmistakable. 'He can't call you back, sir. He says he's in a phone booth at Heathrow airport, London. He's on his way to some place in Wales. He said something about buying a car.'

13

'Jesus!' John looked back at his clients and arranged his features into an apologetic smile. 'Sorry, gentlemen, you'll have to excuse me for a moment. I've just had a very urgent call. The minister must talk to me now.' He shook his head in mock despair. 'These politicians, eh? Can't be kept waiting a second. Um ... Annette will bring in some refreshment. Coffee or tea? Yes, tea, of course.'

He nodded to the three Chinese who were standing by the model watching him. Mr Li had taken off his glasses and was polishing them vigorously with a special optical cloth which he had produced from his inside pocket.

'I won't be a moment,' John repeated and quickly put the receiver back on the deck. He didn't notice that in his haste he'd pressed the 'conference' button.

His secretary was standing by her desk, phone in hand, her face flushed. She was anxious to get to the washroom and run some cold water on her wrists. *Next week,* she promised herself again, *I'll go to the doctor and get some of that hormone treatment. Never mind what Mother says about it.*

John grabbed the phone from her hand. 'Go and get them some drinks. Non-alcoholic. Give them that green tea we bought in Chinatown.'

She nodded and went towards the little office kitchen. She was not upset with her boss. He was, unusually in her experience, very easy to get on with and not a bit arty considering that he was a prize-winning architect. *If anything,* she thought, as she opened the kitchen door, *I'd rather be at work than home with Mother.*

14

John sat on Annette's desk and loosened his tie. 'Matt? What's going on, for Christ's sake?'

Eight o'clock at night at Heathrow was as busy as eight o'clock in the morning at any other airport. The holiday season was in full swing and people were thronging the concourse of Terminal Three, noisily expectant and excited. Matthew Williams leant against the cover of the phone booth and placed a booted foot on top of his bulging rucksack. He was wearing the standard student outfit of jeans and sweatshirt, with a waterproof jacket tied carelessly to one strap of his rucksack. He was fair and blue-eyed like his mother. People, seeing the family together, often remarked that he was the image of her, looking in vain for some hint of John's Welsh genes in his son. There was none. Except, sometimes, the stubborn set of his head and the way he planted his feet firmly apart when he was about to challenge his father. He was taller than John, but not noticeably so because the older man was heavier, with big shoulders and strong arms, a legacy of generations of farmers.

'Hi, Dad. Well, I guess I did it.'

'Did what? Where the hell are you?'

Matthew gazed out at the concourse and heaved a sigh. 'You know where. I told Annette. Anyway, I'm spending the night in London and then going on to the farm in the morning. I collected the deeds and the keys from the attorney, yesterday. Oh, and in case you're worrying, I've got dough. I took my savings out.'

'Jesus!' John raked his fingers through his thick, greying thatch of hair, then brought his hand

15

down with a thump on the secretary's desk. He leant over and quietly opened the door to his office and took a peek inside. The clients were now standing by the window looking out on the Toronto skyline. They seemed to have lost interest in the model. He closed the door.

'Look, Matt, I'm in conference now and it's important. Get the next flight back and we can talk about this when you get home. You can go to Wales for a holiday at the end of the semester. It's only a few weeks.'

An elderly tourist whom Matt had beaten to the phone stared relentlessly at him. When Matt turned to look at him, the old man made a little play in sign language of urgently wanting to use the phone. Matt grinned and returned to his conversation. 'No, Dad. I'm not going back to college. It's a waste of time. I'm not interested in being a lawyer; you know I despise all that sort of crap. I'm going to work the land like Grandfather did. He knew I would. That's why he left me the land – not you.'

The muscle in John's cheek twitched and Annette's pencil, which he'd been tapping nervously on the edge of the desk, snapped in his hand. 'You stupid bastard.' He didn't bother to keep his voice down and Annette, just emerging from the kitchen, retreated abruptly, preferring to keep out of the way while a row was going on.

'How can you be so idiotic? You never met your grandfather and you know nothing about farming. Now get the next flight back like I told you and don't argue. God, haven't we had it up to here with your bloody stupid behaviour? How

16

can I ever get anything done when I have to spend most of my time bailing you out of prison or apologising to the various authorities you seem to enjoy upsetting? Now, for once, do as I goddam tell you.'

Matt leant down to pick up his rucksack. 'Sorry, Dad, nothing doing,' he said and nodded at the tourist who was still waiting. 'I'll be in touch. Tell Ma.' He replaced the receiver and made a mock bow to the old man before jauntily walking out onto the concourse.

In the outer office John stood with the dead phone clenched in his hand. He felt like tearing the machine out of its socket and throwing it violently against the wall. His face worked as he struggled inwardly to regain self-control, and it took several deep breaths before he was able to slowly and deliberately replace the handset.

Annette bustled out of the kitchen bearing a tray loaded with cups and saucers. She shot a nervous glance in his direction and a flush suffused her face and neck. He watched motionless as she juggled with the tray, trying to manage it with one hand and open the office door with the other.

'Here, let me,' he said finally, opening the door to his office and ushering her in before him. He arranged an enthusiastic smile on his face and tightened up his tie before striding into the room. 'Now, gentlemen,' he said, 'I haven't yet explained fully the solar heating plan.'

Chapter Two

Later that afternoon, Lydia Williams sighed and sat up in bed. She was an attractive woman, naturally blonde, although that was fading a little, now that she'd entered her forties. But her figure was good, helped by regular sessions at the gym and her ability to live permanently on a strict diet.

Her clothes, a smart royal-blue suit and silk slip, hung tidily in the open wardrobe. Underwear lay on a chair, on top of her leather purse. High-heeled shoes were placed neatly, side by side, beneath the chair. The room in the Pine Lodge Motel – a cheap overnighter on the outskirts of the city – might be basic, but she had her standards.

Beside her in the rumpled bed, the young man who had just made inexpert love to her lay on his back staring at the grubby ceiling. He reached out to the bedside table and opened a packet of gum. Lydia watched out of the corner of her eye as he withdrew a strip, unwrapped it and carefully folded it into his mouth. She gave an imperceptible shudder as he proceeded to chew, noisily and with his mouth open. No one could claim that he was sophisticated or even basically well bred, but then that didn't matter. That was not what she wanted. She drew the sheets above her breasts and glanced quickly at her wristwatch.

The boy turned to look at her. 'Gee, that was great, Mrs Williams.'

Lydia clucked her tongue and glared at him. 'Jason, will you for Christ's sake stop calling me Mrs Williams! This is not some scene from *The Graduate* and I'm not Mrs Robinson.'

He looked puzzled. She was always talking about things he'd never heard of.

'Mrs Robinson?'

'Oh God! Don't tell me you've never heard of *The Graduate?* Dustin Hoffman. Simon and Garfunkel music. It was a movie.'

He considered, chewing harder and drumming his hard young fingers on the rickety bedside table. 'I don't think I caught that one. I saw Paul Simon on the TV a couple of years back. He's the same guy, ain't he?'

'Yes. Yes, he is,' Lydia sighed, wondering whether to explain further. She decided against it. 'Oh, never mind.' She got out of bed and walked over to the chair where she took her purse from under the tiny pile of underwear. Opening it she withdrew her mobile phone and switched it on. 'Will I see you here next Friday?' she asked, turning back to the bed and her twenty-year-old lover.

He looked embarrassed and sat up, allowing the bedclothes to fall away from his body. Lydia silently sucked in her breath. He was beautiful to look at.

'The thing is,' he said nervously, 'I got football practice starting this weekend. Coach says that if I want to make the first team permanently, I gotta give up outside interests.' He paused and looked at her pleadingly. 'Just for the season.'

Lydia slowly picked up her pants and bra and started to get dressed. She gave a short laugh. 'Well, I could be called lots of things, I suppose. Outside interest is as good as any.' She went to the wardrobe and unhooked her suit. There were a couple of tiny flecks of grit on the jacket. *Must have come from this filthy room,* she thought angrily. She gave the suit a shake and flicked her slim, well-manicured fingernails at the dirt. 'It was getting boring, anyway, Jason. Let's just call it a day.'

His cheerful reply came just too quickly for comfort. 'Oh great, Mrs Wi– I mean, Lydia.' He jumped out of bed, grabbed his jeans from the floor beside him and dragged them on.

She watched his muscles ripple and flex as he slid into his T-shirt then bent over to pull on white socks and tyre-soled boots. His hair was too short to require combing, but she knew that his haste to get away would have negated that exercise anyway. She shrugged and zipped up her skirt, smoothing it over her neat hips and pulling it straight over her flat, girlish abdomen.

The sudden trill of her phone broke the silence and she hurried over and picked it up. 'Hello? Yes, John, it's been switched on all afternoon. It's that damned company you bought it from. It's never worked properly.'

She listened for a while and then broke in. 'What? In England? Wales? What the hell is he doing there?'

Jason had finished dressing and stood awkwardly by the bed, listening to the one-sided conversation. If he got a move on, he could get out a movie and drive over to the guys' apartment before they went out for the evening. He couldn't drink, now he was in training, but he and the guys knew how to have a good time. He wandered towards the door, making sure to knock against the bedside table so that Lydia would look round and see him.

She was pulling on her shoes, holding the phone under her chin. 'Well, you know whose fault it is,' she was saying scornfully. Jason thought that the 'John' must be her husband. She never mentioned him, but one of his friends knew the son from Little League days. Stuck-up kid, he'd said, always wanting to be different.

'It's your fault, yours and that ridiculous old man who gave him the land. You wouldn't listen to me when I said that Matthew should sell it straight away.'

She was frowning, obviously furious, and Jason was now really anxious to leave. In this mood, she reminded him of his Math teacher and that wasn't a good memory. He put a hand on the door handle and looked back over his shoulder. She was looking at him.

'Anyway, we'll discuss this when I get home. Yes … I've finished. The project has been put to bed and I was just getting up to go.' She smiled at Jason and waved her hand dismissively before returning to her conversation. 'Yes. I'll be home in half an hour.'

Jason heard the beep of the phone being switched off, as he went through the door. He wondered briefly about returning to say goodbye but rejected the thought almost at once, and

21

hurried to his car and freedom.

Alone in the dingy motel room, Lydia walked into the bathroom and sat on the round plastic stool in front of the fly-specked mirror. She could smell mould and looked up at the ceiling above the shower cubicle. There it was, grey and spreading, unattended by the negligent owners of the cheap establishment. She flinched and looked down, meeting herself in the mirror. Her face, always so animated in company, stared back. It was flat and solemn in repose, mouth turned down and eyes blank. The neon light didn't help, of course. It showed up ageing lines and cast odd shadows, and made her almost unrecognisable to herself. Was this the person she had become?

She took a brush from her purse and smoothed her fine blonde hair into a neat bob. Her eyes looked bluer again after she had reapplied eyeliner and mascara, and lipstick brightened her face. But it was only when she changed her expression that she looked glamorous again. She smiled at herself as she straightened her jacket, and taking a last look round the room, she picked up the keys and left.

Three thousand miles east and four hours on, it was late evening.

'Come on, be a sport.' The drunken guitar player pulled vaguely at the beaded jacket of the young woman standing next to him on the crowded festival field. She ignored him and continued to push her few belongings into a dirty green rucksack.

'You'll love it on the Isle of Wight, best gig ever. Better than Glastonbury.' He sat down suddenly

22

as his legs crumpled under him. He'd been drink-ing all day; cans of lager bought with the few quid he'd earned busking on his way to the festival. He would carry on until he either passed out or ran out of money. Earlier, he'd bought some pot, but that had been stolen within minutes of his putting it in his pocket and he hadn't bothered to get any more. He preferred to drink, anyway. Now he watched the girl.

She had finished her packing and straightened up. 'Well, I'm off,' she said, with a slight smile. 'Have a good life.'

'Oh please, don't go.' His whine was pathetic.

She looked at him, wondering now why she had stayed with him for so long.

Now he started to cry, drunken, blubbering tears which fell unwiped onto his beer-splattered T-shirt. People standing and sitting close to them looked briefly at him but soon turned away, more interested in the faraway band and the giant TV screens.

The girl gave him one last look before thread-ing her way slowly through the crowd. It was dark, the floodlights had come on around the field and the noise was overpowering. A lorry, having unloaded several hundred crates of lager, was struggling across the churned-up track behind her and she moved aside to let it pass. It was without really thinking that she put up her thumb as it drew level.

'I'm only going to the depot, love,' the driver said kindly, 'but it'll be a few miles on your way.'

She heaved a great sigh and settled into the padded cab seat. 'That'll do,' she said.

Chapter Three

Matthew made good progress up the motorway, easily following the road signs and enjoying the sense that he was on an adventure. The weather was fine, a cloudless sky and very little wind. When he stopped at the motorway restaurant, he pulled off his sweatshirt and turned his face to the sun so that the warmth soaked into his body. He felt a little jet-lagged and would have stayed on in the Bayswater Road hotel for another day if it hadn't been so expensive. It would have been fun to look around London and take in the tourist sites, but after a few moments' indecision, he decided to get on with his mission. So, after a surprisingly good breakfast, he had taken the Tube to a garage in Hendon, recommended by the Asian owner of the hotel. There, with a minimum of fuss, he handed over two thousand pounds and received in exchange a four-year-old Citroën.

The car went well, swaying a little when passed by the enormous trucks which were pounding their way north, but otherwise keeping up a steady seventy-five miles an hour without any strain. He put his favourite CD in the slot and drove along, totally unconcerned about the impact his sudden departure would have on his parents.

When he thought about how he'd left, he grinned. He'd done it well, in his opinion.

Planned and executed in the space of three weeks, and without anyone finding out. The attorney had tried to be difficult, wanting to check with John or Lydia before handing over the deeds and keys to the farm, but Matthew had attended enough lectures at Law School to be sure of his ground. He'd pointed out that he'd reached his twenty-first birthday and was of sound mind, and then made mild threats about confidentiality. The young attorney made no further objection and produced the documents. He had briefly considered telling his principal, knowing that the two families were friends, but within a week he had been transferred to the Ottawa office and forgotten all about it.

Organising the money had been easy, too. He'd used the education fund arranged by his parents years ago. They had continued to supply him with a regular generous allowance but had stipulated that he couldn't use the capital until he had reached his twenty-first birthday or had finished his education. Well, his birthday had been in May and he had decided to leave university. The money was now his, to do with as he liked. And, he thought, looking out of the windscreen at the view ahead, he was going to enjoy himself.

It had been a warm year so far in southern Britain and now, in June, early summer was well advanced. The oak and sycamore trees which studded the fields on either side of the motorway were flourishing. Pinkish-coloured young shoots had changed into bright green; the trees were full and spreading and on this early afternoon were casting fat shadows on the fields. Black-and-white cows grazed peacefully on verdant meadows, and villages and farm settlements dominated the skyline. Matthew thought that the whole area looked like one of the pictures from the English Heritage calendar that his criminal law tutor had on her wall. She was English and, although married and resident in Canada for twenty years, had kept up her connections, It was views such as this that he had stared at whilst trying to keep awake during her boring seminars. Now he was driving through one. *It's like jumping into a picture,* he thought, with a shiver of excitement. *Anything might happen.*

It was on the roundabout just west of Shrewsbury that he saw her: a tall figure in dirty combat trousers, army boots and a T-shirt. She had a small backpack slung easily over one shoulder and stood watching the traffic with a thumb out for lifts. All the cars passed her by without, it seemed, a second look, but she appeared not to care. She just remained on the grass verge, upright and determined. The most remarkable thing about her, Matthew noticed as he approached, was her hair. It was long and knotted into untidy dreadlocks and dyed red and green in patches.

Wow! Matthew thought as he passed her slowly and saw the ring through her nose. *Cool!*

He had gone a few yards up the road when he decided to stop. *What the hell,* he thought, *she might be interesting.* He leant out of the window and yelled over his shoulder, 'Want a ride?'

She walked up to the car and nodded. 'Thanks.'

'I'm heading for North Wales,' Matthew said. 'I

can drop you off somewhere on the way. Where d'you want?'

The girl opened the passenger door and got in. She arranged the backpack on the floor beneath her feet and fastened the seat belt. 'Just carry on driving,' she said. 'I'll let you know,' and she closed her eyes and settled back in the seat.

'Oh.' Matthew felt cheated. He wanted to talk, to tell someone what he'd done and what he planned to do. It wouldn't have mattered who he told; she would have done as well as anyone. But she wasn't going to play ball. Looking over a few minutes after he'd set off again, he saw that she was asleep. That was not fair. Definitely not fair.

At the same time as Matthew was driving over the border into Wales, his parents were facing each other across the granite-topped kitchen table in their house in Rosedale. This had been their home for the last fifteen years, an over-large house in a smart suburb of Toronto which they had decorated and furnished with care and great style. It had been featured in several magazines as an example of modernity blended with comfort, and Lydia loved it.

At first it had been a hobby, a way of filling the hours of spare time she had after Matthew started school. She loved trawling the small shops and craft centres in the city looking for special pieces and interesting fabrics. Soon she was travelling further afield, to other provinces, and in the last few years had flown three or four times a year to New York to look in and sometimes buy at the exquisite stores on Fifth Avenue. A few of her

27

friends had asked her advice on their homes and she now had a small, exclusive interior-decorating business. But her main concern was her own home; she loved decorating it and making it as comfortable and beautiful as possible.

The objets d'art didn't come cheap, but John was doing well and wasn't mean. If he'd lost interest in the house, he didn't let that limit Lydia.

Now they sat in their much-photographed steel and granite kitchen, a place where very little cooking took place, nursing tall, thin glasses of vodka. Lydia took swift puffs of her cigarette, holding it delicately in her fine fingers.

'Well, what have you done about it?' she asked, rattling the ice cubes in her glass and staring at the pattern on the table.

'Nothing, yet.'

'Nothing, yet,' Lydia mimicked. 'Typical!'

'What d'you want me to do? The boy was twenty-one last month. He owns the farm; the money he's taken out is his.' John took a pencil out of his pocket and wound it in and out of his fingers in a familiar gesture that Lydia found more and more irritating. 'Anyway,' he continued, 'I'm no longer responsible for him, thank Christ.'

Lydia puffed harder on her cigarette. 'The boy? The boy? It's your son we're talking about. *Our* son who's throwing his life away. Not some jerk with no prospects or education.'

'Oh, don't be so dramatic.' John was wearily scornful. 'He's not throwing his life away. He's just ... well, he's just gone away for a while.'

'Jesus! Away for a while?' Lydia's voice cut the

air and her thin mouth curled in contempt. 'You sound like a commercial for a cheap funeral parlour. Matthew has walked out of his university course. He's gone off to some deadbeat farm in the wilds. What about his degree? He was only months off getting it. What about that job I had lined up for him in Fred's company? You know how I worked to get him that.'

'Yeah, we all know what you did to get him that job!' John pushed himself out of the wood and steel chair and walked towards the door to the living room. Lydia followed him, her shoes tip-tapping on the marbled-tiled floor.

'Oh God, John. Shut up, will you?' Her voice shook a little. 'I've told you a dozen times that there's nothing between Fred Eland and me. He's my best friend's husband, for Christ's sake. I see him every week.' She grabbed hold of John's arm and looked up into his face. 'At least he has Matthew's best interests at heart. You never made any effort for his future!'

'I suppose paying for his expensive education was no effort?'

'Big deal. Trust you to only think in terms of money.'

John laughed. 'It seems to work for you, sweetheart. You're not exactly Mother Teresa when it comes to ignoring bodily comforts.' He waved his arm around the room. 'We didn't pick up all this in the charity shop.'

Lydia's face fell. Her hand went swiftly to her mouth and her blue eyes widened and filled with sudden tears. 'Bastard!' she said quietly.

He sighed, sorry that he had hurt her. He

29

wasn't normally a sarcastic man and she didn't deserve this. The mess that they had got into in the last year or so wasn't entirely of her making; he was to blame also. And he knew that. He touched her shoulder gently, noticing with slight surprise how thin she was.

'Look,' he said, 'we've said everything there is to say about the subject and I've got work to do if I'm to save the Li Park project. Right now, that is far more important than Matthew having another of his flights of fancy. Face it, Lydia, this is just this year's rebellion. We've lived through him saving whales and supporting the Inuit way of life, and what was it last year? Demonstrating against university fees. Jesus! Demonstrating against university fees? The boy has never paid for a goddam thing in his life, never done a day's work, and judging by the various causes he's taken up and dropped, demonstrates zero staying power. He'll be home in a month. Stop fussing.'

'Go to hell.' She spat out the words and shook off his hand. Turning her face away, she carefully dabbed the remains of her angry tears with the corner of a small handkerchief, then returned to her seat in the kitchen and picked up her glass.

John walked away, through the living room and down the side corridor to his study. There, in the one room in the house that had never been photographed, he lowered himself heavily into his leather chair in front of his old desk and stared blankly at the papers and drawings spread out in front of him.

Lydia had been quite right, of course. It had

30

been years since he'd really had much interest in Matthew's life. They'd grown apart, as fathers and sons do; a lack of understanding on both sides. Teenage pursuits had never figured largely in John's own life. In those far-off times helping on the farm and studying had exhausted all of his time. Even at university he'd had to take a job to supplement his grant. Not for him the carefree evenings of his friends who hung out in the university bar drinking away their grants, relying on their parents to plug the money gap. He'd known that his father could supply him with nothing. Instead he'd depended on the clothing factory where he'd packed and stacked crates on regular, eight-hour shifts.

Matthew's life, in contrast, had been frivolous. He'd never been short of money and had a good brain which allowed him to pass exams with the minimum of study. That left plenty of time to indulge himself in causes. Worthy causes, no doubt, but taken up without much thought and abandoned when the next interesting prospect came along.

'Oh God.' John groaned beneath his breath and wiped a hand heavily across his face. Just lately his life seemed to be falling to pieces. If the Li Park project failed he would be in trouble. There was nothing else on the horizon; he'd turned down other shopping precinct designs, desperately hoping to be offered something more fulfilling. But when he'd had the chance of designing a low-density housing estate and a new university building, he hadn't offered a proposal for those, either. It would have involved too much effort.

'Jesus, what's the matter with me?' he asked the portrait photographs which gazed sightlessly at him from the wall over his desk. Their reply was the same as ever: disapproval. Dad, buttoned up in his dark Sunday suit, stiff hair cut short and face set, was staring at the camera. This was a look John remembered well. The after-school look, when tea was finished and the two of them could think of nothing to say to each other. The same face that had said goodbye in the farmyard when John had left for Canada: few words exchanged but disappointment and anger thick in the air.

John sighed and looked across at Mam. She was actually smiling, cautiously giving the lens the benefit of her straight teeth and the little dimple at the corner of her mouth, but her eyes were sad. And she was stick-thin. She'd sat for the photographer in Llanfair the winter before she died. Dad had suggested that she should, telling her that a new shop was opening and that they should support it. Nobody believed him, of course. Even Mam, who hadn't been told the facts by the doctor, knew that she was dying and that this was just a method of having something to remember her by.

'Old fool, he is,' she'd said to John as they'd examined the studio photograph one January afternoon, 'wanting a picture of me.' He remembered her pulling at the baggy sleeves of her cardigan so that her bony wrists were covered. 'He should have waited till the summer when I'll have a bit of a tan. I look like death now.'

John, aged twelve but knowing, had gulped and

looked across at Dad. He had turned abruptly and walked into the yard, muttering about checking the sheep, leaving John and Mam sitting by the open kitchen fire, watching the pine logs spit and send aromatic smoke up the old chimney.

She'd flinched slightly as the kitchen door slammed shut in the wind but hadn't looked away from the flames. 'He'll need some help around the house, *bach*. You'll be a good boy now, won't you?' The words were said matter-of-factly as though she were talking about him taking on more chores as he got older. He had chores already, feeding the dogs, keeping the log basket full and helping with the washing-up, so what Mam said didn't sink in at first. But slowly, as they sat in the darkening kitchen, he began to realise that she was warning him, intimating that she would be leaving.

'Oh Mam!' Tears welled now where they hadn't all those years ago, and the adult John clenched his fists and cried unheard and alone.

In the kitchen, Lydia poured herself another drink and drummed her perfect fingernails on the table. She watched the rain pattering on the curtainless window and shivered.

Chapter Four

The road which led to Llanfair wound back and forth around the mountains, and Matthew slowed down as he carefully negotiated the bends. The sun was low in the sky now and it was noticeably cooler than it had been earlier in the day. In some places, where the road narrowed and the hillside rose up directly from the unfenced verges, the grey rock faces were covered in wire netting to prevent falls. Matthew eyed them nervously as he passed. Despite the grandeur of the scenery, he couldn't help feeling that it was all on a small scale and too close. He remembered a holiday the family had taken in the Rockies. Jesus, those were mountains. Magnificent snow-capped ranges, viewed safely from the windows of the RV as Dad had driven them west.

He glanced again at the girl beside him. How she could have remained asleep on this twisting road was a mystery. Not only were there constant gear changes, but the alternating light was confusing, first brilliant when the sun had been directly ahead or, as now, in shadow of the deepest purple. Then, rounding another bend, he was suddenly bathed in a golden glow of sunset as the road fell downhill into the valley. And still she slept. It was unnatural.

She had sighed once or twice in her sleep and

uttered a few unintelligible words, snatches really, of what might have been a conversation. The knotted dreadlocks bounced around with every movement of the car and Matthew noticed that amongst the green and red dye, tiny beads were plaited into her hair and even small coloured feathers. Her face was tanned and healthy with a clear skin drawn over fine cheekbones. The nose ring glinted in the sun, though, and he looked away. For all his taking up of causes and rebelliousness, Matthew had never wanted to be associated with the wilder elements of student life. His girlfriends had always been upper-class young women who loved the fact that he was a daredevil. The idea of being with someone who was more outrageous than he was novel, but... He looked at her again and grinned. The idea was not altogether attractive. Unfortunately, there was another novelty: she smelled.

Suddenly, almost missing it, he saw the village sign standing up amongst the cow parsley and willowherb which thronged the left-hand verge. Llanfair, it read. Llanfair, this was it. The excitement he'd felt earlier today returned and he was grinning widely as he drove into the village and came to a halt in the small square.

The houses were a uniform grey stone with slate roofs, dull now in the evening sun, but he imagined they would glisten like glass when wet with rain. He noticed a shop which had a Post Office sign, and two churches. The larger one had a spire and was stone-built like the village houses, but the smaller one opposite was constructed of shiny brick and had windows with painted black frames and a black noticeboard. 'Salem Chapel' the noticeboard said, followed by the name of the minister and times of services. There were other words in Welsh which Matthew couldn't read.

Facing the car was a pub. Again it was a stone and slate building with small square windows. Hanging baskets, expertly filled with pretty summer flowers, were attached on either side of the arched doorway, and two tables with folded umbrellas stood on the wide pavement in front. The tables were in shadow now but Matthew thought they would be a great place to sit at lunchtime, maybe with a bottle of beer. On a post, a brightly coloured hanging sign announced that this was 'The Miner's Arms' and depicted men with hammers in a mountain scene. They were not coal miners, he could see that. Quarrymen, perhaps.

He gave the girl a push on the shoulder. Her eyes opened instantly and she sat up. Matthew looked at her and grinned. 'We're here. At least, this is where I'm stopping to get further instructions.'

She yawned and stretched her arms and looked casually through the windscreen. 'Further instructions?' she said quizzically. 'What are you, a spy or something? On a mission?'

Matthew faked a short laugh. 'Ha, ha. Very funny. No, I'm not sure where the place is I'm going to. I'll go in this bar and ask.' He opened the car door. 'I guess you can get another lift here.'

The girl nodded and got out of the car. She

bent over and pulled out her rucksack, revealing a gap of tanned but dirty flesh between her T-shirt and combat trousers. Matthew wondered when she'd last had a wash. She caught his eye and straightened up and looked about. 'Yeah. Thanks for the ride.'

Matthew stood uncertainly beside the Citroën looking at the pub. The girl moved to stand beside him and put out her hand towards him. 'I meant that,' she said smilingly, revealing straight white teeth, 'and for letting me sleep.' She tossed the mass of matted hair away from her face. 'I hope you weren't looking for sparkling conversation; I was too tired for that. I can be quite entertaining when I'm not quite so knackered.'

She swung the rucksack onto her shoulder and looked about the empty square. There was a bus stop sign outside the stone church and she turned towards it. Matthew grabbed her hand. 'Hey,' he said, suddenly attracted by her grin and her throwaway words. 'How about you come into the bar with me? I could use a drink and I bet you could too. We could have a beer and you can demonstrate your conversational arts.' He looked again at the pub, noticing for the first time the faces in the small window who were looking back at him. 'Maybe they do food too.'

She hesitated for a moment and then smiled again. 'Thank you.' Her voice was less casual now, deeper and more genuine. 'I would love a drink. And I'm desperate for a pee.'

The pub was full of customers and noisy. It was obviously the hub of the village, the place to meet, exchange gossip and do business. Young farmers in blue overalls or jeans stood at the bar, laughing and downing pints. They'd finished work for the day and were now planning the weekend. Llanfair had an amateur football team and some of these men would be on a coach tomorrow morning for an away match at Aberystwyth. A few of the team members were drinking orange juice, but most weren't, and the supporters were busy debating how many crates of beer, a necessity at away matches, they could get into the coach.

There were little tables around the room, surrounded by polished chairs and upholstered stools. The pub had recently been refurbished and, whilst not losing its traditional look, was certainly cleaner and more comfortable than it had been. The old men sitting at the table by the window, nursing their half pints, had grumbled at the changes, bemoaning the loss of the tobacco-stained walls and the thin, greasy carpet. But it hadn't stopped them coming in at their usual times and now, six months into the new landlord, they no longer talked about the renovations.

There had been a sudden pause in the noisy conversations when Matthew walked into the bar. This was not a tourist village and strangers were unusual. He saw their eyes on him, examining his clothes and shoes, and heard without understanding comments followed by short bursts of laughter as he strode towards the counter. Then the laughter stopped and there was a curious sound like a collective indrawn breath. It was a bit disconcerting, but Matthew had never been shy and quite enjoyed the attention.

The smoothly plump man behind the bar

watched his arrival. He would have been good-looking if his jowls had been less full and his gut less prominent. An overfed zoo panther with a drooping black moustache, was Matthew's first impression.

'Hi.' Matthew gave his most charming grin, the one that generally ensured him popularity.

The fat panther was silent.

'Hi!' Matthew repeated. 'We're looking for beer and some information. I guess this would be the place to get both.'

The landlord's dark eyes looked at him briefly and then flicked over Matthews shoulder to concentrate on the girl who had walked in after him.

'I don't serve travellers.' He picked up a pint glass and a bar towel, and, with surprising elegance considering the breadth of his sausage-like fingers, proceeded to polish the glass to perfection, before placing it carefully on the shelf above the bar.

'Excuse me?' Matthew looked confused.

'Travellers. Like her.'

The other customers were silent, attentively watching the byplay as Matthew turned round and looked at his companion. She shrugged and gave a little smile, then hoisted her rucksack and turned to go. Matthew grabbed her arm. 'Hang on. What's he talking about? What is a traveller?'

'It's me. Or rather, people like me. It's my hair and clothes.' She nodded to the listening farm workers. 'They think I'm part of a gang and I'll cause trouble. People say that travellers' dogs bother the sheep.' She lowered her voice and smiled at him. 'You must have noticed that this is sheep country.'

'But are you one of these "travellers"?'

The girl looked back at him and spoke in a deliberate voice. 'I have been. I'm on my own now.'

Matthew nodded and turned back to the landlord. 'OK. You heard her. She isn't a traveller. She came with me, in my car.' He looked over to the window where the old men were sitting, straining to follow the conversation. 'They saw us. We arrived together.'

One of the old men rapped the stem of his pipe on the small square of windowpane and called out in a thin, wavering voice, 'He's right, Griff Parry, boy. We saw them, me and Huw. They came in that car there.' He sharply rapped the glass again, bringing a scowl to the landlord's already bad-tempered face. 'Just the two of them there was.'

Griff Parry, newly arrived in Llanfair and unwilling to upset his customers more than was absolutely necessary, gave the girl another suspicious look. It had only been three or four months since the villagers had managed to get rid of the traveller camp which had appeared overnight on the lay-by beside the village sign. They'd been a nasty bunch. Mostly young men, probably responsible – though it hadn't been proved – for the spate of minor thefts that had occurred around that time. Worse than that, they had destroyed fences, using the wood in their fires, and their lurchers had wreaked havoc amongst the young lambs. The police couldn't shift them and it had taken the combined efforts

40

of the football team and other villagers to bodily lift the vans and trailers off the verge onto the road so that they could be moved on. It had left a nasty taste.

And this girl looked like the few women who had accompanied the last lot. He looked at the multicoloured hair and the nose ring with distaste. What a waste of a good-looking woman. He felt a movement at his side and a voice whispered in his ear, 'Let them in, Griff, love. It'll be all right.'

It was his wife, Llinos, who had quietly come into the bar from the pub kitchen. She was a small, serious-looking girl, as dark as Griff, but slight where he was bulky and more adept at thinking on her feet. 'We don't want to be turning customers away.'

The frown disappeared like snow off a roof and the landlord turned to Matthew with his professional smile. 'Right then. What can I get you?'

Matthew sighed with relief and grinned cheerfully at the girl before turning back to Griff. 'Well, I guess I'll have a beer and my friend would like...' He waited for her to speak up.

'An orange juice, please.'

'She'll have an orange juice. And do you do food?'

Griff looked at Llinos, who nodded and pointed to a chalked board nailed to the wall above the fireplace where various snacks and sandwiches were offered.

Conversation in the bar resumed and more orders were taken, but the event would be savoured for later retelling.

41

Matthew studied the chalked menu and turned to the girl. 'What would you like?'

'Oh, just a sandwich, I think. Ham.'

He looked at the list of dishes. He was starving and there was steak on offer. 'Are you sure? It's my treat, you know.'

The girl smiled and Matthew was struck by her looks. Once you ignored the hair and the nose ring, she was really pretty. He wondered how old she was. 'I'm having the steak; do you want to change your mind?' He nodded to the landlord, who was standing by with an order pad in hand.

'No, I'll stick with the ham. And salad, if I may.' She looked around the room and spotted the 'Toilets' sign in the far corner. 'I'll be back in minute.' She picked up her rucksack and wove a path through the assembled customers towards the sign, unconscious, Matthew was sure, of the heads that turned to watch her or the murmured comments.

Llinos took the order and disappeared into the kitchen, leaving Griff to man the bar.

Matthew eyed the handpumps along the counter and looked at the landlord. 'I guess you haven't got anything lighter. A bottle beer, maybe?'

'Well, sir,' Griff Parry grinned slyly, 'I think we can find something to please the transatlantic palate. Will this do?' And from under the counter he produced a bottle of Budweiser. 'My favourite, this,' he said, placing it carefully before Matthew and putting a highly polished glass alongside it.

'Great!' Matthew beamed with pleasure. Ignoring the glass, he upended the bottle and took a long drink.

'That'll be three pounds and ten pence, with your girlfriend's drink, of course.' Griff put a tall glass loaded with ice and juice on the counter.

'You'll have to take it out of that.' Matthew reached into his pocket and drew out a handful of change. 'I haven't got the hang of the coins yet.'

Griff counted out the correct money and pushed the rest back across the counter. 'We don't get many American visitors in here. You on holiday?'

Matthew pointed to the bottle for another.

'I'm Canadian, and no, not really. I've come to live in a house I inherited, in this village I think, or close by.'

The conversation around him suddenly paused again.

'You might know it. It's the Cariad Elin farm.'

Beside him, one of the young men in blue farming overalls slammed down his pint mug with such force that the beer splashed over the top and onto the counter. He was bigger than Matthew, tall and thickset with a mop of untidy brown hair which flopped over his face and low on his collar.

'Cariad Elin? That was old Geraint Williams' place. Died last year, in the field, poor bastard. Not a soul from the family came to his funeral. I know, I was there. We're in the next farm.'

'He was my grandfather,' Matthew said, suddenly aware of the interest he was attracting. 'He left me the house and the land.'

'Good God Almighty!' Griff leant back against the optics and then hurriedly scooted through the connecting door to the pub kitchen.

'Where was the family at the funeral, that's what I want to know?' the young farmer asked angrily, looking round at his friends, who nodded their support, before turning back to Matthew. 'The poor old bugger was put into the earth without one fucking member of his family there. We know he had a son.'

Matthew nodded, 'Yeah, my dad. He didn't know till later. Grandfather had apparently got rid of any papers with my father's address. The lawyers found us.'

'Bloody hell. What a way to run a family!' The young farmer snorted his disgust.

One of the old men by the window got up and walked unsteadily towards the bar and put his glass down, waiting for Griff to return.

'Geraint Williams would argue with a fence post,' he said, with a drunken cackle, 'even with that sick little wife. And the son, poor bugger. Couldn't wait to get away.'

Several of the older men in the room nodded, and Matthew, holding onto the neck of the beer bottle, shifted uncomfortably as he heard them agreeing with the cruel assessment of his grandfather. It was with relief that he saw the girl coming back from the ladies' room and waved his hand. She looked different. Her hair was now tied back in a ponytail and she had changed out of the grubby shirt. The baggy white one she wore now was at least clean, if crumpled. Matthew noticed little curls of reddish blonde hair which had escaped from the dreadlocks and clustered damply around her neck and temples. She

44

had obviously taken the opportunity to have a quick wash. He pushed the orange juice towards her.

'This mine? Thanks.' She smiled and drank deeply. 'Lovely!'

Griff came back to his position behind the bar carrying two sets of cutlery and a cruet set 'D'you want to eat at the bar?' he said, looking at Matthew and then at the girl.

'Yeah, whatever.' Matthew nodded and then asked, 'Who's going to tell me how to get to the farm?'

'Oh, I wouldn't go there tonight, boy,' Griff said urgently. 'It's been empty for a year and God alone knows what condition it will be in.'

The young farmer barked a laugh and looked round at his friends, who were visibly sniggering. 'Bloody hell, Griff Parry,' he said. 'God might move in a mysterious way, but Cariad Elin's condition is no fucking secret round here. And you should know, if anyone!'

'Hey, what's going on here?' Matthew was beginning to get angry. He glanced at the girl, who was listening carefully to the exchange, and was encouraged by her slight nod.

The landlord made a placatory gesture of peace with his fat hand. 'Nothing. No, nothing to worry about. It's just that some of us have been running our sheep on the land. A waste of good grazing, it was. And the stone from the barn has been used a bit.'

'The stone has been used a bit?' Matthew looked round at the assembled company. 'How the hell do you use stone ... a bit?'

'You pinch it, that's how, and sell it to the garden centre. For fucking rockeries.' The farm worker laughed out loud and, fixing his small brown eyes on the scowling landlord, downed his fourth pint in a dismissive gesture.

Griff Parry pointed his finger at him and then waved it in an arc, encompassing all the younger men who were grinning at him. 'You stop making trouble, Elfed Jones, or I'll bar you from this pub. And that goes for the rest of you!'

At that moment, Llinos glided in from the kitchen bearing a tray of food which she put down on the bar in front of Matthew and the girl. She put a small warning finger on Griff's arm before disappearing back into the living quarters.

'Look,' said Griff, simmering down and arranging the knives and forks on either side of the plates, 'there's nothing gone that can't be replaced, and we can come to some arrangement about the grazing. After all, you won't want to use the land yourself. Just doing up the house for holiday lets, is it?' A calculating gleam came into his eyes. 'Or maybe you want to sell it?'

Matthew attacked the steak eagerly and savoured a mouthful before replying. 'Nope, I don't want to sell it, and you can find somewhere else for your sheep. I'm going to work the land. Like my grandfather did.'

There was another general indrawn breath.

'Christ!' said Elfed. 'And there was me thinking Yanks had more sense.'

Matthew grinned and nodded to Griff for another beer. He turned back to the girl, who was slowly eating her ham baguette.

'Well done,' she said quietly, for his ears only, putting the sandwich down on the oval platter and neatly gathering a forkful of salad. 'They understand bold, these sort of people.'

Matthew's earlier euphoria reappeared and he ate his meal happily, ordering another juice for the girl and coffee for them both to follow. 'OK,' he said to Griff when they'd finished, 'now you can tell me how to get to the farm.'

'I'll show you,' said Elfed. 'It's just up from our place and I'm going home now.'

'Great, thanks.' Matthew got up and bent down to pick up the girl's rucksack. It wasn't very heavy. He spoke quietly so only she could hear. 'Come with me tonight, just for company.'

Her eyes, he noticed for the first time, were amber-coloured with little flecks of green and blue. He thought of the semi-precious stones that his mother had collected once at the shore and had polished and set into a bracelet. Some of those stones had looked like these eyes. He had never seen anything like them. As he stared they widened and then crinkled as she gave him a smile.

'OK,' she said simply. She turned to Griff and Llinos, who were watching their departure, and said, 'Thank you. The meal was lovely. Good night.'

Chapter Five

By the time they left the pub, the light had just about gone. The bright afternoon sun which had dominated the trip to Wales had fallen behind the mountain and dropped gently into the Irish Sea, and heavy clouds had rolled in from the west, bringing spiky rain which spattered noisily on the windscreen of Matthew's car.

The road out of the village ran uphill, still winding and narrow, but now there was the problem of overhanging trees to contend with, making the business of following Elfed Jones' old Land Rover hellishly difficult. Matthew swore gently under his breath as yet another leafy branch smacked into the car, giving him a fright and making him grip the steering wheel even more tightly.

The girl made a sympathetic sound and then said, 'Look, I have to say that this is good of you. To give me a place for the night, I mean. I don't think I could have found a lift at this hour and I'm very grateful.'

'It's OK,' said Matthew, concentrating on the road ahead as the Land Rover disappeared round a bend but then relaxing as he saw its tail lights ahead. 'We seem to be in this together.'

He took a swift look at her. In the dark car she didn't seem quite so strange. He couldn't see the multicoloured hair, and her profile with its straight nose and finely drawn jawline was quite attractive. 'I never asked,' he said suddenly, 'what's your name?'

There was a pause and then she said in a low voice, 'I'm Lark. That's what I'm called.'

'Lark?' He laughed. 'As in the bird?'

'Mm.' She gave a little giggle. 'Lark.'

He nodded his head. 'Nice, I like that. I'm Matthew Williams. Matt.'

'As in, the cat sat on the...?'

'Yeah.'

They sat comfortably together in the darkened vehicle driving through the tunnel of trees towards Matt's inheritance. The mutual teasing had made them friends and Lark felt surprisingly excited, for no reason that she could think of. Maybe a suggestion of Matthew's youthful exuberance had rubbed off on her, but there was something else. Something deeper. She sighed. The last few months had been difficult and yesterday she had taken the second biggest decision of her life. For all that it had been akin to unloading a huge burden, it had still been hard and had left her exhausted.

'Hey, look.' Matthew pushed on the brakes. 'We're stopping.'

They had come to a halt beside a collapsing five-bar gate at the head of a rutted, overgrown drive. Two crumbling stone pillars stood to either side, and on one of them Lark could see a small wooden board. The writing, white painted but flaking, read 'Cariad Elin'.

'Is this it?' she asked, but didn't need to. She knew.

Matthew got out of the car. The rain fell faster

49

now and plastered his hair onto his head. He zipped up his waterproof jacket and stood beside Elfed, looking with dismay at the heavy chain and padlock which fastened the gate. 'How the hell are we supposed to get through this?' He was tired and suddenly exasperated and wondered if he should have found somewhere to stay in the village, just for the night. It would be easier to cope with this sort of situation in daylight.

'No problem, boy.' Elfed grabbed hold of the gate and easily lifted it off its hinges and dragged it to one side. 'Same as everyone else, see.'

Matthew took a deep breath and looked down the track. In the little light that was left, he could just make out the outline of the house and buildings. The rain was now drifting away, and behind him a pale moon was making its nightly track to its zenith. It cast a weak glow on the hillside and silhouetted the twisted shapes of fir and rowan trees, growing sparsely where there was enough soil for them to put down roots. The scene was not welcoming and he wasn't sure he liked it much. He looked back to his car where Lark was sitting patiently. 'I guess this is it.' He watched her get out of the car and said hurriedly, 'You're still coming in with me, aren't you?'

'Yes, of course,' she said. 'You drive through and I'll put the gate back.'

'Don't bother, love.' Elfed gave her a pat on the shoulder. 'I'll do it.'

He waited until Matthew had returned to the driving seat with Lark beside him, and started the engine. 'I'll drop you off a pint of milk in the morning,' he called, 'and I expect my mam can find you some bread. If I were you I'd go to the Tesco's in Bangor tomorrow to get your groceries. Cheaper than the fucking village shop.'

He waved his hand as they drove through the open gateway and called 'ta-ra', the local form of goodbye which Matthew was to get to know very well over the coming months.

The rutted driveway gave way to an overgrown farmyard, potholed and littered with bits of wood and rusting metal. The house was to one side, a stone and slate cottage with a lean-to annex, added on sometime later. Opposite, a range of buildings – barns, pigsties and machine sheds – loomed, hard to see in the light from the headlamps, but not, as far as Matthew could tell, in very good condition. He couldn't see the sheep but he heard them, bleating restlessly on the hillside, disturbed by the arrival of the car.

Lark got out of the car and stood beside it, peering at the house through the darkness.

'Jesus, it's a mess.' Matthew was dismayed by the view of his inheritance.

'Yes,' Lark said softly, 'but a lovely mess.'

'D'you think so?'

'Mm. Especially in the moonlight. It's mysterious. A lonely house, full of secrets.'

Matthew looked at her doubtfully. 'Is that a quote, or something?'

'No. At least, I don't think so. It just looks like that.' She lifted her eyes again to the barren hillside behind the house. It reminded her of ... well, she wasn't sure. Maybe it had been a painting in the little gallery down the street from where her

51

parents lived, although the man who owned it generally preferred still lifes, and modern still lifes at that. But she knew it from somewhere.

Matthew had gone round to the boot and lifted out his rucksack. He took out a large torch and directed the beam onto the front of the house. A wooden Victorian porch had been added to protect the front door but it was leaning slightly, and some of the paling strips that made up the sides had disappeared. As he moved the torch back and forth over the front of the building, Matthew noted with dismay the broken window frames and missing tiles, and the grass and weeds growing out of the cracks in the stone walls. 'Oh God,' he said in despair, 'it's a ruin!'

'I don't think so.' Lark was more optimistic. 'It's probably just neglect. Anywhere could get like this after a while without an occupier I expect it will be all right inside,' she added sympathetically and then walked towards the front door. 'Have you got a key?'

'Yeah.' Matthew shoved his hand into the pocket of his rucksack and produced a stiff yellow envelope. From amongst the papers within, he pulled out a small ring which carried two keys. He looked at them and then shone the torch onto the door. 'I don't think either will fit in here,' he said doubtfully. The old door didn't appear to have a keyhole at all, and when he pushed it didn't give an inch.

'There's a door in the side, there,' said Lark, pointing to the annex.

The larger key worked, and the door opened stiffly into a small scullery with an old Belfast sink, crowned with high arched taps. The light from the torch led them through into a large room with a Rayburn range which had originally been cream but was now scratched and dirty and icy to touch. Beside it stood a grease-encrusted electric stove, piled high with battered saucepans. Matthew gave a weary sigh and directed the flashlight further into the room. There was a pine table surrounded by four pine chairs in the centre of the room. It looked dirty and marked with scratches and patches of grease. He couldn't imagine ever eating a meal off it.

At the far end of the room, a huge inglenook fireplace took up most of the wall. On either side of the grate were two seats, one a wooden rocker with a fringed cushion and the other, opposite, a large winged chair. It was covered in ginger-coloured leather, torn in places so that the stuffing showed through. On the floor beside it was a pile of newspapers and a wooden crate which contained a piece of tartan rug. Could it have been a dog's bed? Matthew was beginning not to care.

There was a door in the centre of the wall opposite the windows and Matthew went towards it, shining the torch on the walls, desperately looking for a light switch. 'Aha!' An old-fashioned round switch was on the wall beside the door. He eagerly pushed it up and down, and then again, before turning back to Lark in dismay. 'It doesn't work!' he cried in disappointment.

'The electricity is probably switched off at the mains.' Lark had followed him through the kitchen. 'We should look for the box.'

'Oh God, it could be anywhere.' Matthew leaned wearily against the wall.

Lark pushed past him into a narrow passageway. In front of her she could see the main door, bolted top and bottom with hefty two-hundred-year-old iron bars. No wonder they hadn't been able to get in that way. A room led off to the right of the door and a narrow staircase led to the upper floor.

'The main switch is usually under the stairs in old houses,' she said. Feeling along the wall beneath the staircase, her fingers came across the latch of a small door. 'Shine the light in here.' She bent down and crouched her way into the cubbyhole.

Matthew heard the click of a heavy switch and her muffled voice called, 'Try now.'

A dull yellow glow from a single hanging bulb brought sense to the main room and Matthew grinned with relief. 'How did you know how to do that?' he asked, switching off his torch.

She laughed. 'I've hidden talents.'

They explored the house, switching on lights and finding that in some places the bulbs were dead. The room by the front door was a complete contrast to the big kitchen. Here the floor was carpeted in a thick patterned Axminster and the windows were dressed in dark red velvet. Too much furniture filled the room, but most of the pieces were old – antique, Matthew thought – and elegant. It was obvious that nobody had sat on the chaise longue for many years and that cups and saucers had been banned from the tiny rosewood wine tables. But there was a layer of dust that covered everything. Matthew picked up a photograph frame and studied the face peering dimly back at him. He had no idea who he was looking at. The young man in a World War One uniform was unrecognisable.

Upstairs, there were two bedrooms, both just as ordered as the front room. The larger one had a walnut suite of double bed, wardrobes and dressing table; the smaller, with a brass bedstead, was more sparsely furnished. The beds in both the rooms were covered in starched white lace counterpanes and the dressing table in the main bedroom had pretty crocheted doilies placed carefully underneath the china pin boxes and hairbrushes.

Lark went into the kitchen again and examined the cookers. She tried the taps in the scullery and nodded resignedly when they didn't emit any water. In the cupboard under the sink she found the stopcock and after a struggle managed to turn it on. When Matthew came downstairs after examining the cold but tidy bedrooms she had already filled a kettle with water and set it on the electric cooker to boil.

'You seem to know how to do everything,' Matthew said, watching her as she searched a cupboard and found a tea caddy.

'Tomorrow, you should try to light the Rayburn. It will heat the water and you can cook on it.'

'What the hell is the Rayburn?'

'This is.' Lark indicated the cast-iron stove. 'I'll show you how it works. If you like.'

Matthew, suddenly really tired, dropped into one of the kitchen chairs and rested his head on his hand. 'Jesus,' he said wearily, 'is there no end to your talents?'

'No.' She laughed and put two spoonfuls of dusty-looking tea into a chipped brown pot which she'd found under the sink. 'I'm brilliant. Have some tea.' She put a tin mug in front of him. 'There's no milk, but it will be warm.'

'I hate tea. D'you think the old man had any coffee?'

She shrugged her shoulders and looked through the cupboard again. 'Sorry.'

'Oh, all right, I'll try it.' He took a cautious sip and pulled a face full of disgust and pain. He put down the mug. 'Oh Christ. I guess I'll go to the supermarket tomorrow.'

Lark sat opposite him at the big table and took a gulp from her mug, seemingly not minding the stale grey tea. She looked about the room, taking in the mess of old magazines and papers pushed into the gap between the upper and lower cupboards beside the fireplace and the filthy rug in front of the hearth. 'You've got some work ahead,' she said. 'I'll bet the farm is just as bad, too.'

Matthew grimaced. 'My ma would hate this. I remember once, when we took a cottage on the islands one summer. God, it was a million times better than this, but she wouldn't stay. She made Dad book us into a hotel.' He laughed, thinking about it. 'After a couple of days she went back to Toronto leaving Dad to get on with his fishing. She said a week at home on her own looking at the washing machine was more restful than competing with roaches for the shower.'

'So you and your dad had a men only holiday,

56

did you?' Lark smiled, seeing the young man before her as he must have been as a child.

Matthew snorted. 'God, no. I went home with Ma. I'm not into all that country stuff!' He only had to look at Lark's raised eyebrows to realise what he'd said, and his face coloured in embarrassment. 'Well, I wasn't then,' he muttered, 'this is different.'

Lark nodded and then yawned suddenly. 'I'm tired,' she said. 'I've been at a festival for a week and you don't get much rest there. I'll kip in that chair, if you don't mind.' She got up and took the mugs to the sink in the scullery. Matthew followed her. 'Don't be dumb,' he said gently, 'take one of the beds. They look OK, no rats or anything.'

'All right, thanks.' She picked up her rucksack and headed towards the stairs. Matthew followed her down the little hallway. On the bottom step she turned. 'I wouldn't be too sure about the rats, you know. They say you're never more than ten feet away from one. I expect they're holding a union meeting right now deciding how to get you out!'

Matthew shuddered and his mouth turned down. 'Oh hell, don't talk about things like that,' he groaned. 'If I thought that, I'd never get any sleep.'

She laughed and started up the stairs. 'Good night, Matt.'

He smiled and then turned back towards the kitchen. He sat again at the table and looked around the room. This time he ignored the mess; he'd regained the feeling of triumph, the pleasure

57

of striking out on his own. He smacked a fist into his other hand and grinned to the empty room. *Now let him call me immature*, he thought.

Chapter Six

At the Miner's Arms, all was quiet. The last customers had been shoehorned out of the bar and Griff and Llinos, with well-practised efficiency, had cleared up and gone to bed.

Their bedroom was comfortably furnished. The thick mushroom-coloured carpet, which was bliss to walk on, was complemented by heavy pink and cream curtains. Llinos had chosen the colour scheme after reading all the superior home decoration magazines and she was pleased with the effect. Griff loved it too, although he'd had no input, other than paying for the furnishing of this room or indeed any part of the pub. But that was all right, Llinos had the brains and the taste. She was his most valuable asset.

But now, as Griff wandered round the king-sized bed, undressing fitfully, first his shirt thrown into the wicker laundry basket, followed by vest and socks, he was a worried man.

Llinos was already in bed, her glasses on her nose and a book propped up in front of her. Her bedside table had a neat pile of books. A few novels by well-known women writers were at the bottom of the pile, but the ones that were obviously most frequently read were computer manuals and popular paperbacks on accountancy and management. At the moment she was deep into an explanation of conducting business via the Internet. She had plans for expansion, plans that her husband was more than happy to go along with.

Griff was hopping around at the end of the bed, taking off his trousers. He looked miserable and Llinos knew that she was never going to be able to read more than a paragraph that night. He was naked now, a great plump baby with a hairy chest and shoulders, but not unattractive and always devoted. She was content and their marriage worked well. His devotion and her dispassionate affection had lasted longer than the whirlwind romances of some of her friends.

'Did you see them, Llinos love?' he said, pulling on a clean T-shirt and climbing heavily into the bed. 'The Williams boy and that hippie girl?'

'Yes, I did.' Llinos kept her eyes firmly fixed on her book.

'Bit worrying that, isn't it? Having them at Cariad Elin.'

'No.'

'But it is, can't you see that, sweetheart? He said that he was planning to work the farm. That'll put a stop to me running the sheep up there. Free grazing, I was getting.'

She turned over a page and spoke without looking up. 'Don't look to me for sympathy. I told you last year that it was a bad idea. Tantamount to stealing, that was.'

'No, no, not stealing, *cariad*. No one else was using it and our sheep were keeping the grass down.' He folded his arms and nodded his head towards his reflection in the mirrored wardrobe. It was a good argument.

Llinos snorted. 'Our sheep! I like that. They're *your* sheep, boy *bach,* nothing to do with me. Anyway, you can move them, or sell them.'

'Sell them? Jesus, no. Well, the lambs, yes. But not my ewes. They're good stock, those ewes.' He groaned and slid down in the bed, staring miserably at the ceiling. 'They're prizewinners, them. I can't sell them. I won't sell them.'

Llinos took off her glasses and looked up from her book. 'Find some new grazing. Try the other side of the mountain, or...' She thought for a moment. 'Why don't you sell a share or two to the young Williams boy? He won't know anything about running sheep and you could make a few bob and still have your bloody prize ewes.'

Griff lay still for a moment and then sat up with a jerk, dislodging the duvet and bouncing Llinos' book from her hands. She clucked her tongue impatiently and reached out her hand to retrieve it but Griff grabbed it and threw it over the side of the bed. He turned towards her and kissed her lovingly on the cheek. 'Yes, yes! Clever old girl. I'll go straight round in the morning. That Yank will be putty in my hands.' He put his arms around her and pulled her down into the bed. 'Come here, my lovely girl,' he crooned, 'come to your grateful husband.'

She giggled as his hands reached inside her pyjama top. 'Amazing, the things that turn you on. Archetypal Welshman you are, excited by sheep! And,' she added from beneath him as he moved his fat legs over hers, 'stop calling him a Yank. He's a Canadian!'

'Same fucking thing,' he grunted, now losing interest in Matthew Williams, 'same fucking thing.'

Llinos stretched out an arm and switched off the bedside light. She grinned smugly into the darkness. That was the best idea she'd had all week.

In Toronto that late afternoon, the weather was still very warm. There had been no respite after last night's storm; indeed the morning had dawned steaming, and the day had gradually heated up to near record temperatures. The residents of the lakeside city were beginning to feel that they'd had enough, and some even harboured yearning thoughts of winter.

John Williams sat at his desk in his air-conditioned office. Facing him were the members of the Hong Kong delegation, small, neat men who refused to remove their suit jackets despite the heat and the casual attire of their host. John had given up wearing suits and ties years ago, preferring polo necks in winter and open-neck cotton shirts in summer. At fifty, his figure was still good, spare but strong and well muscled. He had continued to play squash, first learned at university and now kept up three times a week at a club in the city. In the winter, he cross-country skied, a sport he'd grown to love but which he had to enjoy on his own. Lydia hated outdoor activities, and Matthew, since leaving school, had dropped out of most sports.

Sitting now in the uncomfortable silence of his

61

office, John would have given a lot to be out on one of the forest tracks, winter or summer. At least the solitariness would have been of his own choosing, unlike now, when he felt exposed by disapproval.

'I'm not sure I see the problem, Mr Li.' John broke the silence, his voice rather louder than he had intended. 'You liked the model, you liked the site, and as you know, there would be generous tax concessions from the government, if you located here.'

Mr Li, the central figure of the three, nodded in agreement. 'Yes, yes, Mr Williams. That is all true.' He looked down at his small, carefully man-icured hands and tapped one finger into the opposite palm. His fidgeting was compelling and John felt he couldn't tear his eyes away.

The tapping stopped. 'You have no partner. You work alone,' continued Mr Li.

This unexpected remark took John by surprise and when he looked up, it was to see the three men now staring at him, smilingly waiting for his confirmation. 'Yes ... I've always worked alone,' he said slowly, wondering what this change of tack might mean. 'I have associates, of course, people I can consult for special problems.' He stood up and walked nervously around the room. 'But ... I ... I can't see the difficulty there.'

Mr Li turned in his chair to follow John's pere-grinations. 'We would be investing many, many millions in this project. We would need to know that it had your full attention.'

John stopped beside the model of the shopping mall. 'But it would. Entirely.' He put his hands out expansively and waved imaginary work away from him. 'I've put everything else on hold to concentrate on the Li Park centre.'

'Very commendable.' Mr Li gave one of his tight little smiles. 'However, we were thinking more about your personal problems.' He glanced from side to side at his companions, who rewarded him with imperceptible nods. 'What if you were called away on family business?'

John frowned and came back to his desk. He sat down and stared at Mr Li. 'I have no personal problems that could in any way interfere with this project,' he said firmly.

'At our last meeting, when you had to take a phone call from the "minister", you inadvertently pushed a button on your phone deck.' Li spoke slowly, giving time for the flush which started on John's neck to spread hotly into his hairline. 'Your conversation was overheard,' he continued. 'We apologise for listening, of course.'

John wiped his hand over his face, almost as if he could wipe his mortification away. He coughed. 'Ah, well, most embarrassing. But I can assure you, gentlemen, in that regard. My son's activities will have no bearing on my work.'

'I'm sure that you hope that they won't. And we know that all families have difficulties. But, in the interests of our shareholders, you must accept that we have to be careful before we invest such a large amount.' The smooth voice took on a colder tone. 'We have done a preliminary investigation...' As the pit of John's stomach churned, Mr Li got up from his chair, promptly followed by his companions. 'We discovered that last year you had to take time off to collect your son from a detention centre in the Yukon. And that earlier this year he was arrested for demonstrating in front of the parliament building. He was mentioned specifically in the newspaper as being your son.'

John sat back, suddenly exhausted. 'My son has ideals.'

Mr Li smiled, his eyes disappearing behind his thick glasses. 'Ideals are always commendable, aren't they, but I think more comfortable from afar.'

He put out his hand to John, who, with an effort, pushed himself out of his chair and took it.

'We will meet again next week after I have reported to my backers,' Mr Li said, as John accompanied the delegation to the door. 'It will give us both time to think.'

The sun was slowly disappearing and downtown Toronto twinkled with electric light before John left his office. He had taken a nearly full bottle of whisky out of the bottom drawer of his desk and found a glass in the kitchen. Returning to his office, he sat heavily in the chair, swivelling it round so that he could watch the light fade through the window. The alcohol was comforting and so was the dark. As he drank he saw the sharp forms of the skyscrapers melt into the twilight and become the hills behind Cariad Elin. He knew that if he opened the window, he would hear the owls calling from the oak trees behind the barn and smell the musty aroma of hay which he'd helped Dad stack that afternoon. He stretched his legs; they were so tired. But Dad had promised to come upstairs and rub them after he'd done his night round of the farm. The only trouble was that he might go to sleep before he came. The glass dropped onto the polished block floor as his head dropped onto his chest.

In the farmhouse, Lark slept peacefully. She had chosen the smaller bedroom with the brass three-quarter bedstead and the starched white counterpane which she had taken off and carefully folded over a chair. Rumpling it would have been a crime. She liked the room, although it had little furniture. Besides the bed there was just a bookcase, a small wardrobe and a wooden chair.

She had examined the contents of the bookcase which stood against the wall and smiled with remembered pleasure on reading the titles. The books, some of which had been her own favourites – *Treasure Island, The Hobbit* and lots of Enid Blyton – were arranged alphabetically. Interspersed with these were the choices of the owner as he grew older: Asimov, Joseph Heller and Ian Fleming. She liked the way that he hadn't rejected his earlier loves as he'd grown out of them. Perhaps, as she had done, he'd found himself re-reading the Narnia series at seventeen and eighteen, when he should have been swotting for exams. It was a he, she was sure of that, for on top of the bookcase there were model planes, carefully made from balsa wood and cement and arranged as though drawn up at an airport. This must have been Matthew's father's room, probably unused for years.

Before getting into bed, she had stripped off

her clothes, wrinkling up her nose at the sour smell that wafted off the long-unwashed combat trousers. She had found soap and a towel in the little bathroom at the head of the stairs, and although the water was freezing, she had washed herself all over. It was cold, getting into bed naked, and the sheets felt just slightly damp, but she was cleaner than she had been in months and exulted in the sensation.

She hadn't waited for sleep long. Vaguely, in the distance, she thought she could hear the hoot of an owl. It was a peaceful sound and mingled happily with the soft pitter-patter of rain on the window. A jumble of thoughts filled her head, each vying for attention and eager to keep her awake. But tonight they seemed strangely un-important, and her eyes fell shut within five minutes and dreamless sleep overtook her.

A noise woke her before dawn. It was the sound of the lavatory flushing and she guessed that Matthew was awake. She looked out of the window. It was still dark outside, although per-haps there was just a slight lightening of the sky. Nevertheless, it was very early, and she wondered if he had been to bed at all. She turned on her side and looked towards the door. She could hear his footsteps on the uncarpeted landing, his bare feet slapping on the linoleum-covered floor. Then there was a slight tap at her door, and before she could speak, the handle had turned and he'd pushed open the door.

'Are you awake?' He came into the room and stood uncertainly at the end of the bed. Lark could make out that he had draped a blanket over himself but couldn't see his face.

'I am now,' she said.

'Sorry.' He walked over to the window and bent to peer out. 'I can't sleep. Jet lag or something.'

Lark yawned. 'Perhaps you're just excited. It's been quite a day.'

He walked back and sat on the end of her bed. 'Could be.' The blanket slipped off and he pulled it back over his shoulders. Under it he still wore his T-shirt of the day before and a pair of boxer shorts. 'I'm used to watching TV in bed or playing on my computer until I'm tired. And where I live, there's traffic at night. It's very quiet here.'

Lark listened sympathetically and looked at his boyish figure and the bent head. 'Come in here with me,' she said gently.

Matthew looked up. 'I didn't mean that.'

'I know. But the offer stands.'

He got up and stood at the end of the bed for a moment and then slowly walked round towards her. She smiled and pulled the covers open and moved over to let him in. For the briefest moment he stood and looked at her naked body, slender and pale in the near-dawn light, and then quickly threw off the blanket and got in beside her. She put her arms around him and he sighed as he snuggled towards her. 'I wasn't looking for payment for the lift,' he said softly, his mouth against her neck.

'I know.' She held him close and felt him beginning to move against her. 'This isn't payment. It's companionship.'

He slept before dawn, still in her arms, tension relieved and equilibrium restored. And when she

67

awoke again and eased herself from under him, the rain had gone and brilliant morning light had flooded the room.

Chapter Seven

Lark dressed quietly in her T-shirt and pants. The dirty trousers were left in a heap in the corner of the room, as were the socks and boots. For some reason, she couldn't bear to put them on, although she hadn't anything to replace them. Her rucksack contained only the one dirty shirt, two pairs of pants and the beaded jacket. She'd realised early on, when travelling, that there was no point in trying to hang onto her belongings. Theft was endemic amongst the travelling community, for all its much talked-about ideals.

Matthew was sleeping, his face pushed into the pillow and his body bare from the waist up where the sheet had been pushed away. His back was smooth and tanned and he exuded good health and previous good living. Lark shook her head slowly, the contrast between Matt and Stewie couldn't have been greater. The last time she'd seen Stewie without his shirt, his ribs showed through yellowed skin and he was covered in septic flea bites.

She crept downstairs to the kitchen. It was bright with morning light and she went to the scullery door and opened it wide. The air was like nectar and she closed her eyes and breathed in deeply.

She could hear birds, house martins or swifts maybe, whistling by the barn and when she opened her eyes, saw them, swooping and diving in an orgy of insect-feeding. Her gaze drifted to the mountain. It was green this morning, refreshed by the overnight rain, and sheep wandered across the expanse of hillside, pulling eagerly at the moist grass. The summit was covered with bleached wisps of ever-changing cloud which now and then shredded in the high breeze to permit a tantalising view of a craggy peak. Lark thought of the Chinese paintings her mother loved, watercolour images of dreamlike landscapes – and here was one in front of her. *I could stare at that forever,* she thought, and a tear unexpectedly welled in the corner of her eye.

She stepped forward as though dragged towards the view, but knocked her bare foot on a cardboard box which had been dumped on the porch. 'Ow!' She winced and, dream feelings gone, bent down to pick up the offending carton. Inside, there was a bottle of milk and a loaf of white bread wrapped in a piece of tissue paper. There was also a packet of butter and a jar of home-made blackberry jam. Elfed Jones' mam had been generous. The contents of the box were designed to make anyone feel hungry and Lark was no exception. With a last look at the hillside and a mental promise to look again, she turned and carried the box into the kitchen.

She boiled the kettle and made some tea and then carefully laid a breakfast table with cups, saucers and plates which she found in the cupboard. A butter dish, white china decorated with

dark blue pansies, was at the back of the cupboard. It had obviously not been used for years,
but she took it out and wiped it with a tea cloth
from a drawer and placed the butter inside. It all
looked lovely and she sat, quiet and alone, eating
her jam and bread and drinking the dusty tea
with more pleasure than she'd known for a
couple of years.

When full, but still thirsty, she poured another
cup of tea and looked around the room. This
must have been where the old man lived in his
later years, perhaps even sleeping on the burst
leather chair by the hearth. The other rooms were
untouched, tidy but ignored, the necessity of
using them long since gone. In this room, he had
eaten and read the paper and his *Farmers Weekly*
magazine – there was a pile of them on the floor
beside the chair – and then slept. She looked up.
On the mantelpiece, tucked beside a stopped
clock, there were photographs. She got up, cup in
hand, and went to look at them. She recognised
a teenage Matt straight away, standing upright on
skis, his fair hair brushed to the side and his teeth
white as the surrounding snow as he grinned at
the camera. The other picture, taken in the
summer, showed a man and a woman, standing
in a garden beside a barbecue. She was small and
fair, her hair done in a smooth bob and her
bright, confident smile just like Matt's. This was
a woman obviously in charge of her life. She was
wearing pale cream-coloured shorts and a
sleeveless white top. For all their plainness, Lark
could recognise that they were not cheap. Mrs
Williams wore designer clothes.

The man wasn't smiling. He stared at the camera with the same studied pose as the young First World War soldier she had seen last night in the elaborate frame in the front room. He was several inches taller than the woman, with broad shoulders and well-developed biceps showing through his short-sleeved shirt. His thick dark hair was cut short and already sprinkled with grey. His eyes – she held the photograph towards the light and looked closely – were hazel, she thought, or maybe grey. She couldn't decide, the picture wasn't sharp enough. So these were the parents. Far, far removed from this neglected farm and not only in air miles. How strange.

She put the pictures back and had another look around the room. It was dirty, and despite the warmer weather outside, it felt damp. The Rayburn caught her eye and she wandered towards it, cup still in hand. She lifted one of the lids and then opened the lower door. It was crammed with cold ash and clinker which tumbled out messily onto the stone-flagged floor. *I'll give it a go*, she thought, and went to the scullery to find a brush.

When Matthew came downstairs two hours later, yawning and scratching his hair, the kitchen looked quite different. She had cleaned out the ash box of the range and found kindling and anthracite in a metal store behind the house. Matches had been more difficult to track down, but after half an hour of fruitless searching, she was rewarded with an unused box on the shelf above the sink. Most of them had been too damp to use, but eventually she had got the kindling to light,

71

and now the anthracite was burning. She had boiled water on the electric stove and filled the sink with hot water and soap. First, she washed up her breakfast dishes and then proceeded to wash the table and wipe the chairs and the old pine sideboard. She needed more hot water for the cooker and the floor and wished for sterner cleaning materials. The sun was climbing in the sky now and she opened the windows and let the warm air into the room.

'Hi.' He startled her, his bare feet making no sound on the stone floor.

She turned away from the windows and smiled. 'Good morning. Would you like some breakfast?' She indicated the table, which she had relaid with bread and jam and milk. 'Still no coffee, I'm afraid,' she grinned. 'I don't suppose you want to try the tea again. There's milk this morning.'

'Nope, I'll give that a miss, thanks. Milk would be good, though.'

They sat facing each other at the table and she watched him making his way through the loaf. He looked round the room and nodded his head approvingly. 'Looks better this morning. I don't mind telling you that last night I could have wished to be a million miles away. Well, anyway, at least in that pub in the village. This place sure is a mess.'

'I don't think there's much that can't be fixed with a bit of effort.' Lark spoke encouragingly. She had seen his disappointment last night.

He nodded and then sniffed the air; something was burning. He got up and went to the Rayburn and put his hand on one of the lids. It was slightly warm. 'You've got this thing going,' he said and looked at her admiringly. 'It looks such a bastard.'

'Mm,' Lark agreed, getting up to stand beside him. 'It's got a boiler attached and will heat the water when it really gets going. And you can cook on it. I'll show you how it works before I go.'

His face fell and he went to the scullery door and looked out. 'You expected somewhere?' he asked, his voice casual.

She hesitated. 'No, not really... I thought I might go and see...' – she hesitated again, wondering how to phrase it – '...some people in Cheshire.'

He kept his head turned away but his shoulders straightened a little and when he spoke, she could hear his normal confident tone. 'Why don't you stay here for a couple of days? Show me how to work that bastard.' He turned round and indicated the range. 'Anyway,' he warmed to his theme, 'there might be other hidden under-stairs switches and under-sink faucets to find. You know you are the undisputed champion at that.'

Lark laughed, but still hesitated before replying. He came over to her and put a hand gently on her shoulder. 'I'll stay in my own bed tonight, if you prefer.'

She was touched; he really was a decent person. She put her own hand on top of his. 'That was nice last night,' she said, 'very ... comforting.'

'Jesus! Comforting?'

She giggled. 'Well, maybe comforting is the wrong word. But you were lovely.'

Matthew leant towards her and kissed her. 'You'll stay then?'

Lark made up her mind. 'All right then ... for a couple of days.'

They walked outside after he'd finished eating, picking their way barefoot across the puddles in the potholed yard, making towards the hill. Matthew looked round, taking in his inheritance, wondering how much land two hundred and ten acres covered. He had been left the farm buildings, the land and the contents of the old man's Post Office account. The money wasn't much, less than eight thousand pounds, but he still had the equivalent of another five thousand in traveller's cheques. That must be enough to get started, he thought. Perhaps that guy from last night – what was his name? Elfed, or something weird like that. Anyway, whatever, maybe he could give some pointers.

The sheep started walking towards them, used to people arriving at odd times with extra feed. Lark watched them as they carefully trotted down the hillside. The ewes were steady and slow with blank faces, following each other, never deviating from the narrow, well-worn tracks. But the nearly grown lambs jumped from rock to rock and joined together in spontaneous gangs to race joyfully up and down. Lark smiled at their antics and wondered why it was that they lost their pleasure in the world so early in life.

'They think we're going to feed them,' she said. 'Perhaps we'd better move away.'

'Guess so.' Matthew stretched his arms up to the cloudless sky and gave another huge yawn. 'I think the jet lag is really catching up with me now.'

'You tired again?' she asked sympathetically.

'I'm starving, really,' he said. 'I need some meat.'

When they were back in the kitchen he said he would go and buy food. 'I'll go to that Bangor place,' he said. 'D'you think you could tell me what we need?'

She found a piece of paper and a pencil and wrote a list while he was upstairs getting dressed.

'You know, I just realised, there isn't a TV set anywhere in this house.' He was back in his jeans and boots and studying the list. 'I could buy a little set this morning. Bound to be a store that sells them.'

Lark pursed her lips and shook her head doubtfully. 'We're in the middle of the mountains here,' she said. 'You might not be able to get any reception.'

'Oh God, I never thought of that.'

'Well, you could go for satellite, if you really want one.' He looked miserable, as though he had been refused what he wanted for Christmas, and she felt sorry for him. 'Of course, I could be wrong,' she said quickly, 'perhaps your grand-father just didn't like television.'

'Yeah.' He looked relieved. 'Anyway,' he added firmly, 'I gotta farm to run.' He stuck out his chest and pretended to tuck his thumbs in imaginary braces. She burst out laughing and he grinned and did a funny farmer's walk towards the door.

'Come with me,' he said as he went to the car, but she shook her head.

'No. You must find the shop yourself.'

'You will be ... I mean ... you won't...' he started.

She nodded, 'I'll be here. Don't worry, I won't go without telling you.'

He got into the car and started the engine. 'Lark,' he called, leaning his elbow out of the open window. 'Yes?'

'That's not your real name, is it?'

She shook her head.

'Thought not.' He grinned and drove out across the bumpy yard.

Chapter Eight

It was just as well that the road was empty on that Sunday morning when Griff Parry drove towards Cariad Elin. His mind was working overtime and had no space available to deal with traffic. He had discussed the farm and the implications of Matthew Williams' arrival again with Llinos as they sat over their breakfast. She was certain that her idea would work. After all, it was pretty obvious that the boy knew nothing about farming, and that girl – well, she was just some hippie he'd picked up on the road.

'All you need is to let him get involved. His money will be more than useful, and just think...' She sipped at her orange juice, making sure that she kept her eyes averted from the sight of Griff plunging a forkful of bread into his under-fried egg.

76

'Yes, my love,' he mumbled, yolk dripping onto his Mexican moustache.

'Well, think. He'll be on the spot if anything goes wrong. It won't be you going out in the middle of the night if a sheep runs into a car or wanders into the village.'

'Good point, *cariad,* good point.'

So, her plan was realistic and he would go along with it, but there was something else. Something that Llinos didn't know about yet, because he hadn't worked out the most advantageous way of telling her. He admired her enormously and acknowledged to anyone who asked that she was the brains of the partnership, but the thing was, he took advice from other people as well.

On his trips to the brewery and the Cash and Carry he came in regular contact with other small businessmen. Two months ago he had met Sean Harper, a builder from Leeds who had re-located to North Wales. They'd drunk together in the small bar at the back of the castle in Caernarfon, a place Griff preferred to Bangor. He never liked to run the risk of meeting up with his old friends from his home town. None of them had moved on like he had and they were altogether too fond of reminding him of his poverty-stricken youth.

'What's life like out in the sticks?' Sean had asked as he downed his third pint.

Griff shrugged. He was nursing his first and would make it last however long the session might be. He was not fond of alcohol, particularly beer – a huge asset for a publican, but something that had assured that he was never 'one of the boys'.

'Oh, it's all right, you know. The countryside is very choice.' He wondered what was coming next.

'Mm.' Sean eyed Griff's plump face, his gaze lazy but calculating. The man looked a pushover. 'How about you keeping an eye out for any land coming up for sale? I'm planning to build some holiday places. Log cabins, all mod cons and a view. Got to have a view.'

'Oh.' Griff immediately thought of Cariad Elin. The tumbledown farm had the best view in the valley. 'There is a place,' he said hesitantly. 'It's not on the market yet, but it might be soon.'

Sean took a long pull from his glass and put up his finger to the barmaid to indicate a refill. He lit a cigarette, puffed out the first gasp and took Griff by the shoulder. 'You know, squire,' he said confidentially, 'I'm always prepared to pay a finder's fee.' He nodded and paid for his fourth pint. 'A substantial fee, my friend.'

Griff had thought about that meeting often and had formulated a plan. He knew who the owner was, of course. Absentee landlord in Canada. The grandson of the old man, who was probably some fancy businessman who wouldn't want to be bothered with a stupid little farm on the side of a hill. He remembered a geography lesson in school where they'd been shown pictures of great ranches in Canada – or maybe it had been America, but it was bound to be the same thing. They were vast, flat acres of wheat, utterly different from Cariad Elin.

So when Matthew Williams had walked into his pub last night, nobody could have guessed the shock that first meeting had caused. Even Llinos didn't know that he had instructed his solicitor in Bangor to write a letter to the owner, offering a reasonable bid for the land. Why shouldn't he sell the land to Sean Harper? He would make more that way than just accepting a finder's fee. Now the plan would have to be changed. And that required thought.

He was so engrossed that he nearly missed Matthew's car coming cautiously round the bend away from the farm. The moment he realised who it was, he hooted urgently until the young man stopped alongside Griff's Land Rover.

'I was coming to see you,' Griff said straight away. 'We have to talk about the sheep.'

Matthew nodded. 'Sure, but not now. I have to get food from the town. Hey, am I heading in the right direction?'

'What? Oh yes, ten miles on. The supermarket is on the edge of town.'

'Thanks.' Matthew paused and looked admiringly at the Land Rover. It was newer than Elfed's and didn't have all the scratches and dents. 'Do you all have these?'

Griff looked surprised. 'I suppose so, most of us. Useful, see, on the bad roads.'

Matthew grinned. 'Cool vehicle. Love it. See you later.'

'But the sheep? When do we talk about the sheep?' Griff felt desperate; he didn't seem able to get this boy's full attention.

'Come later on. Come to the house. We'll talk about it with Lark.' Matthew drove off, leaving Griff sitting in his car, wrapped in frustration.

There was something lacking about this young man. He had no feeling for the urgency of business. But he was glad to see when he reached the farm gate that Matthew had closed it behind him. At least he had some sense.

Lark saw Griff climbing into the field as she stood at the scullery door. She had stayed in the yard after Matthew had left, looking about, noticing the hole in the wall of the big barn. That was where the stones had been taken from, she realised. Then she noticed the hen house – empty, of course, but in better condition than many of the odd sheds and pens that surrounded the yard. But her eyes were once again dragged to the mountain. The froth of cloud which had obscured the summit had gone, melting away as the sun rose warmly into the noontime sky.

Now the rocky peak stood out sharply in the solid blue, pointed like a pyramid with a chunk taken out of its side. Lark could see two birds circling higher and higher on the thermals. Within no time they were black dots in the sky and then disappeared from view. She was fascinated, a fascination which had no reason but was intense, and she gazed at the hillside with almost aching pleasure. *I will climb that before I leave,* she promised herself.

Griff walked carefully amongst his sheep, sizing up the lambs as they frolicked around their mothers. The bigger ones were ready for market and he would have to get on with that in the coming days, no matter what arrangement he made with Matthew. Then there was the shearing and dipping, already organised but not yet paid for. If he played his cards right, he could make a profit on that.

He looked towards the farmhouse and saw the girl walking out towards him. He frowned to himself. What did she want, and, more importantly, how much influence did she have over the Williams boy? Nothing much, if Llinos' estimation was right. But Matthew had just said that Lark – did he say Lark? – would be present at their meeting. Maybe Llinos had got it wrong. The girl might be rather more important than they had realised and he arranged his face in a welcoming smile as she reached the gate. He waved his podgy arm in greeting.

Lark had run upstairs and reluctantly dragged on the dirty combat trousers when she saw Griff driving into the yard. She thought he might come to the house and had no wish to be caught simply wearing a T-shirt and knickers. The trousers were grossly smelly, having been worn every day for six months and never washed. The smell hadn't offended her until the last few weeks; in fact, she hadn't noticed it. The group she lived with existed in exactly the same state. Opportunities to wash clothes were rare and generally not taken up when they occurred.

'Hello!' Lark smiled.

'Hello to you, miss.' He grabbed hold of a lamb and made a play of weighing it in his arms.

She watched him. 'Are these yours?' She indicated the flock which was milling around his legs.

'Yes.'

'The lambs look good. They must be about ready for market. What are they? About five

81

months or so?'

'Yes, thereabouts.' Griff put down the lamb, climbed over the gate and jumped down to her side. He noticed that she was as tall as he was, above average height for a girl. He also noticed the smell emanating from her clothes and was glad that his Llinos was so particular about their laundry.

'They must be worth a bit.' She grinned.

He was affronted. 'A bit, perhaps. But then, what business is it of yours?'

'Oh, none at all. I'm just curious.' Lark walked alongside him as he went back towards his car. He opened the door and sat on the seat while he pulled off his wellington boots and replaced them with shiny grey slip-on shoes.

'I met your young man on the road just now. We're going to have an old talk later on. To sort things out. He said you would join us.'

'I don't know about that,' she said, shaking her head. 'After all, as you just said, it's none of my business.'

Griff bent over to put the boots in the back of the car. 'He said your name is Lark. Have I got that right? Lark?'

'Mm.'

'Very unusual.' He gave a little cough and tried a small joke, 'And very flighty.'

She smiled briefly and then said, 'Talking about names, tell me. What does Cariad Elin mean?'

'Cariad Elin? Oh, it means Darling Elin. Elin, you know, a girl's name.'

'But that's lovely!' Lark was enchanted. 'Was the Elin Matthew's grandmother?'

'I've no idea,' Griff started his car. 'I suppose she could have been. But I'm not a local. Bangor, me. Not a fucking Joskin.'

'Joskin?'

'Joskin, that's a local,' he called as he started to drive off, 'one of the bloody village idiots.'

It was the first bath she'd had for six months and it felt wonderful. She didn't mind that the old iron tub was narrow and scratched and felt gritty when she sat in it. The mere act of lowering her body into hot water and letting it swish between her legs and up as far as her small breasts, was unbelievably blissful. She heard herself groaning out loud in pleasure, her voice echoing in the little bathroom and probably throughout the empty house. Lying back and savouring the warmth, she thought about the reasons that had prevented her from enjoying this sensation for such a long time, and the pleasure retreated a little. All that had happened was her own fault, her own lack of judgement. Nobody else was to blame. She knew that. Her father had told her that, when he finally tracked her down to the camp in Somerset.

'I can only assume that you are having some sort of nervous breakdown,' he'd said, sitting gingerly on an upturned oil drum beside the ancient van which was her present home.

She'd shaken her head and laughed rather tensely. Other members of her group were lying around, ostensibly chatting to each other or busy with their own affairs, but she knew that they were listening. Stewie was openly attentive, watching her father with consuming interest.

'I'm all right, Dad. This is what I want to do. I'm happy.'

'You'll never get me to believe that.' He looked pointedly at her torn and grimy shirt and cut-off jeans. Her feet were bare and, like her hands, callused and dirty. Her companions, the ten or twelve people sitting or squatting on the dusty and littered grass of a roadside verge, were in a similar state. 'God knows,' he said with undisguised contempt, 'this is no Shangri-La.'

Someone sniggered and she blushed, embarrassed that her father, even in the midst of his pleading for her to come home, couldn't hide his scorn for an alternative lifestyle. If he heard the laugh, he ignored it and continued with his diatribe. 'You've let your mother down as well as me. What d'you think we say when people ask us about you? And as for Christopher, well... You've wrecked him.'

She was curious about that. 'Why didn't he come with you? Didn't he know you were coming?'

He snorted. 'Of course he knew.'

Before he left he pulled out his wallet and produced five ten-pound notes. 'Hang onto this, it'll get you home when you want to come.'

She was going to refuse, but Stewie grabbed her arm as she walked with her father to his car. 'Take it,' he muttered.

The money had gone before the day was out, a bit on food but mostly on drink and a few joints. Then they moved on, further south, and if Dad had come to see her again, she never knew.

She ducked her head underwater, trying to wash the dirt of two years on the road out of her hair. It was impossible.

Later she sat, wrapped in a towel, looking at herself in the mirror in the big bedroom. Her face looked different, older than she remembered, and despite the riotously coloured hair and the nose ring, more serious. She reached up her hands, nails rough and damaged and knuckles still red from the chilblains she'd suffered last winter, and removed the ring and put it slowly on the dressing table. Matthew's wash bag was lying in front of her and, unzipping it, she examined the contents. It was with relief that she found the nail scissors and, with a determined grunt, started cutting, sawing at the dreadlocks. In some places she had to cut nearly to her scalp, but by the time she'd finished and looked properly at herself again, it was as if ten years had dropped off her. That last year in school she'd finally decided to have her long hair cut and had emerged from the hairdresser's with a bouncing cap of curling gold hair. Here it was again, and she grinned in relief.

'You're free,' she whispered to herself. She jumped up from the dressing stool and twirled around, letting the towel fall to the floor, loving the sight of her smooth, clean body.

She had a sudden thought and started to search the drawers and wardrobe. In one drawer she found some women's clothes, neatly folded, with fragrant lavender bags pressed between the layers. There were underclothes, cotton knickers, old-fashioned interlock, washed smooth and

85

threadbare in places. She put them on and was glad that the elastic waistband held them in place, for they hung freely around her hips. The brassiere was too large and was carefully replaced in the drawer. But a flowery cotton blouse did fit and a skirt, though short and above her knees, looked pretty good. Best of all, she found a pair of white sandals, a size too big but wearable. They were standing forlornly on the floor of the wardrobe next to a pair of men's Sunday black shoes, still brilliant in their polish, and she wondered how long it had been since they were last worn.

When Matthew came back three hours later, his arms full of shopping, she was in the yard bringing in more anthracite for the Rayburn. He stopped in his tracks, staring. For the briefest moment he didn't recognise her, but she turned and smiled at him and called 'Hello' in Lark's voice.

'Hi,' he said shyly, almost scared of this new person.

'Let me help you.' She put down the bucket of coal and took a couple of plastic carrier bags from him. 'You've bought masses of stuff.'

'I can't believe it, you look so different,' he said as they put the shopping on the kitchen table.

'I hope you don't mind,' she said, her face a little pink. 'I found these clothes upstairs. If it's OK I'll borrow them for a while until I've washed my own.'

He shook his head slowly. 'It doesn't matter, take what you like. I guess I would have to get rid of all that stuff anyway.' He looked at the pattern of small pink and lilac flowers on the blouse and the white buckled sandals. 'Jesus! They're old-fashioned. They must have belonged to my grandmother and she died nearly forty years ago.' He grinned. 'They look good on you.'

'Perhaps they're back in fashion.' Lark smoothed down the skirt and studied her feet in the sandals.

Matthew stared at her and then tentatively put out a hand and touched the cropped red-gold hair.

'I felt like a change,' she said defensively, wondering if he was sorry that the hippie he'd picked up had disappeared while he was out shopping.

'You look fantastic.' He pulled her to him and kissed her, nuzzling his face into her neck and running his hands over her narrow body. 'Oh, just the greatest.'

Chapter Nine

Lydia Williams had chosen the restaurant with care. This was a rather special occasion and she had no desire to bump into any of her usual lunchtime cronies. Consequently she'd avoided the fashionable bistros and wine bars where the girls usually gathered. If she were seen eating out with someone, it would be noticed and remarked upon. It wouldn't matter that the person was a family friend and an acquaintance she had known since her girlhood years. The mere fact would be remembered and could be mentioned to John. And God knows, she didn't need that hassle, specially now. So she had arranged to meet in one of the major hotels, one of the smart downtown tourist palaces, where none of her set would lunch. When she walked into the expensively decorated dining room at exactly twelve forty-five, she was relieved to see that her fellow diners were all strangers.

She smiled to herself as she was shown to a table in a discreet corner of the room. This was fun. Assignations, expeditions into inappropriate relationships, were what she adored. The sex at the end of it was good, but not nearly as exciting as the preamble. In truth, she preferred the chase. The capture, she had discovered, was generally boring.

Today it would be fun and would only involve the chase. Neither she nor Fred were ready for more at the moment, maybe they never would be. The flirtatious nature of their relationship, conducted, not quite recklessly, at cocktail parties or at barbecues at each other's houses, when their respective partners were busy getting drinks or bringing out the napkins, was far too enticing to give up. That was why they had sustained the banter and occasional stolen kisses for so long.

'Lydia, honey, this is a pleasant surprise. I thought we weren't supposed to meet in public.' Fred's loud and confident voice carried easily to the nearby tables, and Lydia reddened and glanced quickly around.

'Don't be a dope,' she hissed, turning up her face for his greeting kiss. 'I never said that. It's just better to be careful, that's all.'

The waiter arrived and handed them menus

88

which were printed on enormous white cards. Their faces were immediately hidden from view, but that suited Lydia for the moment while she considered what to order, and more importantly, how to direct the conversation. The meeting had been at her instigation and she had no desire to appear desperate. She temporised by deciding to have a drink and gained more time as the waiter took their order for double vodkas and left them to mull over the varied choice of deliciously described dishes.

Fred gazed with pleasure at Lydia She looked so cool and smart in her lime-green linen suit, perfect for the continuing sultry weather. He sighed as he thought of his Edith, so well bred and so badly dressed. Her idea of hot-weather clothing was to change her normal sweatshirt for a T-shirt. She only made an effort when she was showing one of her blessed horses. Then she would dress up in her tweeds or velvet jacket and Lycra jodhpurs and tie her hair into a netted coil and really look the part. He felt quite proud of her on those occasions, even though he knew that the outfit was merely a part of the show. She, personally, couldn't care less and would fling off the show clothes and be back into her old jeans within minutes of them returning home. Then she would be off to the stables, leaving him to head for the drinks cabinet before going back to the office to catch up on work missed.

'What have you found on the menu?' he asked, looking across at her and admiring the small, pale fingers, the nails expertly polished, which clutched the menu.

'It's surprisingly interesting,' she replied slowly, 'but I think ... just something light.'

The waiter reappeared, setting down the drinks, and waited, pencil poised, to take their order. Lydia looked up and smiled. 'Grilled chicken and salad, please. No dressing.'

'And I'll have a steak and...' Fred paused and considered for a moment, 'er, no ... better not. Bring me the same as the lady. Thanks.'

He watched the waiter walk away and then grinned at Lydia and patted his belly. 'Gotta watch the weight.'

Lydia shook her head. Fred had no excess pounds. Perhaps he wasn't as fit as John and didn't have the muscled physique of that last boy – what was his name now?... Oh yes, Jason – but he was still worth a second look.

She laughed and said in her pretty, musical voice, 'Your figure is fine. You've no worries on that score.'

'Or on any other, I hope.' He made a little mockery of leering and she giggled.

'Whatever can you mean?' She had raised one eyebrow and looked at him in that cutely arch way that he found achingly attractive. He wondered again why he hadn't noticed her at all. She must have been there at the same time, even if she was a couple of years younger than he was. He knew she hadn't been one of the cheerleaders; they had been big, athletic girls. Why, his partner's wife, Meg Bronsky, had been one of them. He grimaced, thinking about her now. She had run to fat and was bossy and loud-mouthed and made Dick Bronsky's life hell on wheels. No,

Lydia certainly hadn't been one of Meg's set.

'Anyway, sweetheart, what did you want to talk to me about? It sounded pretty urgent on the phone.'

Lydia tore nervously at a bread roll. 'Not really urgent, Fred. I just need a bit of advice, and, I guess, someone to talk to.'

Fred looked concerned. Lowering his voice slightly, he asked, 'John hasn't found out about us, has he? I mean, not that there is anything that he could actually accuse us of, but he might not like our ... well, our attachment.'

'No, no, nothing like that.' Lydia put out her hand and patted his wrist. 'Well, maybe he suspects something, but even if he does ... it's of no consequence. He doesn't seem to care about anything much these days. Everything is too much trouble to him. Me, work and Matthew. Matthew most of all.'

Fred picked up his glass and drank slowly. 'How's the Li Park project going? I've been hearing rumours that they aren't satisfied.'

'I don't know. He never tells me, and I'm not interested anyway.'

'He could lose it, you know, and that would be a big blow to him. Word spreads and once one contract goes, others follow.'

Lydia nodded impatiently. 'Yes, I'm sure you're right, but Fred, I want to talk about Matthew.'

'What about him?' Fred sat back in his chair as the waiter appeared with their lunch and started to dish it out.

'He's gone,' said Lydia. 'Flown to England, well, Wales ... to that stupid little farm John's

91

father left him. He says he's not coming back.' Her voice broke a little at that point, her veneer of calm deserting her for a moment and causing Fred to look up from the plate of grilled chicken he'd been contemplating. He watched her hand shake as she picked up her knife and fork and saw the fork poised above the rocket salad on her plate as she ignored the chicken. It was not like her to be out of control, and he wasn't sure he liked it.

'Matthew?' he said casually. 'I can't believe it. I thought the kid had calmed down after that last business. I had him marked down to come into my office.'

'I know,' Lydia said earnestly, 'and we were so grateful. But he's just thrown up college and gone. I'm at my wits' end, but John – well, John is hopeless. He won't talk to me about it and seems totally uninterested. All he says is that Matthew must do what he wants.'

A tiny piece of rocket was picked up on Lydia's fork and delicately put into her mouth. Fred noticed that she swallowed it without chewing and that the small piece wasn't followed by another. His Edith would have cleared that plateful in a trice and be looking round for dessert by now. Edith might not dress very well but she did appreciate her food.

Lydia broke into his thoughts. 'I hoped you might have a suggestion.'

Fred took a large forkful of chicken and ate it while looking round to indicate to the waiter to bring more drinks. He swallowed and paused before replying. 'I don't know, Lydia. Not having kids is one of the pleasures of my life and I have no idea how people manage them.'

She sighed and put down her fork, then pushed her plate away. Her hair, thick and blonde, a genetic legacy of her Scandinavian grandparents, drooped over her face as she leant forward to pick up her glass. 'I'm sorry, Fred,' she said after a while, 'I know it's not your problem and I shouldn't have bothered you. It's just that with John being so distant and unconcerned, I needed to talk to someone else.' She smiled wistfully. 'You drew the short straw.'

This was better; she was smiling again and beginning to joke. Fred attacked his chicken with gusto and then, after gaining her small nod of agreement, set about her rejected plate. 'You know,' he said, after the waiter had taken away the plates and brought coffee, 'I would be inclined to leave him for a while. Let him phone and write and be nice back. Give him time to get sick of it. You know he will – he's a city kid through and through, despite his excursions to the Arctic.'

'But then what?'

'Then, after a few months, start giving him incentives to come back.' She looked puzzled and he leant forward to expand his theory, 'Offer him some money, get him a nice apartment. I can help you there. You could say something like ... er, does he know of anyone back home who would like this great apartment? You've heard that the owner is looking for a tenant. Downtown, right in the centre of things, you know. But don't push now.'

'Well,' said Lydia, doubtfully at first but then warming to the idea, 'I guess it's worth a try. Yes, I'll do that, but I won't tell John. The mood he's in, he would make every effort to go against me.'

'Just between us, eh?' Fred smirked.

'Yeah.'

He put his hand over hers, and under the table pushed his foot between her crossed ankles. 'That's how I'd like it best,' he said thickly, his solid brown eyes widening and slightly bulging, 'something just between us.'

Chapter Ten

It was one of those rare days in Snowdonia, when the weather is fine and hot and the cloud lifts clear from the mountain tops. The peaks stood out sharply, dark rock cutting a jagged outline against a bright blue sky. Below the craggy summits, the hillsides were green and lush. The pastures had grown well in the wet spring and provided good grazing for the hundreds of sheep which polka-dotted the steep fields. Buzzards were spiralling lazily in the thermal currents above the mountain top, calling out now and again their high, mewling cry. They circled in the air with their heads pointed earthwards, watching rabbits scamper and play amongst the rocks and tufts of grass. Mice and voles running busily through the fields were mere specks on the earth from the great height that the birds had achieved and remained blissfully unaware of the eyes in the sky above. For some, their first indication of danger would be their last, as they were swept away from their labours in one perfect, plummeting dive and uplift, and carried off to provide supper for the anxious mouths of buzzard chicks.

Down in the valley, even the farm looked good. The puddles had dried up and the stone buildings took on a warmer glow in the late-afternoon sun. Lark and Matthew had made a pile of scrap and rubbish from the yard and set fire to it, and from where they now stood, three-quarters of the way up the hillside, they could see smoke from their bonfire spiralling in a thin plume straight up into the open sky.

Matthew took off his shirt and tied it carelessly around his waist. He was already tanned from his early summer at home and his body glowed and rippled with youthful strength and good health. He wiped some beads of sweat from his forehead with his arm and rubbed at the short hair on the back of his neck, which was wet with the effort of climbing. 'This is wonderful,' he said, as he stood to admire the view. 'I hadn't imagined that Wales would be so warm.'

Lark, who was walking ahead of him, stopped and turned. 'It isn't often,' she said, breathing hard and pulling at the front of her T-shirt to let some air pass through it. 'Didn't your father tell you that it rains a lot in these mountains? You wait,' she grinned and wagged a gentle finger at him, 'there will be days when the cloud will drop down over the hill and you will almost forget what the sun looks like. Even the farm will disappear in the mist.'

'I know you're exaggerating.'

'Well, maybe. But I would enjoy a day like this while you can. It's special.'

Matthew climbed towards her, reached out and grabbed her round the waist. He tugged her close and, kissing her slowly, pulled them both gently to the ground. They sat, shoulder to shoulder and hand in hand, kissing with eyes open, dizzy with the exertion of the climb and the sexual energy which had developed so quickly between them. 'I don't know about special weather, Lark, but all I can think of is the last few days we've had together. They've been special. Whoever would have thought that I would find you here waiting for me?' He stroked her cropped hair then moved his hand down her neck to the V of her shirt.

She shifted nervously and took hold of his hand, stopping him from going further.

'Matthew, I wasn't waiting for you. We just happened to meet up. Don't make us more important than that.'

He looked away from her, towards the west and beyond the mountains to where the hazy blue form of Anglesey lay, slumbering quietly in the glittering sea. He drew up his knees and wrapped his arms around them, his face suddenly boyish and hurt.

'But it feels more important,' he muttered. 'I don't want you to go.'

She sighed and shook her head, then in a sudden movement, got to her feet and started walking on up the hill.

Matthew sat for a minute and then scrambled

up and followed her. 'Stay on here,' he called, 'at Cariad Elin. It's as good a place as any. And you like it. I know you do.'

The tall figure ahead of him stopped again and with her back still turned, said quietly, 'Yes, I do. But...'

'But what?' He was beside her now, grabbing her hand and looking into her face and the curious, pebbly eyes, which seemed to have lost some of their colours as she struggled with her indecision.

'But I move on. That's what I do. Stay nowhere for long.'

'Why?' he demanded.

'I just do. And I'm not going to tell you why, so don't ask me.' Tears sprang up, suddenly, washing the pebbles so that greens and browns lit up and startled him with their intensity. He bent his forehead against hers and said nothing for a while.

Eventually he looked up and put his hands on either side of her face, forcing her to look into his eyes. 'Lark,' he whispered, 'you seem to belong here, somehow. I won't ask you again, I promise, but stay with me ... for a while.'

She was still for a moment, biting her lip and looking up towards the top of the hill where a little puff of cloud was beginning to gather. She wanted to say yes – it would be so easy, and already the farm had taken hold of her heart. But might she be making another mistake? She didn't know.

Below them the farm was beginning to fade into shadow as the afternoon sun dropped behind the smaller hills. Dragging her eyes away from the hilltop, she gazed down to the valley. As she watched, she noticed, for the first time, holes in the roof of the big barn and could even see birds flying in and out, catching insects in the warmed air. *That must be mended before winter,* she thought, we'll need to bring the sheep into that barn for lambing. But even as she thought it, she gave a little laugh. *We – who's we, you idiot? It's Matthew's farm. You should be moving on.*

Matthew gave her a little hug, encouraged by the laugh. He couldn't remember when a girl had excited him so much. Maybe it was her remoteness that was so attractive, her ability to be with him physically, yet keep some part of herself secret. Yet she seemed so open on the surface, full of practical ideas, and so generous in bed. Their lovemaking in the last week had been, at times, explosive, driven by his desire and her greater experience. And afterwards she had been gentle and ladylike as though the things they had just done, which almost made him blush when he thought of them now, were nothing more than to be expected.

'It is so lovely here,' she said suddenly, her voice low and almost indistinct.

He grinned, encouraged. 'A few weeks ... please, we're so good together. We are, aren't we? I can't let you go now.'

She looked at him and reached up to his sweating forehead to push the damp blond hair out of his eyes. Her gesture, though almost motherly, served yet again to excite him. He had her full attention and he loved that.

'All right,' she said, sighing deeply as she rested

her hand on his bare shoulder. 'For a while. But Matthew,' her fingers tightened into a grip and she stared directly into his eyes, fixing his gaze so that he was almost mesmerised by the intensity of her eyes, 'listen to me. One day I will want to leave, or one day you will want to, and that will be it. No recriminations, no begging to stay for either of us. Remember, we aren't going to the top of the hill.'

He looked puzzled, unable for a moment to understand her metaphor, but then fastened onto the notion that she was going to stay and whooped out loud. 'I know, I know,' he shouted, still unsure of what he knew, 'and I agree. You staying is going to make this whole thing just great. I know we can make this farm work.' He stretched his arms out wide, encompassing his inherited acres, and spun slowly round. 'This is what I've always wanted.'

Lark smiled and raised an eyebrow. 'Always? Goodness, Matt. Always?'

He laughed and gathered her into his arms again and swung her round. 'Don't be mean,' he murmured into her neck. 'I'll make a go of it... Promise.'

They stood, two people alone in a perfect world, watching the great orange sun sink into an untroubled sea. He took her hand and started to pull her down the hill.

'Come on,' he said, 'let's go back to the house. We have to celebrate our decision, and the way I want to celebrate, I can't do in front of all these fucking sheep. Anyway,' he yelled, as they ran, slithering on the scree and pounding heavily through the pasture, 'you said we shouldn't go to the top of the hill.'

A few days before, they had discussed the farm with Griff Parry. He had come back to Cariad Elin later on in the afternoon as he had promised, driving confidently into the farmyard, forgetting that he no longer had free run of the place. Matthew and Lark had watched him bring the Land Rover to a halt in front of the barn. They were standing in the yard staring in dismay at the accumulated rubbish, the bits of corrugated iron, wooden fence staves and all sorts of half-empty cans.

'God, it's awful,' Matthew had said miserably and kicked angrily at a can, sending it flying across the yard and landing by the field gate. 'How could he have lived like this?'

'I expect he was old and tired,' Lark said. 'He was on his own and it didn't matter.'

'But how am I going to get started? What am I going to do with all this crap?'

They had investigated the barns. Only half a wall remained on the north side of the biggest barn. The stones had been carefully removed, leaving the structure, incredibly, still erect but allowing the elements to whip through unchallenged. Two smaller barns – sheds really, Lark decided – were structurally sound but crammed full of ancient machinery. She wondered how old most of the stuff could possibly be. It was covered in rust and ancient bird droppings and neither of them had any idea of what the various pieces were used for. The only thing she recognised was a mangle, its 1940s green paint showing through the rust, and probably still in working order.

'This might be useful,' she said, pushing away a box of rusted castration instruments and lifting out the mummified carcass of a blackbird which was stuck in the broad spokes of the large wheel which worked the handle.

'What the hell for?'

Her explanation was greeted with a snort of disgust.

'Jesus, I'm not using that load of junk. They sell washing machines here, don't they?' She nodded. 'Well,' he continued, 'I'll go into town and buy one.'

Out in the yard again they had discussed the piles of rubbish.

'You could get a skip,' Lark suggested and then had to describe the uses of a skip. 'We could load all the unburnable stuff into it and then make a bonfire with the rest.'

'Yeah,' he said despondently, 'that sounds cool. Will you phone and arrange it?'

'No problem,' she agreed and then looked up as Griff's Land Rover turned into the yard.

Matthew nodded his head towards the plump figure who was sitting in his vehicle with the door open, putting on his boots. 'He's coming to discuss the farm,' he said in a lowered voice.

'Yes, I know,' said Lark. 'Be careful.'

She followed slowly as he walked over to meet Griff. She didn't particularly want to be part of the discussion, but Matthew had asked her to join in. 'You understand this guy better than I do,' he'd said, 'he just seems like an idiot to me.'

'He isn't that,' she warned.

Matthew and Griff leaned over the gate and looked at the sheep who were milling about, expecting some sort of activity. Lark perched on the wall, her long legs dangling against the old stones. Griff looked at her suspiciously. He hadn't yet worked out the relationship between the newcomers and couldn't decide how much influence she had. Matthew seemed to want to include her in the conversation, even looking at her for approval when he said something smart. He was looking at her now, although he was addressing his remarks to Griff.

'I guess I'm not that sure,' Matthew said. 'I planned to do this by myself. I hadn't reckoned on getting a partner.'

Griff tugged thoughtfully at his Zapata moustache with a podgy finger and thumb and then said slowly, 'Well, yes, I can see that, and if you're not interested, then it's no trouble for me to move the sheep. The lambs are nearly ready anyway and will be going to market. Tidy sum, they'll fetch. And the ewes can go across the mountain. I know of some grazing there.'

'Which you'll have to pay for,' Lark interjected with a grin. Matthew nodded.

Bitch! Griff thought, but kept his voice pleasantly calm. 'Perhaps,' he agreed, 'but I might not. There's an Englishman bought the land over there. He'll want the grass kept down, so we could come to some sort of arrangement.'

Matthew climbed onto the wall beside Lark and looked down at Griff. 'Would we be fifty-fifty in this, if I agreed? I mean, would I get a share of the lambs as well as the ewes?'

'Certainly,' said Griff, encouraged but still cautious, 'if you put up enough money.'

Matthew turned to Lark, putting a hand casually on her thigh, half exposed below the short old-fashioned skirt. Griff saw that she didn't seem to mind. Indeed, she patted his hand gently and gave it a little squeeze. It was obvious what was going on there, he decided, no matter what Llinos thought.

'So, what d'you think?' Matthew asked, looking at the girl for guidance.

'It's your land, Matt. You must do what you want.'

He shook his head, the thick blond hair flopping untidily, looking like every American teenager Griff had ever seen at the cinema.

'But do you think it's a good idea?' Matthew demanded.

She placed her foot gently against the back of a curious lamb and smiled as it jumped over its mother and ran around to the rear of the flock. 'I think it might be,' she said slowly, considering her words carefully. 'It would be one way of learning the business, and if the deal is drawn up to each party's satisfaction, then why not?'

Griff almost clapped his hands in delight. 'She's right, you know, your lady friend,' he said excitedly. 'I wish I'd had someone to help me when I first started. You can make mistakes, terrible mistakes, and the bloody vet costs a fortune.'

Matthew looked again at Lark and lifted his eyebrows quizzically. She nodded and he grinned.

103

'OK,' he said, making up his mind. 'You write out the deal and we'll give it the once-over and if it looks cool, I'll sign up.'

Griff, unable to keep his relief a secret, released a huge sigh. Leaning across, he grabbed hold of Matthew's hand and shook it vigorously. 'Good lad, good lad,' he said, grinning so hard that little flecks of saliva gathered at the corner of his mouth and trickled onto his chin. 'That's the ticket, that's the bloody ticket! Now, Llinos, my wife, will write out an agreement and I'll bring it round in the morning. No reason to waste time, is there?' He turned away from the field. 'Well, I've got to get moving. The bloody pub doesn't run itself.'

He started walking towards his Land Rover, and Matthew and Lark jumped off the wall and followed slowly behind him. Suddenly he stopped and turned, and put a finger to his head as though he'd just remembered something. 'Would you like to buy some chickens?'

Matthew shook his head. 'No, thanks, I went to the supermarket this morning. We've got plenty of food.'

Griff laughed. 'No, not dead bloody chickens. Live ones. You've got that empty hen house over there.' He nodded towards the small building closest to the back garden and Matthew and Lark followed his eyes. 'It's doing nothing, and I know someone trying to get rid of half a dozen Rhode Islands. Good layers, they are, and just think of those lovely brown eggs. I could buy them from you for the pub, and I daresay the shop will take a few.'

Matthew was charmed. This was the beginning of his adventure. Within twenty-four hours he would be the owner of a flock of sheep and some hens. Who at home would believe this? Matthew Williams, urban activist, transformed overnight.

'Yeah,' he said, as casually as he could, 'good idea.'

Griff got into his vehicle, forgetting, for once, in his excitement, to change out of his boots so that he inevitably smeared mud over the previously unnaturally clean pedals. 'Good,' he said, 'I'll bring them up tomorrow with the agreement. You'll be a farmer by tomorrow night!'

After he'd driven away and Lark had closed the gate behind him, she and Matthew walked slowly back to the house.

'What did you do in Canada?' she asked, watching him tread carefully between the potholes. 'I bet it wasn't farming.'

He laughed. 'However did you guess? Nope, as far as I can remember, I've never been on a farm before in my life. I was at college. Studying law.'

She shrugged and looked around with a smile. 'Well, this'll be different.'

'There's no chance that you know about farming, is there?' he asked hopefully.

She shook her head. 'No chance, I'm afraid, but it can't be that difficult.' She nodded towards the road where Griff's car could still be heard in the distance. 'If that halfwit can do it, then so can you.'

Chapter Eleven

Fall had come and nearly gone in Toronto and the weather was getting very cold now that it was November. An icy wind blew down from the north and tiny white flakes danced in the air, hardly visible now, but omens of the future. Lydia guessed that the first real blizzard of the season would be on its way soon, for having been born in this city, she knew its ways. Like the old-timers who shuffled about the cheap bars by the waterfront, she could smell snow in the air long before it arrived. But she didn't mind it. Winter was her favourite time of the year, when she felt at her best and most alive. There was something about the frost which brought colour to her face when it was draining out of others.

The snow, in its blanketing awkwardness, excited her. She loved its whiteness and sparkle, and even as a small child had spent hours staring at it from her window, admiring the new patterns it made on roofs and exulting in the difference a night's snowfall could make to the street outside. Escape to Florida or the islands, which attracted so many of her friends, had never interested her. She was a true Canadian who loved her country because of and not despite of its weather.

The street lights were on this afternoon as she drove home from the city. In the trunk of her car were several carrier bags and boxes from some of

106

the best shops downtown. She had spent the day shopping for her winter wardrobe, alone as she preferred, so that she could concentrate her expert eye on the best and most fashionable pieces. The prize purchase among many was a cashmere coat, expensive but so exquisite that she had known she would have it from the moment the sales assistant had tentatively taken it from its plastic covering. She thought about it lying there behind her, snugly wrapped in tissue paper in a glossy cardboard box. At one time, she could have fed the family for weeks for the price of that coat, but that had been years ago and now she spent as she pleased. John wouldn't ask the price; in fact, John wouldn't recognise it as anything new. These days, John barely noticed her existence at all.

They had lived almost as strangers in the last several months. He was either at his office or sitting alone in his study, concentrating, she supposed, on his Li Park presentation. But she, too, had spent a lot of time out of the house. She had a new man, a social worker who, despite his youth, was the director of the homeless project where she worked as a volunteer. All her friends dabbled in charity work and homelessness was her chosen field. It was often surprisingly fulfilling. She was quick and intelligent and able to cut easily through waffle, and thanks to contacts made through John's work, she knew many of the right people in housing who could help. The clients didn't particularly interest her but their problems did, and solving them was fascinating.

'You should do this professionally,' Kevin Burns

had said, when he had taken up his new post and discovered which of the wealthy volunteers made any meaningful contribution.

Lydia had waved her beautifully manicured hand dismissively but had appreciated the remark and warmed to the young man. The discovery that he had once been a priest and that those pale eyes and black hair had been given over entirely to God for nearly seven years, came as a delicious surprise. She wasted no time in ensuring that he no longer kept to his vow of celibacy. If he had been a little nervous at first, well, she had sorted that out. Now he couldn't get enough and she glowed in the continual compliments he paid her. Her sex life was presently very satisfying.

As she drove into her avenue, she smiled. Kevin would appreciate the sight of her in the coat and she had a little gift for him in another box. She would be surprised if he had ever owned a cashmere scarf.

John's car was in the drive, parked on the slant with the windows down and the lights left on. She reached inside the open window and switched them off and then used the key on her ring to close the window and lock the car. A niggle of worry bit into her previous good humour and she looked towards the house, wondering what he was doing.

There were no lights on in the hall when she stepped inside, and leaving the shopping bags by the door, she walked quickly through the dark rooms to John's study. The door was shut and she threw it open with a crash, frightened at what she would find.

He was there, sitting at his desk. In the gloomy light from the window Lydia took in the unopened briefcase lying on the floor beside him and the open whisky bottle on the desk. In his hand was a half-full glass which he raised awkwardly in greeting as she stepped into the room.

'You left the lights on in your car and it wasn't locked,' she said, noting in disgust that he had spilt drink down the front of his grey polo-neck sweater. His hair was untidy and needed cutting, and as she snapped on the lamp by the door she saw that he appeared not to have shaved that day.

'Hello, Lydia,' he said drunkenly. 'What's new?'

She wrinkled her nose, sniffing the alcohol fumes which rose from the open bottle, the glass, and most of all, his clothes. 'Unfortunately, nothing,' she said evenly.

John slopped another drink out of the bottle and put his hand up, feigning shock. 'Now that is surprising. I called you at the charity centre. Remember you said you would be there all day? Funny, those voluntary workers, none of them could recall seeing you after about eleven o'clock. Hell of a lunch you must have had.' He sat back in his chair and looked up at her, his eyes wavering unsteadily as he tried to hold her gaze.

It was she who looked away first. 'I was out on a field trip.' She suddenly needed to examine her nail polish. 'Inspecting temporary housing. I'm the only one who can do it. You know that. It's my expertise, after all.'

His laugh was mirthless. 'Oh yeah. Clever old Lydia. Test the beds, too?'

Lydia did what she always did when attacked – hit straight back. 'Oh God,' she said, 'here we go again. Look, John, you're drunk. Go to bed.'

'No,' his voice was getting louder, 'I don't want to go to bed. That's your department. I want to sit and talk to my expert wife. I want to talk about our son.' He riffled amongst the papers on his desk and with a grunt of satisfaction, lifted up an envelope with a letter half-pushed into it. With clumsy fingers, he dragged out the letter and awkwardly held it up to the light. 'Yeah,' he continued, 'I want to talk about our son, who in five months says he has become a sheep farmer. An expert sheep farmer.' He smacked the letter with the back of his hand and turned round again to gauge Lydia's reaction.

She shrugged her shoulders. 'What's the matter?' she asked, using the patient voice that she invariably employed when speaking to the less intelligent clients at the shelter. 'Feeling more than usually sorry for yourself today?'

That seemed to have hit a nerve, for he paused in his diatribe and took another swallow of whisky. His voice was quieter when he continued. 'Nice of you to leave this out for me to read, although he only seems to address his remarks to you.'

'What d'you expect?' she replied scornfully. 'Last time he phoned, you could barely bring yourself to talk to him. Other than telling him he was stupid, you couldn't have been less interested.'

He looked at her for a moment and then let the piece of paper drop to the floor. 'You know,' he said, 'it isn't anything to do with what I say or do.

Nobody cares what I think. So it's just two experts talking to each other and leaving out the one who isn't.'

The catch in his voice was obvious now and he cleared his throat in a vague effort to disguise it. Lydia moved from the doorway and came to stand in front of him. His whole air was one of dejection, no ... rejection.

'You've lost the Li Park project. That's what this is all about.' She grabbed his shoulder and shook it. 'You have, haven't you?'

He caught his breath and winced but was otherwise silent, staring at the letter which had landed by his feet on the edge of the bright Turkestan rug. The lamp by the door made a soft pool of light, otherwise the room was now quite dark. The bookshelves which lined the walls disappeared into the shadows and only the sharp sleety rain, rattling on the windowpane, made any sound. Lydia dropped her hand from John's shoulder and sat heavily on the leather chair beside the wall. When John spoke, it was with a sigh. 'I lost the Li Park project weeks ago.'

'You idiot!' Lydia snapped, making no attempt to hide her contempt. 'Why didn't you go into partnership with the Jackson Associates on this one? That's all that was necessary.'

He shook his head and tapped his finger on the desk. 'There you go again, being an expert. Now I wonder how you came up with that one. It couldn't possibly be that Fred Eland is their lawyer and this is a little case of pillow talk? No...' The tapping finger folded into a fist and he crashed it down onto the pile of papers with such

111

force that Lydia jumped and then shrank back into her chair. 'No it couldn't, because there's nothing between you. You've told me ... at least twice. It's just clever old Lydia. The expert. Expert screw!'

She got up, the colour draining from her face and her hands shaking. She had never known him to be like this and didn't like it. He was not a violent man, barely ever raising his voice to her; in fact, his even temper had long ago become boring.

He moved in his chair and she flinched. His hand was still curled into a fist and she watched it nervously. But as she watched, it straightened and reached forward, towards the bottle. She let out her breath silently and stood up.

'You're not worth arguing with, John, and I'm tired of the constant battle. We're going nowhere, so let's stop pretending.' She walked towards the door, then stopped and looked back at him. 'I'm going out for supper; you can drink yours.'

He sat on in the shadows, sipping slowly from the glass and allowing his passion to subside. His hands were shaking and his heart was still pumping hard. She should have been kinder; she should have asked what was the matter with him. But then, perhaps, he should have told her. Another wave of nausea flooded through him and he closed his eyes. If she had only answered his phone call and come to the hospital this afternoon they might, just, have got... He didn't know what.

They had taken him to the ER even though he'd said he was OK.

'You gotta have a check-up,' the paramedic said, after he'd done all the tests that John would permit in the street. An interested crowd had gathered, watching a policeman examine the young man who was unconscious on the sidewalk. The fact that he, John, had a stab wound in his arm didn't seem to bother them, but when the paramedics arrived, one of them noticed blood running onto his hand

'You're through to bone there, man,' the medic said and quickly dressed it with a pad of gauze and a pressure bandage.

The policeman was now more sympathetic. 'Tried to mug you, did he?'

John nodded.

'What d'ya use to deck him?'

John pointed to his briefcase which was lying on the ground beside the young man. The officer picked it up and tested its weight. It was heavy. Besides the Li Park papers, John had packed his laptop. He'd told Annette he was going to work at home, and taking the laptop made the excuse more feasible. In reality, he just wanted to get out of the office, a place where he no longer felt comfortable. He would go home and sit in his study. He was safe there.

But a man had stood in front of him as he was coming out of his building and asked for money.

'No, go away.' John had scarcely looked at him, used to the beggars who were becoming a familiar sight in the city. He was shocked, then, when the man produced a knife and held it up in front of John's face.

'Give me your fucking money!' He was only a

boy, really, no older than Matt, but with wild, mad eyes and yellowed teeth. The knife had a serrated blade on one side and holes in the handle into which the boy's dirty fingers slotted. He waved the knife backwards and forwards in front of John's face, grinning stupidly as he did so and making little pretend jabs at his eyes.

Rage started to overtake fear. *Christ, how much more do I have to put up with?* he thought, and in a split second he swung his briefcase upwards and caught the mugger with a fierce blow under the chin. From then on, events seemed to happen in slow motion and he watched as the kid's head snapped back and the flailing arms fell towards him. The knife flew out of his fingers and spun up into the air before falling slowly, its point and serrated edge tearing through John's coat and coming to rest with a slow clatter on the sidewalk. The boy fell beside it and a woman passer-by who had witnessed the whole event opened her mouth and started to scream.

He rode to the hospital in the same ambulance as the unconscious boy, sick with the fright which he'd managed to put aside during the event and conscious of the growing pain of his wound. The paramedics quickly hooked him up to a saline drip and then left him alone as they worked urgently on their other patient. John sat on the opposite bench, watching as an airway was inserted and oxygen administered. Once during the short journey, they lost the boy's pulse and John watched in horror as they ripped open the filthy shirt and smacked the defibrillator paddles onto his thin chest. The yell 'clear' and the subsequent shock had John shaking and vomiting into a cardboard bowl handed to him by a sympathetic medic.

'You'd better get someone to take you home,' the ER medic said, once they'd reached the hospital, after his wound had been stitched and a couple of injections given. 'I guess you're not fit to drive.' But Lydia wasn't at the centre and there was no one else. After he'd given another statement to the police, he got a taxi to the office car park and drove himself home, imagining the feel and taste of whisky dribbling down his gullet and the warm, comforting glow that would follow.

He knew Lydia hadn't realised that, during this latest row, he had been just as frightened as she. Her selfishness would never have allowed her to credit him with emotions as important as hers. And of course, he hadn't told her about his mugging or the wound. It ached, the split muscle unanchored and the superficial stitching tugging at his skin. He sighed; he was dog-tired. Too exhausted even to get out of his chair and go to bed. Today's events had become just one more episode in a life which was falling apart.

His eyes fell on the letter and he bent down to pick it up. 'We've moved the sheep down to the lower fields,' Matthew had written, 'where the grazing is better. The cloud hangs low over the mountain now and it seems to have rained non-stop for weeks.'

John carefully folded the page and looked up at the faded sepia photograph hanging on the wall above his desk, between the formal portraits of his parents. It was too dark in the room to see it properly but he didn't need to; the picture was impressed forever in a rarely opened compartment of his mind. He could see the stone farm buildings in the background and the smiling figures of his parents standing by the front door of the house. He was the solemn little boy standing shyly between them, one hand clutching his mother's skirt and the other held safely in his father's hand.

The adult John closed his eyes and a tear slid slowly down his face. That picture of family happiness was not a large part of his memory. If he tried extremely hard he could remember Mam's face when it had been plump and round and framed with curly dark hair. But his memories of her then were mostly snatches of things. The flowered cotton apron wrapped round her stout body and her short legs stuffed into black wellington boots. And the cigarette which hung constantly from her lips. Even when she was out in the yard, pegging the washing on the line, or helping his father drive the sheep down from the hillside, the cigarette would be in place.

The picture began to swirl in a moisture-laden mist. Rain was sweeping down the mountain, drenching the fields and turning the yard into puddles of mud. *Why don't they go inside?* he wondered miserably, looking at the little family who still waited by the front door, smiling happily at the camera.

'Oh Christ,' he cried out loud to the empty room, 'what's happening to me?' The tears fell freely now and he laid his head down on the desk and sobbed until he slept. He dreamed that he

116

was laughing, running down the hillside waving to his mother as she brought out a bucket of mash to the chickens. The young dog ran beside him, leaping up excitedly and scattering the sheep and the new lambs, making them run about wildly in the field and crash stupidly into the drystone wall. The waving arm hurt so much, and out of the corner of his eye he could see Dad watching them, shaking his head in anger. He had to stop running.

Chapter Twelve

They drove through a mud-sleeked road towards the village. The rowan trees on the hillside, which had been so full and colourful in the summer and autumn, now stood in desolate nudity, stripped of leaves and shivering in the wind. A few Scots pines, elegantly branched, braved the cold, wet weather, stoics among trees but black against the skyline. Only the plantations of conifers showed up green, but it was a dull colour. The planting was too dense to allow any light to filter through the pine needles so that the regulated blocks of individual trees became an unlovely uniform whole.

On either side of the road, straggling rows of alders stood with their roots in the ditches. Their gentle greeny-grey of the summer had gone now and rain dripped steadily off the bare branches joining the swift streams of water which ran

117

across the road into an overflowing gully. This would empty into the river at the next turn and Lark wondered whether it had burst its banks yet. Elfed had said it would, when he came over yesterday evening.

'You'll be all right,' he'd assured them, 'and you'll have no trouble getting into the village. It's the people down the other side of the valley. Fucking flooded, they'll be.' He laughed grimly, enjoying the idea of misfortune striking someone other than him.

'Does it ever stop?' Matthew asked him. He was sick of the rain which had poured relentlessly from a slate-coloured sky for the last couple of weeks. Memories of the long summer were fading fast. He could barely recollect the heavy, indolent days of only three months before when he and Lark had drifted about the hills and fields, discovering the boundaries of the farm and exploring their own growing relationship. She excited him more each day, both sexually and intellectually. He had never met a girl, or a man for that matter, like her. Her intelligence was equal to his in every way, which surprised him, for although he was lazy and generally showed little application for study, he was naturally bright and had passed every exam he had ever sat.

But Lark had a different kind of thought process. She knew things and could present them in an entirely novel way, so that talking to her about anything – literature, mathematics or even rock music – became a new experience. She had laughed when he told her this and dismissed his admiration. 'Anyone can think like this,' she said,

118

'it's just learning how to do it. Like anything else.'

But he doubted it. It was as if she possessed a special type of freedom that allowed her to wander outside the normal patterns. Yet when he pressed her about her education, she was vague. She had been to university, yes. She'd had a job, boring. It was when he asked about her previous relationships that she really clammed up. 'Don't ask me, Matt. I won't tell you.'

He had wondered about her as they lay in the sweet-smelling fields, sucking the nectar out of purple clover flowers. Who was she and where had she come from? He had no idea. All he knew was that she was Lark, and that she had been hitching a lift on the way back from a festival.

She had money. When they went into Bangor, he had waited in the car while she had gone into a bank and withdrawn some cash. And she wasn't mean with it. She had bought food for them and never minded spending her money on small necessities for the farm.

She was older than him, by a few years he reckoned, and from the way she spoke, like the well-to-do women in those British films and TV series he had seen, she must have had a privileged upbringing. But where?

He found himself talking about his home a lot, all his causes, his friends, and occasionally, his parents. But although she listened and laughed with him at his reminiscences and asked pertinent questions, she never volunteered anything about herself.

'You remind me of my father,' he said once,

'he's a clam too.'

She laughed and rolled onto her back, undoing the buttons on the old blouse she'd found in his grandmother's drawer and exposing her small breasts to the sun. It was done without guile and as natural as anyone wanting to enjoy warmth on their body, but Matthew found it utterly entrancing. He swallowed hard; the desire to take her was never far below the surface.

'I think I'll buy some more land,' he'd said, picking another petal off the flower head and dropping it so that it landed on her naked breast.

She smiled sleepily and lay still while he dropped more petals on her. 'Good idea,' she murmured as he bent his head and started to blow gently on the petals before putting his lips on her creamy flesh. 'Go for that piece by the river. It used to belong to this farm.'

It was only later that he wondered how she knew that and when he asked, she was vague. 'I must have heard it somewhere,' she said.

Now the summer had gone, and the coming winter was an uncomfortable prospect. The house was cold and Lark suggested that he buy some Calor gas heaters. They made a difference, but it wasn't the same as living with central heating and double glazing. Every morning, Lark got the big fire going in the kitchen and she kept the Rayburn well stoked up with anthracite. He had offered to help, but he could never get the fire to light and would invariably drop anthracite all over the kitchen floor when he tried to fill the hopper, so by mutual agreement, those had become Lark's tasks.

When they weren't out on the land, they lived in the kitchen. Most evenings, tired out from the reconstruction work on the barns and walls, they would sit quietly reading or talking. They went to the pub once or twice a week where they chatted with the locals, and Matthew had been to a football match one Saturday afternoon. He tactfully got out of going to another. He had never played and didn't understand the rules, and the Llanfair village supporters broke into Welsh at moments of drama, which made it all the more confusing. No, they preferred their own company at the moment.

Faced with the lack of television, Matthew compensated by working his way through his father's bookshelves, rediscovering the books he'd ignored as a teenager. Lark read the *Farmers Weekly* and some old books on sheep husbandry that had been in a cupboard beside the fireplace. They fascinated her but they were forty years out of date. Often the recommendations suggested in the worn volumes were directly contradicted by articles in the modern magazines. She debated these with Matthew but he was not hugely interested. He depended on Griff Parry for his information.

It was Lark's ideas on the care of their flock that had partly instigated this morning's trip to the village. She was becoming more and more certain that the farm was being run on uneconomic grounds and that it wasn't entirely due to Matthew's inexperience. Griff hardly came near Cariad Elin these days, preferring to conduct business by telephone, issuing

121

instructions about moving the sheep to different pasture or suggesting that they got in extra feed, now that the grass was dying off. So far, all their major purchases had been made out of Matthew's savings, and the money for the lambs sold in July, or for the eggs sold to the pub, had not been forthcoming.

Yesterday, Griff had phoned to say that he had ordered some feed pellets from the merchants in Bangor and that Matthew was to watch out for the delivery. 'They want paying on the spot, boy,' Griff had said. 'No cheques, mind.'

Matthew had been glum. He sat at the kitchen table, holding the scrap of paper which the truck driver, who had delivered the thirty bags of pellets, had given as a receipt for cash. He added up the amount per bag and compared it with the driver's total. It tallied but was still more than he'd bargained for, and he was fed up. All his money had gone lately on stuff for the farm. He couldn't remember when he'd last bought something he really wanted – new clothes, CDs, or even a trip to the movies.

'He's screwing me, you know,' he said, throwing the receipt back on the table and zipping up the red fleece jacket which on these cold damp days he wouldn't take off.

'Yes,' said Lark. 'You'll have to say something.' She spoke over her shoulder as she stirred grated cheese into the pan of onion soup she was making. It smelled wonderful and he was starving. He looked up at her. She was very changed from the person he had picked up on the bypass. Her hair, which she had cut almost to the scalp with his nail scissors on that first strange morning at the farm, had grown and was curling around her neck. He loved the colour, a light red, almost gold, much brighter than the dyed dreadlocks that had first brought her to his notice. She had lost most of her summer tan and her face was translucently pale, although now as she stood over the Rayburn, her cheeks were suffused with pink.

'I hate having to complain,' Matthew grumbled.

Lark was sympathetic. 'I know,' she said, 'but you don't want him to get away with it.'

So, here they were this morning, on their way to Llanfair village to confront the Parrys. Matthew was driving a long wheelbase Land Rover, an early purchase which had made a substantial hole in his savings but which he justified easily as a necessity to a hill farmer. He loved it, especially when he went to the market with Griff. It made him feel accepted, as though he had the right clothes or equipment. It made him one of the gang.

'D'you think he'll listen to me?' he asked as he negotiated a bend, carefully avoiding the flooded part of the road.

Lark shrugged. 'Probably not at first,' she said, 'but insist.'

Matthew drew up in front of the pub and turned off the engine. He sat for a moment, dangling the car keys from one finger. 'Come in with me,' he pleaded.

'No. You start. I have to go into the shop; I'll come in after.' She squeezed his arm. 'Go on. You'll be fine.'

123

Matthew still looked doubtful. 'What if he says no?'

'He can't. You're partners.'

They got out of the Land Rover but Matthew still hesitated. Lark stood in front of him and took his hand. 'Did you or did you not put several thousand into this venture?' she said firmly.

He nodded.

'Right. Go on in then. I'll follow in a minute.' She gave him a little push towards the pub door and stood in the square watching him until he went inside. Then she turned and went across the road towards the village shop.

Beti Rowlands was the granddaughter of the original owner of Llanfair shop. He had been a Ukrainian emigrant who had peddled fabric and ribbons around Welsh villages, barely speaking English let alone Welsh. But eventually he had made enough money to settle at Llanfair and bring up his family. They were now so thoroughly integrated that Beti had forgotten that her ancestors had walked across Europe to escape the Cossacks and was as Welsh as any of the Llanfair population.

Her shop was always busy. Grandfather had believed that successful business involved supplying the customers with what they wanted, and his son and granddaughter faithfully followed that maxim. Apart from the Post Office counter, there was a huge range of groceries and ironmongery. Lark was constantly amazed by the variety of goods stocked and was a frequent customer, despite the fact that shopping in Llanfair was more expensive than in the supermarket in town.

When she entered the shop and picked up a wire basket, a couple of the women shopping nodded to her. She and Matthew had become well known in the area.

'She looks better, with normal hair,' said a young woman at the checkout. Her friend nodded.

'Yes,' said another, older woman, 'not half so common. Pretty girl, give her her due.'

They spoke in Welsh, which was their normal way of speaking to each other, but it also allowed them to discuss the English incomers and visitors to the area without giving offence.

Beti rang up the amount owed by the first woman and waited while she groped for change in her purse. 'She's older than him, I think,' she said, looking slyly at Lark, who was examining the aisle of dried goods. 'He's not much more than twenty, and she's got, well ... five years or more on him. Not thirty, but heading that way.'

The others agreed and the middle-aged farmer's wife said, with a giggle, 'He's lovely, that boy. I wouldn't mind him in my bed one night.' The others laughed and she continued, 'He'd be a bit more active than my old fool. He thinks that a Saturday night fumble after seven pints at the Miner's is all that he's supposed to do. Christ, Harry Pugh's ram has got more sense!'

Lark approached the counter, smiling, as the three women gave little squeals of laughter.

Beti, choking back her giggles, turned to Lark and spoke in English. 'Hello, love. You got all you want?'

'Yes, thank you, Mrs Rowlands – oh, except for some kidney beans. Do you keep them?'

'I do normally, but we've run out just now. Be a delivery on Friday. Shall I put a bag aside for you?'

Lark nodded gratefully. 'I'll come in at the weekend. Thanks.'

The women watched her as Beti passed the shopping through the checkout and then one said, 'You settling in all right at Cariad Elin?'

'Yes, it's fine.'

'Good land, that,' said the older one. 'Geraint Williams worked hard on it until he had his stroke.'

'Did you know him?' Lark asked as she packed her shopping into a plastic carrier bag.

'Oh yes, *cariad*, I knew all of them up there. They went to my chapel, see. Geraint and his wife. She died young, poor thing. And the boy, John.' She bent to pick up a potato which had fallen off the counter and popped it into Lark's bag before continuing. 'Your Matthew's father, that would be. Now he was a clever boy. Passed the scholarship and went to the grammar in Bangor. Then to college, I think.'

Beti nodded her head. 'He did, and he never came back. Hated the farm, everyone knew that.' She sighed. 'Shame, really, old Geraint had no one to take over.' She rang up the amount and put the correct money that Lark had given her into the till.

'Well, Matthew is here now,' said Lark cheerfully, 'he's keen to carry on.'

'We hear he's in partnership with Griff Parry,' said Beti, giving a quick glance to the other two customers as Lark picked up her bag of groceries

126

and turned to go. She stopped and looked at the women.

'Yes,' she said cautiously.

'And it's working out all right?'

'Well, I think so.'

The shopkeeper looked at the other two women and then leaned closer to Lark and spoke in an unnecessarily lowered voice. 'Don't take this wrong, love, but tell your young man to watch that Griff. Old cheat, he can be.'

The others nodded their heads in agreement, and the younger woman whispered, 'One or two people have found themselves short after dealing with him. Not Llinos, though. She's clever, mind, but straight as a die.'

Lark was surprised and touched at being taken into their confidence. She was an outsider and hadn't, until now, mixed socially with the village. But they seemed to like her and take for granted that she wouldn't be offended by their interference. For a moment, she was lost for words as she stood there looking from one to the other.

Beti said comfortingly, 'Nothing bad in him, really. Just a bit cunning, see.'

Lark pushed away a lock of hair which had curled into her eye and grinned at the three women. 'Thanks for the warning,' she said. 'We had rather got that idea and we are being careful.' She lifted her finger and tapped the side of her nose. 'We're not that green.'

They all laughed and Lark turned to go. 'Thanks again,' she said, and then paused. *'Diolch yn fawr,'* she said pleasantly, and walked through the door and out into the square.

There was consternation on the faces of the three women left behind. The girl had said 'thank you very much' in perfect Welsh. How much more had she understood?

Chapter Thirteen

While Lark was surprising the village women in the shop, Matthew was attempting to make progress with Griff in the pub.

They were in the big kitchen behind the bar where Griff was busily preparing sandwiches for the lunchtime customers. This was one task at which he was supremely efficient. He quickly sliced crisp baguettes in half lengthways and loaded them with various fillings, ham, beef or tuna, packed them with salad and wrapped them individually in greaseproof paper packets. They smelled wonderful and Matthew suddenly felt ravenous.

He was leaning against the large commercial fridge which dominated one end of the kitchen, moving now and then when Griff needed to get more ingredients. His boots and anorak were muddy and would have given any health inspector who might have come into this kitchen cause for alarm, but neither Griff nor Llinos seemed to care. She was sitting at the other end of the table, away from the sandwich preparation, working at her computer. Matthew would have loved to have gone and stood behind her and watched what she was doing. He wasn't nosy for information; he just wanted to see her set-up. Computers had been his passion since childhood and he missed his like crazy. But, he sighed, he was here to discuss sheep.

'If I've time,' Griff said, loading the sandwiches into a plastic box, ready to set on the bar, 'I'll come up at the weekend to look over the ewes. They've had a couple of weeks on the good grass, haven't they? And did the feed pellets arrive?'

'Yeah, well, that's what I wanted to talk to you about. The bill was much more than I was expecting. Lark has been reading about costs in that magazine. It looks as if we're paying over the odds.'

Griff shot a look at Llinos and then carried on with his sandwich preparations. 'I don't think so, boy.' He shook his head. 'Animal feed has gone up something terrible in the last few months. You're just having to pay the same as everyone else. Isn't that right, Llinos?'

'What?' Llinos looked up from her computer and Griff repeated what he'd said. 'Yes.' She sighed. 'Everything's gone up.'

'Then there's the ram.' Matthew was remembering all the things Lark had told him to say. 'What sort was it?'

Griff looked up from his chopping board. 'What the fuck d'you mean, what sort was it? It's a sheep, that's what sort.' He looked at Llinos and shook his head.

Matthew persisted. 'Yeah, yeah, but what breed? Was it a Welsh Mountain or a Cheviot or the other one? Um … I can't remember the name

129

just at the moment.'

'What does it matter? It's Harry Pugh's tup. It works all over the mountain, knows the business.' In his exasperation, Griff fumbled with his knife as he was slicing into another baguette and cut his finger. 'Shit!' He went to the sink, turned on the tap and dangled his finger under the cold water.

Llinos looked up from her computer and took off her glasses. 'It's a Welsh Mountain, actually,' she said soothingly, 'they all are round here, very hardy.' She turned back to her screen and said with a smile, 'It's no good asking Griff. He's a city boy, barely knows a sheep from a bloody cow. He's only learned the business since we've been here.' The glasses went back on as she concentrated once more on her work.

Griff shrugged and dried his hand with a tea towel. He didn't seem to be offended in any way.

'Well, that's my point,' said Matthew. 'Lark's been reading about it. She thinks we should have been careful about choosing the ram. We want big lambs, don't we?' He was pleased with himself. He hadn't let Griff fob him off and Llinos was on his side, he could feel that. Lark couldn't have done better herself.

'It is a good ram, believe me,' Griff said, his head halfway into a cupboard as he looked for some Elastoplasts. He found a box and tore open the end of a packet with his teeth. Withdrawing the plaster, he wound it carefully around the cut. 'The last lot of lambs were brilliant,' he continued. 'We got good money for them.' He caught his breath as soon as the words had left his

130

mouth and he looked quickly over to Llinos, who was frowning and shaking her head.

Fortunately for Griff, Matthew was standing in front of her and couldn't see her, but he did pick up on the words 'good money'. 'That's another thing,' he said deliberately, his voice slow and his normally cheerful face stern. 'We haven't had our share yet.'

Griff was at his most placatory. 'I know, I know, and you will. Llinos has just got to work out the percentages properly,' he nodded to the computer, 'and then take out the amount for Pugh's tup and–'

He broke off as Lark came into the room. She was still smiling, remembering the faces of the women in the shop. Griff was suddenly struck by her appearance – bright hair, clean jeans and navy sweater. So different from the first time he saw her. No wonder that boy kept her with him. Anyone would.

'Hello, Lark, love,' he said, grateful for the interruption. 'Got your messages?'

'Mm,' she said, noticing the look on Matt's face and guessing that he was having trouble.

'The tup is a Welsh Mountain breed,' he said to her, 'very hardy.'

She nodded. 'Well, that's OK.' She glanced at Griff and then at Llinos, who had stopped typing and was following the conversation closely. 'Matthew just wondered if next season he should buy his own ram. I'm told that Pugh's animal is a bit overworked. It would be easier in the long run and we wouldn't have to wait until it's available.'

131

'Just what I told Llinos,' Griff said eagerly, ignoring his wife's raised eyebrows, 'but it's a bit late for this year. Clinton has done the business.'

'Clinton?' said Matthew.

'The tup.'

Matthew burst out laughing. 'Jesus,' he said and the tension in the room was broken.

Llinos took advantage of the change of mood. 'I'll do a printout of all the figures, Matt. Let you see the costs and all. If you agree with it, I'll make out a cheque for you.'

Matthew could never keep angry for long and nodded in agreement. He went over to look at the computer and saw that Llinos had a spreadsheet on the screen. 'Is this the sheep business?' he asked.

'No. It's the pub. Got to keep on top of it, see.'

Matthew leant over her and examined the hardware. 'I like your set-up,' he said admiringly. 'What are the specs?'

Llinos rattled off the specifications like a mantra and Matthew whistled in delight. 'Wow, cool,' he said. 'All that in a laptop.'

'They get better every month, don't they?' Llinos finished what she was doing and stood up. 'My desktop is upstairs, barely used now and only bought two years ago. Top of the range, then.'

'And cost a fucking fortune, too.' Griff came back into the kitchen after arranging the bar, ready for the lunchtime invasion. He hoped that Matthew and Lark would go soon. He had to open up, and anyway, he'd had quite enough of their interference.

Matthew sighed. 'God, I miss my computer. I hope Ma hasn't sold it.'

Llinos looked shocked. 'She wouldn't do that, would she?'

'No, I guess not,' Matthew agreed, 'but my dad might give it away. Just out of spite.'

Lark took his arm. 'We'd better get back,' she said. 'We've got work to do and these people want to open the pub.' She turned to Griff. 'Matt would be grateful for the figures and for his cheque as soon as possible. Wouldn't you, Matt?'

He nodded, eyes still on the computer. 'Yeah.'

Llinos put her glasses away in a black case and pondered for a moment. 'Matt,' she said carefully, 'why don't you borrow the other computer for a bit? I've got some games you can have, and as you can't get the telly, it'll give you something to do in the evenings.'

Matthew grinned with pleasure. He felt as though someone had just given him a surprise Christmas present. 'Excellent!' he crowed. 'If you're sure... I'd love it.'

'Come on then,' she said, 'help me get it down. You might as well have it as soon as possible.' She led the way through the door into the private quarters and Matthew hurried to follow her.

Lark watched them go. She felt uneasy, as though somewhere she had lost track of the conversation, and even the situation. Matthew was easily swayed and his good nature always won over his best intentions. But, she shrugged, it was his life, not really her business.

Griff put a fat hand on her shoulder, making

her jump, for she had forgotten that he was in the room. 'Bit of an insult to you, love,' he said with an undisguised smirk. 'Young chap like that needing other forms of entertainment in the evening.'

She shook his hand off and turned round to face him, fixing her stone-coloured eyes full on him. He paled. Previously, when he'd thought how pretty she had become, her eyes were a soft amber colour, but now they were like flint and he felt as though they were drilling a hole in his head. But when she spoke, her voice, though scornful, was light and unthreatening.

'Not at all,' she said, 'life doesn't revolve around sex.' She smiled, not letting him off the hook. 'And I've got plenty of reading. I've got all those figures to go through as well, when we get them.' She paused and then stared at him again, 'Like tomorrow, please.'

Griff swallowed quickly and moved away to clear up the remains of his sandwich-making. When he was at the far end of the kitchen, loading plates and knives into the dishwasher, he spoke over his shoulder. 'We did think you would have moved on by now. Your sort get bored easily, I'm told. Can't you hear the pastures new and roast hedgehogs calling?'

Lark, hearing the heavy footsteps of Matthew and Llinos coming down the stairs, grinned. 'No, not so far. I must be deafened by bleating.'

Llinos and Griff watched them drive away. The computer and screen had been safely loaded into the back of the Land Rover and a hugely cheerful Matthew had thanked Llinos again.

'What did you give him the computer for?' asked Griff angrily, still uncomfortable after his encounter with Lark.

'I didn't give it. I lent it,' Llinos corrected.

'Well, why did you lend it, then?'

She turned and tapped him gently on the forehead. *Really,* she thought, *sometimes I wonder if he'll ever understand anything that isn't spelled out in words of one syllable.* 'Use your head, stupid.' She spoke in her patient schoolmistress voice. 'That boy is mad on computers. He'll go home, set it up and spend the next month playing games. He'll lose interest in the sheep and then the farm.' She expanded her point. 'The girl is getting bored with him. Christ!' she said, with more passion than she intended. 'There has to be more to life than sex. She'll go and then he'll go, and Bingo, you've got your bloody farm.'

Griff took a few moments to let the explanation filter through his slow-working, brain, but when it did, he performed a little caper of delight on the pavement in front of the pub. 'Oh, clever, clever girl,' he crooned, giving her a hug and attempting to land a wet kiss on her turned-away mouth. 'How does the country run without you in charge? It will be the Welsh Assembly next.'

Llinos smiled and turned to go inside. 'In time, cariad, in time,' she said.

Chapter Fourteen

In the weeks before Christmas, the weather improved. It was cold but brilliantly sunny and the air was fresh and sharp – so sharp that sometimes Lark found it hurt to breathe, especially when she chopped wood or took great bales of hay out to the ewes. The days were very short now and the farm was in twilight by four o'clock every afternoon, for although there was a cloudless sky, the sun sank quickly below the surrounding mountains and disappeared. One afternoon, Lark climbed the hill behind the farm, breathing with difficulty the freezing air but enjoying the exertion which made her feel dizzy and alive. The higher peaks around her were covered in snow, and when she lifted her eyes upwards she could see that the top of her hill also had small pockets of snow in crevasses shaded from the sun.

She reached the flat rocks where Matthew had sat, begging her to stay, that first week. They were slippery with frost but she perched gingerly on an edge and turned her eyes west to watch the dying sun fall in an icy turquoise sky. It had turned into a great orange ball and the sight was so entrancing that she lingered, shaking with cold, until it seemed to gather speed and slip into the Irish Sea. The red and purple haze over the water darkened and Ynys Mon, the magical isle of

Anglesey, faded into the night. When she looked down, the farm was in darkness. She felt a slight frisson of alarm. She had never been on the mountain at night and for a moment wondered how she would get down. As she stood, confused by the growing darkness, a vixen barked in the valley and concern for her hens cleared her head and allowed her to breathe easily again.

Of course she knew the way, and with growing confidence she retraced her footsteps, carefully following the trail down the hillside until she was once again in the lower fields. The sheep, gathered for shelter by the stone wall, bleated hopefully as she walked amongst them. They knew her now and were comforted by her presence. She could smell the warm aroma of lanolin and hay as she pushed her way through and she spoke gently to them, assuring them in their ignorance that they would be under cover soon.

Matthew looked up briefly as she came in. 'Been feeding the hens?' he asked, eyes back again on the computer screen before she had a chance to reply.

'Yes.' There seemed little point in saying that she had been out for nearly three hours. He hadn't really noticed her absence and now she knew that their relationship had changed. As she filled the kettle and set it on the Rayburn to boil she could feel the arrhythmia in her chest. Her heart already knew that her time at Cariad Elin was nearly up. It was just her head that had to come to terms with it. Her mistake had been profound.

'I'm starving,' Matthew said suddenly, and she

tightened her grip on the handle of the kettle in order to pacify her shaking nerves. Her reply emerged as calmly and matter-of-factly as if this was any normal day.

'I'll give you a coffee in a minute and some cake. That should keep you going until supper.'

'Yeah, great,' he said. 'Thanks.'

The tardy winter sun rose the next morning, promising another fine day. Lark got up and started loading clothes into the washing machine. She was eager to get on with things now that she knew, what she had to do and hurried around the house, cleaning the rooms and sorting out belongings.

Matthew came down later after she had fed the hens and taken extra hay out to the sheep.

'They'll have to come inside soon,' she said, placing a plate of bacon and toast before him. 'You'll have to finish fixing the barn.'

'I know,' he said reluctantly, 'I'll get onto it after the weekend.' He took his plate and mug of coffee and went to sit at the short end of the table where he had his computer set up. Lark watched as he switched on and loaded a CD game into the drive. She sighed, and for once he heard her and looked up. 'I will, promise,' he said, producing one of his charming grins. 'No need to nag me.'

Later that day, she stood on the little lawn where the line hung and unpegged the washing. Her arms were full of dried clothes and she buried her head in them, sniffing the clean, cold scent of washing powder and fresh air. It was a

138

smell of which she never tired.

She heard a sound and, looking up, she saw the figure of a man standing in the yard. He stood with his back to the sun and she couldn't see him properly, just a dark shape which seemed to have appeared from nowhere. For no reason, her heart was beating faster and the breath caught in her throat. In an effort to clear her eyes, she squeezed them shut and then looked away up to the hilltop. For the first time in days, cloud had begun to gather around the peak, shreds and wisps of white tissue which swirled and dipped like a circle of dancing figures. Her mouth opened and she breathed a small gasp of pleasure. It was a lovely sight.

She looked back at the man, eager to include him in her discovery, but in that split second he had moved forward and was standing in front of her. 'Hi,' he said.

She took a step back and looked at him again. Now she could see him properly and nothing was as strange as it had been a moment ago. He was just another tourist like the ones who had often come to the farm, asking for a drink of water or directions.

'Hello,' she answered and smiled. 'Are you lost?'

He shook his head. 'No,' he said slowly, 'I wouldn't say that. I know exactly where I am.'

There was something in his voice that was familiar and in the way he stood, feet firmly planted. He was thin, with short dark hair which was liberally flecked with grey. He stared evenly at her as though into a camera lens.

'Oh,' she said, recognition dawning, 'you've come at last. You're John Williams. Aren't you?'

'Yes, I am.'

'I knew,' she said, smiling. 'I've seen your photograph.' She paused and stared up into his face. 'They're grey. Your eyes.'

He nodded and they stood for a moment, face to face on the drying green, examining each other's looks until Lark, shivering in the biting wind, regained the initiative. She shifted the bundle of washing onto one arm and held out her right hand.

'Welcome home!' she said.

He took her hand in both of his and shook it, feeling the strength of her fingers and the roughness of her knuckles. 'Well, thanks,' he said, and then letting her hand go, added, 'er ... you have me at a slight disadvantage. You know who I am, but ... er ... I don't know who—'

Lark broke in. 'Oh, I'm so sorry,' she apologised. 'I thought he'd told you. He said he would. I'm Lark. I live here, with Matthew.'

John allowed the surprise to show on his face. He wondered if this news was something that Matthew had told Lydia and the pair had not bothered to pass on to him. He thought probably not, if she'd known she would have used it as a further reason for getting Matthew home. Never having seen the farm and unable to imagine it, as humble as it was, she would have cast this girl in the role of gold-digger. He gave a short laugh. Lydia would loathe this place.

'Lark? You did say Lark?'

She nodded her head.

'Unusual.'

Lark picked the peg basket off the line. She shot a quick glance up to the peak but the dancing clouds had dispersed and a heavy bank of grey cumulus was rolling in from the sea. The sun had been hidden and it was getting dark and cold.

'Come along in,' she urged. 'I'm sure you'd like a cup of tea or coffee and a bit of a warm-up.' She grinned, her small, straight teeth bright in the dull light. 'I think Matthew is going to get a surprise.'

John nodded and picked up the holdall he had dropped by his feet and followed her. He flattened his palm against the stone wall beside the door as they passed through it, remembering the feel and texture of the granite as much as the look. His stomach churned. He had some difficult hours ahead.

Lark dumped the washing in a basket by the scullery door and hurried through into the kitchen. It was dark in the room. Matthew hadn't moved from the computer screen for hours, concentrating so much on the game he was playing that he hadn't noticed the light fading. Lark switched on a lamp with a shade the colour of a terracotta pot as she walked through, and a warm glow suffused the room. Moving swiftly to the inglenook, she took three logs out of the basket and threw them onto the red embers of a dying fire. Sparks of light shot up the chimney and the dry wood crackled and spat as tongues of flame curled around the logs. Within seconds, the logs were burning merrily and sending a welcome draught of heat into the room.

'Matt, Matt,' she called. 'Close that down.'

'Yeah, in a sec, honey. I'm just beginning to beat these bastards.' He smiled grimly as he spoke, his fingers frantically working the buttons on the mouse.

Lark glanced at John who was standing in the doorway to the scullery. He almost seemed to be afraid to come into the room but when he caught her eye, he gave a resigned shrug, understanding, better than her, his son's obsession. She smacked her hands together, dusting off wood debris, and walked over to Matt. She put a hand over his on the mouse and said firmly, 'Stop. We have company.'

He dragged his eyes away from the screen, looking up at her angrily with a childish expression of spoilt fun. She jerked her head, indicating for him to look behind him, and he turned in his chair. The shock couldn't have been greater. His mouth dropped open and he stared at his father as though he was seeing a ghost. He slowly got to his feet.

'Dad? What the hell are you doing here?'

John cocked his head to one side and grinned. 'I thought it was time I paid you a visit.'

'But,' Matthew was still confused, 'Ma didn't say. I spoke to her on the phone, Monday.'

The grin faded from John's face. 'She didn't know.'

Matthew stared at his father and then turned his head to the side and glanced at Lark. She smiled encouragingly back at him and jerked her head almost imperceptibly, implying that he should go over and greet the visitor. The slight reluctance to move would have been obvious only to a close observer. John was still adjusting his eyes to the simple light in the room, but Lark noticed and felt embarrassed. When Matthew did move it was with one of his charming grins.

'Well, hi, Dad,' he said, going over to the older man and giving him a hug. 'Great to see you.' He took the holdall from his father's hand and dropped it on the floor, then pulled out a chair from under the table. 'Sit down,' he said. 'Tell me all the news.'

Lark walked back and forth around the kitchen, making tea and coffee and putting a plate of buttered currant bread on the table in front of them. She sat with them as she poured the tea but didn't join in the conversation. John took tea with her and seemed to enjoy it, for he asked for more and Matthew looked surprised.

'I thought you didn't like tea,' he said. 'I hate it.'

'This is good,' John said. 'Like I used to have.'

'Hear that, Lark?' Matthew laughed sarcastically. 'You're not the only one who likes to drink poison!'

She smiled and then got up. 'I'll go and see to the hens and have a look at the sheep. Let you and your dad catch up on things.' She took her coat from the peg and picked up a torch from the shelf above the sink.

They waited until she had gone out and closed the door and then John said, 'Good-looking girl. Who is she?'

Matthew looked surprised. 'That's Lark. Didn't she introduce herself?'

John nodded and helped himself to another piece of the currant bread. 'Oh yes, she did. But who is she? A girlfriend?'

Matthew paused before he answered, wondering what his father's reaction would be. 'I guess so,' he said. 'We've been together ever since I came here. She's good with the stock and she keeps Griff Parry in line. And,' he added with a rueful shrug, 'she knows how to do things.'

'Like what?'

'Oh, I dunno. Like, well ... she knows about fuse boxes. She's great at those. And she can work that bastard.' He pointed to the Rayburn which even now was emitting a comforting smell of the casserole which Lark had prepared earlier on in the afternoon.

'And you can't?' John said.

'Christ, no!'

John shook his head. 'Oh dear,' he said. 'Big gaps in your education, I feel.'

Matthew waited for a moment, wondering if his father was being serious, then he noticed John's mouth trying not to break into a grin and he burst out laughing. 'Yeah. Not educated for the simple life.'

'And who is Griff Parry?' John asked after they had stopped laughing.

'He's my partner, I wrote to Ma about him. Didn't she show you?'

John nodded, 'Yes, I remember now.' He leant back in his chair and looked round the room. 'Well, how are you enjoying it here?'

Before Matthew had time to formulate an answer, John had got up from the chair and was wandering around the room. He looked at the big fireplace and threw another log onto the burning ash, then watched it catch alight and throw off sparks with a kind of satisfaction. He turned and walked across to the door which led to the hall. As he opened it, a draught of freezing air came into the room and he shut it quickly. 'Jesus,' he said, 'I'd forgotten how cold it was.'

Matthew laughed. 'Ma would hate it,' he said.

'And you love it?'

'What?' said Matthew, and then hurriedly added, 'Oh, yeah, sure. It's cool.'

Chapter Fifteen

In her comfortably heated house, three thousand miles away from the privations of Cariad Elin, Lydia Williams was walking aimlessly from room to room. She had just returned from three marvellous days in New York, shopping and having utterly satisfying sex with her lost priest in the Plaza Hotel. She had come home rejuvenated and calmer. Indeed on the plane, when an exhausted Kevin was sleeping, she had decided to try making a real effort to patch up the problems between her and John.

But just now she had walked into an empty house. More than that, a house which contained a goodbye note. He had left. He had given her no time to prepare her recovery plan, and in one

145

move, had completely taken the wind from her sails. She felt a surge of blood flush into her face. Her friends, who knew or guessed her infidelities, would laugh, though not to her face, of course. Several who had marvelled at her ability to juggle her various attachments and keep her marriage intact, would enjoy her downfall.

She had the note in her hand now as she walked through the pearl and silver painted lounge which led into the dining conservatory. She loved this room – it was one of her greatest successes and had been photographed many times for different magazines. The plants needed watering and were wilting in the overheated atmosphere, but for once she didn't notice them. The note needed to be read again.

'Dear Lydia,' he had written, in his neat architectural script,

I have gone to Wales to see Matthew. I will try and persuade him to come home because I know that is what you want. You were right when you said he must finish his education. Despite his age, he is still very much a child.

Our lives have changed lately and I'm not sure I know you, really, any more. But I am sure that you want Matthew here and that is the least I can do.

As for me, I don't know. I find work increasingly dull and although I understand that people must shop, I cannot bear to design another mall or precinct. Perhaps time out to think is necessary, so that is what I will do for a few months.

At the moment, we are not short of money, so if you keep your head you will not be destitute and at least

146

you will be able to live your own life for a while, without having to look over your shoulder for me.
Will be in touch.
John

A sharp lump was taking up too much space in her chest and she felt nauseous. For a horrible moment she wondered if she was having a heart attack; these symtoms sounded very like the ones described in the health-promotion adverts she had seen on TV. Shock was supposed to be one of the reasons for sudden death, wasn't it? She almost cried in fright and tears did start to escape her lids, but only tiny ones, squeezed out without the accompanying sobs and running nose that went with heartbreak. She swallowed and coughed and the lump began to dissipate. She was angry, not dying.

'Damn you!' she said fiercely to the empty house and walked swiftly, heels tip-tapping, to the kitchen. She poured herself a large drink and lit a cigarette before taking the phone off the wall and punching in a familiar number. Her call was answered quickly and she drew a lungful of smoke in and breathed it out before speaking. 'Fred? Good, I'm glad you picked up. Edith out at bridge?... Yeah, I thought she would be.' She listened for a moment and took a large swallow of her Jack Daniel's, then interrupted his flow and said, 'Fred, listen, you'll never guess. John's gone...Yes, flown off to the UK.' His surprise was evident and she allowed him a few moments before saying, 'Fred, honey, come round. Let's talk about it.'

At Cariad Elin, John and Matthew were still sitting at the kitchen table when Lark came back in. She looked cold, the tip of her nose was pink and a halo of tiny gold curls on her hairline had sprung up in the frosty air outside.

'Everything OK?' asked Matthew.

'Yes,' she said, going over to the fireplace and warming her hands.

The two men stared unconsciously at her and then John asked, 'When are they due to lamb?'

Lark turned round. 'End of January, aren't they, Matt?'

'Yeah, guess so.'

John shook his head sympathetically. 'That'll be hard work.'

Something about the tone of his voice irritated Matthew and he was quick to reply. 'There'll be two of us, you know, and Griff will help. Anyway, he says that they more or less know how to do it themselves. You have to be prepared to lose a few.'

John opened his mouth but then thought better of it and sat back in his chair. It was years since he'd been anywhere near a live sheep, and anyway, what went on here was really none of his business. But catching the look that passed between Matthew and Lark, he somehow felt obliged to recover the earlier mood of good humour. 'Oh well,' he said, 'I guess you know what you're doing. My memory is only that sheep are bastards. They like to have you up all night, just for the hell of it.' He grinned and Lark gave a relieved little laugh. After a second, Matthew joined in and the tension was eased.

The fire crackled and glowed in the cosy room and after a while, John took off his coat and relaxed in his chair. Lark opened the door of the Rayburn and took out the casserole. She took a spoon and tasted the meat and then added some more seasoning before returning it to the oven. 'I hope you'll stay for supper,' she said to John. 'There's plenty of stew and I'm sure you and Matt have lots to talk about.'

John looked cautiously at Matthew who nodded his head eagerly. 'Yeah, stay, Dad.'

'Well, thank you... Lark. That's very kind of you.'

She smiled. 'Why don't you go and sit by the fire whilst I peel some potatoes? It won't take long.' And she went into the scullery and returned with a plastic bowl full of earth-covered potatoes, a sight John hadn't seen for years. He wondered if the supermarkets in Toronto ever carried vegetables in the raw these days. He couldn't remember Lydia ever buying anything remotely like these. When they ate at home, they had little scraps of meals, prettily served on fine china. Lydia always said that the look of the meal was just as important as its taste.

Obeying Lark's instructions, he got up and walked over to the fireplace where the logs burned fiercely red, exuding a sharp, sweet aroma of autumn bonfires. He sank into the leather armchair and stuck his legs out in front of the fire. A vision of his father's feet encased in heavy grey socks, in exactly the same position, forced itself, unbidden, to his mind. He looked at

149

the floor beside the chair, expecting to see the untidy stack of newspapers and *Farmers Weeklys* that Dad never wanted moved. It wasn't there, but looking across to the other side of the hearth, he saw a few copies of the magazine piled neatly on a small table beside the rocking chair. *That table used to be in the parlour,* he thought sleepily, *beside the display cabinet. I must take a look in there before I leave.*

'He's nodded off,' said Matthew in a low voice.

'Mm. I expect he's jet-lagged. You can wake him later.' Matthew switched on his computer and sat down, happy to be back in fantasy land.

Later that evening, when John had woken, the three of them sat around the kitchen table and demolished the casserole. John produced a bottle of whisky from his bag at the start of the meal and, after pouring a large amount into his water glass, offered a drink to Matt and Lark 'Are you sure you won't have one... Matt... Lark?'

They shook their heads. 'You know I don't like whisky, Dad, and Lark doesn't drink spirits.' Matthew watched as John poured himself another large drink and sat holding his glass almost as if he was scared that someone would take it away from him. He couldn't remember his father drinking much before; this was something new.

'Oh well, doesn't matter,' John said. 'Thought I'd offer.'

There was a lemon tart to follow which John ate with evident enjoyment. The whisky glass had been refilled a couple more times and when he

150

turned to speak to Lark his voice slurred slightly. 'That was a very nice meal. Thank you. You know, it seems ages since I had a home-cooked dinner.' He swished the whisky around in the glass so that it sparkled in the caught light. 'I've been eating out a lot,' he added.

Matthew grinned. 'Ma was never that keen on cooking. Sounds as if she's given up altogether. That it?'

'Something like that,' said John shortly.

The room was quiet. Everything that John said seemed to put a halt to the conversation and the three of them sat surveying the wreckage of the meal in awkward silence.

'D'you want to phone Ma, let her know you're OK?' Matthew said finally.

John shrugged, his eyes fixed on the shining liquid in his glass. 'Perhaps later,' he said. 'I left her a note; she knows where I am.'

Matthew looked at Lark and silently shook his head. He didn't know his father like this. Angry, yes; sarcastic and indifferent, often. But a sad old drunk? No. He could never remember Dad like this. He wondered what to do next, how to carry forward the conversation. Lark came to his rescue. She started piling the dinner plates together and got up from her chair to take them to the sink.

'Why don't you go and have a look round while I do the dishes?' she said to John. 'I'm sure you'd like to rediscover your home.'

Matthew breathed a silent sigh of relief and looked eagerly at his father, hoping that he would get up and go for an exploratory trip around the house, but John didn't move.

'Guess I should,' he said, not getting out of his chair but pouring another drink into his glass. 'To be honest, there doesn't seem to be a lot changed.' He looked around the room. 'It's cleaner, of course, but apart from that,' he waved a hand vaguely towards the computer, still in place at the far end of the table, 'it's just the same.' He lifted the glass and swallowed the drink in one gulp. 'Christ,' he said, his voice louder. 'I almost expect the old man to walk through the door and yell at me!'

'Why?' asked Lark, from the sink.

'What?' said John.

'Why yell at you?'

John shrugged. 'Yelling? That's what he did. Unsatisfactory son, I guess.'

'Tell me about it,' said Matthew, not quite under his breath, and John raised his head from his examination of his now empty glass and frowned.

He stood up unsteadily and pushed the chair away from the table. 'Will you excuse me for a moment,' he said politely and then, turning to Matthew who was standing uncertainly beside the table, watching his father in dismay, 'Is it still upstairs, the bathroom?'

They stood silently by the sink, waiting until John had gone up the narrow stairs and they could hear his footsteps on the small landing above. Matthew scowled and muttered angrily, 'Christ knows what he's up to.'

'What d'you mean?'

'Can't you see? He's weird. And the drinking.

This isn't him, you know. He's obviously come here to make me go back, but ... somehow he seems to have lost it. God, I thought he would try and drag me out and throw me in the car. That's how he normally is.'

'Well,' Lark spoke practically as she quickly washed the dishes, 'he can't do that. You're too old now.'

Matthew snorted. 'He wouldn't care about that.' He picked up a cloth and started to dry a plate, then a sudden thought struck him.

'He thinks he's staying here tonight!'

'Of course, where else? Anyway,' she added, nodding towards the half-empty whisky bottle still on the table, 'he's not fit to drive.'

'Oh shit!' Matthew groaned.

They listened to the noises upstairs. The lavatory flushed and they heard movement as John wandered into another room.

'Look,' said Lark, 'take his bag into the little bedroom. I've aired the bed, so he'll be warm, and I expect he'll crash out any moment.'

Matthew sighed, but was resigned. 'OK,' he said. 'But I'm phoning Ma later. I'll find out what's going on.'

Chapter Sixteen

Lydia was in her bed staring at the eggshell blue of the painted ceiling. The colour was exquisite, just what she had hoped for when she picked it out of the ring of paint cards and held it against the swatch of fabric she had chosen for the curtains and bedcover. It reminded her of the sea in that small bay in Mexico where she and John had vacationed once. No other sea looked like that, she was sure; it was too pale and much too calm, almost unreal in a way, but the colour was just right for her bedroom.

The pattern on the curtains was one of mixed spring flowers, lemons and pinks and watery greens. Her bed was painted ash wood, pale stone colours, antiqued professionally in New York and admired throughout the decorating world of North America, which had been privileged to see photographs of her, gracefully reclining on the quilt and standing by the matching built-in wardrobes.

John had frowned when he'd been shown the pictures. 'What sort of person wants their bedroom displayed to the eyes of strangers?' he'd said in disgust, but she had laughed and said that it was flattering to her, at least. Then he'd said he didn't like the colour scheme anyway. It reminded him of the patterns on the front of Easter egg boxes. She ignored that. It had long since been obvious to her that he had very little concept of modern decorating trends.

But now, lying naked on the crumpled bed, she looked at the ceiling and then at the walls again and wondered if he had been right.

The water ran softly in the bathroom and she dragged her eyes away from the walls and looked towards the closed door of the en suite. She had crossed the Rubicon this afternoon, and whilst entirely necessary and comforting for the moment, it might prove, in the future, to have been a wrong move. She thought fleetingly about Kevin: she would have to let him down gently. She was fond of him, but she couldn't afford for her life to get too complicated. She shrugged her thin shoulders and rolled over so that her tanned back with the narrow white bikini line around her smooth backside met Fred's eyes when he stepped back into the room. He gulped. He had never thought that this day would actually come and she was offering again.

'I wonder what John's up to now?' she thought, not realising that the words had come out loud. 'Who gives a shit?' he replied and grabbed at her flesh urgently, not seeing or caring that he was leaving red marks on her sides and breasts, in his overwhelming desire to take her again. Lydia closed her eyes and forgot about John. This wasn't as bad as she'd imagined. More than simply bearable, and so useful for her future plans.

John put his head round the door of the large bedroom at Cariad Elin. It had been his father's room and he had rarely been inside it, except on those occasions when he'd been sent running upstairs to fetch something his father had forgotten. The room then had smelt of tobacco and damp clothes, especially after his mother had died. Dad often forgot to open the curtains and the room always seemed dark and sad, a constant reminder that the happier times had gone.

Now it looked better. Matthew and Lark had painted the walls white and Lark had put apple-green curtains across the little window. The bed was fresh and clean with a sweet-smelling white duvet and plain white pillowcases. A mahogany towel rack stood against the wall opposite the bed and on it lay the lace spread that had covered the bed when they had first arrived at the house. John fingered it cautiously. Dad had kept all these pieces of linen in the ottoman on the landing. He'd said that they were too special for everyday and the beds had been covered in blankets and rough sheets and the finer linen hidden away for guests. He smiled ruefully at that thought. During the time he was growing up, a guest had never stayed in the house. He looked around again. There were books and lamps on the bedside tables, evidence that the room was used for more than sleep. And sex. He preferred not to think about that. How did any parent come to terms with their children's overt sexuality?

He sat heavily on the bed, his legs giving way and his head reeling. He knew he was drunk and felt suddenly ashamed, wondering what his father would have said about his condition. Even

156

at his worst times, after Mam died, Dad hadn't taken comfort in the bottle. He'd kept his grief to himself and carried on. In his father's old bedroom, John groaned silently, scared that he would start crying again, and he worked his face hard to keep it from crumpling up. He got up quickly, staggering against the dressing table, knocking over a plastic tube of hand cream that Lark had left there. The bottle of whisky had been left on the kitchen table and he needed it now.

He was noisy descending the stairs, and Matthew and Lark were standing side by side with their faces turned towards the door when he walked unsteadily into the kitchen. 'Jesus, this house is small, isn't it?' he said loudly, shattering the silence. 'I'd forgotten. The rooms could have been designed for pygmies.'

Matthew's eyebrows drew together and his lower lip stuck out like it had done when he was an aggrieved youngster. He couldn't bear to have his house criticised, specially by his father.

While he was formulating a suitable reply, Lark spoke. 'It was designed for people with few possessions, probably.'

If it had been meant as a put-down, it worked, and the fatuous smile which John had worn to enter the room left his face abruptly. Matthew grinned approvingly and gave Lark's arm a little squeeze. The look he gave John was almost challenging and the older man cleared his throat nervously and looked at the table to where he'd left the bottle. It had gone. His eyes wandered the room: it wasn't on the dresser or the mantelpiece, and the sink and draining board were cleared and empty.

He turned his eyes towards Lark, noticing that she was almost as tall as he was and also for the first time catching a glimpse of the pebbly eyes. He felt worn out and desperate for a drink. He gave an apologetic little bow. 'Yes, you're right,' he said, wondering how to broach the subject of the bottle. 'I stand corrected. My materialistic values are getting the better of me.' He prayed that she wouldn't want to get into a debate; he didn't know how much more he could take of this enforced politeness.

Lark, who had recognised what he had been looking for, now watched his face collapse into exhaustion. 'It doesn't matter,' she said gently. 'Look, why don't you go up to your old room? I'm sure you must be tired out. I've aired the bed and you should be quite warm.' She put out a hand and touched his arm softly. It was almost too much and he bit his lips fiercely in an effort to hold back the ever-ready tears. Out of lowered eyes he saw Matthew pick up his case and carry it towards the stairs, passing the grandfather clock in the hall as it started striking the hour.

'Yeah,' he said, 'you're quite right. It's far too late for philosophical discussions and I am tired.' He turned towards the door, suddenly almost beyond staying awake and forgetting about the whisky. He remembered his manners again. 'Thank you,' he murmured, 'for the excellent meal. Good night.'

'Good night,' she said quietly. 'Sleep well.'

Matthew was waiting for him on the landing,

indicating the open door to his old room as though he was, visiting the house for the first time. 'Got everything you want?'

John nodded, sinking onto the bed and pushing off his shoes. 'Thanks, son.'

'Well, see you in the morning, I guess,' Matthew said awkwardly, unable to come to terms with playing host to his father.

'Sure thing.'

John's eyes were closed and Matthew said, 'Good night, Dad,' and clattered down the uncarpeted stairs without waiting for a reply.

Lark was sitting at the kitchen table. She was tired, too; the day had been long and she was aching to go to bed. She had made some tea and a mug of coffee for Matthew and they sat looking at each other as they quietly drank their nightcap.

'Oh God,' Matthew muttered, afraid that his voice would carry upstairs. 'What is going on?'

Lark shook her head silently.

Matthew drained his mug and stood up. 'I'll give him a few minutes to get to sleep and then I'm going to phone Ma.'

Lark sighed. 'He looks so sad,' she said.

Matthew was scornful. 'He's old. It's the same thing.'

She drew in her breath suddenly, taken aback by his dismissive words. He was usually so easy-going and laid-back that she found it hard to believe that he could be so contemptuous of his father. Her voice was reproving when she said, 'My God, Matt, he's not that old. What is he, about fifty?'

Matthew barked a small laugh. 'Yeah, about

that. Ancient!'

A worm of doubt started to crawl into the outer reaches of Lark's mind but she continued to argue. 'You're cruel, Matt,' she said softly and deliberately, 'give him a break.'

'Yeah. Like all the ones he gave me.'

He went into the hall. The telephone was on a little table and he picked it up, stretching the cord so that he could sit on the floor in the kitchen with the door to the hall shut. Lark watched as he dialled the number, and then she got up and walked into the scullery. She pulled her coat off the peg and quietly opened the door to the yard.

The moon was very bright and the night starry and cold. She walked to the hen house and rattled the lock on the door, ensuring that it was safely closed. Inside, the chickens clucked softly, annoyed at being disturbed, and she left them and stepped carefully across the yard to lean against the field gate. The moon lit up the top of the mountain and she stared at it, watching enthralled as grey streaks of cloud fled across the peaks, weaving and dancing in the icy night-time breeze. She shivered and held her coat close across her body, but still looked upwards. She knew she should go back inside; it was too cold to stay here in the quiet yard. There was ice forming on the puddles and the muddy tracks were hard beneath her feet. Now the wind was getting up, cracking the bare branches of the ash tree and tearing through the rafters of the big barn. But still she lingered. Despite her chattering teeth, she kept watching. It was hard to give up such a beautiful sight.

John watched her from the small window of his room. He had lain on the bed after Matthew had left, too tired to undress. He hoped sleep would come quickly; he could no longer cope with the myriad thoughts which tumbled haphazardly one after another through his head. What was he doing here? Why had he left? The answers multiplied and confused him.

He turned off the lamp. It was new and he liked it. The plain mahogany stalk was topped with a dark blue coolie shade which appealed to his sense of design and colour. He wondered briefly who had chosen it, perhaps they'd gone together to the store, like he and Lydia had done, in the old days. But that thought led to others and he was wide awake again. He sat up, his head reeling, and took several deep breaths. There was aspirin in his holdall and someone, Lark probably, had thoughtfully left a carafe of water and a small glass on the bedside table. He didn't bother to put on the light but groped in his bag and found the bubble pack of tablets.

Holding the glass in his hand, he stood up and walked to the window. New blue curtains dressed the small opening and he pulled one aside and looked out. He gasped in surprise, it was so light. All around, the countryside was bathed in moonglow, brilliantly lighting the yard, the buildings and the fields beyond. He could see the white shapes of the sheep, huddled for warmth against the wall, their vacant faces staring at nothing and their mouths working mechanically. Light shimmered on the freezing puddles, suddenly darkening as a stream of cloud hurtled across the face of the moon and then gleaming again as the cloud passed.

He remembered standing at this window so many times in years past. As a child he would listen for the soft shriek of the barn owl and then wait silently for the white-breasted bird to flap heavily across from the trees on its nocturnal hunt. The excitement could be breathtaking. But the memories that superseded all others and still made him ache with despair were of the guilt-ridden nights when he had stood, head pressed against the small cold windowpane, wondering how to tell Dad that he was leaving.

There was movement in the yard, and as he watched, he saw the girl, Lark, walking towards the house. He pressed closer to the window, staring at her tall, straight figure and assured step as she walked without caring, through the icy puddles, across the yard. The moonlight shone suddenly on her hair, picking out the gold lights which seemed to dance and sparkle in the frosty air, leaving the rest of her body to fade into the gloom. It was like a sepia print, with just a small part coloured in. Somewhere, at the very back of his mind, a forgotten memory stirred. He tried to form a picture, something to act as a hook to capture the shred of thought.

'Look up, look up,' he whispered, stupidly anxious that she, perhaps even anyone, should acknowledge his presence. He was shocked when, as if she were capable of telepathic thought, she paused in her journey and slowly lifted her face towards his window. For a moment they stared at each other, before he shrank away, confused by sudden stirrings of alarm. When he dared to look again she had turned her face away and continued her walk towards the house.

He left the window and turned towards the small chair. With almost mechanical movements he took off his clothes and placed them neatly on it before getting into bed. Sleep came immediately, and if he dreamed, the dreams were stolen and replaced with the type of peaceful rest he hadn't known for months.

Chapter Seventeen

When he woke the next day it was to the comforting smell of bacon and hot bread wafting up from the kitchen below. He lay dozing, warmly wrapped in the blue-checked duvet, listening vaguely to the half-forgotten sounds of a farm morning. The chickens were about. He could hear faint clucking and the occasional louder squawk as small squabbles erupted between rivals in the yard. The sheep were in the bottom field, he knew that; he'd seen them there yesterday when he arrived. But, even without sight, he could pinpoint the direction of the urgent bleating. Matthew must be taking out extra feed. He remembered the feel and smell of the ewes, their heavy bodies reeking of lanolin, pushing against his legs as he broke apart hay bales and strewed them in the field by the water trough. It was always his chore, feeding the ewes and the calves when they'd kept them. Funny, he hadn't thought of the cattle for years. How the cows had bellowed when the calves were taken away and how the little Welsh Blacks had shivered and huddled together in the calf shed. When he'd gone out to them, they had looked up eagerly, slobbering and fighting for attention, their warm little noses plunging deeply into the milk buckets. He'd loved them. But after Mam died, Dad had got rid of the cattle; had to scale down, he'd said.

He lay thinking for a few more moments before throwing off the duvet and getting out of bed. The room was cold and he hurried to get dressed, before going across the narrow landing to the bathroom. By the time he reached the kitchen he was famished and looked eagerly to the Rayburn, expecting to see the old black frying pan which Dad used to fry their breakfast. But there was nothing to be seen. A bright fire was burning in the grate but the room was empty.

Lark was in the yard, sprinkling seed and grit for the chickens. They stepped about her feet, delicately pecking at the grains and fluffing out their feathers to greet the day. She looked down at them carefully, examining each one, noting their feathers and beaks, and, most important in this icy weather, looking for the first signs of frostbite. In the last few months she had become quite knowledgeable about her poultry and enjoyed working with them.

Matthew disliked the fowl and would never go near them. She didn't mind; they were little

164

trouble and if nothing else, Griff Parry had no hold over them. The sheep were a different matter.

Already this morning she had taken out a bale of hay and a sack of pellets to the field. The ewes were hungry and the pasture, even in this lower field, had just about finished. She wondered yet again why Griff had insisted that the tup must go in so early. The sheep were now well on in their pregnancies and the weather was getting colder. All the articles she'd read recommended indoor lambing, and the barn roof hadn't been repaired, and neither Matthew nor Griff seemed inclined to get on with it. She looked at it speculatively as she fed the chickens. Perhaps she could borrow a ladder from the Joneses next door and do something about the roof before she left. And then, if Matthew saw her struggling, he would be forced to help.

'Good morning!'

She looked down. In her concentration on the barn, she hadn't noticed John coming out of the house. He was standing by the hen house, shivering, although he was wearing a warm coat and had put on a blue fleece baseball cap. His face was pale and he looked ill, she thought. Maybe it was just exhaustion, but she wasn't sure. There was something wrong with him. 'Hello,' she said, smiling. 'I thought I'd leave you to have a lie-in. You looked so tired last night.'

He noticed that she hadn't mentioned seeing him at the window and wondered miserably if he had imagined it. Anyway, she looked so different in this clear morning light, just an ordinary girl,

165

with roughened hands and a matter-of-fact manner. She was wearing jeans and a heavy sweater, but over those she was wearing an old-fashioned wrap-around apron. He found himself staring at it and had to force his eyes away in order to speak to her. 'You're up early,' he said.

'Yes, I suppose so, but I like this time of day. Before everything has been ... used.'

He nodded. It described a feeling perfectly and he appreciated it too. He looked over to the fields and then back at the house. 'I didn't see Matt in the kitchen. Where is he?'

She upturned the bowl of chicken feed and dusted the grains off her apron. She grinned. 'He's still in bed. He's not an early bird, but you must know that.'

He snorted and said sarcastically, 'Nor a late one. I saw you closing up last night.' The words sprang out of his mouth unthinkingly. He'd wanted to hide the fact that he'd been watching her. It was Matt's fault, as ever.

He watched her nervously, wondering what she would say. In truth, he found conversation with her difficult. Not only was she years younger than him, but how did a man speak to someone his own son was screwing?

She shrugged. 'He had things to do.'

She started walking to the house and he fell in beside her. 'Things to do, like phoning his mother?' The remark was less than a question, but he expected a reply.

She ignored that, but paused and opened the big pocket on her apron, inviting him to look inside. She was carrying five large brown eggs.

166

'Are you hungry?' she asked. 'I did some bacon earlier. It's in the bottom oven. I can crisp it up and cook these eggs to go with it.'

'Sounds great.'

He stopped at the door to let her go in first. As she passed, he put his hand out and touched the skirt of the apron. The material was smooth, threadbare nearly, the result of many years of washing, and his fingers made contact with her leg beneath it. She froze and looked down and he snatched his hand away. 'I'm sorry.' He could feel the blood rushing into his face. 'It's just that ... well, my mother had an apron like this. Absolutely like this. It ... it brought back a memory.'

'I think this must be the same one,' Lark said slowly. 'I found clothes in a drawer in the bedroom. Matthew was going to dump them. But they're good enough to wear and I love some of the patterns.' She put her hand into the pocket and pushed her fingers gently between the eggs. 'I hope you don't mind.'

'No. Of course not. Why should I?'

He looked at it again, seeing his mother digging in the vegetable garden, pulling misshapen carrots from the stony soil and putting them with a laugh in that same pocket. The desire to hold the material again was almost overpowering, but as if she could read his mind, Lark suddenly twitched the apron away and went inside.

They sat together at the scrubbed pine table. John devoured the bacon and eggs followed by toasted rolls and greengage jam. It was the biggest breakfast he'd eaten for twenty years, but he sat in front of the thick white plate as though it was the most normal thing to do and enjoyed every mouthful. Lark had sat with him, drinking tea and breaking off little pieces of roll and pasting them with butter and jam before popping them in her mouth.

'Don't you eat bacon?' he asked, nodding as she indicated another cup of tea.

'Oh, I do. Had mine earlier.'

He sat back and looked around the room, brighter now in daylight, even though the sun was low in the December sky. He noted the patches on the leather chair, and the brass and copper jugs and the toasting forks which decorated the fireplace were now well polished and gleaming. The rug was clean and the cushions on the rocker looked different. Perhaps they were new. Even the walls and ceiling had been painted, a creamy white which contrasted well with the old black ceiling beams. Lydia would have been charged a fortune to achieve this look, he thought.

'You've made this room much more comfortable than it used to be. It's cleaner and warmer. And I like the pictures.' He pointed to a series of photographs of the farm and surrounding countryside which had been framed and arranged on the wall between the two windows.

'Oh, Matt took those in the summer. I made the frames out of bits and pieces I found in the barns.' She smiled. 'He's good at photography.'

'Yeah, he always was. Even as a child.'

Lark stood up and started piling the plates together. She had taken off the apron and thick sweater and had on a long-sleeved grey T-shirt which covered her jeans almost to her hips. John watched her as she went to the sink. She walked so smoothly it was almost like gliding, and yet she was a tall girl with long legs and strong arms. He wondered again about her relationship with Matt. The few girlfriends his son had brought to the house were quite different from this girl. Not that they had been all of one type, Matt was too easily bored for that, but they had been similar in their prettiness. Lark could never be described as pretty. She was too beautiful for that.

John cleared his throat. 'Where are you from?' he said.

'Oh, here and there.' She kept her back to him as she washed the plates and cleaned out the bowl which she had used for the chicken feed.

'You're not Welsh,' he persisted.

'No.'

John got up from the table and wandered over to the fireplace. He picked up a Welsh language grammar and waved it at her. 'Who's learning?'

'Me.'

'For Christ's sake, why?'

'I like learning new things.' Lark turned to face him, wondering if he would follow up with a sarcastic remark, but he had turned back to the table and was examining the other books.

Beside the copies of *Farmers Weekly* there was a new book on poultry-keeping, open at the section about incubators. He was about to move away when he caught sight of a tattered little book lying on the floor beside the table. He picked it up and opened it to the title page. He really didn't need to; it was a book he knew by heart. 'A Collection of Welsh Legends', he read

169

and carefully pulled aside the tissue paper leaf that partially concealed the picture opposite. The coloured plate had been drawn at the turn of the last century and showed a maiden in mediaeval costume leading a small herd of cows across a lush green meadow. The mountains in the background of the picture were misty blue and lilac-coloured, fading into obscurity so that one's eye was drawn entirely to the willowy girl in the foreground. 'Angharid and her Magic Herd' was the caption at the bottom of the picture and John gazed at it in pleasure. There had been many evenings when he had sat on the rug in front of the fire poring over this and other stories in the little book.

'I remember this,' he said joyfully and flipped the pages, halting now and then to study the half-forgotten pictures.

'Do you still speak Welsh?' Lark asked suddenly. She had finished her work at the sink and was putting the plates away on the dresser racks.

'What?' John was still turning the pages of the book but looked up when she spoke.

She repeated the question.

'Um ... I don't know. I shouldn't think so. I left here twenty-six years ago and I haven't spoken a word since.' He put his head on one side and looked speculatively at her. 'You're learning – try me with a sentence, see if I understand it.'

She laughed and shook her head. 'My accent would defeat you, even if you remembered the words.'

He laughed too and walked over to stand in front of her. 'Go on ... be brave.'

Lark opened her mouth and then shut it as she struggled to formulate the correct words. He felt that he could almost see the wheels moving and waited, grinning encouragingly, for the sentence to come out. She took a deep breath and opened her mouth again, but before she could speak, Matthew came into the room. He was barefooted and wearing only underpants and a sweater. He looked rumpled and boyish, obviously only just awake.

'Hi,' he said to the room, 'how goes it?'

'Fine,' said John, oddly resentful that his banter with Lark had been interrupted.

Matthew sat at the table and Lark poured a mug of coffee from the filter machine and put it in front of him. He drank it slowly, and looked over his shoulder to see if there was any more in the jug. Lark brought him a refill and he nodded his thanks while yawning and stretching his arms. She put a small pot of yoghurt on the table with a teaspoon and while he ate it, made him a plate of toast. All this was done without a word passing between them and John, who had come to sit opposite, barked a short laugh. 'No wonder you don't want to come home.'

He said it lightly, trying to make a joke, but Matthew's face hardened. 'What d'you mean?'

'Oh, nothing, really.' John retreated, sorry he'd spoken, knowing that Matthew sensed familiar parental criticism. What would be the point in having a fight with him?

Matthew wasn't prepared to let it go. 'I guess you didn't get your own breakfast,' he said, his voice heavy with scorn.

'No.' The tension between them thickened the air, spoiling the earlier mood, and John tapped his fingers nervously on the cover of the little book that he was still carrying.

Matthew put a piece of toast in his mouth and chewed slowly. 'I phoned Ma last night. She said she hadn't known you were coming here. You just left a note or something.' He looked at his father curiously.

John shrugged. 'So?'

'Well, I guess it seems a bit mean.' Matthew was indignant and turned his head to see what Lark thought of it. He would have liked her to join in with condemnation but she wouldn't meet his eyes. This was his argument.

John stopped tapping. 'You didn't tell us that you were coming here.' The words fell heavily into the quiet room and Matthew scowled.

'That's different,' he said. 'Anyway, whatever, she's pissed!'

Chapter Eighteen

'I think I'll go for a walk outside.' The atmosphere in the room was charged and John felt unable to stand another row. 'See what's changed and all that.' He went to the scullery and took his heavy coat off the peg. For a moment he hesitated, a remembered habit forcing him to look for his rubber boots, but of course they weren't there, and with an embarrassed cough, he opened the door and went outside.

'Jesus!' Matthew exploded as the door shut. 'I can't stand much more of this.'

'Of what?' Lark looked at his sulky mouth and angry blue eyes. In the few hours since John had arrived, Matt had grown younger. The man who had made such headstrong love to her in the fields and on the mountainside, and who had lain in her arms every night, was suddenly disappearing. A boy was replacing him. She bit her lip as the breath caught in her throat. It was nearly finished.

'Can't you see? He wants to take over. He's come here to drag me home, make me do what they want.'

She took hold of his arm and reproved him gently. 'Don't be stupid, Matt. He hasn't said anything like that, and anyway, he can't do it. It's your farm.' Her exasperation showed and he glared at her, suddenly seeing her in a different light. At this moment, she was one of them.

He shook off her hand and walked over to the window. He could see John walking in the lower field, moving easily amongst the ewes in the manner of one used to the land. He wasn't even sightseeing, but striding authoritatively across the pasture as though he had never left. Somehow he looked different out there. No hint of the trembling, tearful man who had sat drunkenly in the kitchen last night. That person had frightened Matthew. He was a stranger who bore no resemblance to the determined and forthright father he had known all his life.

As he watched, John began to climb higher on

the hill, scattering the sheep who had been following him, hopeful of more feed. 'Dumb bastard,' Matthew growled. 'He's spooking the sheep.'

Lark looked over his shoulder at the scene through the window. She could see the distant figure clambering up the hillside and lifted her eyes beyond him to the peak. The clear skies which had lasted for over a week had gone now, hidden by dense grey clouds which drooped low over the hills. She felt an urge to run out after him, to race into the cloud and disappear, anywhere other than here and the difficult days which were to come.

She made an effort. 'Don't worry.' Her voice was soothing. 'It'll be all right.' But she wasn't sure what or whom she was talking about, and Matthew wasn't listening anyway.

'He's spoiling the place. I want him to go.' This was a teenager speaking. Lark shook her head impatiently and left the window. He was behaving in an extraordinary way. It seemed as though everything that had happened between them before John arrived had been wiped out and that she was becoming a stranger.

She walked over to the hearth and carefully banked up the fire with several logs, and brushed away the dust and twigs which had fallen onto the grate. It would burn unattended now for a couple of hours, which would give them some leeway to get on with the outside work. Perhaps that would help to get over the awkwardness which had grown between them. Matthew was strong and could work well when he was in the mood.

'There's work to do,' she said, going to get her coat. 'The barn roof has to be fixed; so we'd better get on with it.'

Matthew stood for a moment, his back rigid with annoyance, and then turned towards her. 'I'm going to get dressed,' he said, not looking at her, 'and then I'm going into Bangor. Meeting Griff there.'

'What for?'

'I gotta bit of business to do.' He said it in a way that was deliberately meant to exclude her and she held her breath as a chill of indifference started to swamp the room. She wondered if he was hurt because she hadn't joined in with his bad-tempered remarks about his father, but that surely couldn't be the only cause. In twenty-four hours he had changed. Maybe she had too.

'OK.' She struggled to keep her voice calm. 'I'll see what I can do.'

Matthew stood for a moment after she had gone out and looked around the room. His eye lit on the book his father had been holding and had left on the table. He remembered seeing Lark reading it. He went over and picked it up. 'A Collection of Welsh Legends', he read, and opened the title page, seeing the picture of Angharid and her Magic Herd.

'Jesus,' he snorted contemptuously to the empty room, 'they're as bad as each other!' He tossed the book back onto the table and hurried out of the room and up the narrow, shaky stairs.

After he was dressed, he opened the wardrobe and fished out his rucksack. In the little pocket on the front was his bank book and he took it out

175

and examined the balance for a moment. The cheque from Llinos for the lambs had been entered and he still had a bit of Grandfather's money left. He grinned and smacked the little book against his hand before stuffing it in the back pocket of his jeans.

When he came out, she was in the yard, dragging a large piece of corrugated iron towards the barn. He heaved an audible and irritated sigh. She was beginning to push him, just like everybody else. 'Leave it,' he said, 'you can't do it by yourself. I'll be back too late to do it today, but I'll start tomorrow.'

'Right.' She dropped it and stood waiting, hoping he would change his mind and ask her to go with him, but he walked quickly towards the Land Rover, swinging the keys impatiently in his fingers. He stopped for a moment to examine the rented Vauxhall which John had brought in from the road, and then jumped into his vehicle.

'See you later,' he called and drove swiftly out of the yard.

Lark swallowed. The lump in her throat was huge and she knew that she was going to cry. Her eyes flickered around the yard and then up to the mountains. How quickly the time at Cariad Elin had passed. Why, it could have been yesterday when she'd first caught sight of the cloud on the hilltop and remembered how it felt to fall in love. It was over, she knew that. The magic had gone for him and it was only a matter of time. Tears swam in her eyes and dropped carelessly on her cheeks and coat. The sheep were quiet and even the few winter birds, the jackdaws and the red-beaked choughs who normally called their strange cry from the hillside, were silent. The farm was retreating from her.

'I'd forgotten how sharp the wind could be.' John's voice broke into her desolate thoughts and she turned round to find him standing behind her, breathing rapidly, his face flushed in the damp, chilly weather.

She answered automatically, her voice low and hoarse. 'I thought it would be colder in Canada.'

'Different kind. Dryer.'

She nodded and bent to pick up the piece of corrugated iron. It might as well go back to the pile. There was no way that Matthew would be mending the barn now.

'Here, let me.' John pushed her away and grabbed the end. 'It's too heavy for you.'

She led him to the stack of useful iron and wood that they'd put aside for mending the barn and showed him where to drop it. It fell with a clatter, showering the rubbish heap with flakes of rust. He looked at the pile of garbage with dismay. How on earth could she and Matthew hope to use any of it? Surely it would be better to get the barn repaired properly? He wondered briefly if he should offer to pay for the work. They were probably quite hard up, and even if they were affronted, it might be better to get it done and then have the row later. He looked at her, considering how best to broach the subject, but was taken aback at the desolate pallor of her face. The tears had dried on her cheeks and she bore a look of such sadness that he stared at her in consternation. Was she ill, or perhaps not quite normal?

He began to feel concerned for Matthew and looked round, wondering where he was. 'Matthew gone somewhere?' he asked casually, nodding to the space where the Land Rover had been.

She nodded. 'He's in Bangor for the day. He'll be back later.' She rubbed her face with her gloved hand and drew in a deep breath which was released with a shuddering sigh.

'Are you all right?' John asked, watching as she took a green woollen hat from her pocket and pulled it over her frosty gold hair and low over her ears.

For a moment she was silent and then in a small voice muttered, 'Yes, I'm all right ... whatever all right is.'

They stood, two people in the lonely farmyard in the quiet valley, neither able to speak, until she gave herself a little shake and turned and gave him her sweet smile. 'I thought I'd go for a walk on the hill.' There was no invitation in the statement and John wouldn't have joined her anyway. He had no desire for her company.

'I'm going to stay for another couple of days,' he said, 'if you'll have me.'

'It's not up to me, really. It's Matt's place.'

'I know. But I don't think he'll mind. I've come all this way and I haven't said... Well, we have things to talk about.'

She nodded. 'I'm sure it will be fine.'

He reached in his pocket and drew out his car keys.

'I thought I'd go into Llanfair, have a look at the village. Is there anything you need?'

She shook her head. 'No, nothing.' She looked up at the mountain, suddenly very anxious to get away. 'Thank you.'

'Right, I'll get off.' He unlocked the car door and got in. 'See you this evening.'

He looked in the rearview mirror as he swung out of the yard. She was walking up the hillside, her face turned up towards the summit. The mist was low and it was beginning to drizzle but she was not deterred. Her smooth progress across the uneven pasture and up through the rocky outcrops was totally sure.

The square in Llanfair village looked exactly the same as it had in the old days when he had breathlessly skidded to a halt on his old bike after cycling the three miles from Cariad Elin. Then, he'd propped his bike beside the shop and run inside to choose sweets, watched carefully by Mr Aarons and old Johnny Peddler. Give them their due, they never suspected the local children of stealing; it was too small a village and parents would have been ashamed if their child was accused of being light-fingered. No, the Aarons were worried about clumsy little fingers disturbing the display, or worse, spilling the pick-and-mix onto the floor.

John wondered if the Aarons were still there and thought he might go in to see if they remembered him. The shop front was covered in advertising slogans, and newspapers were displayed on racks under the porch, just as they used to be, but when he looked up at the sign, it read 'Rowlands' and he was disappointed.

He parked in front of the Miner's Arms, relieved that the pub looked unaltered, although perhaps the garden at the side had been tidied up and the sign newly painted with a garish representation of slate splitters. Actually, he couldn't remember what had been on the sign before, but he was sure it hadn't been like this.

A sudden spurt of rain spattered on his windscreen and obscured his view so that he didn't notice the battered red van pulling up beside him until it had stopped, and one of its occupants had got out. He was a young man, wearing a waxed jacket with his head covered by a tweed cap. He was talking to the other person in the van and gesticulating towards the heavens as though to remind him that it was raining outside.

John looked away and concentrated on his own confused thoughts. The trip to Llanfair had been taken partly to get away from the farm and that girl, Lark, who had been visibly upset and acting strangely. Earlier this morning he had been quite taken with her, not only with her looks, which he thought striking, if unusual, but with her easy and cheerful temperament. So different from Lydia and all her girlfriends. None of them would be prepared to be seen without make-up or in patently old-fashioned clothes. No, that wasn't true. Fred's wife, Edith, didn't dress up. Lydia and her friends had a lot of fun discussing Edith and her lack of fashion. The fact that they were supposed to be best friends had never stopped Lydia, and she could kiss the air next to Edith's cheek in greeting while happily winking at another expensively coiffured pal, without turning a hair. But then, Edith wasn't in any way good-looking and she had a caustic tongue which was used freely. John sighed. No wonder Fred looked elsewhere, poor bastard.

He wondered what to do now. He could go into the pub and take a look at the landlord, who he had been told was Matthew's partner. But that would be interfering. Or he could go to the shop and ask about old Johnny Peddler and Mr Aarons. Now that he thought about it, for the first time in years, he realised that they had been kind to him when Mam died. Quite a few people in the village had been good, but he hadn't appreciated them at the time.

The rain started up again and spattered against the windows, running down the red bonnet in waxy rivulets, and he reached over to the back seat to get his baseball cap. There was a sudden sharp rap on the window and he turned back, startled. Outside was another, older man standing beside the youngster, making an urgent winding motion with his hand. For a second John was wary. Normally, he wouldn't open his car to a stranger – it was far too dangerous – but this wasn't the city and the guys looked harmless enough. He wound down the window. 'Hi, something I can do for you?'

The man pushed his head in through the window and gave a snort of laughter.

'Bloody hell, John Williams, you're not going to pretend you don't know me. Insulting, that is.'

John was baffled. He desperately searched the large face thrust in front of him for clues. He could find none. The stranger was broad and weather-beaten with a few thin strands of hair blowing across a tanned pate. His mouth, when he grinned disconcertingly at John, was missing several teeth and those that remained were crooked and tobacco-stained. There was something familiar, perhaps, about the eyes, but he couldn't pinpoint it and gazed helplessly back at the grinning mouth.

The man snorted and drew his face out of the window, looking over his shoulder towards the younger man. 'The old bugger can't remember me,' he said sneeringly. 'Spent too long living the good life.'

John followed the glance towards the younger man and suddenly recognition blasted him upright and he felt his mouth spreading in a delighted and somewhat relieved grin. It was only later that he realised that he had understood the Welsh they had been speaking. 'Robert?' He spoke cautiously. 'Is it you, boy?'

'Of course it bloody is, you bugger.'

'Christ, who would have thought it?' John got out of the car and grabbed Robert Jones' extended hand and welcomed the other man's clumsy and eager embrace.

Robert pointed towards Elfed. 'You only knew me because of the boy here, didn't you?'

'Well, he is like you.'

'Fucking spitting image.'

John laughed out loud and punched Robert lightly on the arm. 'Bigger than you, mind.'

'Get away, boy *bach*. I've shrunk a bit, that's all. It's the hard work.' He stood back and looked at John, his neighbour and school friend from all

182

those years ago. 'Anyway, look at you. All that grey hair. Like an old badger, you are.'

John rubbed his hand slowly through his grizzled head. 'At least I've got hair. Up on you, man.'

Robert laughed and turned towards his son, pushing him forward. 'This is my lad, Elfed. Running the farm with me now.'

'Still at Bryn Goch?' John asked while shaking the young man's large hand.

They both nodded, suddenly looking very alike and bringing the buried past alive for John. God, the times he and Robert had had. Searching the mountain for birds' nests and recklessly diving into the quarry pool when they were sure no adults were about. Later, as teenagers, they had spent endless hours in Robert's barn, slowly leafing through tattered and swapped copies of *Playboy*, breathlessly excited at the brazen array of nudity. The American pin-ups, staring provocatively back at their acned faces, became just as real as other adults, and for more than two years John and Robert were wrapped in a half-life fantasy, talking entirely of Miss September or Miss June, and thinking of very little else.

Robert came out of it first, after starting to go out with a girl from the village, but John hung on alone for a few more weeks, not easily able to let go. It was from then that their friendship weakened. Keeping it going had become too difficult, specially now that John was studying for his exams and Robert was working his way through the village girls. But it had been Robert who had driven him to the airport and had awkwardly

183

shaken hands with him in the departure lounge after the last call for boarding. John cleared his throat, surprised at the sudden wave of emotion. He hadn't thought about that last afternoon for years.

'We've met Matthew and his girlfriend,' Elfed was saying. 'In fact, I see them nearly every day. They're trying to make a go of it.' He paused and looked uncertainly at his father, 'At Cariad Elin, I mean.'

'Yeah, I've been there overnight. I've seen what they're doing.' John shrugged. 'I'm not sure they're getting the best advice.'

'Nothing to do with me, man.' Elfed jerked his head towards the pub. 'It's that bastard in there, running the show.'

John nodded. 'So I gather.' He shivered slightly; the rain was still beating down and dripping insidiously into his collar. The pub looked very inviting. It would be warm inside and he could get a drink. 'I thought I'd go in and see him. Not that it's any of my business,' he added quickly.

'He isn't there,' Robert snorted. 'I saw him and your boy driving on the Bangor road earlier on.'

'Oh.'

Robert gave him a careful look and sensed rather than heard the tone of despondency in John's voice. He'd have known his old friend anywhere. There'd not been many in this valley that tall or with the same finely drawn face. Old Geraint had looked much the same, even old and sick. And they were tough, normally. 'We're going home for a spot of dinner. Come with us.' He ignored Elfed's look of surprise; the plan had been to go into the Miner's first and the boy was looking forward to his first pint of the day. 'Bethan will kill me if I don't bring you round.'

John hesitated. He wasn't ready for an old pals act, or talk about the old days, but as he stood wondering, Robert got into his van, followed reluctantly by his son.

'You know the way,' Robert shouted from his wound-down window, 'see you up there,' and he careered off, the van rattling noisily as it took the corner out of the square and headed up the mountain road.

Was it just a hint of relief that John felt as he climbed back into the hired Vauxhall and started the engine? Someone else had made a decision for him, and although he grumbled to himself that this was going to be hellish, he obediently followed the road out of the village and drove towards the mist-covered hills.

Chapter Nineteen

The yard at Bryn Goch was as muddy and pot-holed as the one John had left at Cariad Elin, but he scarcely noticed it. He was wrapped in his own thoughts and had followed Robert out of the village and up the mountain road as if in a dream of years ago. He knew the way, of course, and such was his now-renewed bout of helplessness that he didn't bother to look at the small new housing estate on the edge of the village, or the nascent industrial area where the council hoped to attract new business and employment.

He and Robert had been as close as brothers growing up; both only sons. Robert had a sister, but she didn't count, being quite a lot older and already at work in the quarry offices when John and Robert were teenagers. They were always equally welcome at each other's homes. Even after Mam died, Dad had accepted Robert as a normal adjunct to the family, and at Bryn Goch John was just another person to be fed and nagged at when necessary.

He parked beside Robert's van after splashing heavily through huge puddles, and stepped warily out of his car. His heavy shoes coped well with the mud but would need a good cleaning later tonight. Boots would have been better, he thought.

There were several vehicles in the yard, some looking beyond repair with their redundant parts spread untidily about, adding to the general mess of empty feed bags and plastic bottles of un-known origin and use. But in one corner, oppo-site the calf shed, a rickety car port covered a newer car, clean and waxed and looking totally out of place.

'Bethan's,' said Robert, nodding to the pristine vehicle. 'Very particular, she is.'

And Bethan's influence was obvious as soon as they walked through the back door. Elfed and Robert hastily removed their boots, and Robert's dog who had jumped out of the back of the van didn't even attempt to follow. He trotted past the door and made for an open barn where John presumed he had his bed. Another dog stood in the doorway of the barn, sheltering from the rain and wagging its tail furiously. John felt obliged to remove his shoes also but Robert gave him a slight shake of the head before leading him into the kitchen.

It was so different to Cariad Elin and to how he'd remembered Bryn Goch. Modern kitchen units stood on a spotlessly clean plastic floor, and the pine table which had always been covered in papers and bits of machinery now bore a china jug of flowers and a single broadsheet newspaper folded to the crossword section. A plump, dark-haired woman sat in front of the paper, pen in hand and a look of concentration creasing her pretty, fat face.

'Bethan, *cariad,* look who's here.' Robert spoke cautiously, but with a certain amount of pride. Elfed had carried on out of the room and John could hear his footsteps going upstairs.

She got up and came towards him, smiling. 'It's John Williams, isn't it?' She shook her head wonderingly. 'Image of your dad, you are.'

A wave of release came over him. Her cheerful face, the presence of his old friend and the sur-roundings of Bryn Goch, even altered as they were, almost brought tears to his eyes, and he struggled with rising emotions which threatened yet again to overwhelm him.

'Come and sit down, stay for dinner. Robert is mad to hear about life over there.' The instruc-tions tumbled one on top of the other and John was drawn cosily into the family circle and sat at the scrubbed table, glass of beer in hand, describ-

187

ing his home and life in Canada while Bethan expertly made mushroom omelettes and an onion and tomato salad that Robert's parents would have died rather than eaten.

'You didn't grow up in Llanfair,' John said shyly to Bethan. He couldn't remember her at school, but then he hadn't remembered Robert, and he might be making a dreadful mistake.

'No, love. My dad came as the new headmaster after you left. I was in college then, didn't come here for a few years.'

'Bethan is the deputy head teacher at the grammar school,' Robert said proudly. 'Brains of the family.'

She laughed. 'I don't seem to have passed them on, if that is the case. Our Elfed is only interested in farming and football and Megan wants to be a top model, for God's sake. And she's got exams this coming year.'

'John had the brains,' Robert said, dubiously looking at his friend and then at Bethan. 'They took him away. That's what always happens.'

There was a silence while the remark was digested. John shook his head. 'It wasn't only that,' he said slowly, mopping up the remains of the salad with a piece of bread. 'Dad and I ... well, you know how it was.'

Robert sighed. 'Your old man was an unforgiving bastard. I couldn't believe it when I heard that he'd cut you out and left the farm to Matthew.'

'He cut me out years before that, Rob.'

'Yes, he did, boy, fair play.'

There was a contemplative silence then as Bethan digested the remark and Robert and John remembered the old arguments.

'Matthew's a nice boy,' she said brightly, bringing them back to the present. 'And Lark, well, she's lovely.'

'Do you think so?' John was curious to know their opinion. 'I find her slightly strange.'

'Different, mind, I'll give you that, but we like her, don't we, Rob?' Bethan looked at her husband who was nodding in agreement.

'Got a head on her shoulders, that girl. Picks up what you tell her in no time. Really got a feeling for the sheep.'

John sighed. 'But Matthew hasn't,' he said heavily.

Robert shook his head. 'I think he's under the influence of that Griff Parry,' he said, the contempt he felt for the pub landlord obvious in his voice. 'That bastard barely knows one end of a sheep from the other.'

'Elfed thinks he's up to no good,' Bethan added. 'He saw him in Caernarfon with that builder, Sean Harper. The one that puts up all those log cabins. Maybe he's after Cariad Elin. It's so beautiful, it would be perfect for holiday lets.'

The architect in John considered the idea. Done properly, it could work. He could see cabins set neatly on the mountainside, nestled amongst the rowans and pines. From the verandas, the views would be magnificent and a keen naturalist would have a welter of bird and animal life to enjoy. If built to face west, the visitors would be able, on the good days, to watch exquisite sunsets while they sipped their pre-dinner drinks. It was an attractive prospect and he was pretty certain it would be a money-spinner. He thought about materials. Local wood used liberally and fitted out to the highest specs. Low density was the key. Those sorts of people liked privacy.

'Ruin the farm.' Robert's voice broke into his thoughts and brought him up short. 'Sheep and tourists don't mix. Never have, never will.'

'Mm...' John wondered if his face had given him away and shrugged dismissively. 'Nothing to do with me, really. It's Matt's place now.'

Bethan got up and went to the range. She took an apple pie out of the plate warmer and set it on the table in front of them. There was cream and sugar to go with it and John, with an eagerness unlike his normal self, sniffed the air and savoured the aromatic taste of autumn apples flavoured with cloves. He had loved this meal and had been comforted by the presence of two unquestioning friends who didn't hold his every remark up to examination. Even when Bethan asked about Lydia he managed to answer calmly. 'No, I don't think she'll be coming over. I'm only here on a flying visit. Wanted to see what Matt was up to. He gave up college for this, so I hope he makes a go of it.'

Robert and Bethan exchanged a quick glance. 'It won't be easy,' Robert said. 'You know there's no money in hill farming now. If it wasn't for Bethan's salary, we'd be fucked!'

Bethan blushed hotly and gave her husband a small punch on the arm. 'Language, Rob, language.'

'He's heard it before and used it too.' Robert grinned and John laughed out loud, remembering their teenage days when they had, for devilment, hidden behind rocky outcrops and yelled foul words at unsuspecting weekend walkers.

'What about Elfed?' he asked, still grinning. 'He's in farming.'

'Oh, he's not as thick as Bethan made out. Got himself a nice little sideline in drystone walling and building fences. Only part-time here now.' He looked round. 'Come to think of it, Beth, he hasn't had any food. Where is he?'

'He's all right. I took him a sandwich. He's out at a function tonight in Bangor. He didn't want much.'

'Oh yes, the sheepdog trials committee. I'd forgotten.' Robert turned to John. 'He's wonderful with the dogs, just like my dad. Won cups, that boy.' His face beamed with pride and John was ashamed of himself for feeling envious. Matthew had done well enough in school but had never made an effort to be anything other than one of the in-crowd. Even the protests and demonstrations he'd been on were just exercises for relieving boredom. Matthew was not an achiever.

He felt his face dropping and quickly smiled and nodded in admiration 'Good for him,' he said. 'There isn't a dog at Cariad Elin now. At least, I haven't seen one.'

'Geraint's old dog was put down.' Bethan sounded genuinely sad. 'He was grieving so much and wouldn't eat, no matter how hard Elfed tried. We kept him here for weeks but he kept going back. Sent for the vet in the end.'

'How does Matthew manage without one?' John suddenly wondered out loud. 'They must have trouble moving the flock about.'

'They've borrowed Elfed and his dogs so far.' Robert snorted. 'And barely a thank you, let alone payment.'

In the embarrassed silence, Bethan got up and cleared the table. She laid cups and saucers out and put the kettle on to boil.

John cleared his throat. 'Did he suffer much? My dad. You see,' he added, catching the look that passed between them, 'I really don't know what happened. The lawyer only told us that he'd died, and that was months after, and that the farm and land had been left to Matthew. I was left out of most of the discussion.' His voice trailed away as he stared out of the window to the muddy yard and the bare hillside beyond.

'He'd got old,' Robert said awkwardly, 'but he was a stubborn old bastard and would hardly let anyone help him. You know how he was. So proud.'

John nodded, still looking out of the window. He didn't think he would be able to hear about Dad's last days without breaking down and was glad that the light was going and the room getting dark.

'I went there all the time,' Robert continued, 'and Bethan took meals up there and batches of scones.' He sighed. 'The place went downhill. He couldn't manage it and wouldn't give up. Oh, the stock was well enough, he never ignored them, but the buildings ... well, you've seen them. They're a mess still, despite Matthew and Lark.'

'And the end?'

'He was in the bottom field, trying to mend the wall. That's where our Elfed found him.' Robert looked towards Bethan who was pouring tea into the cups, her normally cheerful face solemn and concerned, and then back towards his friend. 'He had fallen, or sat down, maybe, against the wall and couldn't get up. The doctor said he'd had a massive heart attack but Elfed said he was conscious and talking when he got to him. He was looking up at the mountain. He said...' Robert's voice hushed to a whisper as he reluctantly finished the story, 'he said, he could see her coming for him.'

The room was quiet and dark in the December afternoon. The rain had stopped and the clouds had parted enough to let a weak glow of sunlight shine on the puddles. The wind had dropped, too, and John thought it would get quite cold tonight.

'He was probably just wandering in his mind, see,' Bethan said comfortingly, 'thinking about your mam.' She handed him a cup of tea.

'Yes, probably.' John cleared his throat again and turned to smile at her, grateful for her kindness, but his eye caught Robert's and he knew that his old friend didn't believe that.

He drank his tea in one swallow and stood up. 'Look, I'd better go. I have to have a bit of a talk with Matthew. I've been putting it off but it has to be done.' He looked at Bethan and smiled. She was just the sort of wife Robert needed, a helpmate.

'Thank you for my dinner,' he said, 'and for the chat. I needed that.' He suddenly realised that he had indeed needed the chat. It seemed ages since he'd had a normal conversation with anyone.

'Come and see us again soon, John, love.' Bethan took his hand and gave it a squeeze, 'And under no circumstances dare to go away without saying goodbye. D'you hear me now?'

John grinned. 'Yes, ma'am.'

Robert walked him to his car and opened the door for him. 'You going to make him go home?'

John got in and rolled down the window. 'I'm going to try, yeah. He's just wasting his time here. You know that as well as I do.'

'What about Cariad Elin?'

'It's up to him. Guess it'll be sold.'

Robert sighed. 'Shame, that. Been in the family for generations.'

John nodded as he started the car. 'Things change, Rob. They have to.'

Chapter Twenty

Matthew drove carefully, keeping an eye on his rearview mirror, checking on the van with its trailer which was following him along the winding road towards Cariad Elin. He'd had a good day in Bangor, and although elated and excited about his latest purchase, the prospect of explaining it to Lark was heavy on his mind. These days, she was getting just as critical as Dad used to be. And now as he drove along, he remembered that Dad would be there too, and judging by this morning's performance would be his usual carping self. *Jesus, that's all I need,* he thought, and scowled to himself in the darkness.

Griff and the salesman had been totally certain that he was getting a terrific bargain and he was sure of it himself. Apart from it being entirely useful, it would be fun, and fun was something he was short of these days. He scowled again, picturing Lark's face. She would grumble, or rather she wouldn't actually say anything, but would, with a gesture or a look, make sure that he knew she disapproved. Let him know that he'd done something childish or stupid, when she, the sensible one, would never have spent money in that way.

He glanced quickly again into the mirror. The van was still behind him, its headlights bleary with mud and only emitting a vague yellowy glow. That van was pretty old, Matthew knew that. It had taken him no time to work out the registration system of vehicles in Britain when he had first arrived, and he had been surprised to discover how old most of them were in this part of Wales. He loved cars, all cars, all means of transport really, and now, as he watched the first flicks of rain on his windscreen, he thought about the silver and black jeep, a present from his parents for his twenty-first birthday, which he had so recklessly left behind in Toronto. Dad hadn't mentioned it yesterday and he had never spoken of it when he'd called Ma on the phone. *I suppose they just stuck it in the garage,* he thought. The idea that they might have sold it never occurred to him. No one would do that.

An hour before, John had pulled into the yard and parked his car beside the barn. It was nearly dark now and icy rain was spitting in the air. A smell of burning wood wafted from the chimney, an aroma so reminiscent of his childhood that he stood for a moment, picturing the old kitchen. They'd still had oil lamps when he was a boy; the electricity didn't come into the valley until just before Mam died. On winter evenings they never moved from the kitchen. The rest of the house was far too cold. Mam and Dad would sit in the two chairs in front of the big fire and the child John would lie on the rug between them, playing with his Dinky cars. At about nine o'clock on those cosy evenings Mam would make a big pot of tea and a plate of toast which swam deliciously in salty local butter. He had to sit up then to eat it – she would make a fuss if he let butter drip on the rug.

And then they would all go to bed. No television then – or now, he suddenly realised. Then, they had been too poor to buy a set, Dad being dead against hire purchase even before he'd realised that reception in this valley was impossible. It must still be the same, he assumed. *I should buy them a satellite system,* he thought, and as he walked towards the back door he considered how to broach the subject without appearing patronising. But then the other thought that had possessed him on the short trip back from Bryn. Goch overrode the satellite prospect. *Why would they need a television when I'm going to persuade them to leave?*

'Hello,' he called as he went in through the back door and hung his coat on the peg, 'it's only me.' Why had he said that? It sounded so dumb, just like his mam's friends when they used to come into the house without knocking when she was ill, putting a casserole in the stove, or calmly walking through the hall and running upstairs with a pile of freshly ironed sheets. It had driven his father mad. 'Use the place like the bloody Chapel hall,' he used to say, knocking his pipe angrily against the stone hearth and making himself scarce so that he wouldn't have to talk to them.

These memories were so strong now, and growing more frequent with every hour he spent at Cariad Elin. Even when he had been cleaning his teeth that morning, swilling his mouth with plaque-removing wash, he had been suddenly overwhelmed by a long-buried recollection. The face in the mirror hardened as he found himself smelling the sickening odour of disinfectant and medicine and hearing the unstifled cries of Mam, bursting from behind the closed bedroom door, as the district nurse helped Dad turn her to a more comfortable position. It had taken several deep breaths and a handful of cold water thrown on his face to bring himself back to the present.

He walked into the kitchen with these thoughts swimming in his head, sniffing the applewood smoke from the open fire, and found Lark sitting, curled into the rocking chair, staring intently at the dancing flames. Her concentration appeared absolute and he cleared his throat noisily, not wanting to shock her as she'd patently not heard him call. 'Hi,' he said gently.

She turned her head slowly and smiled at him. Her cheeks were pink from the heat of the glowing wood and the light reddened her hair, picking out the tiny curls which clustered around her temples. The desolate look in her eyes which had so alarmed him that morning had gone. Now they were calm and grey and exuded peacefulness. 'Hello,' she leant over and pushed some magazines from the other comfy chair, 'come and sit down and get warm.' She looked up at the clock on the mantelpiece. 'We'll wait a bit for Matthew, then I'll do supper. Or would you like a cup of tea now?'

He shook his head and settled gratefully into the leather chair. He felt tired, exhausted by emotion, more draining than any physical energy he had ever expended. He sighed and drummed his fingers nervously, on his knee, unaware that his foot was tapping at the same time.

Lark watched him from beneath lowered lids. 'Did you enjoy your day here?' she asked carefully. 'I always find being in the mountains so relaxing. It makes everything else seem so...' she paused, 'well, so little.'

He barked a laugh. 'I hadn't got you pegged as an amateur psychologist.' He made no effort to keep the sarcasm out of his voice, and on another day Lark might have been hurt. But she'd spent several hours of the misty December day on the hillside, walking through the scrub and scree until she'd reached the summit. At the top she'd sat on the flat rocks and watched the blue haze of

198

coal fires rising over the villages of Anglesey. She'd looked at tiny Puffin Island and at Penmon, and thought about Llewellyn the Great and his faithless wife who eventually came to love him, and of all the other people, important and simple, who had lived and died within her vision. Icy squalls of rain sped in from the Irish Sea and frequently drenched her, but they passed almost unnoticed. She worked out her problem and was now at peace.

John was the one who felt embarrassed. He was annoyed with himself for being angry and rude and not a little disconcerted when she didn't take offence. He made an effort at conversation. 'I had lunch with an old friend. Perhaps you know him – Robert Jones?'

'Oh yes. And Bethan and Elfed. They're lovely people and so helpful. I've learnt most of what I know about sheep from them.'

'Hill farming seems to be in desperate straits, doesn't it?' John posed the question, already knowing the answer. It was a way of introducing her to his current thinking. If he was to persuade Matthew to leave Cariad Elin, he would have to get Lark on side.

She nodded. 'Yes, I know. It is so hard for people to make a living.'

'Absolutely!' The twitch in John's leg grew stronger. 'It's an utterly pointless occupation. Christ knows why people persist in trying to make a go of it.'

She was silent for a moment but then said, 'Perhaps because hill farming takes place in the most beautiful parts of the country. It would take

199

a lot to give up living in a place like this.'

'Not for everyone.' His voice was low and bitter. 'It could be the easier option.'

'Well, yes,' she agreed. 'You did.'

They sat silently then, not angry, but contemplative, until Lark stretched her arms over her head and peeled her slim body off the chair. She stood up and moved towards the pantry. 'I suppose I'd better start supper,' she said. 'Matthew should be home any moment.'

A card had fallen from the chair as she stood up. She must have tucked it beside her after reading it. John leant forward and picked it up. It was a snow scene in a countryside setting, on heavy, glossy paper, and when John opened it he noticed the sender's address printed below the Christmas greeting. A note added in ink read, 'Come home soon, much love, Mum and Daddy!'

'This from your parents?' he asked, standing up and placing the card beside the clock on the mantelpiece.

She looked up from the sink where she was peeling potatoes and nodded. 'I phoned the other day and told them where I was.' She saw his look of surprise and added, 'I've been away for a while.'

'And will you? Go home soon, I mean.'

'I don't know. Maybe. I will go somewhere.'

John's laugh had a cruel note. 'I bet you're tired with your nannying job. I'm not surprised. Matt can be a real pain in the ass.'

They heard the commotion in the yard at the same time and both looked expectantly at the back door. Matthew bounded through, excitement etched on his face and all memories of this morning's arguments seemingly forgotten. 'Hi,' he said eagerly, 'come outside and get a load of this!'

In the dark farmyard the van driver walked round to the trailer and put down the back ramp. Matthew had left the lights on in his car so that they illuminated the scene, and John and Lark peered into the trailer and saw the object of Matthew's excitement: a quad bike. As they watched, the driver undid the restraining straps and allowed Matthew to start up the engine.

'Isn't it great?' he yelled, driving it in a circle around the yard. 'This is what they all use nowadays. Much better than a dog for getting the sheep in, and it can pull a trailer.'

'But it must have cost a fortune,' Lark said, watching him and allowing irritation to break through her newly found peace.

Matthew drew up alongside her and looked over his shoulder to the truck driver, who was listening with great interest. 'It's my money,' he hissed. His voice had returned to the petulance of the morning. 'I can spend it on what I like.'

John said nothing. He watched as the van driver closed up the trailer and got into his cab.

'Have you paid him?' he asked Matthew.

'No. I'll see to it now.'

'Don't bother. I'll do it.'

John walked over to the van and Matthew turned to Lark. 'It isn't new, you know,' he said pleadingly. 'It didn't cost that much.'

He was relieved when Lark smiled and patted

the mudguard of the bike. 'It looks like fun,' she said after a short pause and turned towards the kitchen door. 'Supper in about half an hour.'

The meal passed without argument. John ate automatically, his mind busy with the conversation he intended to have with Matthew after supper or tomorrow morning at the latest. This extra purchase could make things more difficult. Unravelling his son's life at Cariad Elin would be much harder than he had imagined.

Matthew was still excited about his purchase. 'I drove it all round the cattle market this afternoon,' he said with a grin, pushing the blond mop of hair away from his head with his long, pale fingers. John noticed how clean and soft his hands were compared to Lark's and wondered yet again if his son ever did any work on the farm. 'Griff got it for me at a bargain price. All the guys at the pub agreed.' He forked the fried potatoes clumsily into his mouth, not noticing that he was the only person talking. 'They say that dogs are finished on farms. I guess Elfed Jones is flogging a dead horse with those sheepdog trials.'

After supper Matthew went out again to drive his bike around the yard. John offered to help with the clearing up, but his offer was refused and he sat stiffly on the leather chair. He was aware that he had upset Lark by calling Matthew a pain in the ass and also aware that he hadn't had the guts to offer an opinion on the purchase of this latest vehicle. He was sick with anger and thought about the bottle of whisky which he'd left on the table the evening before. Where on earth had she hidden it? he wondered. It was certainly not on view.

'He wouldn't have lasted five minutes here, without you to help him.' The words burst out of his mouth and Lark turned from the sink, a plate and drying-up cloth in her hands suspended in mid-air. 'Even his adoring mother recognises that he hasn't any staying power.' John punched a fist into his other hand. It stung and his eyes pricked with sudden, hot tears.

Before he could say any more she was standing in front of him, the plate and cloth still in her hand. When he looked up he flinched. The pebble eyes were flashing with anger and scorn. 'I don't know why you care,' she said, her voice cold and unemotional. 'He's an adult now; he's not your responsibility. He does things his way.'

'He's just a dumb kid, playing at being a farmer.' His voice shook.

'He's not such a kid. Not as far as I'm concerned.'

She could have meant anything and he looked at her face, trying to interpret her words. Did she mean in terms of business, farming, or worse, sexual activity? He swallowed and pulled his eyes away, sinking down into the chair. 'I was going to persuade him to go home,' he muttered. 'For his mother's sake.'

'I know.' Her voice had softened. 'But it's not up to you anymore.'

'You're telling me that I'm redundant. Is that it?'

She shrugged. 'I wouldn't have put it that way, but perhaps, yes.'

John sighed and closed his eyes. He was totally

weary and unable to argue any more. 'My use-lessness is the general consensus these days.'

Lark leant over and touched his shoulder. Her sudden flash of temper had gone and she now saw his overwhelming depression and hopeless-ness. A muscle twitched in his thin cheek and the skin drawn tightly over his cheekbones seemed papery and fragile. 'I'm sorry,' she said softly. 'I didn't mean to hurt your feelings.'

'It doesn't matter. I'll go tomorrow. I've out-stayed my welcome.' He looked up at her and then around the room. 'I want to go. I always hated this place.'

The logs on the fire crackled in the otherwise silent room, sending spirals of pale smoke and sparks up into the chimney, and Lark watched them for a moment before returning to the far end of the room.

Matthew noticed nothing when he crashed into the room a few moments later. 'That machine is great,' he enthused, 'the best thing I ever had!'

Chapter Twenty-One

John slept badly, not only because he had gone to bed in his now usual state of consternation. Lying awake in the small room which had been witness to his youthful anxieties and fears, he shivered and drew himself into a tight foetal posi-tion. He still couldn't believe how cold it could be at Cariad Elin, and after a while he got up to find a sweater. Then sleep came fitfully until about two hours later when he got up again to put on some socks. It was then, when his travel alarm showed it to be just after four o'clock, that he remembered that Lark had shown him the extra blankets in the chest of drawers. Wrapped in a stiff beige utility blanket, which had been so thoroughly washed that the pile had lost any elasticity, he finally fell deeply asleep.

When he woke it was after eight o'clock and he was confused and imagined for a moment that he was his teenage self and late for school or for doing his chores. He shot out of bed with a small cry of alarm and stood up shakily, beside the window. It was the sight of the modern cars parked in the yard below him that brought him back to reality, and he sat back heavily on the bed. He stared at himself in the mirror propped on the chest of drawers. The man looking back at him was his father, the careworn face angry and disappointed. *When did I get so old?* he wondered, looking away from the reflection in distaste. He thought about getting back into bed and drawing the covers over his head, but after a few moments he pulled himself together and made his way to the bathroom. He collected his washing things and brought them back to the bedroom. He thought he might pack his bag now and take it down with him. There was absolutely no point in delay.

Matthew and Lark sat together at the kitchen table eating toast and drinking their usual tea and coffee. A smell of washing powder pervaded the air as the old washing machine Lark had bought in Bangor noisily entered its wash cycle and dribbled soapy water onto the quarry-tiled floor. This was the second batch of the day, for Lark had been awake early and had started on her preparations for departure.

Matthew stared moodily into his coffee cup. 'Why are you going?' he grumbled. 'Nothing's different, is it?'

She sighed. 'I told you I'd go one day. This is the day.'

'But why?'

Lark shrugged. 'No reason. It's just time to move on. Past time, really.' Now that she had made the decision it was imperative that she get on with it quickly and not allow time to weaken her resolve. She had foreseen Matthew's argument and knew that she would be able to cope with it. That was the easy part. But the mountain and the farm? How would she be able to leave those? She drew in a quiet breath, controlling a shudder.

Matthew had grabbed hold of her arm and was looking closely into her face. 'Don't go,' he pleaded, 'I love...' She held her breath, surprised and not expecting this. 'I love having you here.' She relaxed; he hadn't surprised her after all.

'You're so good with the animals,' he added, his voice expressing desperation as much as admiration.

She smiled a little but turned her face, which was beginning to crumple, to the ceiling. 'Don't forget to shut the hens in tonight, or the fox will get them.'

'I know, I know.' He got up and walked around the room, his hands plunged deeply into the pockets of his beloved red fleece. 'You don't need to tell me. I'm not dumb.'

Above them they could hear John moving about and Matthew jerked his head towards the sound. 'It's his fault. I told you he'd spoil things.'

'No. It's just a coincidence.'

He grunted disbelievingly and picked up the motor magazine he had brought home from Bangor and turned to the page featuring off-road vehicles. The discussion had already bored him, and the fact that Lark was going was now settled in his mind. There was nothing more to be said. He was now thinking about changing his car.

He heard her get up and recognised the rattle of cutlery as she laid a place for John. He groaned inwardly. Another day of disapproval was in the offing. He heard John's footsteps on the stairs and looked up to see his father enter the room. John was carrying his valise and oddly, despite his previous irritation, a pang of homesickness swept over Matthew.

'So you're off too, I suppose.' He jerked his head towards Lark, who was putting a fresh pot of tea and a plate of toast on the table. 'You know she's leaving?' An unattractive whine came into his voice. 'I'll have Christmas all by myself.'

It was the opportunity John had been waiting for. He could encourage Matthew to come home with him for the Christmas holidays. The boy would leap at the chance and then, once Lydia had got to work on him, there would be no way he would come back. But just as the persuasive words formed in his mind he heard himself saying sarcastically, 'You won't mind. That's what you came to Wales for. You know, finding yourself, and all that.'

Matthew immediately put up a defensive front. 'I didn't say that,' he protested and glared belligerently at his father, ready to continue the sudden fight.

Lark felt sorry for him and angry with John. Why had he been so mean? There was absolutely no call for that, and she couldn't bear to have her last day at Cariad Elin spoilt. She stopped pouring tea into John's cup and leant over to put a comforting hand on Matthew's arm. 'You'll be OK,' she said kindly. 'Griff and Llinos are having a party at the pub. And I bet Bethan will ask you for Christmas dinner.'

Reassured, he nodded slowly and she resumed pouring John's tea. He thanked her but she ignored him and went to the back door. She took her coat from the peg and went outside. Through the window, John could see her opening the hen house and letting the birds out for the day. After a moment he saw her with a bowl of grain, scattering it on the muddy yard, and noticed her mouth opening as she made chucking noises to her chickens. His mam used to do that. Dad said she was mad.

The tea was scalding, as he liked it, and he drank thirstily and piled raspberry jam on a piece of toast. He was hungry this morning and felt as though he needed to refuel.

'Why's she going?' he asked, picking crumbs from his plate with a dampened finger.

Matthew didn't look up from his magazine but casually flipped over a page. 'Who? Lark? Guess she wants to.'

John hated this sort of indifference. 'Haven't you tried to persuade her to stay? Don't you care?'

His son shrugged. 'Of course I care,' he said, 'She's great on the farm.'

The words sounded so callous that John sat and gazed at his son. Was this an act? John didn't know; Matthew had always been a mystery to him. He tried again.

'I meant,' he said, his voice steely, 'I meant personally. You. Don't you care?'

'Oh, sure.'

'Jesus!'

The expletive ripped angrily from John's mouth and Matthew finally looked up.

'What?' he shouted. 'Why do you care? Leave me alone. Lark's my business, not yours.' He slammed the magazine shut and threw it across the table, not caring that it slid along the pine and slapped with a flutter of shiny pages onto the floor. With an exaggerated scrape he pushed back his chair and stood up. His voice was calmer when he spoke. 'I'm going to get the sheep into the lower field. Try out the quad bike.' He went to get his coat. 'You'll hang on till I get back, won't you?'

John nodded, unable to speak and aware that he'd blown his chance to talk Matthew round. If Lydia knew, she'd believe that he had done it on purpose. She would think that he preferred his son to be on another continent. He swallowed the lump in his throat guiltily. Maybe he did.

In the yard, Lark was looking carefully at the hens. They had gone off lay and were quietly pecking at the specks of grain she had scattered. A few days ago she had decided to get in some more layers, but it was pointless now. Matthew would barely remember to feed the ones that were here and she hoped fervently that Robert or Bethan would come and take them away. She heard the raised voices from the kitchen and looked up to see Matthew slamming out of the back door. Without speaking to her, he went over to the barn and presently she heard the sound of the quad bike engine revving up.

She was unpegging the washing when he rode over and stopped beside her to grin a greeting. The wind was ruffling his pale hair and he looked young and healthy and seemingly without a care in the world.

She smiled. 'I'll go before lunch. Perhaps your dad will give me a lift to the station.'

'So you mean it then?'

She nodded. 'Yes.'

He reached out and took her hand, causing the pegs she had been carrying to scatter onto the damp lawn. She looked down at his hand and gave it a gentle squeeze.

'It was good, wasn't it?' Matthew said.

She bit her lip and worked hard to stop the tears which threatened to overflow and drop onto the wet grass beneath her feet. She managed a smile. 'Yes. I've loved these last months. I'll remember this,' she looked around the farm and up to the cloud-blanketed hillside, 'for the rest of my life.'

'And me?' He sounded slightly put out and she found herself beginning to laugh.

'Of course. Every time I mend a fuse or bring in coal, I'll think specially of you!'

She giggled and after a few seconds he joined in, glad that she wasn't going to cry. He would have loathed that. He sat back on the seat of the bike and casually lifted one of his booted feet up onto the mudguard. He wished he could see how he looked and for a millisecond considered asking Lark to go inside and get his camera. But the thought was fleeting; even he recognised that it wouldn't be appropriate.

'Where will you go?' he asked, mildly interested.

She sighed. 'I'm not sure. I might visit my parents for a while. I'm a lot calmer now than I was and we won't upset each other as much. I think everyone's forgiven me now for walking out on...' She paused but his curiosity was now aroused and he wanted more.

'On who? On what? Lark?'

She turned her back on him and continued unpegging the washing. Each piece was folded carefully and put into the plastic basket with the pegs, and Matthew thought that she wouldn't tell him any more. But after a moment she continued. 'I was married, Matt. I had a home and a husband and a job. We were doing well, Christopher and me. He was a junior partner in my father's firm. Solicitors. He and Dad ... lawyers, you know, like you were going to be.'

'And you?'

'Oh, I was at university.' She looked over her

shoulder at him. 'No, not a student, a lecturer. History.'

He was baffled. He remembered the first time he'd seen her, thumbing a lift on the Shrewsbury roundabout with the dyed dreadlocks and the filthy T-shirt. These latest revelations were hard to believe. 'Well, what the hell were you doing walking along the road, with,' he gestured towards her face, 'the fancy hair and the ring?'

The washing was all in the basket now and she picked it up. 'I can't explain ... well, I could, but you wouldn't understand.'

'I might.' He spoke slowly, his mind struggling with the picture of her as a respectable married woman and college lecturer. 'Try me.'

She looked up at the mountain, heavily laden this morning with grey cloud. Thinking back to those days was something she had refused to do for a couple of years. Her brow creased as she attempted to explain. 'My life was too secure, too comfortable,' she murmured. 'I was scared. Scared that it would never be any different. Christopher wanted us to have a baby and then what would have happened? I'd have been trapped in the wrong place.' Her knuckles whitened as she grasped the basket and her eyes looked bleak. 'I met an old friend and left. At the time it seemed the best thing to do.'

She started walking towards the house but Matthew turned the bike to ride next to her. 'Is that it?' He was disbelieving. 'And you'll pick up where you left off?'

Somehow her explanation had annoyed him. All the time they'd been living a free and

212

bohemian life at Cariad Elin, she'd had a decent house and a loving family to fall back on, exactly like he had. He felt let down. She'd pretended to be so different.

He examined a scratch on the handlebar of the bike and spoke without looking up. 'I expect they'll welcome you with open arms.

She heard the disappointment in his voice and was sorry. He hadn't understood.

'No, I don't think so. Christopher has gone, found someone else now, and my job no longer exists. If I go back, things will be entirely different.'

She went into the house and left him on the bike. For a moment he sat, thinking about what she had told him and trying to imagine her standing in front of a class of students. Had she looked the same? Did the students find her sexy and flirt with her while she tried to teach? He couldn't imagine it and for a moment decided that she'd made it all up. But Lark didn't tell lies, did she?

He looked up to the hillside where a few stray sheep were grazing on the poor grass. They had to come down to the lower field and he would have to take them extra feed. It would have been a bore yesterday but now he had the bike. He grinned and with a yell of 'Yippee!' revved up and set off excitedly to the fields. Lark and her stories slipped to the back of his mind and even her impending departure had lost any importance. All that mattered at the moment was the bike. He was going to have fun.

At the Miner's Arms, Griff was behind the bar loading mixers onto the shelves and getting the pub ready for the day. Llinos sat in the kitchen behind him, at her computer, studying the spreadsheet she had loaded. She stared at the screen for a moment and then made up, her mind. 'Griff,' she called. 'Come here a minute.' She leant back in her chair and took off her glasses. It was necessary to play this carefully.

'Look,' she said as her husband bent over. 'you must take a cheque up to Cariad Elin. Wait...' She cautioned him as he began to splutter an objection. 'Wait, Griff. We didn't give him half enough for the lambs. I've put it down here as an introductory fee, but the dad's visiting, and according to what Elfed said last night, he and Robert Jones are old friends. He's bound to find out the prices.'

Griff nodded slowly; her logic as always was impeccable. He didn't need Robert Jones blabbing about him all over the valley. 'You're right, my lovely girl, right as ever. How much d'you think we should give him?'

She took a green chequebook from a pile of papers on the table and wrote the amount. He whistled when he saw it. 'That's quite a bit, *cariad*. Are you sure?'

She nodded her head firmly. 'I am. We've still made quite a profit and this will ensure that if the father asks, he won't find anything wrong.' She tore the cheque from the book and gave it to her husband. 'Tell him it's a government subsidy. He'll be none the wiser.'

Later, as she watched him get into his Land

Rover, she patted his hand in a rare spontaneous gesture of affection and he wriggled with pleasure. 'I bet Lark will have something to say about the quad bike,' she said and parted her lips in a sly little smile.

Griff laughed. 'Stroke of genius, that, my love. Will Hughes couldn't believe it when the boy agreed the price straight away. Mad on gadgets, he is. What with the computer and now with the bike, that farm will be a bloody nuisance in no time. It'll be on the market within a year. Mark my words.'

'Partners get first refusal.' She took away her hand and prepared to go back into the pub.

'Rules of the game, rules of the game,' Griff repeated, as if it were a mantra, and then added, as though he was trying to convince an unseen listener, 'Fair play, now.' He had another thought and his plump brow creased into heavy lines. 'That Lark could cause trouble, mind. She thinks a lot, that one.'

Llinos shook her head slowly. 'Mm, maybe, but I'm not sure. I think she's getting restless. Other than the sex, there's not much to keep her with that boy. It gets boring for women after a while. And of course, at his age, he'll be looking else-where.'

Griff wasn't entirely sure what she meant – the wheels moved slowly for him – but he extracted the fact that Llinos had stayed with him despite her lack of interest in sex and that was more than enough.

'Lovely, lovely girl,' he said happily, putting the Land Rover into gear. 'Keep saying things like that, make me a happy man.'

He was happy all the way to Cariad Elin and was still grinning as he pulled into the yard. John and Lark were by the hired car, his valise in the open boot and stowed beside it, Griff noticed with surprise, her old green rucksack. He then saw that she was dressed in her coat with the woolly hat pulled low over her ears and had the leather bag that she now used for shopping slung over her shoulder. 'God Almighty,' he whispered to himself, 'she's going.'

It was only then that he noticed that they were not looking at him, the visitor, but up at the hillside. There was a concern and urgency in their expressions that drew his eyes to the same place. Matthew was on the mountain driving around on the quad bike. The sheep had scattered; some were still running, leaping over rocks and bashing headlong into the stone walls. He had given up any pretence of gathering them in. The task seemed impossible, certainly the way he was going about it, but it was apparent that he was having a great time.

As they watched, he drove straight up the hillside and turned slowly for another run down. They could hear the motor revving as he raised a triumphal arm and set off at top speed for the gate. John opened his mouth to shout a warning, but got no further when with a sickening crack the quad bike hit a rock and the horrified spectators saw the red-jacketed figure flying through the air and hitting the ground several feet below, and rolling over and over. The bike bounced after him down the hill, crashing against rocky outcrops so that great pieces of metal flew off and scattered across the field.

Did ages pass, John wondered, before he moved? His feet felt rooted to the frozen ground and in his mind he was watching a movie where his only participation was in the viewing. But then, with what felt like slow motion, he started running. As he ran, he screamed terrified prayers and imprecations and begged God for the life of his son.

Chapter Twenty-Two

The waiting room next to the Intensive Care Unit at the hospital in Bangor was empty when John and Lark were ushered in. They had stood in the Emergency Department, unable to sit or even keep still, while Matthew's condition was assessed by an ever increasing team of doctors. John had still been dazed when he scribbled his permission for surgery and even now wasn't entirely sure what he had agreed to. Lark had been silent, watching the comings and goings, her luminous eyes glittering green in distress but carefully following every movement. Somehow, John found her presence reassuring and was glad she was there.

'He'll be going into the Intensive Care Unit after surgery,' the young house surgeon had said. 'Perhaps you'd be more comfortable waiting there.' She paused, waiting for John to answer, but he seemed confused and she turned to Lark. 'I'd go to ICU,' she repeated.

'What are they doing, exactly?' Lark said. She had heard the consultant's diagnosis and his plan for surgery, but she needed, as much as John, to hear it again.

Dr Monk sighed. She had two kids in cubicles waiting for stitches, an old man needing to be catheterised and a pile of paperwork that would keep her in the department until well after her shift was officially over. *They never listen,* she thought, too new at her job to realise that bad news had to be told over and over again.

'Matthew has a smashed pelvis and a broken thigh and ankle. We think that there are four ribs broken also. His head injury is not particularly significant – as you saw, he has come round – but,' she paused, to make sure they were listening, 'the scan has shown that he has an internal injury ... a ruptured spleen. That has to be removed.'

John groaned and looked at Lark in despair.

The young doctor tried to be more sympathetic. 'He is seriously ill, Mr Williams, but is getting the best of care. Please go up to the ICU waiting room. There really is no point in you staying here.'

Lark went over to the chair where they had dumped their coats. She picked them up and returned to John and Dr Monk. 'John,' she said softly, using his name for the first time. 'John, come on. Let's go.'

He turned obediently and followed her out of the department and along the corridor. She didn't ask directions but followed the signs until they were met by the nurse in charge of the ICU.

'Come in here,' the sister said, putting a plump arm around John's shoulder and opening the door into a comfortably furnished room. 'Now, would you like a cup of tea, or coffee maybe?'

They were quiet for the first hour, each mentally reliving the event from the first crash to the ambulance arriving at the farm. 'The mist wasn't on the tops,' John said suddenly. His voice cracked. 'I looked up, you know, when he was lying on the grass.'

Lark swallowed and gripped the arms of the upholstered chair in which she had sat without moving for the last hour. 'Yes,' she whispered, 'it was a clear morning.'

'No, I mean, she didn't...' He stopped in mid-sentence, aware that she was looking strangely at him. He glanced over to her, nodding slowly, and his face softened as though the state of the weather had a calming effect. They were silent again for a while until John, his thoughts breaking into words, said, 'I wondered when I would meet Griff Parry. He was quick off the mark, phoning for the ambulance, fair play.'

Lark wondered if he knew that he had spoken the last phrase in Welsh or that he had used his native language to the paramedics. Probably not, she decided. 'Yes,' she said, 'he was useful, for once.'

They lapsed into a silence, which was not awkward or embarrassing but almost therapeutic. It was as though they both needed the time to absorb the shock and come to terms with it.

The door opened suddenly and the consultant they'd met previously strode in. He was still in his theatre greens, mask undone and hanging on his chest. John stood up, almost unable to breathe for the thumping of his heart in his chest. He felt Lark's hand sliding into his and he held onto it as if it were a lifebelt. If there had been a worse moment in his life, he couldn't remember it.

The doctor had a booming voice and a broad smile which exposed a mouthful of expensively capped teeth. 'He's on his way back from theatre,' he announced. 'I thought I'd just fill you in with what's been going on.' John listened breathlessly while the consultant ticked off on his fingers what had been done.

'Spleen's out, all bones stabilised and blood transfusions still in progress. I think he'll do, but he's been bashed about a bit, so we'll watch him carefully for a few days.' His cheerfulness seemed out of place, but this time John understood and followed the explanation.

'What about his head injury?' he asked, grateful that the words were coming out sensibly.

'There was nothing on the scan, seems to have been just concussion. Considering what I understand of the accident, he was lucky he didn't break his neck.' The words were chilling and John and Lark both stood rooted in horror.

'Even so, it will be many months before he's up to speed. We'll keep him here for a while and then he's going to need physio in the biggest possible way. Still,' he paused, recognising that he was beginning to lose them, 'that's for the future. The next couple of days are what we have to get through.'

They could hear voices and the trundling of a heavy bed in the corridor and the consultant opened the door. 'Here he is.'

They followed him out of the room and were immediately faced with the barely recognisable form of Matthew lying naked, except for a small sheet, in the middle of a large bed. Lark swallowed as she took in all the tubes and lines which connected to various parts of his body. His face was swollen and black around his eyes and there were livid bruises developing all over his body. He looked smaller and shrunken and she felt slightly sick as she put her hand out and touched his shoulder. It had only been a few hours since she had noticed how young and healthy he looked.

John leant over the bed. 'Hi, son,' he said gently. 'How ya doin'?'

Matthew's eyelids flickered briefly but he remained still and John looked up worriedly at the doctors and nurses who surrounded the bed.

'Don't worry, Mr Williams,' one of them said. 'He hasn't come round properly yet and we've sedated him.'

'Right.' The consultant snapped his fingers. 'Let's get him into ICU and connect him up. We can't hang around here in the corridor.'

It was after midnight when they left the hospital and drove back to Cariad Elin. Matthew had woken up and whispered a few words to his father, and when Lark bent to kiss him, he tried to grin. 'Guess I got it wrong again,' he breathed and she nodded and kissed his swollen cheek.

'Go home,' said the sister in charge, coming to stand beside them at Matthew's bedside. 'He's pretty stabilised and will be drifting in and out of sleep for the next few hours.' She looked at their white and strained faces. 'You two look as if you could do with some yourselves.'

'Yes, I expect that is the best thing to do,' said John, reluctant to leave his son's side but recognising the logic of her words.

'You can come back tomorrow, he'll be more awake then.' She turned to Lark. 'Take your dad home, love, he looks all in.'

Lark stared at her, uncomprehending at first and then wondering if John had heard that last remark. He didn't flinch as she had done, but the nurse, noticing his quick indrawn breath, coloured and turned away. They had all assumed that Lark was the sister. She made a mental note as she watched them walk out of the ward, to find out exactly what the relationship was between the three of them.

It was very dark as they drove back towards Llanfair. It was after midnight and the road was deserted. John, behind the wheel of the hired car, drove quickly, knowing the way as if he had been backwards and forwards this way forever. His mind was in turmoil. The accident had ramifications which would alter all his plans and Matthew's, should he recover. Oh God, that last thought was dreadful and he felt his stomach turning over. 'Sorry,' he muttered as he stopped the car. Lark watched him being sick at the side of the

222

road and gulped.

'Sorry,' he said again as he got back in, wiping his face on the sleeve of his jacket. 'Something just came over me.'

'Yes,' she said sympathetically. 'It's been a horrible day.'

The clouds cleared as they turned out of the village onto the mountain road. A watery moon shone through the trees and Lark was reminded of the first night she came to Cariad Elin. 'I came here at night, the first time,' she said suddenly. 'I had no idea how beautiful it was until the next day.'

'Did you?' John was now thinking about Lydia. He should have phoned her from the hospital. 'I must let Matthew's mother know.'

'Of course. Um ... perhaps you'd better leave it until tomorrow. It would be awful for her to have to think about it all night. It is evening now in Canada, isn't it? And anyway, I'm sure there'll be better news to give her then.'

He nodded. This girl was full of sensible ideas. He turned his head to look at her. She was staring ahead at the road, in profile, older than he'd re-membered, and the moonlight shining in through her window bathed her head in an unearthly glow and made the little curls clustered around her face sparkle like tiny metal wires. He shivered for a moment, but the light changed as they went around a corner and when he looked again, she seemed entirely normal.

He cleared his throat. 'I ought to thank you for being with me today. It helps to have company on occasions like this.' The words were stupidly formal and he wished he could relax and sound more genuine, but he was too tired, and anyway, he barely knew her.

'I couldn't have been anywhere else,' she said simply.

When they arrived at the farmyard, Lark noticed with gratitude that the hens had been locked up for the night and that there was a lamp on in the kitchen. Inside, a note from Bethan was propped up on the table. 'There's a lobscouse in the pan, just needs heating up. Elfed put the sheep in the lower field. Hope the news is good.'

Lark held the note out to John and he nodded slowly. 'They're good neighbours.'

'Do you want to eat?'

He shook his head. 'I could do with a drink.' He looked around the room. 'Is there any left?'

She opened the cupboard under the sink and brought out the half-full bottle of whisky. Taking a glass from the dresser she put them in front of him. She didn't say a word but the granite eyes were cloudy and narrowed when she turned away towards the stove and the kettle. He looked at the bottle and the gleaming amber liquid.

He could taste it, rolling around in his mouth and sliding smoothly down his throat, warming and comforting as it settled in his stomach. It was just what anyone would need after a day like he'd had. Nobody would deny that. His hand went to the screw top and as he released it, the warm peaty smell drifted into his nostrils. God, it was wonderful.

Lark was pouring boiling water into the teapot and the bubbling noise made him look up. He thought then of Matthew lying hurt on the hard white bed surrounded by tubing and machinery and possibly even now struggling for life. It was no effort to screw up the top and push the bottle away. 'Better not,' he said hoarsely, 'there might be a call.'

It was only after he'd climbed wearily up to bed, gratefully clutching the hot water bottle she'd made for him, that he remembered that his bag and her rucksack were still in the back of his car. 'They can stay there,' he sighed out loud as he got into bed, after making sure that he had left the door open in case the phone rang, 'the morning will do.'

Lark, lying alone in the large bed, heard him sigh, but thought that, like her, he was crying.

Chapter Twenty-Three

Lydia was in bed when she got the phone call from John. It was nine o'clock in the morning in Toronto and although normally an early riser, she had been at a party the night before and only got home in the early hours.

At first, she couldn't understand what he was saying: 'Matthew seriously injured and in hospital.' She rolled over and sat up in bed. On her bedside table there was a bottle of spring water she had put there specially the evening before. It was flat and warm and made her feel slightly worse, but at least it was liquid. Her hand shook as she held it to her mouth.

'Say that again,' she groaned, mopping clumsily at the drops which had fallen onto her nightdress and peering at the pretty French carriage clock which sat on the dressing table. Her head ached dreadfully and she closed her eyes again and leant back on the pillows.

John repeated the bad news, expanding on his earlier statement, explaining what had happened and the extent of Matthew's injuries.

She couldn't take it in at all. 'I don't know what a quad bike is,' she said, after a moment.

'Jesus, Lydia,' John yelled down the crackling phone line, 'it doesn't matter what it is. Just accept that Matthew is in the Intensive Care Unit with several broken bones and an abdominal injury.'

There was silence now and John thought he could hear a moan. He was sorry then that he had shouted and started again, more gently, with fuller descriptions and with the name and phone number of the hospital ward so that she could speak to them herself.

'Should I come over?' she asked when he had finished.

'You could ... but there's nothing that you can do. He's in really expert hands.' He paused and then added slowly, 'It's up to you, of course.'

There was another silence while she took this in. He hadn't begged her to be with him on this critical occasion, so it couldn't be that serious. Maybe he was just making a fuss – he'd been gone less than a week and his behaviour had been so bizarre in the weeks before that he could easily be exaggerating. Matthew had told her on the phone the other night that his father had drunk nearly a whole bottle of Scotch with his supper and had been embarrassingly tearful. She decided to play it cool and see what happened.

'I'll call the hospital myself,' she said. 'I'd like to hear what they say.' She became businesslike. 'Give me the name of the doctor in charge; I'll get the real story from him, I guess.'

John told her, glad that she was apparently now taking the news well. He was finding the conversation difficult. Their relationship had deteriorated so much that it was like talking to a stranger and he seemed unable to impart any reality into the situation. 'How are you?' he asked formally, feeling he shouldn't ring off without enquiring.

'I'm fine.' Her voice was similarly detached. 'I'm going to spend Christmas with Fred and Edith in the Caribbean.'

'Oh.' What could he say to that? She had obviously reckoned on him not being home soon. 'That should be good.' It was like having a conversation with his secretary. That reminded him. 'Will you give Annette a cheque from the business account for her Christmas box? Make it for five hundred dollars. Tell her I'll be in touch in the New Year.' He cleared his throat; the morning at Cariad Elin was cold and misty and he felt as though he had a cold coming. 'I'll hang on here for a while.'

'Are you thinking of becoming a farmer?' She laughed without humour. 'I would imagine you'd be worse than Matthew!'

She phoned the hospital later when her headache was better and she was ready for the day. The consultant wasn't available and she refused to speak to anyone else. 'No, I won't bother with the juniors,' she'd said to the sister who answered her enquiry. 'I think I'll wait until I can speak to the head man.' The woman had said that Matthew was 'comfortable'. That couldn't be too bad. Comfortable was good, like a country hotel was comfortable.

It was late in the evening when she managed to speak to the consultant.

'He's doing well, considering,' the doctor said in his bluff way, quite unaware that he was misrepresenting the seriousness of Matthew's condition. 'We'll have him on his feet in no time.' His understatement, which would have been recognised amongst his peers, didn't work over the phone or, particularly, transatlantically, so Lydia was left assured that her suspicion that John had gone over the top was correct. It was a wonderful relief.

In the middle of the afternoon she'd begun to have a horrible feeling that something was really wrong and had been on the point of phoning the airline and booking a seat to the UK. No need for that now, and she could go ahead with her Caribbean trip without worrying.

'Thank you so much, doctor,' she said in her low, attractive voice. 'May I call you again?'

'You may and you must, dear lady.' He had a strong impression that she had been flirting with him over the phone. 'Any time!'

Her throaty goodbye as she replaced the re-

228

ceiver remained with him for the rest of the evening.

She picked up the phone again immediately after that and arranged for a basket of fruit and flowers to be sent to Wales and then, satisfied that she had got to the bottom of the matter, went out.

Earlier, Lark and John had eaten a quiet breakfast. She had been up and seen to the chickens first, then, as she was getting a bale of hay from the barn to take up to the sheep, John had emerged from the kitchen door. He had been phoning the hospital.

'He's doing pretty well this morning,' he called to her. 'The transfusion has been discontinued and they've given him a bit of breakfast.'

'Great!' She grinned at him. 'I'll come in and make breakfast for us when I've done this.'

'Let me,' he said, taking the bale from her. He carried it out to the field where, remembering his tasks from years before, he plucked handfuls of the aromatic hay from the binding string and spread them around. On returning, he'd taken their bags from the back of his car and stood them by the door to the hall.

'I'm staying on,' he said as they ate scrambled eggs and toast. 'Someone's got to keep an eye on things.'

She nodded. 'If you don't mind,' she said cautiously, 'I'll stay for a few days too. I'd like to visit Matt in the hospital.' She was buttering a piece of toast as she spoke and so missed the cloud that came over his face. He had hoped she would go, and leave him alone in the house. The last thing he wanted in his present mood was to be with a stranger. It had been surprisingly comforting to have her with him yesterday, but he still wasn't sure what to make of her. He thought back to the other morning when he had been shocked by the wild and desolate expression on her face. Then, he'd wondered if she wasn't a bit mad and had intended to warn Matthew, but well, events had overtaken him.

Lark was speaking again. 'It seems ages since I brought that rucksack down.' She nodded towards the bags by the hall doorway and sighed. 'Yesterday was a long day.'

'Yeah,' he agreed, 'I wouldn't like to go through that again.' He took another piece of toast. 'Christ, I'm ravenous today.' He looked at her and his thin cheeks flushed a little. 'Look,' he said, 'I am sorry about being sick last night, I, er...' He was going to say that he was usually more composed than that but she probably wouldn't believe him. His behaviour since being in Wales had been anything but stable.

She shrugged. 'It doesn't matter, you know. It could easily have been me. Shock affects people in different ways.'

They smiled politely across the table, like people sitting opposite each other in a train. There was an awkwardness that hadn't been relieved by their emergency companionship yesterday. John was struggling to find more to add to the conversation when there was a swift tap on the door and Robert came in, followed by Elfed.

'Good morning John, Lark,' Robert nodded in her direction. 'Good news from the hospital this morning, isn't it?' He beamed happily, exposing the gaps in his lower set of teeth.

'Well, yes,' John nodded. 'He's come round and sitting up. Having a bit of breakfast. I'm going to see him this afternoon.' He looked puzzled. 'How the hell did you know?'

'Our Elfed's young lady. Been on night duty on the ward, hasn't she?' He chuckled and Elfed grinned. 'Phoned us this morning, knew we were neighbours, see.'

He found a mug and poured himself some tea. 'We've come to see what you want doing. That barn, of course, would be number one. Then the sheep. Several are limping, I noticed yesterday. Got to have their feet done.' He turned to Lark 'Did Matthew arrange their injections?'

She shook her head. 'No, I don't think so. Griff never said anything about injections.'

Robert snorted and drained his mug. 'That bastard. Knows nothing about sheep and the bit he's picked up he gets all wrong. Those animals are about six weeks from lambing, right? Well, they need jabs. You can get the vet to do it but he's fucking expensive. The best thing is to buy the stuff from him and do it yourself. I can show you how.'

John looked from Robert to Elfed and then to Lark. He was bewildered; too much had happened in the last twenty-four hours. First he was leaving, then there was Matthew's accident and now ... all this. He sucked in a deep breath and glanced at Lark again. A hint of a smile was on her lips. He frowned.

'Jesus!' he said, getting up from the table and

automatically taking his plate and cup to the sink. 'I'm an architect, Rob. I was only going to hang around to keep an eye on things. I hadn't planned to start working on the farm.'

'Someone has to.' Robert looked speculatively at Lark. 'What about you, love?'

She flushed. John probably wanted her out of the house as soon as possible, and after all, she had been leaving yesterday. She and Matthew had been finished. She was surprised to hear herself saying, 'I don't mind. Just for a while.'

Robert grinned; he'd known she would stay. That girl was becoming a really good shepherd. Instinctive, it was with her. He glanced at John. He was standing by the sink with a miserable look on his face. Bethan had said the other night after John had left them that she thought he was ill, or something. Nervous breakdown was what she'd said, but he'd dismissed that theory. Not John Williams, he'd said with a derisive laugh. But now, he wondered. 'Come on, man.' Perhaps gentle persuasion might be the best way. 'It's either you or that bastard, Parry.'

Later, when he'd spoken to Lydia and realised that there was no point in him trying to go home, John was relieved that he had agreed to get involved. It would be something to do, something to stop him thinking. At the hospital he was able to tell Matt that he had agreed to chop bits off the sheep's feet and was pleased when his son managed a weak laugh. 'Way to go, Dad.'

Lark waited in the corridor while John sat with Matthew and only made her short visit when he came out. She had spoken to the sister and learnt that Matthew was already everyone's favourite patient. 'A right charmer,' said Sister Davies, 'we all love him.'

She watched closely when John came out and held the door open for Lark. The relationship between the three of them had been a source of interest to all the staff. The girl was most unusual-looking, 'stunning' was the anaesthetist's opinion. He had been one of the party who had brought Matthew back from theatre. 'But older than the boy and a lot younger than the father,' said Sister. 'And not related,' added one of the nurses.

John spoke to the consultant, who came into the ICU as John was waiting for Lark to complete her visit. 'He's been lucky,' Mr Fielding said, serious for once. 'There were a few hairy moments when we didn't think we could stop the internal bleeding, and of course, the compound fracture of his thigh was a bloody affair. We're not out of the wood yet and you must prepare yourself for many months of recovery.'

John nodded. This was what he had expected, so the prospect, although worrying, was not a surprise. 'I've let his mother know,' he said. 'She's at home in Canada.' He paused and thought for a moment. 'She's going to call you. Please don't frighten her – she's on her own there at the moment.'

'Got you. I'll play it cool.'

On the way home Lark and John stopped at the supermarket in Bangor to stock up on supplies before setting off for Cariad Elin.

They were through the checkout before John

realized that Lark had paid and hurriedly pressed two twenty-pound notes into her hand. 'Did you and Matthew have some sort of arrangement, financially?' As soon as the words were out of his mouth he realised that they sounded dreadful. 'I mean,' he continued hurriedly, 'did you share the cost of food and stuff for the house?'

She shook her head. 'Nothing formal, I'm afraid. Whoever went to the shops, paid.'

'I'm sure that can't be fair – after all, you're not earning. Unless,' a thought struck him, 'you were in partnership?'

'No. Just a hanger-on.' She didn't mean that to sound bitter, but it came out wrongly and caused them to travel in silence for the rest of the way.

The weather had turned cold and flakes of snow swirled in the gleam of the headlights. *Oh God,* John thought as he drove through Llanfair, *these next days are going to be hell.*

Chapter Twenty-Four

The next few days *were* hell in a way and certainly the most physically exhausting that John had experienced for many years. There were times when he was ready to give up, and one early morning, lying in his cold, dark room, he seriously thought about repacking his case and driving the hundred or so miles to Manchester airport. He could be home in Toronto within a day and pick up where he had left off.

He shifted uncomfortably in the small bed, suddenly embarrassed by recollections of his behaviour in the last months. The way he had treated Lydia had been unforgivable, despite his suspicions of her. He couldn't remember now when they had first started to drift apart; he couldn't even remember when he'd first started to actively dislike her. Or why. Nothing had triggered it; no huge fight or even, at the beginning, a particular disagreement. The animosity between them just grew, insidious, like an infection which hadn't been treated. And then there was work.

He hadn't been to any meetings in the city, had ignored most of the committees he was supposed to attend and had generally dropped out from the professional life he had worked so hard to achieve. And in place of all that, what had he done? 'Nothing,' he groaned out loud to the empty room and grimaced to himself when he heard the word echoing around the newly painted walls. The healing scab on his arm itched and the muscle through which a slice had been gouged, ached. It was all the lifting and carrying he'd been doing. *Hardly work for a man in recovery*, he thought piteously. *No one knows what I've suffered.*

He lay there waiting for the usual wave of depression to swamp him, as it did most of the time when he thought about his life. But this morning, even thinking those words sounded dumb, and besides, other ideas kept getting in the way.

There was nothing to stop him tendering for one of several contracts which he knew were on offer. The housing complex he'd turned down last spring could be fascinating. When he had briefly thought about it before, some ideas had surfaced which would be interesting to explore, particularly the use of materials compatible with the area. That approach had always been important to him, and he loathed buildings which looked as though they had been airlifted in from another continent. It would be the same with the holiday cabins that Robert had been talking about. You could lay a heavy bet that the builders of those would go for the cheapest wood available and end up with houses that looked little better than garden sheds.

He turned on his side and looked at the window. The curtains were still drawn but he could see that it was beginning to get light. It must be after seven o'clock and the girl, Lark, would be up and laying the fires. He groaned and sat up and reached for his socks. It was too cold now to go to the bathroom without getting almost fully dressed. He swore to himself that if he had to stay here longer than another couple of weeks, he would have heating put in. And a shower, he added mentally, as he washed himself down in the icy, lino-floored little bathroom.

Lark was sitting at the table eating breakfast. She had riddled the ashes from the range and filled it with anthracite. Then, as the kettle was boiling, she had cleaned out and relit the big kitchen fire. An acrid smell of cool new coal and logs pervaded the room, and blue smoke billowed back down the chimney as the wind rose in the valley, but she hardly noticed it. Her mind was fully occupied with the situation at Cariad Elin. It had become very awkward, her staying on. She knew that Matthew's recovery would take months and even when he was back on his feet, the idea of him coming back here and running the farm would be out of the question. On his own, anyway. And she was no longer, really, any part of it. She had just stayed, well ... to help John. But it was obvious that he would rather be here alone.

Matthew didn't need her now. She couldn't nurse him; his care was too specialised and the staff of all grades were spoiling him already. As he made his initial recovery after the first dreadful hours, his infectious charm had returned, drawing people to bend closer to hear his whispered jokes. When Lark had seen him last night, she'd thought he'd never seemed so good-looking, his face pale and thinner in the five days since the accident and his blond hair flopping heavily over the stitched cuts on his forehead. He looked like a Victorian painting of some mediaeval knight wounded in battle, so handsome and noble.

'You helping the old man?' he whispered.

She nodded. 'We're mending the barn. He ordered the wood and slates and somehow persuaded some builders to come out straight away. And we've wormed the sheep.' She was going to tell him more. How, under Robert's instruction, they'd also pared away the horny growths from the ewes' feet, a job which had been waiting for a while, but she could see that he wasn't really listening.

'Fantastic machine.' He jerked his head painfully towards the morphine pump which delivered a set dose into his drip when he pressed the little button clipped to his pillow. 'And all the others.'

Lark looked at the machinery which surrounded the bed. With that and the ever-attentive nurses he was in another world now and had lost interest in the farm.

'I hear that you're moving into a ward tomorrow, so you must be on the mend.' Her voice sounded bright and artificial, like her mother's did when she visited elderly relatives. Lark had hated going into the residential home where her grandmother lived. Looking at all the old people sitting in chairs and staring blankly at the opposite wall had sickened her. 'That's not the way I'm going to die,' she had promised herself.

He was speaking and she leant forward. 'It'll be a few months before I'm out. They told me, the doctors.' She nodded and watched as he lay back on the starched pillows, an almost contented smile on his face, and she knew then that he was loving every moment of this situation. He was getting what he craved for most: unlimited attention.

She was still in a dilemma over her next move when John came into the kitchen. He nodded good morning and sat down opposite her, grabbing hold of the teapot and pouring steaming tea into the mug before him. She got up and went to the Rayburn where a plate of scrambled eggs was keeping warm. 'No bacon today, sorry. We've run out.'

'I've never eaten so much in my life,' he said

through a mouthful of eggs, and took another piece of the granary toast and pasted it with butter.

'It's the fresh air, it has the same effect on me.' She smiled and thought suddenly that he looked better than he had when he first came to the farm. Despite the fright over Matthew, he had put on a little weight and had lost the deep shadows around his eyes. Now, when he came into a room or walked about the farm, he seemed to be more powerful and definite in his movements, as though he had gained a purpose and wasn't just going with the flow.

'Thanks,' he said, putting his knife and fork together, 'that was good.' He sat back in the chair and looked at his plate. It was time he said something. 'We ought to have a talk.'

'I've been thinking.'

They spoke together and then stopped and each gave an embarrassed little laugh.

'You first,' he said.

She ducked her head, deferring to him, but he insisted and she said, 'I've been thinking. It's time I left. Matthew is going to be in the hospital for a while and then when he comes out, he won't be coming here. He couldn't manage it. And,' she drew in a breath before continuing in a rush, 'he and I were finished anyway, so there's no point in my being here.'

The last words came out with a small choke and John remembered the day before the accident when she had looked so desolate. She didn't want to leave, that was obvious. *She must love Matthew a lot,* he thought. *What a fool that boy is, not to want this fantastic girl.* His thoughts echoed in his brain. Fantastic girl? Only an hour ago he'd been lying in bed resenting her continued presence. Now he was condemning his son for giving him an easy way out.

'Now you.' She passed a hand over her face quickly, hoping that the tear which had sprung into her eye wouldn't be noticed. It was, and John frowned. Perhaps when Matthew came out he would want to try again with her. After all, there was no one else and – his stomach lurched – maybe Matthew would think that his father had sent her away. He didn't need another rod for Matthew to beat him with.

'Where will you go?'

'I don't know, maybe north for a while. I'll be all right. I'm used to travelling.'

He shook his head and leant forward. 'How about you stay here and help me for a while? I know that you think that Matthew doesn't want you here any more, but things could be very different when he comes home. He'll need you then.'

She sighed and turned her head so that she was looking straight into his face. Her eyes were grey and cloudy as though a tiny mist had blown over the pupils and obscured her real thoughts. 'I don't think so, John. It was just a summer romance, something to remember in later years.'

'But you love the farm.'

'Yes,' her voice trembled. 'I have been happy here.'

'Then stay. Help me.'

If he'd known that he was echoing the words his

son had spoken six months ago he wouldn't have believed it. He didn't know why it was suddenly so important that he should persuade her to hang on, but he knew he must. For Matthew's sake. 'We'll start anew. I think we got off on the wrong foot last time. I've been in a funny mood lately.' He paused, then said reflectively as though realising this for the first time, 'Behaving out of character.' He grinned, not Matthew's grin but all the more humorous because it broke up his normally solemn face. 'I'm quite a nice guy, really.'

She gave him a little smile. 'I know, but...' It was the same thing all over again, but why should she put herself through the agony of making the decision to leave? The wind howled in the chimney and a wispy branch of the winter jasmine trailing round the side of the house knocked furiously against the window. They both looked up, and John got up and went over to the fireplace. He threw some more logs on the fire and riddled at the cinders with the long poker.

Lark got up too and moved to the window. She looked out across the yard and up the hill. Dark clouds were scudding across an ice-blue sky and tiny flakes of snow danced this way and that in the swirling wind. On the tops, the mist drooped like heavy grey lace, hiding the summit for a moment and then giving tantalising glimpses of the rocky outlines. It was entrancing.

'You won't be trapped.' The idea that this would matter to her suddenly came into his mind and the words were out of his mouth in a trice.

'I will never be that again.' Her back was still

towards him and her voice was low and thought-ful, but the words were articulated with utter assurance. John wondered what else to say to convince her, but it wasn't necessary, because she suddenly turned round. 'I will stay, if you're quite sure. I'd like to see the lambs.'

The wind had dropped and the room was quiet, and they stared at each other across the cosy kitchen. John was surprised at his feelings. It was as if something momentous had happened, though when he retraced the conversation he could recognise only the ordinary.

'Let's give work a miss today,' he said, cheerful now in a way he'd forgotten he could be. 'I need some working clothes if I'm going to live at Cariad Elin for any length of time, and I'm going to buy heaters.' Lark raised her eyebrows quizzically and he added defensively, 'I'm too old to rough it. It's ridiculous to be comfortable in only one room of the house. Anyway, the place needs central heating. I'll talk to Matt about it when he's feeling a bit better.'

He chattered on as she cleared away the break-fast things, talking about how the house could be improved without spoiling its character and which materials he would use. She listened, nod-ding now and then but adding nothing to the conversation. She was still battling with her deci-sion.

'I'm going to turn this in too,' John said later as they got into the rental car. 'I can use Matt's Land Rover. What d'you think?' She had her face turned away, looking out of the window, and he realised that she had barely spoken since telling him she would stay. His new-found cheerfulness started to dissipate, trickling away in the face of her continued moody silence. *My God,* he thought desperately, as they drove out of the yard and onto the road to Bangor. *Have I exchanged one difficult youngster for another?*

'Good idea,' she broke her silence, 'it must be costing you a fortune. I was thinking about that this morning.' She pulled her gloves from her pocket and put them on, covering her work-damaged hands. 'While you're looking for clothes, I think I'll get something new as well. Do you mind if I go off and meet you later in the car park?'

At three o'clock, John was waiting in the car. On the back seat were several bags containing warm sweaters, shirts and trousers. He'd also bought heavy boots – they were already on his feet, imparting blissful warmth on this cold December afternoon. In the boot, he'd loaded two electric fan heaters and a thick cotton rug for the bathroom floor. All that was needed now was food, and they could get that on their way to visit Matthew. It was getting dark and the neon lights in the car park were popping on, casting their orange glow on the shoppers, hurrying to get home before it got really dark. He noticed a man carrying a lopsided Christmas tree and remembered that the festival was only a week away.

He thought of Lydia. She loved Christmas and decorated the house extensively, changing the theme and colour of the decorations each year. They always held open house on Christmas Eve and their friends and neighbours looked forward to seeing what she had done each year. He couldn't remember when he hadn't accepted compliments on Lydia's behalf and he was proud of her flair.

'She is so talented,' friends would say and he would nod modestly and laugh off the effort as 'just Lydia putting a few ideas together'. But last year, when he was fetching another bottle of champagne from the crate in the garage, he had overheard a less flattering remark. A neighbour, leaving by the back door and probably having drunk more than her share, told her husband what she really thought. 'Thank God that's over. Wasn't it awful? How does that poor man put up with these ridiculous shows year after goddam year. Christmas decorations? There's nothing Christian about them. It's just another excuse for her to show off. And I'll lay you a bet, they don't have a Christmas dinner tomorrow. She'd die rather than eat a proper meal!' As John shrank into the shadow of the door so that they could pass without noticing him, he heard her companion's chortled laughter and his condemnation of the Williams' marriage. 'Who do they think they're fooling?'

John's face burned miserably now as he sat alone in a strange car park. Lydia would have been heartbroken had he told her. But even he wasn't that unkind; they had too much history for that. He shrugged. There would be nothing for the neighbours to snigger at this Christmas. The house would be bare and empty for the first time in twenty years.

He looked at his watch – it was five past three

and there was no sign of Lark. Maybe she'd changed her mind and was, even now, on the train, speeding away from Wales, leaving her few belongings behind in the house. Girls like her didn't carry baggage. They picked it up wherever they chose to stop.

'Hello!' Lark opened the passenger door and got in. She had an armful of parcels and leaned over to put them beside John's on the back seat. Her clothes and hair smelt salty from cold seaside air and he sniffed appreciatively. He liked the way she absorbed the scent of the outdoors. He'd noticed it from their first meeting: lanolin from the sheep and hints of heather from the hillside. It was so different from the waft of expensive scent that followed Lydia, or the cloying aroma of violet and roses that surrounded Annette.

'Thought you weren't coming,' he said, trying to make a joke as he put the car into gear, 'decided to leave us to our own devices.'

'No.' She grinned cheerfully as they drove out of the car park and onto the busy streets. 'You don't get rid of me that easily. I made up my mind this morning, and anyway, I've bought things for the house.'

'What things?' He couldn't decide if this was a good or bad move.

'Oh, a couple of sharper knives, a big saucepan and these.' She reached behind her and pulled over a bag. As she opened it, light from the streets and shop windows made the collection of Christmas decorations she had bought glitter and sparkle in the dark car. 'It's Christmas next week,' she said.

'I know. Should we get a turkey?'

'Bethan told me that goose is traditional in Wales.'

'Yes, it is. I'd forgotten. We'll get a goose.' He paused, 'But a small one, otherwise we'll be eating it for days.'

She laughed and the atmosphere between them lightened and stayed like that as they hurried round the supermarket, before driving on to the hospital.

Chapter Twenty-Five

She had finished her packing and was sitting on the edge of her bed, mentally ticking off a list of clothes and beauty equipment without which travel would be impossible. During the last few days she had trawled the best stores in downtown Toronto, searching for outfits suitable for the forthcoming holiday. The exercise had been hugely enjoyable and entirely successful. She had found the shops full of exciting holiday wear and she had treated herself lavishly, buying couture dresses and swimsuits, without caring about or even looking at the price.

Yesterday, she had had her hair cut in a different style. Marco, a young, gay hairdresser who was new to her favourite salon, had suggested a change and he was right. It was shorter than she had worn it before and flicked away from her ears so that her pretty, heart-shaped face could be seen to its best advantage. It was very flattering, so much so that heads had turned in the underground mall in a way they hadn't for years.

'My God, Lydia,' her girlfriend said, when they met that day for lunch at the new salsa bar, 'you look fantastic. Separation obviously suits you.'

This was the first time anyone had referred to the fact that John had left, and she was relieved that the word 'separation' had been used. It made it sound as though his leaving had been a mutual decision, and the more she thought about it, the more she convinced herself that it had been. She couldn't have stood much more of John's moods, and, above all, his drinking. He'd had to go.

'We needed breathing space,' she said lightly. 'To see where we were going in our lives.'

'He's abroad, isn't he? Edith Eland told me when we met at the college reunion.'

A frown, so fleeting that her companion didn't notice, crossed Lydia's carefully made-up brow. She was surprised that Edith should know about John's whereabouts. Fred was the only person she'd told, which meant that he'd been speaking about her to his wife. Why? Had someone been talking to Edith? She looked at Charlene sitting opposite, idly crumbling a piece of olive bread and sipping at her wine carefully, so as not to disturb her lipstick. She and Edith had known each other since school, and weren't they related in some way? For a moment, Lydia's heart fluttered and she could feel a flush growing on her neck. Perhaps this vacation was a dumb move.

But then, she calmed herself. They'd be bound

247

to speak about her. After all, the three of them were going to share a cottage on the beach for ten days. Of course she would be part of their conversation. She produced one of her brilliant smiles. 'Yeah,' she said brightly, 'he's gone to see Matthew. Did I tell you that my dopey son has had a bit of an accident?' She shook her head in response to the other's raised eyebrows, 'No, nothing much. Broken leg, falling off some sort of bike. Mad kid.'

Now, sitting on the bed, she thought about Matthew and wondered if she had been callous in not flying off immediately to see him. He and she had always been very close. She didn't care that he was reckless and often in trouble; that didn't really matter. His quick wit and charm and his stunning good looks were what she loved. There was nothing she liked better than to hear people say that he was the image of her.

She looked over her shoulder at the phone on the bedside table and then at her watch. It was just before eight o'clock in the evening, time to give Matthew a quick call before the cab arrived. She was spending the night at the Elands' before they all flew off together in the morning.

'Give me Matthew Williams, please,' she asked the startled nurse when she finally got through to the ward.

'I can't do that,' a small voice responded – small but clearly angry.

'This is his mother. I want to speak to him.'

There was a short pause and then the nurse repeated her refusal. 'Mrs Williams, it is nearly midnight. Matthew is fast asleep. I'm not going

248

to wake him up.'

'Oh!' Lydia felt foolish. She'd forgotten the time difference. Why did he have to be so far away? 'Well, can you tell me how he is today?' She didn't apologise for her stupidity and the nurse made a mental note to repeat this conversation to the day shift when they came on duty.

'He's doing well, his temperature is down and the doctors are pleased with him.'

'Is he managing to walk about in his plaster yet?' Lydia heard the word temperature but it didn't register. This girl had a strange accent and it was difficult enough understanding the basics of what she said, never mind the detail.

'There's no plaster, Mrs Williams, he's on traction.' The nurse thought for a moment and then added, 'But he is sitting up in bed.'

Lydia knew nothing about medicine. She had never been ill herself, and Matthew had led a charmed life, apart from a greenstick fracture when he was six, falling off his little skis. Traction was a mystery. 'This traction,' she said cautiously, 'is it dangerous?'

Three thousand miles away, the little nurse nodded to Night Sister, who had come into the ward to do her round. She would have to get a move on. 'No, Mrs Williams, it's quite ordinary. It's the normal treatment for his injury. He's fine. I think his dad saw him this evening.'

Did he? thought Lydia and looked at her watch again. She would have time to phone him and ask about Matthew before she left. 'Tell him I called when he wakes up and to expect lots of parcels. Goodbye.'

'Who was that?' asked Night Sister as she walked through the ward. 'Calling at this time of night, for goodness' sake.'

'Matthew Williams' mother. She's in Canada.'

'And not here, when he's been so ill. Makes you wonder about some people, doesn't it?'

Lydia picked up the phone and dialled the number for Cariad Elin, but before it could be answered she replaced her receiver. The nurse had told her that it was midnight, and she could imagine John's temper if she woke him. *I'll phone in the morning before we go,* she thought. *Fred won't mind.*

At Cariad Elin, John heard the three rings before Lydia put the phone down and swung his legs out of bed, ready to rush to the hall. By the time he stood up there was silence, but he hurried downstairs and stood by the phone waiting for it to ring again. Lark appeared at the top of the stairs looking questioningly at him. Matthew was uppermost in each of their minds, both imagining some terrible scenario in which he had suddenly collapsed and was critically ill or worse.

'It just stopped ringing,' said John. He picked up the handpiece and listened to the dialling tone before replacing it. 'The very next thing I'll buy is a new phone,' he said, looking at the old-fashioned Bakelite set with its ragged, cloth-covered flex. 'And an extension for the bedroom.'

'Should you ring the hospital, just in case?' asked Lark, slowly walking down the stairs.

He dialled and got through to the ward. The nurse was audibly annoyed and told him that Matt was asleep, which was what she had told Mrs Williams when she'd telephoned only ten minutes before.

'Sorry,' John apologised. 'The phone rang and we thought it was you, but obviously not.' He looked up at Lark and gestured with his hand that all was well.

'I expect it was your wife.' The nurse had decided that this was an occasion when she could be rude to a patient's family. 'She thinks this is a good time to make calls.'

'Sorry,' John apologised again, this time on behalf of Lydia, 'she gets mixed up with the time difference.'

They went into the kitchen, neither able to sleep now until the adrenalin surge had died down. Lark filled the kettle and John poked at the red embers of the fire. The room was still fairly cosy, but John carried in one of the new electric heaters from the hall and switched it on. A rush of warm air poured into the room and they both stood looking at it admiringly. 'Modern technology,' John said ironically. 'My dad would have likened it to works of the Devil.'

'Perhaps he just couldn't afford it.' She said it simply, not wanting to offend him, and he understood it as such.

'Yeah,' he sighed. 'Money was always tight when I was growing up. Why d'you think I wanted to get away?'

'It must have been quite lonely here, when you were a child,' Lark said as they sat by the fire with mugs of tea. 'Matthew told me you were an only child, like him.'

'It was quiet,' John agreed, 'just my dad and

251

me, after Mam ... went. But of course, I had Robert and his family. I couldn't have been really lonely.'

'When did your mother die?'

'Oh,' he calculated in his head, 'er ... it must have been about forty years ago. I was just a kid.' He leant back and looked at the fire. 'I guess she had cancer. Nobody said; you just didn't talk about it at the time, but,' he sighed, remembering, 'she knew she was dying. She tried to warn me.'

He thought about Mam saying to look after Dad. *How could she have laid that on me?* he wondered angrily. *Dad wouldn't let anyone help him, ever.*

Lark watched his face change. He looked miserable again and she was sorry she had brought up the subject. She drew the soft blue robe, which she had hurriedly dragged on, closer around her body. It was one of the few items of clothing she'd bought since coming to the farm. Even she found the bathroom unbearably cold.

Matthew had teased her about 'going soft' and she smiled at the recollection. They'd had fun, at the beginning.

She looked again at John. 'I'm an only child too. At least, I think I am. I was adopted.' This was the first time she had spoken about her life for a long time. Christopher had hated her mentioning it and her parents were almost as bad. As far as they were concerned, she was their own child. It had taken months of questioning to establish that she had been left at the back door of a remote farmhouse when she was about two

252

weeks old.

'There were gypsies through about that time,' said the farmer's wife, a woman in her early eighties, when Lark finally tracked her down. 'I expect you were something to do with them. They're particular about who their women go with. Quite respectable, in their own way.' She had paused for a moment and then added with a cackle, 'Or they could have stolen you. Gypsies do that.'

'Hush, *Nain,* you mustn't say things like that.' The old lady's granddaughter was scandalised at the last remark. 'She's very old,' she apologised, under her breath, to Lark. 'She says odd things.'

John was interested. 'Tell me,' he said, and she found herself explaining how she had discovered which adoption agency had been involved, by going through her father's desk and then contacting them directly.

'It's all changed recently,' she said to John. 'Nowadays you are allowed to know something about yourself. But I came to a dead end at that farm.'

'Where was it?'

'Well, in fact, it's only about fifty miles from here. Near Llangollen.'

'Aha!' he grinned. 'You are Welsh!'

She shook her head. 'I've absolutely no idea.'

He looked at her sitting in the soft glow of fire-light. 'And your parents took on a lost red-headed baby.'

She chuckled. 'The earliest photographs show me without any hair. They must have had a hell of a surprise!' They both laughed then, and a few minutes later, when they switched off the lamps and went to their separate beds, the shock of the phone ringing had dissipated and they were able to sleep calmly for the rest of the night.

It was Christmas Eve the next day and Lark put her little collection of decorations around the mantelpiece and dresser. John found holly, laden with bright berries, in the field by the river and cut a few branches and brought them in. Placed in a large vase and draped with a rope of tinsel, it substituted well for a Christmas tree.

Lydia phoned while they were eating soup and bread at lunchtime. She was at the airport waiting for the flight to be called and back to regretting that she had agreed to go with Fred and Edith to the islands. There was a frosty atmosphere between the two of them, and Lydia had an insidious feeling that she might be the cause of it.

'I spoke to the hospital last night,' she said to John when he answered the phone. 'I could barely understand a word they said.' He couldn't work out if she was exaggerating or genuinely meant what she was saying. 'How is he?'

'He's a lot better, really. He's the star of the ward and being spoilt to death.' He waited for her to say something but she was listening to the announcements behind her and looking at Fred to see if he was beckoning. He wasn't. He was sitting beside Edith staring into space while she was talking into his ear.

Lydia spoke absently. 'Did he get my parcels? I did it all by mail order through stores in London.

They were astonishingly helpful,' she added, sounding genuinely surprised.

'Yeah, he has, and the nurses are looking forward to them almost as much as he is. It should be all excitement tomorrow morning.'

'Good.' Now Fred was beckoning, and she waved her hand to let him know she understood. 'I gotta go, John. Merry Christmas.'

'And to you, Lyddie.' The old nickname came out without him noticing and Lydia swallowed a little lump which had suddenly grown in her throat. 'Have a great time on the islands.'

'I will,' she whispered. 'Bye.'

Chapter Twenty-Six

That evening, John and Lark went to the party at the Miner's Arms. Neither of them had planned to go but Robert and Bethan came round in the afternoon and persuaded them that everyone in the valley was going and it would be considered bad form if they remained aloof.

'We're expecting you for Christmas dinner, mind,' said Bethan and was genuinely disappointed when they declined.

'We've bought a little goose,' Lark said. 'John's going to stay the morning with Matthew while I cook it. Maybe I'll go and see him in the evening.' The maybe was truthful. Recently, her visits to the hospital had been brief and unsatisfactory. Matthew and she had very little to say to each other, now that they were no longer lovers. He'd lost interest in the farm, and other than that, they had nothing in common. Oh, Matt was as charming as always, but during her visits he flirted with the nurses, who made a point of coming in and out of his room. On three or four occasions, Lark had found Dr Monk, the junior casualty officer, sitting on his bed, deep in conversation with him. At first, the young doctor had jumped up with a blush, obviously thinking that she was venturing onto forbidden territory, but lately she left with a conspiratorial grin to her patient, aware now that Lark was not important.

'Well, come to us on Boxing Day. We'll have leftovers to finish and lots of pickles to go with them.'

'Thank you!' said John. 'We'll enjoy that, won't we, Lark?'

'Yes.' She was genuinely grateful. 'And let me bring something. I've been baking.'

'Don't you dare! There's enough food for an army at Bryn Goch.'

Robert took John aside and told him about a fence that was down in the field by the road. 'I think it was pushed over last night. Kids home from college, probably drunk and drove off the road. I'll help you fix it, before the fucking sheep get through.'

They went off together as they had all those years ago. John hadn't even paused to wonder at the miracle of a friendship unaltered by twenty-five years' absence, and Robert wasn't given to deep thought.

'How's Matthew?' asked Bethan carefully, watching Lark fold laundry, some of which was John's. 'Still continuing to improve?'

Lark nodded. 'He's fine. Impatient to get on his feet, of course, but otherwise OK.' She concentrated on what she was doing for a moment and then said, 'I don't think he'll be able to come back here for a while.'

'No, love, I'm sure you're right. Bit of a quandary, that.'

Lark looked up quickly but Bethan had bent to pick up a stray sock and when she straightened the moment had passed. 'Well, I'd better get going. Got lots to do this afternoon before we go out.' She took her coat and went to the door. 'See you later,' she called and got into her shiny little car.

Lark followed her out to wave goodbye, then hurried back inside. Bethan had been probing – in the nicest way, but still probing. Perhaps she knew that Matthew and she were finished; maybe Elfed had said something. He had been to the hospital several times. *I won't think about leaving yet,* she told herself, putting the underwear on the hot Rayburn lids to air. *I'll wait until the New Year.*

In the hospital, Matthew was sitting up in bed as far as his traction would allow. He'd just been bathed and shaved and was wearing a clean T-shirt and shorts. Two nurses had been rubbing his back with cream, a daily routine to prevent bedsores and something he was now used to. At first he'd found it and all the other necessary care of the bedridden patient terribly embarrassing

257

and had hated the whole rigmarole. Now it had become normal and everyday and he loved the attention.

The nurses had finished with him and were now sitting on the end of his bed, chatting. Every now and then they would look over their shoulders in case Sister walked into the room.

'Have you been to Hollywood, then?' asked one of them, a plain, fat girl, who had only left her native county once, to go on a school trip to London.

'No, Hayley, I told you that yesterday.'

Matthew winked at the other nurse who shook her head in disgust. 'She's thick, that one,' she said, secure in her prettiness and better education. 'No idea where anywhere is. I know you are Canadian and come from hundreds of miles away from Hollywood. We did geography in my school. She didn't. They don't at the comp.'

The fat one scowled. 'Shut up, you,' she snapped and turned again to Matthew. 'Have you got a girlfriend?'

'Sure.'

'It's never that Lark who comes with your dad.'

'She's just a friend.' It was easy to say this, because that was how he felt about her now.

'I knew that. I thought she was your mam, at first. She's a lot older than you.'

'Nothing wrong with that.' Matthew grinned. 'I like a bit of experience!'

They both laughed and then the fat one asked, 'Are they coming in to have Christmas dinner with you tomorrow? They can, you know.'

'Nope. Just a visit as usual. Anyway, I'd rather

spend the day with you lot. You are going to be on duty, aren't you?'

'No way. Home for me with Mam and Dad and my boyfriend.'

The other nurse got off the bed and came round to plump up the pillows. 'I'll be here, on lates, though, so you'll have to wait for your present.'

Matthew reached out a hand and squeezed her bottom. 'Great, bring the mistletoe when you come.'

As they left the room, giggling, the nurses collided with Dr Monk. 'She's up here again,' whispered the pretty one as they went into the next bay, 'Can't keep her hands off him!'

The Miner's Arms was full almost to bursting when John and Lark arrived at eight o'clock. It seemed that everyone in the village and surrounding valley had come to the pub tonight to wish themselves and each other the best of wishes for the season.

'Jesus!' said John. 'We'll never get a drink.' But Lark had spotted Robert with Bethan and Elfed sitting at a table near the bar and plucked at his jacket to show him. They fought their way through the good-natured crowd and joined their friends. Elfed got up and gave Lark his chair and when a man sitting at an adjacent table got up to get another drink, Robert pulled that chair over for John.

'You look very choice tonight, *cariad*,' said Robert as Lark took off her coat and revealed a long multicoloured woollen tunic worn over narrow black trousers. Her hair almost touched her shoulders now, curling as it grew and gleaming in the coppery light of the old pub. John looked at her and agreed silently. The girl was striking.

She blushed. 'Thank you.'

'Matthew doesn't know what he's missing,' Robert continued and grinned at John drunkenly, 'a little prize, she is. There's plenty here who'd like to take his place.'

'Oh, hush, you old fool.' Bethan put her hand over his mouth and mouthed an apology to Lark. 'He started too early, that's what it is.'

'I'll get drinks,' said Elfed. 'Beer, is it?' He glanced at John and before he got a reply, was off on his fight to the bar. 'You want wine, don't you, Lark?' he called and she nodded, looking round and catching sight of Griff for the first time.

'Oh, goodness, look at him,' she gasped and John turned to follow her gaze. The landlord stood behind his tinsel-decorated bar wearing a Father Christmas hat adorned with a piece of mistletoe. His plump face was running with sweat as he and a cooler looking Llinos served the impatient customers and counted the change. Their fervent hope of this being one of the busiest nights of the year had come true, and the big-screen TV for the bar which would bring in more regular customers was a definite possibility. He caught their look and waved to them cheerfully. 'I'll be over in a minute,' he yelled above the noise. 'Must give the ladies their Christmas kiss!'

'Over my dead body,' said Bethan with a shudder and Lark giggled.

Robert snorted into his beer. 'Griff Parry's making a fucking spectacle of himself. One of these days someone's going to push his bastard face in. God, I hope it's me!'

'I gather you don't like him,' said John, pretending to be serious, and Robert, who was halfway to his mouth with his pint glass, stopped in mid-air and stared. Then he saw the grin hovering on John's face and bellowed a laugh.

Elfed arrived carrying a tray of drinks. 'I brought seconds to save having to try again for a while.' And he left to join his friends, leaving the four of them together.

John sat and watched the crowd. The noise was deafening but good-humoured as the local farmers and their wives celebrated Christmas in the new traditional way. A generation ago, their parents, like John's, had mostly stayed at home, the wives exhausting themselves preparing for the big day, and the husbands and children quietly excited and listening to the radio. The generation before that would not have celebrated at all. The type of Methodism which had dominated the valley in the early part of the last century took little pleasure in partying and none at all in alcohol. But life was different now. The wives worked; they needed to because the hill farms brought in poor returns. And on their way home from the offices and schools or hospital, they bought ready-prepared food. No need now to peel or chop or even wrap the turkey in bacon; it was all done for them in the supermarket. It left ample time for enjoyment.

He smiled. He thought of Lydia and her smart

Christmas Eve cocktail parties. The contrast couldn't have been greater. He wondered what she was doing now; on the beach probably, sipping an exotic cocktail. He hoped she was happy.

'Thinking of your wife?' said Lark in his ear, softly so that Robert and Beth couldn't hear.

John was startled. He turned to look at her. 'Yes,' he said. 'How did you know?'

'You were smiling.'

Griff was making his way through the crowd to their table. He was frequently blocked by customers yelling orders for more drink in his ear, but he ignored the requests and kept walking through. He had a mission in mind. He needed to talk to the father.

'Good evening to you, Mr Williams,' he panted when he'd reached their table and squeezed his fat body into a non-existent space beside them. 'I've been looking forward to meeting you again.'

'And I you,' said John, taking the proffered hand and shaking the sweating sausage fingers.

Griff nodded to the others at the table and then turned back to John. 'I thought we should have a little chat, now that circumstances have changed.' He looked round the crowded bar, 'But perhaps not tonight.'

'Yes, perhaps not.' John kept his voice light but allowed just a hint of steel to edge through. Robert snorted again and Bethan put a warning hand on his arm. Nothing would have improved Robert's evening more than a bust-up.

Griff's eyes flickered towards him and for a moment, a wave of concern passed over his face.

He wondered if he had jumped headlong into a fight. Robert and Elfed, who had now joined their party, had never made a secret of their contempt for him and they were both drunk. But then he looked back to John. This man was different; he had spent years away from the valley and he had different ways of settling affairs. Reassured, Griff carried on, 'I've seen Matthew in the hospital. He wants us to go on as before.' He paused, realising that he probably should have waited until the conversation could be more private. 'But perhaps I should come to Cariad Elin after the holidays and we can have a little chat.'

John nodded. 'Yeah, whatever.'

The casual answer made Griff feel better. Maybe the father was just as detached about the farm as the son. His plan could continue unfettered. He wiped away the little blobs of moisture which had gathered on his temples and grinned down at Lark.

'I haven't wished you Merry Christmas yet, *cariad*.' He leant down and before she could move, planted a kiss full on her lips. She could smell him, sour with sweat and the drops of beer which had fallen on his shirt, and she put up her hands to push him away. But he was gone, already falling as John grabbed the collar of his shirt and pushed him aside.

He landed in Robert's lap, fat and scared, knowing that now he was really in trouble.

'Fuck off,' roared Robert. 'Particular, me, who sits on my knee.'

'You tell him, Dad,' laughed Elfed and grabbed

the hapless landlord and hauled him to his feet.

Griff snarled. 'If it wasn't Christmas, I'd bar you two bastards.'

He turned to Lark. 'No offence meant, Lark, love. Just the Christmas spirit,' and he staggered back to the bar through the hooting crowd and soon disappeared behind a crowd of thirsty customers.

'I expect he wants to discuss the lambing,' said John. 'How much help he's going to give.'

Robert shook his head, 'Don't bother with him, boy. He knows nothing about fucking lambing. Elfed and me will give you a hand.'

The pub started to empty after midnight when Christmas greetings had been exchanged and people began to wander home to put the presents out for the children.

Lark drove home while John sat beside her, happy to let her. He hadn't drunk very much but he was tired and battered by the noise. The night was clear and cold and he gazed through the windscreen counting the stars and wondering at this new turn in his life. When they reached the yard, he got out and stood for a moment, head turned up to the sky and letting the frosty air clean away the beer and smoke odour.

In the kitchen, Lark had taken off her coat and put another log on the fire. 'I'm not ready for sleep yet,' she said. 'I think I'll sit here for a while.' She settled into the rocking chair beside the hearth and he came to sit opposite her.

'Would you like a nightcap?' His brow creased as he looked around the kitchen. 'That elusive bottle of whisky should be here, somewhere.'

She grinned. 'It's still under the sink. You know, Matthew didn't like you drinking. I think you frightened him.'

'I frightened myself.' He spoke to the fire. 'I've been doing a lot of dumb things lately.'

They sat quietly then for a while, on that early Christmas morning, each thinking their own thoughts until Lark broke the silence.

'Do you know why the farm is called Cariad Elin? I've asked, but nobody seems to know.'

'Robert knows. Did you ask him?'

'I asked Bethan. She had no idea.'

'She doesn't come from here. It would be of no interest to her.'

'But you know, don't you?' Lark fixed her amber-coloured eyes on him. 'Tell me, please.' She didn't know why it had become so important to her. It was almost as if it was something that she should have learnt as a child but had missed. Now she had to be told.

He laughed gently. 'It's just a legend, handed down. Not even interesting enough to put in that book you're so fond of.'

The wind sighed in the pine trees and blew softly down the chimney, making the logs crackle and send out narrow tongues of blue flame. John leant back in the leather chair and folded his hands lazily over his narrow belly. Dad had sat like this, he remembered, when he was tired from being in the fields. Often he would drop off to sleep, leaving John to sit alone, with just his book for company. He looked across at Lark hunched forward in her chair with her long legs folded beneath her. Her face was pale despite the heat from the fire but when he looked again into her eyes they were brilliant and alive and impossible to ignore.

Chapter Twenty-Seven

'You've been learning Welsh,' he started, after leaning forward to rattle the poker amongst the embers of the fire, 'so you know what *"cariad"* means.'

'Yes, it means "darling" or "dearest", doesn't it?'

'Yeah, and Elin, well, that's a girl's name. So it's Darling Elin's farm.'

'Who was she?' Lark's chest felt tight, aching to hear him tell what she almost knew.

He started the tale slowly and she heard the reluctance in his voice to repeat what most of his previous listeners had treated as pure make-believe. 'She was a fairy woman... Oh yes, don't smile. There are lots of legends about fairy women around Snowdonia.' He looked across the fireplace at her, expecting to see the dis-believing smirk that had been on Lydia's face when he had told her, all those years ago. Lark wasn't smiling. Her eyes were fixed on his as she waited impatiently for the story. She had that strange expression that had worried him before and he slid his face away to stare at the fire before continuing. He spoke fluently now, his voice low and serious, as though he was rehearsing a story from his own life.

'A long time ago, this farm was owned by a man who couldn't find a wife – too poor or too busy, or maybe just too bloody-minded to have anyone interested: the story doesn't say.

'On an early summer day, a woman came down from the mountain to the farm. She simply walked into the kitchen and started to cook the supper, and when the farmer came in from the fields, she put his food in front of him. Of course, he immediately fell in love with her – she was very beautiful. Fairy women are always beautiful. He asked her to marry him. She refused at first because she said she came from the Fairy Kingdom on top of the mountain and would miss her family if she stayed down on the farm. But he begged so plaintively that she eventually agreed, but on one condition. When her sisters came for her, she would go and never come back. The farmer was so desperate that he agreed and they married and lived happily.

'The farm prospered and the farmer became very wealthy and Elin – yes, that was her name – grew more beautiful and contented. They had a baby son and the farmer was so happy and glad that now there would be someone to carry on the farm, that he loved her even more. Of course, by then he had forgotten the agreed condition.

'Then, after a few years, Elin began to get restless. She would climb halfway up the mountain and stand looking up, as though searching for something or someone, but never saying what it could be.

'One cold misty day, while she was sitting at her

spinning wheel with the boy on the hearth beside her and her husband eating his dinner, she suddenly looked up, tilting her head to listen to the sound of the wind in the chimney.

'"My sisters are calling," she cried in great excitement, and ran out of the house and up the mountain. The mist was very low that day and the farmer was sure he could see figures swirling about in the cloud, their hands beckoning to his fairy wife.

'"Come back," he called. "Oh, Elin, my *cariad*, don't leave me." She stopped for an instant and looked back to him. Her voice whispered on the wind: "I'll come for you," she called, and then put her arms out and disappeared into the mist.

'Oh, he searched for her night and day, refusing to eat or look after his stock, until his neighbours thought he would die, so desperate had he become.'

'What happened then?' Lark was breathless.

'Nothing. He never found her and after a while he learned to live with his loss. But the farm continued to prosper and the son grew up to take over.'

Lark was silent for a moment and then said slowly, 'I didn't think it would be such a sad story.'

John grinned. 'You must realise that Welsh legends are pretty depressing. But look on the bright side: he had a prosperous farm and she had left him a son. He did all right.'

She smiled then, relaxing into her chair again. 'Darling Elin. What a lovely name for a farm.'

'Mm, it is a special name. I always hoped we would have a daughter. I would have called her

Elin, or its English equivalent.'

She looked at him enquiringly.

'Helen, it translates as Helen.'

She made a little choking noise and coughed to cover it.

'What is it?'

'That's my name. My real name. I'm Helen.'

The fire was dying and the room was getting cold, but neither of them moved. It had been another day when too much had happened. Although it was two o'clock in the morning and Christmas Day, the desire for sleep had fled, as they separately mulled over the story. The legend had brought back too many memories for John. His dad had told it to him one afternoon while John walked beside him on the side of the hill. He was only a little boy then; Mam was still alive. He'd rushed in to tell her, but she'd laughed. 'Only an old story, *bach*,' she'd said, 'load of rubbish.' But he'd looked back at Dad and he could tell that he believed it.

John looked up suddenly from contemplating the embers. 'Christmas Day.' He stood up and went over to his coat. 'I've got you a present.' He handed her a parcel, hastily wrapped in brown paper. 'Sorry, I didn't have any fancy paper.'

Lark took it gently and opened the paper. Inside was an exquisitely carved love spoon made of pale ash wood, the handle decorated with little balls of wood held fast in a wooden cage and the bowl carved with a picture of the original tree.

'Oh, it's lovely!' she breathed and turned it up and down so that the tiny balls slid backwards and forwards within the cage.

269

John swallowed. 'It's really something that Matt should give you, not me, but I saw it in the little craft shop and thought you might like it.'

'I do. I really do.' She put the spoon carefully on the table beside her and got out of her chair. She opened the door to the hall, letting a freezing draught rush into the kitchen. When she returned she was carrying a flat package. 'I've got a present for you,' she said and gave him the parcel. 'Happy Christmas, John.'

'Oh!' He was genuinely surprised and tore nervously at the wrapping. In his head he was preparing a complimentary remark for what would be revealed. The only gifts he really liked were the ones he'd bought himself.

'I hope you like it.' She was reading his mind and watched him closely as he pulled the last piece of paper away.

It was a watercolour painting of the farm. The artist had captured it on a high summer day when the sky was clear and the mountain tops stood out sharply against the pale blue. In the valley, the stone buildings, white in the afternoon sun, nestled quietly amongst overgrown hedges and a buttercup meadow. A stranger looking at this scene could only imagine a peaceful existence for the inhabitants of Cariad Elin.

John held the picture up to the rosy light which came from the lamp. He examined the brushwork and composition. It was faultless. The painting was exquisite.

'Lark,' he said slowly, 'this is lovely. Wherever did you get it?'

'I watched it being painted in the summer,

when I first came here. The artist asked Matt's permission to go on the hill. He did several pictures of the farm and the mountains; it seemed to take him no time at all and he didn't mind me watching. When he left, he gave me that picture. Wouldn't take any money, said it was for me.' Her voice trailed away as he shook his head and held the picture out to her.

'I can't take it,' he said, 'it was painted for you.'

She gazed at the picture, remembering the summer day with its cloudless sky and the dandelion heads floating away across the valley on the afternoon breeze. Matthew had lain on the mountainside soaking up the sun, bored with the artist and his work but jealous of Lark's interest. Eventually, he'd gone down the hill, back to the house, leaving her to watch and marvel as the whole vista of Cariad Elin was recreated before her eyes.

'I want you to have it. Please.' She touched the edge of the wooden frame which had been made on the afternoon when she and John had gone to Bangor. 'I want you to look at this when you go back and remember how beautiful your home was.'

He swallowed a lump which had come into his throat. It was true, Cariad Elin was beautiful; he'd forgotten that. In the years since he'd left, only the unhappiness of his lonely childhood and the broken relationship with his father had remained as the dominant memory.

'Oh Christ, Lark,' he said, tears welling in his eyes, 'you sure know how to get to me.'

She smiled. 'Happy Christmas, John,' she

repeated and leaning forward, kissed him gently on the cheek.

The next weeks flew by. The weather closed in, bringing sleety rain and low mist, but they worked through it. The barn was repaired and by the end of January was ready for the sheep. The first lambs were due any moment and despite their never mentioning it, both John and Lark were excited.

Robert and Elfed came over now and then to offer advice and to bring various bits of lambing equipment which they had never used and which John was pretty sure that he wouldn't either. He tried to think back to the times he'd helped Dad with the lambing, but the memories were vague. He had an uncomfortable feeling that he'd mostly let his father get on with it by himself. *God,* he thought, *I must have been a selfish little bastard. Why didn't I do something? How could I have let him work so hard for so long?*

When he really thought about it, he couldn't remember ever making his father a single cup of tea in all the years that they had lived on the farm together. And then, in Canada, he'd made quite a bit of money but never thought to send any home. He shrugged, curling his fingers into a fist, and a muscle in his cheek twitched. The memory was painful, and for the first time in his adult life, he wondered if the problems between him and Dad weren't entirely the old man's fault.

In the uncanny way that she had of reading his mind, Lark asked, 'Did you help your father with the lambing?'

272

He ducked his head and muttered, 'No, I didn't.' With his face turned away from her, he continued with a rueful sigh, 'I let him spend nights in this damned barn alone with the sheep. I guess I always had school work to do.'

He was grateful when she nodded and turned back to arranging bales of straw. He hoped she'd accepted the explanation, otherwise he would appear incredibly mean, and he didn't want her to think that.

She changed the subject: 'I wonder if Matt will be out by the time they start?'

'I don't think so. His physio isn't going as well as it should. At least, that's what the doctors tell me. They might have to reoperate on his ankle.' John looked miserable, as though Matt's lack of progress was in some way his fault. Lately, his visits to the hospital had been difficult. Matt was bored despite the attentions of Karen Monk, and desperate for a change of scenery. Last Sunday John had taken him for a drive, loading him, with the help of his giggling nurses, into the passenger seat of a rented seven-seater wagon. Matt should have been grateful but he wasn't. No matter how carefully the pillows were arranged he was uncomfortable, and with the broken leg stuck out in front of him he wasn't able to turn much to look at the scenery. He only brightened up when John found a McDonald's and bought him a takeaway meal.

'Jesus, that's good,' he sighed when he'd swallowed the last crumb of the burger and wiped the moustache of chocolate milkshake from his mouth. 'I could live on Big Macs.'

John was angry with himself for not thinking of bringing him a takeaway before. Lydia would have thought of it and a host of other useful things, he realised now, and he wondered again why she hadn't flown over to see her son. Was it his fault? Could he have deliberately underplayed the seriousness of Matt's injuries?

'Heard from Ma?' He kept his voice casual.

'I gotta postcard from the islands. She's having a great time.' Matthew stared out of the window at the boats bobbing on the murky grey water of the inner harbour. John had hoped that Matt would enjoy seeing the Marina – it might remind him of the hours he'd spent on the lake back home – but the contrast couldn't have been greater. The January weather was dreary and the sight of a few yachts slapping against each other in the driving rain aroused no happy memories for Matt.

'Wish I was with her,' he'd said miserably.

John shook his head as he helped Lark shift the hay bales. 'No,' he reiterated. 'I don't think he'll be getting out in a hurry.' He straightened up. 'You'll have to put up with just me for a bit longer.'

Chapter Twenty-Eight

Lydia was back in Toronto after a perfectly wonderful time in the Bahamas. She was tanned and fit and swore to anyone who asked that she could thoroughly recommend a winter holiday in the Caribbean.

'Yes,' she insisted with her winning smile, her small teeth looking whiter than ever in her glowing skin, 'I know I always say I love the cold weather, but ... honestly, it was fantastic!'

Her friends shook their heads and looked at each other knowingly, waiting until Lydia left before speculating on who was the new man in her life. It couldn't be Fred, one, who was a very close friend, whispered, that was for sure. Edith had put her foot down after finally realising what had been going on for so many months.

'If you want cheap and available, honey, carry on.' Edith had been firm and left no room for argument, 'But don't expect to stay here or have further access to our bank accounts.'

Fred had experienced a small tremor around his heart and a wave of nausea nearly choked him. That she had found out was bad enough, but her display of threatening disdain was almost frightening. It had an instant effect. The affair with Lydia was effectively over immediately, but more remarkable was the new respect he felt for his previously merely tolerated wife. Good old

275

Edith had brought him down to earth and he was grateful.

Lydia didn't know, of course, but she felt the change. At Fred and Edith's house on the first night, before they were due to fly out, the atmosphere was cool and she nearly decided to change her mind and not accompany them. The holiday could be a disaster. But then she thought about Christmas alone in the house. No Christmas Eve party, no John, and most of all, no Matthew. A sudden tear came into her eye and she allowed it, and the ones that followed, to drip freely onto the overstuffed pillows of the guest bed.

You bastard, you bastard, how dare you leave me. She cried silently into the starched slip and wondered vaguely, for the first time, if there was something she had done to make John go away. Before, she'd always thought it was just him – a drunk having a nervous breakdown and ashamed of his tiresome behaviour. But now she wasn't so sure.

Two policemen had been round only a few days before asking if he intended to drop the charges against the mugger.

'What mugger?' she'd asked, baffled. 'I know nothing about a mugger.' She looked from one to the other, an older one who leant tiredly against the door frame and a tall, gawky youngster who was in his first months on the force.

'Didn't he tell you?' the young cop said, surprised. 'Didn't you see his injury?'

She shook her head and frowned. 'No, he said nothing. Anyway,' she looked down at the older man's feet. His shoes were scuffed and down at

276

heel and plainly hadn't been polished for many weeks. Lydia was angry. John had really let her down and she didn't want these men or their filthy shoes on her doorstep. 'Anyway,' she continued, 'my husband has gone abroad and I don't know when he'll be coming home.'

They looked at each other and the older policeman took a breath before starting to speak. Lydia spoke first. 'I have to go out now and as I can't help you, you'd better go.'

She wondered yet again, as she lay weeping, what sort of injury John had suffered, and how serious. What sort of a marriage had they had when he couldn't even tell her he'd been attacked? Stupid man! Walking around with ... well, with what? Fractured ribs? Head injury? She had no idea.

After a while she calmed herself. It couldn't have been that bad, she reasoned; after all, he hadn't been hospitalised. And then as her anger increased, self-pity receded and the old, strong Lydia sat up in bed and dashed away the last of her tears.

'Damn him!' she swore. 'Let him be miserable in that crappy old farm. I'm going to enjoy myself.'

In the master bedroom a different atmosphere prevailed. 'Look, we can cancel the vacation. Or I'll tell her we don't want her to come with us.' Fred was childlike in his humility and Edith smiled at her reflection in the dressing-table mirror. She hadn't realised just how easy it could be to gain the upper hand in this long and boring marriage.

'No. We won't change anything. Lydia is my

oldest friend.' Her mouth hardened and she directed a venomous look at her husband who was standing by the door, unsure of his welcome into the room. 'She'll just have to understand that things are different now. A few days on the island will give her time to let reality sink in.' *And you too;* the unspoken end to the sentence was not lost on Fred. She turned round. 'Are you coming to bed? We have an early start.'

With his pathetically eager 'yeah, honey', Fred accepted the new facts of life and Edith smiled again. The prospect of making them suffer was a most rejuvenating experience. She would enjoy the trip, if nobody else did.

He was on the plane, three rows back from Lydia, four from Fred and Edith, and Lydia spotted him when she walked to the bathroom to freshen up before landing.

'It's Joe Bithell, isn't it?' Lydia stopped and held out her hand to the heavyset, balding man who, with a huge grin of recognition, attempted to stand up to greet her.

'Lydia Williams, what the hell are you doing on this flight?'

In the thirty minutes left before landing, they had renewed an old friendship, found out about each other's absent partners – in Joe's case, divorced – and discovered that they were destined for the same beach complex. It was the gales of excited laughter that Fred and Edith followed when they looked for Lydia in the arrivals lounge. Fred shook his head and smiled slightly, first making sure that Edith couldn't see him. Lydia was a national treasure, he thought. A one-off.

Two days after Christmas, she and Joe flew on to Panama. He was going to speak at a conference and she was thrilled to be invited along. Fred and Edith were miffed. He was jealous and Edith was annoyed that her planned humiliation of Lydia had gone awry. But Lydia had a wonderful time and hadn't been so entertained in years.

Now she was back, revitalised and once more bursting with confidence. It had been the very best Christmas ever and the affair wasn't over. Joe was determined to go on seeing her. Life was great, and she conveyed her enthusiasm to Matthew when she phoned him at the hospital soon after returning.

'How are you, honey?' she asked lovingly. 'Not out of that damned hospital yet?'

Matt was feeling low. His fractures were taking a long time to heal and in the last couple of days he had picked up a respiratory infection. Coughing hurt and he lay very still, back in bed, refusing to make much effort to help himself. The physiotherapist had reported her concerns to the consultant and Matthew was now on heavy doses of antibiotics. 'No,' he whispered. 'I got the flu or something.'

'Oh, you poor thing,' Lydia laughed, unconcerned. 'It will go soon, don't worry.' She paused for a moment, wondering if she should mention Joe. Matthew might not be aware of the state of his parents' marriage and she didn't want him to be upset when she was so far away. But Joe could be useful.

'I met a nice guy on the island,' she said. 'Joe Bithell. Guess what? He's an orthopaedic surgeon. I told him about you and your accident. He said you must have had a rough time. Honey,' she added with sudden inspiration, 'd'you think it would help if I asked him to talk to your surgeon?'

Matthew had a paroxysm of painful coughing and Lydia waited impatiently three thousand miles away until Matt said breathlessly, 'Yeah, Ma, whatever.'

Later that evening she repeated the conversation to Joe. 'Will you call the surgeon for me, sweetie?' she asked. 'I never seem to understand properly what they're saying. And,' she recalled Matthew's breathless voice of that evening and his lack of interest in her holiday, 'he didn't seem too good today. Said he had the flu ... or something.'

Joe's face creased into a frown. 'The flu?' he asked. 'Are you sure?'

'I don't know, he didn't seem able to talk much.' Suddenly she felt worried and looked up at him. 'Perhaps I should call John. He'll know.'

'Yeah, do that, and then, if you like, I'll call the guy in charge.'

The phone rang in the empty hall at Cariad Elin and echoed throughout the house. For a moment, in the lambing shed, Lark turned her head towards the house, feeling rather than hearing the ring, but then her attention was taken again by the urgency of the situation in front of her.

'This one is twinning too,' she called to John,

who was carrying two, still damp, newborn lambs into a pen at the far end of the barn, followed closely by their anxious mother.

The shed heaved with life. A hundred and fifty ewes, separated into small pens, pulled slowly at hay bales, some in labour and some already mothers, suckling their new lambs. Steam from the closely confined animals rose to the newly repaired rafters and a sweet, earthy smell hung in the air, bathing all the occupants in its aroma.

Outside it was sleeting, and occasional flakes of formed snow whipped through the ventilation gaps near the roof. The wind had been whirling around the mountains for hours now and it was a cruel night for any living creature to come into the world.

John and Lark had been in the shed for three hours now. It was their third night of lambing and they almost felt that they were old hands. On the first day, Robert and Elfed had been enormously helpful, showing them the basics, explaining how to deal with the problems, but on the whole letting John and Lark get on with it on their own.

Thanks to the advice given in the weeks before, the flock was healthy and the lambs were mostly dropped without any difficulties. Now and then a ewe would require help and Lark and John had had to learn on the job. They had lost a couple of lambs and just this evening they had lost a ewe. Lark had tried to get another one to take on the orphan lamb, holding its soft little head to the udder where it tried weakly to suckle. The ewe was suspicious, preferring her own offspring, and kept

281

pushing the tiny scrap away until it stood bleakly in the corner of the pen, bleating a pathetic little cry.

Lark had moved it then into another pen and into a box lined with straw, and fed it with a bottle. Later, when she had a chance, she would take it into the kitchen where it would be warm and might stand a chance of surviving. Just now, however, another ewe was straining to deliver, and when Lark got onto her knees to have a closer look, she groaned at the sight of the jumble of legs which were protruding from the back end of the sheep.

'I think we'll have to sort these two lambs out if she's going to have any chance,' Lark grunted as John came to have a look. 'I could push that one back and get out the first.' She pointed to a leg which obviously didn't belong to the two which were even now dangling down as the ewe made another effort to push.

'Can you manage?' John looked concerned.

'Somebody's got to do something.' She plunged her hands and arms into a bucket of disinfectant before reaching carefully into the ewe and turning the second twin into a delivery position. The mother gave another bleat and, with renewed effort, pushed the first lamb out. The second came with the next push and lay shivering on the straw beside its sibling. Lark and John stood back and watched as the ewe pushed her nose into the lambs and started to lick them. Within minutes, both twins were on their feet and finding their way to their first meal.

'It's incredible, isn't it?' said John, yet again. 'If

they were human they would be surrounded by the latest technology, yet these sheep just lick their offspring into life.'

Lark smiled. 'It's wonderful,' she said. She washed her hands again and then went over to the shelf where she had left a flask. 'Let's have a coffee, keep us awake.'

John looked at her as she poured the steaming liquid into plastic cups. She was dressed in a padded jacket and corduroy jeans and her feet were warmly encased in lace-up boots. Her face was still flushed from the effort of delivering the latest pair of twins and little tendrils of hair stuck to her damp forehead. As she handed him a cup he noticed her hands. They were still red and chilblained, so unlike Lydia's, which were always beautifully manicured. But then, Lydia wouldn't have been able to do any of the tasks that Lark had done throughout these last days. The girl had been a tower of strength and he couldn't imagine how he would have managed without her.

'You could go to bed now, Lark, if you want.' He said it reluctantly. He didn't want to spend the night alone in the lambing shed. But it was the wiser course. At least one of them should be alert in the morning.

She swallowed a mouthful of coffee before replying. 'I'll hang on a bit, I think. There's a couple over there,' she jerked her head to the big holding pen where the ewes were treading restlessly, 'who are ready to pop.'

'I can manage.'

'I know.' She grinned. 'I'm tired as hell, but I

283

don't want to leave. I must be mad.'

John laughed. 'That makes two of us. God, I think if Griff Parry came here now and said he was taking over, I'd throw him out on his ear!'

Lark wiped her mouth with the back of her hand and reached into a box beside the flask, produced a couple of chocolate bars and offered one to John. 'You know,' she said thoughtfully, tearing away the wrapping and examining the chocolate, 'it's funny about Griff. He hasn't been near the place since Matt's accident. You'd think he would still be interested in what goes on here. After all, these are his animals.'

'He isn't really a farmer. It was just a hobby. Perhaps he thought he could make a bit of money out of sheep.'

Lark snorted. 'Well, he must be the only one. No,' she shook her head and sighed. 'I always thought he had some sort of ulterior motive. I just don't know what.'

John thought about what she'd said, off and on, throughout the night. She was right: there was something going on, and Matt hadn't seen it. He remembered Bethan telling him about Elfed's suspicions that Parry was hatching a plan with a builder from Caernarfon. *I'll find out,* he decided as he wiped blood and mucus from a weak little body and set it on its feet under its mother. *I can't let that bastard take over.*

Chapter Twenty-Nine

The phone rang again while Lark was standing at the range making lunch. She had left the barn in the early hours and brought the orphan lamb to the house to lie in its box in front of the open lower door of the Rayburn. She had fed it, but then, too tired to worry, had gone upstairs and fallen into bed. When she got up again at seven to give it a bottle she found another lamb lying beside it. John must have brought it in.

He was asleep now and all was quiet in the barn. She had been out for a look, treading carefully across the slippery yard, where ice had formed on the puddles and freezing sleet had collected in sheltered corners of the buildings.

The mountain was grey this morning, blanketed in a heavy mist which seemed to shut out sound as well as sight. The weather forecast was grim. Heavy snow, unusual even here in the mountains, was predicted, and Lark sniffed at the air. She could smell it coming. The wind had turned away from the west, away from the sea, and the wind which was now beginning to swirl around the roofs didn't carry its normal salty odour but brought an acrid whiff of the quarry workings to the north.

The sheep were quiet this lunchtime. The new mothers appeared content with their offspring, raising their heads warily as Lark bent over to look at their lambs. She watched as the lambs suckled, wriggling their little tails in ecstasy, and smiled. Who could not? Remembering what Robert had said, she examined the ewes to see if they were suckling the lambs properly. A pair of shears was at hand and she wandered amongst the pens clipping wool away from the teats so that they were easy to get at. John had been doing the same, she could see that, and dabbing the lambs' navels with iodine. She laughed to herself as she walked back to the kitchen. Between the two of them, they nearly made one good shepherd!

She took off her heavy coat when she went inside. The house was warm now; John had seen to that. He had attended to the windows, shaving the wood so that they fitted properly and screwing back the hinges where they had pulled away from the frames. Matt had never bothered with any of these tedious household tasks, preferring to simply complain about the draughts, and she had not wanted to appear too involved, so nothing had been done. But, without realising it, she and John had worked on the house and farm buildings as if they were the owners of the property, instead of merely tolerated guests. Cariad Elin was now a comfortable as well as a wonderful place to live.

She was cooking bacon and eggs when the phone rang. *It'll be Robert asking how we've got on,* she thought, moving the pan off the hot plate and hurrying into the hall.

'Yeah, I need to talk to John Williams,' a female voice demanded when Lark picked up the receiver.

Lark guessed who it was, although she had never spoken to Matthew's mother. The peremptory tone with which the demand was made fitted into everything she had come to understand about Lydia.

'I'm sorry,' Lark said nervously. 'He's in bed, asleep, at the moment. I'll ask him to ring you as soon as he gets up.'

There was a pause at the other end of the line and then Lydia said, 'Tell me, exactly, who are you?'

Lark swallowed. It would appear that Matt hadn't said anything about her living at Cariad Elin. 'Um,' she cast about rapidly for something neutral to say – something that wouldn't compromise either Matt or John. 'I'm helping with the lambing. Mr Williams has been up all night with the sheep. I was ... er ... just making him something to eat.' She heard the silence at the other end as Lydia digested this piece of information and then Lark added, 'I can get him to call you when he wakes up.'

'Yeah, well, this is the third time I've tried; I need to talk to him about our son.'

There were footsteps on the landing and, as Lark looked up, John's head appeared over the banisters. She covered the mouthpiece and hissed, 'It's your wife. She wants to talk to you. Now!' He nodded and started down the stairs.

'He's just coming, Mrs Williams.' Lark put the receiver down on the table and returned to the kitchen.

She was making breakfast when he came into the room.

'She wanted to know about Matt,' he said. 'It seems she spoke to him yesterday and something he said worried her.'

John sat wearily at the table and rested his head on his hand. Lark gave him a cup of tea and put out knives and forks for them both. She piled plates with bacon and eggs and put them on the table, along with a warmed granary loaf. They were both hungry and attacked the meal with relish, John finally wiping a large slice of bread around his plate to soak up the final smears of bacon-flavoured egg. He got up and took the teapot from the range. She nodded to his unspoken question and waited while he poured her another cup of tea.

'He wasn't very well at the beginning of the week.' Lark spoke, suddenly. 'You told me that the nurse said he had a spike of temperature. Maybe you should call the hospital.'

He nodded, 'I will,' and then he glanced over to the box where the two orphan lambs lay asleep. 'How are they?'

'They seem fine,' she said, 'I'm going to give them another bottle in a minute.' She collected the plates and took them to the sink. John watched her. Her face was pale and he guessed that she felt just as weary as he did, but she hadn't grumbled, just carried on. He wondered again why she had stayed, but he didn't dwell on it. He was glad that she had.

'I'll ring now,' he said, 'and then give Lydia a call.'

The sister on Matt's ward was glad he'd called. 'I'm afraid he's got pneumonia, Mr Williams,

288

but we've been giving him a course of antibiotics and making sure that the physiotherapist gets his chest working. He's a lot better today. I thought you would be bound to visit, otherwise I would have telephoned you,' she added as an afterthought.

'We're lambing here,' John said guiltily. 'It's hectic.'

'Not to worry, *bach*,' Sister had been brought up on a hill farm, 'he's going to do. Come in when you can and I'll tell him you rang. You can speak to him yourself, but not today. I want him to get some rest.'

Lydia was ready to have hysterics when he told her about the pneumonia, but he calmed her down and repeated word for word exactly what the hospital sister had told him.

'I'm still going to talk to the doctor,' she said, 'and I have an orthopaedic surgeon friend who is going to speak to him too.'

'Another good idea,' said John. Sarcasm wasn't his intention, but he was tired and, without realising it, had fallen back into the same exasperated way of talking to her that he had done before he left. He heard the little gasp at Lydia's end and immediately regretted his last words. 'I mean,' he said quickly, 'you'll feel happier if you get the gen from the horse's mouth, so to speak. But, seriously, Matt's not too bad and I'll try and get to see him in the next day or two.'

'In the next day or two!' Lydia was scandalised. 'Can't you get your goddam ass over there sooner? It's only down the road, for Christ's sake.'

John groaned silently and leant his head against

the oak banister which rose behind the telephone table. She was right, of course, he should go but... 'We're lambing here,' he said, 'it's–'

'Yeah, I know. That girl told me. Who is she anyway?'

He, too, took the coward's way out. Matt obviously hadn't explained about Lark, and now how could he say that he was sleeping in the same house as his son's ex-girlfriend? Lydia would want to know why she was still there and why he was letting her stay. God knows, he hadn't worked it out himself.

'She's a friend of Matt's, helping with the lambing.' He hoped that would satisfy her and quickly changed tack. 'Did you have a good vacation? I saw the card you sent Matt.'

'Yeah, very nice.' Lydia was slightly mollified. 'But I've been back nearly three weeks now.. Which reminds me. When are you coming home?'

He was taken aback. She had asked what, in any circumstance and particularly in theirs, was a perfectly normal question, but he hadn't thought about leaving for days now, so wrapped up was he in the-day-to-day activities at Cariad Elin. Clearly it must seem odd to her.

'I dunno,' he answered cautiously. 'I can't leave the farm right now with the lambing going on, and, of course, I have to stay for Matthew. It'll be a few weeks, still, I think.'

'And you will be coming here, I suppose?'

He paused, unable to tell her something he didn't know himself. 'I don't know, Lydia. I just don't know,' was all he could say.

It was with relief that he left the hall and went

out to the uncomplicated world of the lambing shed, but on the other side of the Atlantic Lydia stood bleakly in her kitchen, holding the silent telephone in her small, tanned hand. She felt rejected and alone and that events were spinning too quickly out of her control. Joe had been comforting on vacation, and more than that, but he couldn't make up for the continuing upheaval in her life.

She caught sight of her face in the little mirrors that were inserted randomly in an art deco lampshade that stood out of place on the kitchen table. Joe had bought it for her earlier in the day, hoping that it would be to her taste. It wasn't. In fact she found it utterly hideous. Maybe it was the coloured glass which made her face look so sickly. She looked away and put the phone back on its hook. As she took a bottle of white wine from the refrigerator, she wondered what to do next. Things couldn't go on like they were.

'She was still worried about Matthew,' John said when he joined Lark in the shed. She was moving the newly delivered lambs with their sheep into a series of pens by the door. Tomorrow, if the weather improved a little, they were planning to take them out to the field by the river, where there was an open stone barn and plenty of shelter.

'How is he?'

His face was glum. 'They say he's had pneumonia, but he's getting better. You know, Lark, I feel bad for not going there this week. He must have been feeling rotten.'

'Go now,' she said. 'I can manage here for a few

hours and you'll feel better for seeing him.'

She was right; he was glad he went, and Matthew was pathetically pleased to see him. He was sitting up against a pile of pillows, his eyes closed. His computer was on a table, pushed to the side of the little room, and his bedside table, which normally held a jumble of magazines and papers, was cleared except for a jug and glass of water. John thought he was asleep and reached for a chair to sit down beside the bed but the scrape of chair legs against the plastic floor made Matthew open his eyes.

'Hi, Dad.' He coughed with the effort of speaking. 'How goes it?'

John leant over him and brushed the pale hair from his forehead. It was hot and slightly damp and when John examined his face, he could see two bright spots of colour on his cheeks.

'I hear you've been sick,' he said cheerfully, trying not to let Matthew see his concern. 'Hospitals are always the best places for picking up infections.' He smiled. 'How are you feeling, son?'

'I'm OK. My chest doesn't hurt so much today, except when that goddam woman comes in and makes me cough.'

'I guess she's only doing her job,' John said sympathetically. He was ashamed with himself for not going in to see Matt for days. The boy looked ill and pathetically young. No wonder Lydia had worried.

'The lambs have started to appear,' he said. Matthew had lost interest in the farm and they never talked about it lately, but today there seemed very little else to say.

'Yeah?' He turned his head and looked at his father. 'How's it going?'

John raised his eyes and shook his head dolefully. 'It's hard. I think I'm getting too old for this sort of thing.'

Matt grinned and lay back as John prattled on about the lambing and how many twins they were getting. 'They're all doing well,' he said, 'even the orphans that Lark is bottle-feeding.'

'She still there?'

'Yeah.'

Matthew said nothing for a moment, letting this piece of information sink in. In the visits his father had made during the last weeks, neither of them had mentioned Lark and Matt had assumed that she had gone. 'She's good with the sheep,' he said finally.

'Yeah,' John agreed and they left it at that. It was something that both of them could think about another day.

The snow had started in earnest as John drove away from Bangor and out onto the mountain road. It was dusk and lights from the few on-coming cars dazzled and worried him. He drove carefully, thinking about Matthew and how ill he had looked. He was glad that he had seen the doctor.

'He's over the worst, Mr Williams, but it was unfortunate that he picked up the bug. Bad time of year.'

John had agreed, but miserably felt that it didn't absolve him from ignoring his son for so many days. Nothing had changed.

It was only as he turned into the farmyard that his mood lightened. The buildings slumbered under their blanket of snow but the mountain peak stood out in a sudden clearing of cloud and its icy summit twinkled in the light of the rising moon. After parking in front of the house, he got out and stood for a moment, taking comfort from the scene. It uplifted him and he found that he was crying in relief. He was glad to be home.

Chapter Thirty

After four snowy days, the weather improved, and for the rest of the month and into the next, it was unseasonably mild. Lambing time was nearly over and Lark, leaning on the water-meadow gate, watched the tiny lambs with an almost maternal pleasure. They still clung to their mothers' sides, but in a week or so they would be venturing across the field on their own and joining the others in mad games of chase. She was still bottle-feeding her two orphans and they were thriving, although housed away from the others, in one of the stables. Robert had said she could put them in the field at the end of the week, where, supplemented with lamb pellets, they would be able to live on the pasture. He had complimented her on their care and she had blushed with pleasure.

'Proper little shepherd, she is, man,' he had said

to John. 'You'd think she'd been born to it.'

John had laughed and agreed. 'I couldn't manage without her.'

He had been bent double, moving a wooden hurdle, so he hadn't seen the lifted eyebrow Robert made to Bethan, who had come for a visit. Lark had seen it and turned away. Were people beginning to talk? she'd wondered. Elfed went to the hospital to see Matt now and then and he could have said something about them not being together any more. *Oh, I hope not,* she had thought desperately, *don't let this all end in a mess.*

John was walking across the yard towards the field and she lifted her arm to wave. His demeanour was changed. He seemed happier, stronger and more upright, despite the lack of sleep during these past nights. He had begun to look like a farmer now and behave like one. When he looked at the fields and the mountainside it was with a calculating gaze as he gauged the quality of the grass and the strength of the fencing. Lark couldn't remember when he'd last grumbled about Cariad Elin, or even compared it unfavourably with life in Canada.

One night, when they had been drinking coffee in the lambing shed, she had asked him about his work.

'Do you miss it?' she'd asked curiously.

'A bit.' He leant back on the hay bales while he pondered the question. 'There's something exciting about a blank piece of paper. You have a list of requirements from the client, but otherwise, the idea for the building is entirely your

295

own, and your imagination begins to fly. There are so many ways to go. Traditional is always popular and generally sells, but I think true architects are innovative. Designing a fascinating building which fulfils the client's requirements and yet enhances its environment is what one strives for.'

He shrugged and smiled rather bleakly. 'I could do it once,' he said, 'and then I lost the touch. But I made a good living on my reputation.'

'You could try again,' Lark said, 'you'll get another good idea.'

He shook his head. 'I don't think so.'

'I know you will.' Her brilliant eyes were staring straight into his and a frisson of alarm seeped from his gut and through his muscles and ligaments until he could feel the tips of his fingers tingling. The look she could produce was mesmeric and he found his head nodding in agreement as he mumbled, 'Yes, maybe.'

The barn was quiet for a while, apart from the bleating of the new lambs and the occasional grunting noises from the ewes in labour.

'What about you?' he said, asking about her life for the first time. 'Have you had a job?'

'Oh yes,' she replied, 'I was a junior lecturer at a university.'

'Wow!' John didn't know why that surprised him so much. She was obviously intelligent, but remembering his dons of thirty years ago, he couldn't imagine any of them being like Lark. 'What was your subject?'

She laughed as she sat amongst the hay bales

and pulled her jacket close around her body to combat the draught from the ventilation holes. The night was cold and despite the steam rising from the milling bodies in the sheep pens the barn was freezing. 'Something entirely useless, I'm afraid,' she sighed, 'French pre-renaissance literature.'

John grinned. 'Not much of a grounding for working a hill farm, I'd say.' He thought for a moment, 'Unless Lancelot or Guinevere had something to say about it.'

That surprised her. Not many people knew much about her subject; even her colleagues at the university had found it utterly obscure, and few of the students who took it as a possibly interesting option followed it for longer than a year. Christopher had been proud of her but didn't ask about her work and had never read any of her papers. The romances of the troubadours left him entirely cold. 'Have you read any of it?' she asked.

'Not much, really, and only in translation. Bits and pieces when I was a teenager, and I guess I've forgotten most of it.'

'Well, you know more than most.' Lark frowned. 'I think I must have become dispirited with it too, in the end. Far too romantic for the techno age.'

He wanted to ask her about leaving the university and ending up here, but she had already moved away and into a delivery pen where she was squatting beside a heaving ewe. 'Think she needs help,' she called, dragging John back to the job in hand.

Now, on this mild early February morning, he leaned close beside her on the field gate and admired the lambs. The sheep grazed mechanically despite the fact that there was barely any grass and they were fed mostly on pellets and hay, but they looked healthy. Robert had told them to get in some kale and John had been on the phone all morning trying to find a supplier.

'I've got it,' he said triumphantly. 'It's coming from Caernarfon this afternoon.' They turned away from the field and started walking back to the house. 'Matt should have put down a few acres of it, you know. Apparently that's what they all do.'

'He wouldn't have known,' said Lark, 'he was relying on Griff Parry telling him how to run things. Robert wasn't consulted.'

'That Parry!' John was exasperated. 'He hasn't come up here once or even phoned to see how the lambing's going, and yet when they're sold, he'll want his cut.'

'He's seen Matt. Last week. Elfed told me.'

'What is he up to?' John wondered as he held open the kitchen door for her to go in ahead of him.

The room was warm and inviting now that John had improved the heating and draught-proofed the windows and doors. He had bought a thick rug which they had thrown over the stone slabs on the floor and improved the lighting with a brighter overhead shade for the winter daytime and attractive lamps which during the evening suffused the room in a warm terracotta glow. The other rooms were better also, warmer and less stark. He had found an antique oak bookcase in a shop in Bangor and had set it up in the alcove beside the inglenook. It was stuffed with the books from his old bedroom, and he and Lark had added more. The house was fast becoming more than merely habitable.

When I've put in the central heating and rewired, I could build an extension, John would think, as he sat quietly beside the fire on those long winter evenings. And then he would think again and remember that Cariad Elin wasn't his, and his brow would crease and the little tic start up in his cheek.

Lark, sitting opposite, would watch and know what he was thinking and break into conversation to divert him. 'Beti Rowlands, at the shop, told me she remembered you when you were a boy. Said you were in the same class at school. Do you remember her?'

'Um...' He looked up, dragging his mind away from the disappointment of Cariad Elin. 'I dunno ... it was old Johnny Peddler and his son who had it when I was a kid.'

'Well, yes ... same family. She told me about her grandfather walking across Europe to escape the Cossacks or something.'

The conversation would flow then until Lark got up to make them tea and a plate of buttery toast which they would eat companionably before going to their separate beds. When the lambing started, those friendly evenings disappeared and meals became snatched affairs taken at odd hours. It had been two weeks of highs and lows.

'There's just a couple left,' John said, throwing himself into the leather chair and stretching his feet out in front of him. 'We'll be through tonight.' He stared at the flames flickering quietly in the windless chimney. 'I think we've done OK.'

'Matt should be pleased,' said Lark from the kitchen table where she was making them hefty beef and mustard sandwiches. 'The flock is doubled, and even in these times, he'll make a bit of money.'

'Yeah. I'll give him a call later on. Not that he's that interested any more. Since that chest infection he seems less and less keen to talk about Cariad Elin. It was all baseball when I went there yesterday. Lydia has been phoning him every day.'

Lark brought him a sandwich and coffee. 'Here, this will do for now. I'll make a proper meal this evening.'

She pot-roasted one of her old chickens later that day and they ate silently, too tired to speak. John marked the arrival of the last but one lamb in his notebook and lifted it up for her to see. Her mouth was full, but she nodded and, after swallowing, grinned. 'Great,' she said.

'You don't need to come out tonight,' John said. 'It doesn't need two of us. You have a rest.'

'Mm, that sounds good. I'll just feed the orphans and then I think I'll have a long bath. I can smell sheep on all my clothes and on my arms and legs. I wonder if anyone in the village has noticed?'

'I shouldn't think so; they all smell the same.' He laughed. 'As long as you clean up before the tourist season starts, it won't matter a bit.'

Her small voice broke the new silence which had followed his joking remark. 'I won't be here then.'

He closed his book and got up from the table. 'Of course,' he said, coughing to clear the gruffness from his throat. 'I'd forgotten.'

She lay in the bath for an hour, luxuriating in soft, herb-scented water. The room was warmed by an electric towel rail which John had had installed. This, and the newly draught-proofed windows, made the brief wash-downs in rapidly cooling water, which she had hated, a thing of the past. Bathing had become a pleasure again. John was planning to install a shower, a surprise for Matt, he'd said, and she loved the thought of that too.

It was after midnight when she rose from the water and took a warmed towel from the rail. She was tired and sat wearily on the cork seat of the wooden bathroom chair and slowly began to dry her legs and arms. They were smooth and strong and still held a hint of the tan from last summer. She thought about those magical days when she and Matt had roamed the fields and hills, exploring a new world. That was when she had fallen in love. It was when she finally found what she had been looking for, all down the years, and knew without any doubt that the feeling would last forever. And now she would have to leave and the prospect was unbearable.

She buried her face in the towel and sobbed.

'Oh Matt,' she cried, 'why weren't you the one?' She had been so sure in those first days. 'How could I have got it so wrong?'

It was an hour later when, cried out and exhausted, she crept down to the kitchen seeking tea or water to combat her dry mouth. The room was unlit except for a low light emanating from the small lamp by the fireplace. She noticed that there were fresh logs on the fire and then saw John's legs stretched out towards it, as they always were when he sat in the leather chair.

'We've finished,' he said quietly, not moving or turning round, 'and the last were twins.'

'Brilliant!' She tried to sound cheerful but her recent bout of crying had left her weak and gulping, and John, who was sensitive to her see-sawing emotions, struggled up and turned to look at her. 'Couldn't you sleep?'

The sympathetic enquiry nearly brought on the tears again. Lark grabbed hold of the kettle and set it on the range. 'I thought I'd make some tea. Would you like one?'

Her voice was still wobbling and he could see that she was deliberately keeping her back to him. 'I think we should celebrate,' he said, getting up. 'If you'll tell me where you've hidden the whisky, I'll pour us a large slug each.'

He watched as her hand went to her face and dashed swiftly at her eyes. When she spoke, she sounded more normal and there was a hint of laughter in her voice. 'I didn't hide it ... it's still under the sink,' and she reached down and drew out the bottle he'd wanted so much on those first days. *How strange,* he thought as he carefully poured the last of the sparkling liquid into the glasses, *I'd forgotten about drinking. It must have been Matt's accident; I had too much else to think about.*

They sat by the fire, nursing their drinks and gazing at the dying flames. Lark had calmed herself and the alcohol had brought some colour back to her cheeks. As ever, after she had allowed a burst of emotion to bubble to the surface, it was followed by the realisation that fate would guide her life and that she had no power to alter it.

'We should be happy,' John said with a yawn. 'Most of the hard work is over and we've done well.'

'I know.' Lark's words sounded hollow and he nodded, acknowledging the sense of anti-climax that had seeped into the room. His glass was empty and he stared at it, wishing he had some whisky left so that he could go on sitting there. Lark had finished hers too and was moving her feet, ready to get up. Suddenly, he didn't want her to go. He wanted to go on sitting by the fire with her beside him, just like in the old days with Mam and Dad.

'I think I'll go...' Lark started to say but he was off his chair and kneeling in front of her with his arms working themselves around her. Her body, inside the blue dressing gown, was taut and shocked and very afraid of this new emotion which was beginning to overwhelm her. Gently, he pulled her down to the rug, and as she turned her face to his, his mouth descended on hers and they were kissing, mouths wide open, tongues probing and saliva passing unnoticed. She could feel his hands pushing away her gown and searching beneath, until one hand cupped her small breast and the other forced its way beyond the elastic of her pyjama bottoms. 'Oh God,' she moaned and pulled him closer.

For the briefest moment he stopped and looked at her. 'Yes,' she whispered, 'yes, do it,' as passion swept away her fears and she tore at his clothes in her urgency to lie beside his naked body. He took her as the dying logs cracked and split apart and ejected fierce spurts of flame up the chimney. She cried at the climax, a low, unearthly wail which he heard only vaguely above his own groans of triumph and forgot immediately.

Afterwards they lay exhausted on the rug, still entwined and unwilling to let each other go. John reached over and dragged Lark's robe to cover them. 'I guess I should say sorry,' he breathed into her neck. 'I didn't plan that, but these last few days I've been feeling...' He left the sentence unfinished, unable to put into words exactly how he'd been feeling. Was it just exhaustion that had produced this overwhelming desire to hold her, feed life from her, even? He didn't know.

'Don't say you're sorry,' Lark's muffled voice whispered in his ear. 'I'm not.'

The fire had died before they got up and made their way up the old stairs. On the landing they paused and John looked at her with a question in his eyes. He wanted to stay with her; he needed to put his hands on her thin, firm body again and to smell the apple scent in her hair. Desire, such as he hadn't felt for years until tonight, was seizing him again and it had to be expiated.

'I don't know what we should do,' he said, holding onto her arm as though to stop her disappearing.

She pushed open the door of the main bedroom and said quietly, 'Come to bed, it's late.'

Chapter Thirty-One

The next morning dawned cloudy but dry. A weak February sun shone over the peaks, lighting up the fields and melting the snow which had clung to the mountain tops for the last few days. The yard was deep with slush and mud, and Lark, picking her way through to the hen house, slipped and landed with a splash in a cold puddle. But even that couldn't wipe the glowing smile off her face. *Don't be so emotional, you idiot,* she tried to tell herself severely, but her mouth kept widening and her heart beat a little faster than normal. *This is what it's like,* she realised, *not what I thought before.*

John had been in the lambing shed to see last night's newborns. The twin lambs were well and their mother contented, so he picked up the two quivering little bodies and took them out to the field. The ewe followed anxiously as he opened the gate, walked to a sheltered part of the field and set them down. Once satisfied that her lambs were all right, she settled down to pull at the poor pasture while the twins, still wobbly on their thin, dark legs, stood in the lee of her body and suckled the abundant new milk. John watched them for a moment and then looked quickly over the rest of the flock. He was not prepared to linger this morning. He was as eager as a school-boy to get back to Lark.

They met up again in the kitchen and went about the morning tasks of bringing wood and making breakfast, not speaking and barely look-ing at each other. They were both suddenly shy and couldn't find the right words to break the ice.

'This bacon is good,' said John eventually, attacking his plate with relish. 'I'm really hungry this morning.'

'I can't imagine why.' A grin hovered around her mouth, and as he looked up, her laugh ex-ploded into the room and he threw down his knife and fork and reached over to grab her. 'Let's go upstairs,' he said, pulling her towards the hall.

'Yes,' she nodded and they ran, like teenagers, throwing the door open and pounding up the old wooden stairboards.

It was as good as it had been the night before. John had rediscovered a potency that he had thought lost somewhere in the regimes and con-straints of middle age. It was as if all the pent-up emotions which previously he had turned into depression and self-pity were now released, and he indulged himself like a man rescued from a famine.

Somewhere, driven to the back of his mind by unadulterated lust, was an awkward feeling of guilt. He was, after all, having an almost unnatural relationship. Lark was his son's girlfriend, and added to that, he supposed, young enough to be his daughter. But it seemed that this notion made what he was doing even more thrilling, and he closed his eyes and allowed his body to be swept along on a tide of passion.

It was equally exciting for Lark. With Matthew she had been the giving one, as she had with Stewie and, she now realised, with Christopher. It seemed that all her life she had been so grateful to people for loving her that she had allowed their desires to overwhelm hers and subdue her own imagination. But with John, it was different. Everything he did, every time he drew his hand down her body or put his mouth on her skin, took her to new heights. She could close her eyes and be dancing wildly on mountain peaks. They were like two pieces of a whole which had been lost and was now rediscovered and joined together.

'Oh Lark,' he groaned happily, 'what have you done to me?' He stretched out on the bed as he felt the weight of years roll away from him. *Is this what it should always have been like?* he wondered.

'I don't know,' she answered, turning towards him and wrapping a long leg around his body so that they were, once again, lying skin to skin and feeling the stirring and movement that presaged another climactic event. 'Shall I stop?' she added with a suppressed giggle and laughed out loud as his grip on her smooth flesh tightened and he growled 'trollop' into her ear.

Later, temporarily satiated, they lay, relaxed and warm under the white duvet, and stared out of the small window as the sun reached its zenith in a pale frosty sky. John thought about his parents who had used this bed and wondered if they had experienced this ecstasy. Maybe they had, or something near it. And he remembered how Dad had struggled to live with his grief and began to understand.

'I suppose we should get up,' said Lark practically. 'There are things to be done.'

'Yes.'

But neither of them moved until Lark, who had been lying quietly, sat up.

'John,' she said seriously, fixing him with her strange eyes, now hazel with flecks of green, 'I think I'm going to be Helen again. Do you mind?' She paused and creased her brow as her thoughts tumbled over each other and sorted themselves into a new order. 'I don't feel like Lark any more. I was Helen when my parents found me and that is what I want to be.' She was thoughtful for a moment and then added, 'Perhaps I should tell you that I've been married.'

'Oh.' He lay back on the pillows and thought about what she'd said. This was something he hadn't guessed and he wasn't sure how to feel. 'What happened?'

'I don't know, really. He's a decent person and was good to me but he was the wrong man.' She bit her lip knowing that she had to be open about her feelings. 'The truth is I was the wrong woman. I should never have married. I couldn't cope with the boredom of suburbia and I ran away. I went with another man and lived on the road. It was an utterly bizarre existence.'

'Will you run away again?'

She turned her head and stared at him. 'I'm at home in Cariad Elin. I don't want to be anywhere else or with anyone else.'

'Good,' said John. 'Because that's how I feel.' He looked at the ceiling, noticing a crack in the plaster and wondering who he could get to fix it. For the first time in years he could see his way ahead and loved what he could see. 'I'm married, still, I think,' he said. 'Lydia hasn't said anything about filing for divorce.' He grinned. 'She will, when she finds out about us.'

He gently stroked a hand along her side. 'My life has been seriously dull compared with yours,' he said with a sigh. 'Utterly conventional.'

'No.' She shook her head and her red-gold hair bounced off her neck. 'You've achieved recognition. Not many have done that.' She leaned over and kissed his forehead. 'Don't put yourself down.' They held each other, aroused again and moving against each other.

It was the crunch of tyres on the frozen puddles in the yard that finally parted them.

John leaped out of bed and looked out of the window. 'Jesus,' he whispered, 'it's that bastard, Parry.' He threw on his clothes, struggling with his socks and shoes, hoping to get downstairs before Griff, in the local and accepted way, walked into the kitchen merely calling out 'hello'.

He made it just in time and walked to the door, as though intending to go into the yard, as Griff put his hand on the latch.

'Hello, John.' Griff stepped back in surprise as John came through the door straight in front of him.

'Ah, Parry,' John said evenly, 'we wondered when we would see you. Lambing's finished, by the way, so don't bother to arrange any nights up here.'

Griff refused to rise to the sarcasm but put on his cheerful landlord's face and nodded towards the river field. 'I've seen them, they look good. Plenty of twins.' He looked back at the kitchen door. 'I don't suppose you could let me use the lav. It's the cold weather, see. Plays the very devil with my bladder.'

His flabby cheeks wobbled pitifully as he spoke and John jerked his head towards the house and turned to open the door. He wondered nervously if Lark had got out of bed yet, for Griff would need to go upstairs, and was deliberately slow as he lifted the latch and led the way into the kitchen.

To his relief, Lark was bending in front of the washing machine, loading it with sheets. She was wearing jeans and a sweater and had her feet warmly encased in thick socks. She looked at Griff with undisguised distaste. 'Long time, no see,' she said coldly. 'Thought you'd done a flit or something.'

He attempted a friendly chuckle, aware that he was treading on eggshells in this house. The girl always made him uneasy and today she appeared more perverse than ever. She also looked more beautiful. Obviously being up nights suited her.

'Well, Lark, love,' he said, 'fancy you still being here. We thought that with Matt being laid up and all...' He let the sentence peter out as her mouth turned down and her eyes fixed him with a cold grey stare.

'I've been helping with the lambs.' She put in the washing powder and switched on the machine. 'Not that it's any of your business.'

'It's upstairs,' John intervened. He pointed the way to Griff, and looking at Lark, said, 'He wants a pee.' She shrugged and picked up the kettle and put it under the tap. John waited until Griff's heavy feet could be heard on the stairs and put a loving arm around Lark's waist. 'How's it look up there?'

'Both our beds are tumbled and my under-clothes are on the floor.' She giggled and lifted up her sweater to show him her small, round breasts, bra-less. 'No knickers either.'

He laughed and put his head down to nuzzle one of her breasts.

'Stop it, you idiot,' she hissed, swinging the kettle onto the range and trying to escape. 'He'll be down in a minute.'

When Griff did descend, after having a quick look round the bedrooms, they were sitting silently on either side of the table. He had the feeling that they were suppressing laughter, but that didn't surprise him. He was used to it in this village.

'Have a cup of tea.' Lark tried to make an effort

311

to be normal and Griff, after looking first at John for confirmation, pulled out a chair and sat down.

He looked curiously at the remains of the breakfast, scattered untidily on the table from hours before. *Never twigged her for a slut,* he thought, and John, following his gaze, said, 'Too busy to clear up, these days.' Lark said nothing, but gathered up the used crockery and took it to the sink.

'Anyway, Parry,' John said irritably, 'what has finally brought you out here?'

'Oh, you know, wanted to have look at the lambs; they're half mine. Fair play, now.' He tried to look affronted, but his face wouldn't assume the right expression. The jowls and the drooping moustache only ever looked foolishly happy or sad.

'We remembered that every night these last few weeks, didn't we?' John looked at Lark.

'Mm.' She was washing up the dishes and added over her shoulder, 'I expect Matt will factor in labour charges for lambing duties, when it comes to the accounting.'

John grinned. 'I must remind him of that when I go to the hospital.'

Griff sucked at his tea through his moustache, carefully wiping the drips with the back of his hand. 'I saw Matt yesterday,' he said slyly. 'We had a good old talk about things.' He noticed John's hand stiffen around his cup and felt Lark pause in her washing-up. 'He's got a long con-valescence in front of him and it won't be easy for him to manage here, on his own. With the plaster and crutches and all.'

He leant back, now vitally interested in the effect that his words were having. How he wished Llinos could be here to properly assess the situation; she could tell him if he was letting his imagination run away with him. Lark came to sit at the table, and as she passed, her hand trailed casually on John's shoulder. Griff watched with growing excitement. It wasn't his imagination; it was obvious that they were, in his mother's parlance, 'carrying on'.

He pushed away his chair and got up. 'Well, must go. Llinos will be waiting for me to take over.' He flashed his fat baby smile at Lark. 'Thank you for the tea, Lark, *cariad;* make sure you call in to see us before you go. You too, John.'

He moved surprisingly quickly for an overweight man and was out of the kitchen door and into his Land Rover whilst Lark and John still looked at each other, appalled at the new turn of events.

'He's guessed,' she said, her voice breaking.

He put his arm round her. 'Maybe, but I don't really think so.' He chewed his lip. 'More important, what has he cooked up with Matt?' He thought for a moment and then said, 'I'd better go and see him.'

'You won't tell him?' Lark was suddenly fearful. 'About us, I mean.' She leant close to him, craving the comfort that he alone could now give her. It was a new and strange sensation, this feeling of dependency. *I used to be so strong,* she thought, *nothing could touch me, and now...*

'I won't tell him, not yet. We won't tell anyone yet. But Lark,' he paused and then smiled and kissed her gently, 'I mean, Helen, this thing between us. It is as important to you as it is to me, isn't it?'

She nodded. 'Yes, oh yes.'

'I'm glad, because I don't want to be apart from you ever again. I know it's only been a day, but I'm more positive about us than I've ever been about anything. I love you, Helen.'

She saw through his eyes into the clear mind beyond. This man was truly the one she had been destined for and her fears receded. The farm had brought them together and would keep them safe.

'You are my love,' she whispered, 'and will always be.'

The sun was sinking in the sky when John went out to take pellets to the sheep and Lark took mash to the hens. She stood for a moment, watching them peck at the feed. They clucked and chattered contentedly, searching the hopper for bits that they liked and then abandoning it in favour of searching the yard for corn and grubs. The wind was beginning to blow in from the sea and clouds had gathered on the mountain, presaging the rain and sleet that would be falling before midnight. Her eyes were drawn towards the summit, now hidden beneath a growing blanket of rolling grey cloud. She smiled, knowing that the cloud would fall lower during the evening, covering the farm in mist, protecting her and John from the outside world.

He came back from the field, striding upright across the yard, easily carrying the half-empty bag of feed. From a distance now he looked like a younger man, strong and capable, quite different from the person whom she had first seen a couple of months ago. As he approached, she noticed his face. The lines had smoothed out and the sharp mountain air had given him some colour. *It must be love,* she chuckled to herself, *that makes me see him differently.*

'I'll dash in and see Matt,' he said. 'I must find out what Parry has been up to.' He dropped a kiss on her upturned face. 'Don't worry, *cariad,* it'll be all right.'

'I know.' She grinned and walked with him to the shed where he stored the pellets. It was beginning to get dark and a few sharp drops of rain, earlier than she had expected, whipped into her face. 'Don't be long,' she said, looking up at the sky. 'I think we're in for a downpour.'

'I won't.' He pushed the bolt on the shed door and produced car keys from his pocket.

They could have had no inkling, as they kissed goodbye and John got into his car and drove out of the yard, that far away, across the Atlantic, Lydia was also in a car, on a journey. Her lover was driving her to the airport. She was coming to Wales to see her son and bring him home.

Chapter Thirty-Two

'They're at it. I tell you, Llinos, *cariad*, they're at it! Plain as a pikestaff. And bold with it.'

'I don't believe you.' Llinos looked up briefly from her computer screen where she was composing a letter to the local MP. Gareth was an old friend from her university days and they were working together on a committee to create more rural businesses. This was all part of her greater plan to enter national politics, a career far more suitable and satisfactory than that of a pub landlord's wife.

'Well, maybe not bold, exactly, but God, Llinos, you should have seen them. Tumbled, they were, tumbled. And touching each other. And the house.' Griff shovelled chips, heavily coated with brown sauce, into his mouth and thought about the kitchen table at Cariad Elin. The remains of breakfast still apparent at three o'clock in the afternoon. 'I think they'd been in bed all day and only just got up when I called round.'

Llinos shook her head; it was quite unbelievable. Lark was a good-looking girl, granted, but she was years younger than John Williams. What could she possibly see in him? There, her theory unwound a little. More than one friend had wondered out loud what she had seen in Griff Parry and she had wondered herself, on many an occasion. Her answer was always the same. 'I

316

matured late, didn't exactly know what I wanted when I married him.' But that wasn't entirely true. He was earning good money when she'd met him and was malleable. He had brought the financial security that allowed her, a plain, bookish postgraduate, to formulate a new persona.

She shrugged. Maybe Griff was right about the goings-on at Cariad Elin. Perhaps Lark had latched onto the wealthy older man for a purpose. But it wouldn't matter to her and Griff's plans. Why should they care if John Williams took a mistress back to Canada? It was up to him ... and maybe his wife.

Griff had finished his chicken and chips and was now attacking a dish of syrup pudding and cream. *His arteries can't last much longer,* Llinos thought dispassionately and returned to her letter, only half listening to the excited babble emanating from her husband's pudding-laden mouth.

'Matthew wants to leave, he told me,' Griff was saying. 'Wants to go home to Canada and have his mam and dad look after him till he can get on his feet. I told him that I would keep an eye on Cariad Elin while he was away.'

He got up and took his empty plates to the dishwasher. 'And, Llinos, what d'you think he said to that?'

She didn't answer, and used to talking to himself, he raised his voice and repeated the question.

'I've no idea,' she murmured impatiently, still staring at the screen. 'What did he say?'

317

'He said "sure" and "whatever", you know the way he speaks. But the point is, he's lost interest in the farm.'

John found Matt in the same mood, when he went into the hospital.

'I gotta get away, Dad,' he said. He was up on crutches, clumsily walking around the day room. He had lost weight during his recent bout of illness and looked pale and drawn and, to John's eyes, somehow shrunken. The bouncing, confident son, who had made John feel middle-aged, had gone, replaced, it seemed, by a whining, hospitalised invalid. It would take months to build him up again, not only physically but mentally, and Matt was right, he would have to get away. It was obvious that he wouldn't be able to come back to the farm until he'd had a few months' convalescence.

'We could fly home any time now,' Matt said. 'I spoke to the consultant and he was willing. You know, he's had some conversations with this guy who knows Ma. He's an orthopaedic surgeon in Toronto and he's ready to take me on.'

This entirely sensible suggestion threw John into a quandary. He wanted the very best for Matt, but how could he leave Lark? It had only been twenty-four hours since he had discovered that she was the one person with whom he wanted to spend the rest of his life and it would be unbearable to be parted from her. He looked away, not wanting Matt to see the doubt in his eyes, and muttered something about having a word with the doctors.

'You don't need to.' Matt was irritable. 'I already did. Jesus, Dad, I'm not staying in this fucking hospital for the rest of my life.'

'Hey. Calm down, son. I'm just trying to work on the logistics of it all.'

John thought for a moment.

'What about the farm? The flock has doubled and the sheep and lambs need looking after. You can't ignore them.'

Matthew didn't have an opportunity to reply to this, because a nurse came into the room with a wheelchair. 'Time to get back into bed, Matthew,' she said, 'you've been up too long.' She took his arm and led him firmly to the chair. He sat down heavily, letting the crutches clatter onto the floor. John reached for them and walked behind the nurse as she wheeled Matt back to his bed.

'Griff Parry said he'd keep an eye on the stock,' Matthew said over his shoulder. 'The sheep are half his, anyway.' He winced as he heaved himself into the freshly made bed and then eased back gratefully onto the pillows. John watched miserably. There was nothing he could do to help. And now he was thinking up ways to hinder Matthew's plans. What sort of a father was he, for Christ's sake?

'You're just trying to make things difficult.' Matthew's words were eerily correct and John could feel a flush coming to his face. He hastily took out his handkerchief and pretended to blow his nose.

'No,' he said, his voice muffled in the hankie. 'I was only trying to work out the best way to

319

arrange it all. Leave it with me. I'll get in touch with your mother.'

Lydia settled into the comfortable first-class seat in the 747 which was going to fly her across the Atlantic. Joe had insisted on buying her ticket and had stayed with her until the very last minute.

'I'm gonna miss you,' he'd said as he brought her another Martini in the departure lounge. 'Don't stay away too long.'

Lydia had smiled. He was a sweetie, even though he got on her nerves. His doglike devotion had remained undiminished from the first, and though flattering and comforting, it so lacked excitement. He was talking about them moving in together and she had considered the proposition from time to time. But only from time to time. She wasn't in love with him.

'Don't fret, honey.' She patted his podgy hand and thought yet again how tasteless his diamond signet ring was. 'I'm just going to bring Matthew home. It'll only take a few days and then he can be put under your care.' She frowned and sipped her drink. 'I didn't realise how ill he's been until you spoke to the doctors over there. Poor Matt,' she sighed, 'I bet he wondered why I didn't fly over sooner. He must think I didn't care.'

'Your husband didn't tell you, I gather.'

'Nope, he more or less said it was a minor accident, and dumb old me, I believed him. God knows what he was playing at.' She finished her drink and he signalled the waitress to bring another.

There were more drinks as soon as the huge plane had climbed to its cruising height, and by the time the flight attendants had brought round a meal, Lydia was tearfully sloshed. She was scared of what she would find at the other end.

Would Matt look different? Nobody had said that his face had been damaged, but then John had pretended that the accident was minor. And even if he looked the same, how did one manage with a smashed pelvis and broken thigh? Poor darling, he must have been in pain. The last thoughts Lydia had, before drifting off to sleep, were angry. John must have deliberately played it down. He was trying to shut her out of his life completely.

'He's fed up and wants to go home,' John told Lark when he was back at the farm and sitting by the kitchen fire. She sat on the rug beside him, her knees drawn up to her chin and her head leaning against his leg. 'Parry has told him that he will mind the farm,' he snorted, 'and we all know exactly how much care he puts into looking after anything.'

She reached up and took his hand but said nothing. He needed to talk it out.

'You know L– Helen, he looked so tired and uncomfortable that I felt bad for not organising his care better. I should have told Lydia and I should have sent him home where she could have looked after him. Christ,' he said angrily, 'I came here specifically to get him home. I lost that plan, somewhere along the way.'

'He couldn't have gone, at first,' she said practically. 'It was only in these last few weeks that he could. But we were busy with the lambing.'

He sighed. He supposed she was right, but the feeling of guilt remained. A small voice at the very back of his mind kept telling him that maybe he'd ignored his son on purpose. Could it have been some sort of punishment in return for all the crap Matthew had dished out in the past? He swallowed and shifted nervously in his chair and Lark increased her pressure on his hand.

'Don't blame yourself, my love.' Her voice was quiet and calming. 'It was circumstances, or...' She paused and stared into the flames, watching them weave and dance like the mist did on the mountain. 'Or fate, perhaps.'

That night, their lovemaking was more profound. That frantic tearing at each other, with the desperation of lust and desire, was over. Now the act was performed with a tenderness and awareness of giving, as well as receiving, pleasure, which first aroused and then satisfied as neither of them had known before. Drained, they slept deeply, and awoke still in each other's arms.

In the cold morning light, John lay, thinking over the events of the last days. He had never been so completely happy and wanted to feel like this for the rest of his life. It was so wonderful that it was frightening. How could this exquisite girl want him? His heart started to beat erratically as waves of doubt swept over him, and he had to know.

'Is it as good for you as it is for me?' he asked, his voice stupidly hoarse, like a teenager's.

'Of course,' Lark murmured, her eyes closed as she felt John's hands beginning to curl nervously around her small bottom. 'Very good.'

He swallowed and opened his eyes to look at her. 'Just, very good?' He was appalled.

She giggled. 'Well, perhaps more than that. I'd say ... very nice.'

He knew she was teasing him and pretended to laugh, but the doubts remained. *Oh Christ,* he thought, *does she mean it?*

'You are truly the most exciting lover I've ever had.' Suddenly, her clear voice cut across his thoughts. 'I have never been happier.'

He drew away from her and propped himself up on one elbow so that he could look at her. She was totally lovely, her red-gold hair bright against the white pillowcase, and her beautifully strange eyes wide open. And it was when he gazed into them, he was finally convinced that she meant what she'd said. They were a soft hazel, the colour of cinnamon, and in this mode, incapable of untruth. She was, at that moment, utterly mortal and his. Tears came into his eyes and she reached up and kissed them, licking the salt greedily as though it were necessary to her very existence. He was transported again and quickly took her, this time hearing her wild call and being thrilled by it.

Later that morning, when they were examining the sheep and lambs in the fields, she took his hand and squeezed it. 'I can't believe I'm so happy,' she said quietly. 'I haven't done enough to deserve it.'

John grinned. 'How old are you?'

'Twenty-eight, twenty-nine sometime in April.'

'Sometime?'

'I told you. I was found. They estimated my birth date. My party was always the same day as Shakespeare's. Dad liked that.'

He nodded. 'Yes, yes. But what I was going to say was, you are too young to have done many "deserving" things. You have most of your life ahead of you.'

She smiled. 'And it will be spent here with you.'

The wind blew hard across the field and the flock sheltered in the lee of the stone wall. A few early daffodil stalks were showing through the poor grass around the edge of the field and John remembered how he used to pick some for Mam to put in a jug on the kitchen table. He would pick some for Helen, next month; she would like that.

They were checking the lambs' navels and painting them with disinfectant when Robert joined them in the field.

'Hello, boy,' he said, clapping John on the shoulder, and gave Lark a friendly nod. 'Lark, love, you're looking very well.' She really was, he realised, as he continued to stare at her. It was as if she had grown younger and softer. Almost girlish. He looked from her to John but his friend was on his knees examining a ewe.

'Take a look at this; it looks infected. What d'you think?' John was holding the wool away from the sheep's rear end and Robert and Lark bent down to look.

With the practised hands of an experienced shepherd, Robert took a firm but careful grasp of the restless sheep. 'Keep still, you bloody half-wit,' he muttered and parted the wool to examine an abscess growing in a vulval tear. 'Nasty!' he said, whistling in disgust. 'I'd get hold of the vet, if I were you. You'll lose her if you're not careful.'

John straightened up. 'OK. I suppose I'd better separate her and her lambs from the rest.'

'I'll do that,' said Lark, 'while you go and phone the vet.'

Robert noted the look that passed between them before he and John turned to walk back to the farm. *Oh hell,* he thought, *there* is *something going on.*

In the distance he could hear a phone ringing; it was the outside bell in the farmyard.

'I must get a cell phone,' John said. 'I keep missing calls.' He looked at Robert's belt where a phone nestled in a leather holster. 'Yeah,' he nodded, 'that's what I gotta have.'

Lydia sighed and put the phone down. She was in a hotel near Manchester airport, where she had booked a room for a few hours to freshen up and organise a rental car. She could never get through to John, and she had wanted to tell him that she had arrived in the UK and would be making her way first to the hospital in Bangor and then to Cariad Elin. *Damn him,* she thought angrily, *he'll just have to be surprised.*

Chapter Thirty-Three

Matthew sat in the day room of his ward, looking miserably out of the window. The view was depressing: the hospital car park in driving rain. He watched vehicles come and go, their tyres splashing over the uneven, though new, tarmac and wished he was in one of them, driving away from Bangor forever. It was nearly three months since he'd been admitted, and despite Dad promising to get him out, he was still here. Of course, it was only two days since he'd spoken to him, but not a word from him today or yesterday, and Matthew was utterly fed up.

Lovely little Dr Monk had moved on to another hospital, her job at Bangor over. She had visited once in the month since her transfer, slipping into the ward late at night and leaning over his bed, just as he was drifting off to sleep. Unfortunately, it was when he was feeling low after the virus which had given him pneumonia, and he could barely manage a friendly greeting.

'Hi,' was his grumpy response to her kiss, 'what the hell are you doing here?'

With this less than affectionate response to her visit, Dr Monk began to regret driving nearly two tundred miles, and although Malt struggled up onto his pillows and attempted to banter as usual, she was suddenly put off. *He's only a kid,* she thought, embarrassed now at the memory of the flirting and snatched kisses in which they had indulged over Christmas. She hadn't visited again and Matthew had forgotten about her.

He did think occasionally about Lark. His most striking experiences during his time in North Wales had usually been with her. He remembered the summer in the mountains, those warm, sparkling days when they had wandered on the hills, stopping now and then to lie together on the stubby grass. The rain drizzling on the hospital-room window now reminded him of an afternoon when they had swam in the deep, dark water of the disused quarry. She had been like a fish, gliding and turning, diving into the glittering pool ahead of him and then reappearing behind him in a splashing fountain of diamond drops. He had shown off, too, swimming powerfully across the length of shining water several times, until they had climbed out onto the rocky sides of the quarry, exhausted, and lain on a flat rock to let the sun dry their naked bodies. *Boy,* he thought now, his handsome face creasing into a grin, *that was great.*

But the grin faded as he recalled her attitude later on. She had tried to boss him around, he decided; that was why their relationship had soured. And she had started to behave as if the farm was hers rather than his, always reminding him to do things and disapproving if he went out with Griff Parry. Anyone would think she was his mother, not a girlfriend.

'Matthew!' A nurse had come into the room but he didn't bother to turn round. It was midafternoon and she would be bringing him his tea.

'Yeah,' he said with a sigh, 'I guess you could put it on the table. I'll stay here.'

Another, sharper voice answered, 'I'll put you on the table if you don't come here and give your poor little ma a big hug.'

'Ma?' He swivelled in his chair and looked up. It was true; she was there, small, expensively perfumed and elegantly dressed, with her arms open to greet him. He struggled up, clumsily levering his crutches, but she hurried across the room, tip-tapping swiftly in her high heels until she was at his side with her arms around him. He could have wept with relief. Now everything would be all right. Ma would get things moving.

'Jesus, this place is like a prison camp!' Lydia said when he was back in bed and she was sitting lightly on the covers. She had wrinkled her nose at the prospect of a cup of hospital tea, and inspected the walls and floors of the ward, all new in the last few years, and declared them dreadful.

'Oh, Ma, it's great to see you.' Matthew settled back on his pillows, listening happily as she brought him up to date with all the gossip from back home.

'People have asked after you, oh, so many I can't name them all. I met that girl – what's her name – Melanie? You know, Judge Fenton's daughter. She was very keen to hear about you.'

'Melody,' he joined in with a grin. 'That's her name.'

'Yeah, well, her. Pretty girl, now working as a buyer for a chain of boutiques. You could do a lot

328

worse than her.' She leant forward and straightened the collar of his pyjamas and brushed the flop of thick blond hair off his forehead, just like she had when he was her little boy. The accident had left him pale and weak-looking, and it was taking all her powers of self-restraint not to gather him in her arms to cuddle him as she'd done when he was a child. If only she'd known, he would have loved her to.

'Now,' she said, her grin a faithful reflection of his, 'how do we get you out of this gulag?'

Matthew burst out laughing. 'Oh Ma,' he gasped, 'you're priceless.'

At Cariad Elin the rain was pouring. It fell steadily from a low, dense cloud which swamped the farm and hid the mountain from view. The puddles in the yard were filling and elongating until, after the second hour of relentless downpour, they had joined together into one lake of rainwater. John could remember nothing like it. He stood in the doorway of the large barn they'd used for the lambing shed and watched as the water washed down the muddy drive, wondering if he should bring the sheep and new lambs in from the meadow. He might lose some of them otherwise, and he didn't think he could bear that.

As he stood, debating with himself, he saw Lark trudging across from the house, high-stepping with her long legs as she waded through the streams of water.

'What's it like in the house?' he said as soon as she reached him.

'It's OK. Whoever built it took care to put it on some higher ground. The water is running past, thank God.'

John looked at the sky, searching for signs of the cloud moving away, but it was as dark and full as it had been all afternoon and promised several more hours of rain.

'Should we bring the sheep in?' he asked. 'The lambs might get washed down to the river if this keeps up.'

She followed his eyes up to the cloud cover. Her face was wet and strands of bronze hair were plastered to her head where they had escaped from the hood of her soaked jacket. She was wet through. In another, urban, society, this would not be work for a woman – nor for a man, for that matter, John suddenly realised, and chuckled. Hill farms were no respecters of people.

'Yes, I think we'd better; it doesn't seem to be stopping.' She looked at him, noticing the smile. 'What? What are you laughing at?'

'Oh, it's nothing, *cariad*.' He smiled again and reached out a hand to brush the raindrops from her cheek. 'I was just deciding that this is no way to treat a lady.'

'I ain't no lady!' Lark laughed and carried on with the quote, 'I'm your...' Her voice died away as she realised what she was saying.

'Wife.' He finished the saying for her and she bit her lip and stared at him briefly before pulling the strings of her hood tighter and stepping into the yard.

'Come on,' she said, 'we'd better get going.'

They were glad they had made the decision

when they reached the field. The lower pasture by the river was already under water and the sheep had gathered by the gate on the higher ground and were milling about anxiously. The lambs were bleating as they kept slipping on the rain-slicked mud and getting squashed beneath the heavier bodies of the adult flock.

John opened the gate and Lark got in behind the sheep and began to urge them out. That part was not difficult – the sheep were somehow aware of the danger and moved eagerly out of the field. Herding them into the yard where the lake was forming was harder. The water was getting deep, up to the flanks of the lambs, and they were frightened and reluctant to move. It took all John and Lark's efforts to persuade the ewes to cross over towards the barn, the sound of their calls and whistles being drowned out by the wind and rain. But before setting out, John had strewn hay and feeding pellets on the barn floor, and eventually the lead ewe smelt them and trotted hesitantly into the shelter, followed by her drenched and shivering infants. And as was their nature, the rest followed.

It had taken two hours to successfully move the flock and John and Lark were exhausted. For a moment they stood and watched the steam rising from the soaked wool backs to disappear into the dark roof of the barn. They watched the lambs snuggle up to their mothers to feed, their little stumps of tails waggling in pleasure, and knew that they had been right to bring them in, no matter how difficult it had been.

Eventually, John said, 'They're OK now, let's go

in,' and they splashed through the water back to the house and fell gratefully through the door into the warm and welcoming kitchen. There was a pan of soup pushed to the back of the range and Lark pulled it onto the hot plate before stripping off her outer clothes. Upstairs, John found them dry sweaters and trousers and brought them down so that they could change in front of the fire.

They were drinking soup and tearing hungrily at a loaf when the phone rang. John groaned and got to his feet.

'I bet that's Robert telling us that the road is flooded. And hey, save me another bowl of soup,' he added over his shoulder as he went into the hall and picked up the receiver. 'Yes, Cariad Elin, John Williams speaking.'

At the other end of the line, Lydia looked up from the payphone and punched her fist slowly into the air. She mouthed, 'At last. He's answered,' to Matthew, who was leaning on his crutches beside her.

'Hi, John,' she said brightly, 'it's me.'

'Lydia, honey, how are you?' John looked back at Lark and raised his eyes to the ceiling. 'How's the weather back home?'

She laughed. 'It was cold yesterday, but today I wouldn't know.' She paused, savouring the moment. 'I'm not there.'

'What? Another vacation already?' John didn't try to keep the sarcasm out of his voice. *Jesus,* he thought, *here's me and Lark struggling to keep this farm going in God-awful weather and she's swanning off again.* 'Where this time?'

'Surprise, surprise, sweetheart!' Her voice was colder than the endearment suggested. 'I'm in Bangor, at the hospital, with Matthew!'

He closed his eyes and leant his head wearily against the banister spindles. A stream of bitter nausea swept up his gullet and threatened to choke him and he coughed, desperately trying to clear his throat. 'What?' he gasped.

'I've come over to see Matt,' she said, 'and just as well that I have, he looks dreadful. It's obvious that he hasn't been taken care of properly.'

She smiled at Matt and shook her head, showing him that she didn't really mean that. He grinned. Ma in a temper was fun. 'How could you have let him be so badly treated?' she added.

'Jesus, Lydia, he hasn't been. He's in an up-to-date, modern hospital. He's had the best of attention.'

'I don't care, anyway.' She spoke quickly, ignoring his defence of the NHS. 'I'm taking him home.'

'When?' John felt dizzy. She was moving too fast, not giving him time to think.

'Saturday.'

'But that's only three days away. You can't. They won't be able to arrange it in time.'

'Crap! I've arranged everything. He's flying home with me Saturday and being admitted for assessment to the orthopaedic ward at the university hospital. My surgeon, Joe Bithell, is going to look after him.'

John listened to her helplessly. She had taken over and there was nothing he could do. He

333

glanced back at Lark. She was sitting at the table, her soup spoon halfway between the bowl and her mouth, her face troubled as she listened to the one-sided conversation. *My beautiful, beautiful Helen*, he thought, *how can I protect you from Lydia?*

He swallowed. 'We'd better talk,' he said slowly. 'There's a lot of catching up to do.'

'Yeah, you can say that again.' It was her turn to be sarcastic. 'I'm leaving here in a minute; someone will give me directions to the farm.'

'You can't come here!' The words were out of his mouth before he had time to think. 'I mean, it's just not right for you. You would loathe it. No, I can't let you come.' His voice rose in desperation, and at the other end of the line, Lydia's heart began to sink. He sounded drunk.

'Matt told me it's kinda primitive out there,' she said, 'but I guess I can rough it for a couple of nights.'

John struggled to take command of the situation. He must stop her coming to Cariad Elin; he wasn't ready to explain.

'The road is out,' he said, suddenly finding the perfect excuse. 'We've got a flood here. It's rained for a couple of days ... there's no way in and no way out.'

'I don't believe you.' She was furious now, recognising the fobbing off.

'It's true, I promise you. Isn't it raining in Bangor? I bet it is.' He had a flash of inspiration. 'Ask one of the nurses; they'll tell you that the road that goes out here is flooded. The river has burst its bank.'

There was silence as she considered this last. It was raining heavily in Bangor and had been since she arrived, so maybe he was telling the truth. And she was tired. The emotional meeting with Matthew, as well as jet lag, was catching up with her and she needed a hotel room with a bed and a shower far more than a fight with her drunken husband.

'OK. I'll book in to a hotel here tonight and get back to you tomorrow.' She put down the receiver before he had time to answer, leaving him staring stupidly at the silent handpiece, quite unable to think of his next move.

He walked back to the kitchen and sat down heavily in the leather chair by the fire. His bowl of soup was left on the table – his appetite had disappeared.

'She's arrived,' he said, not looking up but staring into the flames.

'I gathered.' Lark picked up the ignored soup bowl and spoon and brought it to him, but he shook his head and she put it down on the hearth and sat in the rocking chair beside him.

'It won't change anything, I promise.' John looked up and leant over to take her hand. 'I'll see her tomorrow and tell her.'

'Tell her what?'

'That I'm leaving her. That I'm going to be with you for the rest of my life.'

Lark listened to the wind howling in the chimney and shivered. Things were going to change again.

Chapter Thirty-Four

The rain which had drummed all night on the corrugated roofs of the old sheds eased off as dawn broke. Lark, who was lying awake beside her sleeping lover, listened wearily to the silence. She had been awake most of the night and was very tired. Only yesterday, before Lydia's call, she had been happily content. All the pieces of a jigsaw with which she had been struggling most of her life had finally fallen into place. There would hitches and difficulties, she accepted that; the situation was complicated. But at last things were right. Cariad Elin was where she had to be and John was the man she must be with.

She looked across at him as he slept and then turned her head away again towards the window. Even on the very coldest of nights, she liked to sleep with the curtains open. It was as if she needed to be close to the outside, to have the moon, stars or clouds a part of her consciousness, even when her eyes were shut. Now, as night drifted away, she could see the first grey and yellow streaks of light brightening the heavy sky. The rain had stopped for now but Lark knew that there would be more before the day was out. She thought briefly about her hens, but they were safely away in the barn and she had no worries about the sheep.

John moved heavily and rolled towards her. His

face, relaxed in sleep, was calm and unlined, almost, she thought, as young as the dark-haired soldier in the sepia photograph in the parlour. He was Geraint's young uncle, she discovered, killed on the Somme before he was twenty.

'I was named for him,' John had said when they had looked at the picture together. 'To please my grandmother.' He studied the photo again. 'I guess I used to look like him.'

'And you still do,' Lark said softly to the sleeping form and tenderly stroked the grey hair, grown longer these days, from the peaceful face. John grunted in his sleep but soon the even breathing returned and Lark turned her eyes back to the creeping dawn. She thought about the mountain. It had been weeks since she had been up there, and now, suddenly, she wanted desperately to go.

In a swift movement, she was out of bed. The room was cold and she hopped quietly from foot to foot as she pulled on corduroy trousers and thick socks. John didn't hear her leave the room, or even the back door slam in a sudden gust of wind as she hurried out of the house.

The air was sharp and fragrant with the scent of the sea borne in on the overnight rain. To her relief, she found that the water in the yard was draining away, the lake disappearing almost as quickly as it had been formed. *The field will be better too, by the end of the day,* she thought, *and everything will be back to normal.* But of course, it wouldn't. Things had changed again.

She breathed hard as she climbed up the hillside. The ground was soggy and in places dangerously slippery after the torrential rain of the last few days. Even the sheep track which she normally followed had been washed away in places, leaving patches of loose scree, which moved frighteningly beneath her boots. Suddenly, she fell, her feet sliding away from the uncertain ground, and she tumbled helplessly over pasture and rocks until her flailing hands caught hold of a ledge of slate and she came to rest in a crevice. For a moment she lay there, winded and imagining how a broken back or maybe a fractured leg might feel. How would she bear the loss of freedom?

Cautiously she started moving her limbs, waiting for a sudden stab of pain or loss of sensation. But miraculously, nothing hurt, and breathing a sigh of relief, she scrambled slowly and awkwardly to her feet and looked up to the summit. It was covered in lacy grey cloud, lit from the east with painted streaks of a pale and washed-out yellow. Gusts of wind were moving it, changing the shapes like a kaleidoscope, and now, as the sun rose over the horizon, shafts of silvery light pierced through. It was entrancing and magical and called to her as nothing else in the whole world could.

She abandoned the track and took to the hillside, climbing heavily through soaking tufts of spiky grass and heather. It was madness, she knew that, almost the stupidest thing she had ever done, but she was unable to stop herself. She had to get to the top.

From the farmyard John watched her, a small figure moving on the hillside. He had woken some time after she'd left, alone in the bed and missing her. The kitchen was empty and the barn contained only sheep and her hens, who were roosting restlessly on the rails of the sheep pens. He stood for a moment looking at the sheep, and then a sudden, frightening thought occurred to him, and with his heart pumping, he turned and ran out of the barn towards the car. It was there. She was still on the farm, somewhere.

He knew then where she would be, his Helen, his magical love, and forced his eyes to look up, scanning the distant hillside until he saw her.

'Oh God,' he breathed. The wind from the west was increasing, tugging at his clothes and blowing so fiercely that he felt dizzy and light-headed, and idiotic notions whirled in his brain. She was going to her sisters; she was leaving him. And as he wailed these thoughts, the wind snatched his words away and tossed them carelessly round the mountains so that he thought he'd only imagined speaking.

After a while, the panic subsided and he stood, dully watching. She had always been her own person, she'd told him that. He would never be able to control her, so it would be his lot in life now to be glad that she loved him and not ask for more. He looked closely again. The clouds were blowing away and the peak was clearly visible and gleaming in the weak, early morning sun. She was there, standing by the ledge and gazing towards the sea, but as he continued to stare, he saw her turn and look down towards the farm. She was looking for him, he was positive, and he lifted his arms towards the mountain and waved slowly.

'See me, oh, see me, *cariad*. I'm waiting here for you.' He didn't shout, but spoke quietly to himself, convinced that she could hear him if she wanted to. The relief he felt when a small arm was raised in reply was almost sickening, and he had to move quickly to the fence so he could lean against it.

She came down to the farm an hour later, her legs and lower body soaked and muddy from her climb. Her shoulder and the side of her face were beginning to ache and she suspected that she had hurt herself when she had fallen. But her lungs were full of sparkling mountain air and her whole body felt alive and throbbing.

John was waiting for her by the mountain gate and took her in his arms to help her over. They stood, arms wrapped round each other, he absurdly grateful for her return and she revitalised from her climb and reassured of her role at Cariad Elin.

'Please don't frighten me like that again,' he begged later as they turned the sheep into the yard.

She shook her head. 'I didn't mean to, I just needed to get away and think. Somehow everything becomes crystallised up there. I know now where I'm going.' She picked up a lamb which had climbed onto a pile of logs and was bleating frantically on discovering it couldn't get down. Its small heart was beating wildly and an anxious ewe nosed about Lark's legs until she put the little one down. It dived under its mother's heavy

340

body, urgently seeking the reassurance of the udder.

'Where are you going?' Fear began to curdle again in his stomach.

'Nowhere.' She grinned. 'I was speaking metaphorically. I mean, I know what I want to do.' She put her hand gently onto his face. 'I want to stay here with you. Forever.'

He swallowed as relief surged through him. All the other problems that would flow from this relationship were as nothing. They could be solved. All that mattered was here, surrounding him, and most of all, she was standing beside him.

Lydia arrived at the hospital before nine o'clock, stepping gracefully into the ward as the cleaners started their daily round of mopping and polishing. She drew admiring looks from staff and patients alike as she walked towards Matthew's room, her high-heeled shoes making little sound on the plastic floor but a charming waft of perfume leaving a trail behind her.

'Good morning, Mrs Williams,' said Sister as Lydia passed her in the corridor. 'Did you sleep well?'

Lydia had slept fitfully. She had found an excellent hotel, quite up to her usual standards, and had dined well on locally caught fish. Afterwards, worn out from the flight and the shock of seeing Matthew so pale and crippled, she had dropped into bed and slept restlessly for a few hours. Then, in the small hours, she found herself awake again and went into the bathroom.

She felt cold and had a headache and groped sleepily through her vanity case until she found some aspirin. It was an hour later when she returned to her bed, wrapped in the complimentary white bathrobe, and dropped off to sleep again. Reception, following her instructions, had called her promptly at seven o'clock, and she had got out of bed heavy with sleep but determined to get on with the business of Matthew's repatriation.

In the hotel dining room, she had picked at breakfast, only eating a little bowl of fruit and drinking several cups of black coffee. It tasted sour and she regretted eating so much of last night's fish. She felt heavy and exhausted again and the effort to appear her usual self was almost too much.

But she was determined to take charge. She would speak again to the doctors, organise Matthew's flight and the care necessary for him on the plane, but most of all, she would see John and get their lives back on track.

'Hi, sweetheart,' she said, walking into Matthew's room and giving him a warm kiss.

Matthew was dressed in tracksuit bottoms and a T-shirt and lying on top of the made bed. He looked up with a grin when his mother came into the room and took hold of the overhead chain to give himself a heave up. 'Ma!' he said. 'You're here early. What was it? Uncomfortable bed? Crappy hotel? Not up to your usual standard?'

Lydia's grin mirrored her son's. The cleaner who had popped into the room to replace

Matthew's water jug and glass, looked from one to the other. 'My word,' she burst out, 'like peas in a pod, you two. I'd know this was your mam, *cariad*.' And she laughed, repeating her words in Welsh to the nurse who had come into the room. The nurse said something back and they both went into gales of laughter. Lydia looked at them in astonishment and then raised her eyebrows at Matthew, wanting him to explain.

'It's no good, Ma,' he said, shaking his head helplessly. 'I don't understand much Welsh. Just the odd word here and there.' He grabbed hold of the nurse who was attempting to take his temperature and squeezed her round the waist.

'Go on, Nerys, tell us what you were saying. I know you were talking about us.'

The nurse giggled again. 'It was nothing, Matthew. We were just saying how like your mam you are.' She wasn't going to let on the remark made about John's involvement in Matthew's conception. There was nothing Welsh in this boy's face.

'Jesus!' said Lydia, clucking her tongue impatiently when they were alone again. 'I couldn't put up with all this.'

'It's all right, Ma, you get used to it.'

'Anyway. I'm going to see your father now. Maybe he'll be in a more helpful mood this morning.' She looked impatiently around the room and then at Matthew's bedside locker. 'Have you got a notepad or something in there, to draw me a map of how to get there?'

For a moment Matthew didn't move but then, reluctantly, he reached down and opened the

343

door of the cupboard. Lydia followed his hand as it took hold of a small drawing pad and watched with surprise as he straightened up and put it on the bed in front of him.

'Is this yours?' she said, surprised. 'Are you drawing now?'

'I guess so, a bit. You get bored here. Dad got me the paper and pencils.'

Lydia reached for the pad and opened it. If she had been surprised before, now she was doubly so. As she turned each page of the drawing block, pictures of hospital life were revealed to her: nurses making beds and adjusting drip chambers; doctors standing in a huddle gazing at an X-ray, one of them pointing to a particular place on the image, the drawing executed so realistically that she could almost hear them talking.

'Matthew, honey,' she breathed, 'these are wonderful. I didn't know you could do work like this.' And she turned over a page and gazed at a study of a patient, eyes closed in a hollow face, his cracked lips slackly open, a ribbon of saliva stringed between them.

'I just started, Ma. Dad gave me a few hints, although he said he knew nothing about this sort of work.' He blushed. 'I like doing it, though.' He shifted nervously in the bed. 'D'you think I could do this as a career? I guess I've been thinking about it.'

Lydia was careful. She had planned Matthew's future with Fred Eland at the law firm. There would be plenty of dollars there, and with Fred having no son, well, who knew, Matthew could at least get a partnership. But on the other hand, things with Fred weren't too sweet now and it would be as well to have a fallback plan.

'I don't know, honey, we'll have to think about it. You've got plenty of time while you're convalescing, and in the meantime, I can contact a few people who'll know better than us. Now,' she put on her businesslike face, 'draw me the goddam map.'

Chapter Thirty-Five

Griff Parry was in his usual place behind the bar that lunchtime when Lydia walked in. He had the local newspaper spread out on the bar and was closely studying the lonely hearts column. It was his favourite page and he read it assiduously every week, never replying to any of the adverts but going over and over the descriptions of the women, and imagining them in the flesh. At this moment, he was considering 'Petite lady in middle thirties, g.s.o.h., no ties, looking for fun-loving companion under fifty, for outings, restaurants and theatre. Must be up for anything!' It was this last sentence which was so intriguing. 'Anything' – did it denote anything in terms of cultural entertainment? Sports? Types of food? Or could it be a sexual connotation? Oh, he did hope so.

'Are you Griff Parry?' Lydia didn't waste time on greetings. Matthew had told her to go to the pub; it was easier than drawing her a map and he knew that Griff would be happy to show her the way to Cariad Elin. Lydia liked the idea too. It would mean that she could just turn up at the farm, without first having to phone John and be fobbed off with one of his lame excuses.

'Yes.' Griff looked up slowly from his newspaper. He'd heard the shoes clicking across the wooden floor but assumed that it was one of his lunchtime regulars, Beti Rowlands from the shop. She liked to take a vodka and tonic and sit in the window seat so that she could keep an eye on her store. The 'closed' sign would be up and most villagers knew better than to try shopping between the hours of twelve and one, but there were always the reps and the odd visitors who might call.

But it wasn't Beti. It was a petite, young middle-aged woman who was so attractive that she could be 'up for anything'. His loose mouth dropped open and a tiny dribble of saliva ran from the corner of his lips. 'Yes,' he repeated, taking his handkerchief out of his pocket and running it quickly across his mouth. 'I am. Can I help you?'

'I'm Lydia Williams, Matthew's mother. I'm hoping that you will show me the way to his property.' She gave him her most charming smile, displaying those perfect teeth, so like her son that Griff was left in no doubt that she was indeed who she said she was. He reached over the bar and took her small gloved hand in an enthusiastic shake.

'Very nice to meet you, Mrs Williams, I'm sure.

Yes – indeed. Very nice.' He called over his shoulder to Llinos whom he could hear coming down the stairs into the kitchen. 'Llinos, *cariad*, come and see who's here.'

It was Llinos who took Lydia into the room behind and offered her a drink from their own cabinet. She had calculated the cost of Lydia's pale cashmere coat with the fur collar and the leather boots, gloves and handbag. Beneath the long coat Lydia wore black wool slacks and an oatmeal-coloured silk blouse. Everything was of the best quality and taste and Llinos squirrelled away the memory for later use, when she should have a similar disposable income.

'Let me get you some lunch,' she offered, eager for Lydia to stay a while and impart information.

'Um ... well, that is kind. Just something light, if you don't mind.' Lydia was dubious. The food in this country pub could be horrible, maybe an oval plate loaded with meat and French fries, just the sort of food she loathed. She would never be able to eat it and would have to push it around the plate while making difficult conversation. So the sight and taste of dainty prawn baps garnished with crisp salad came as a huge relief.

'Thank you,' she said, finishing the last piece of bread and draining her second gin and tonic. 'That was delicious.'

Llinos brought a tray of coffee and sat down at the kitchen table opposite Lydia. The pub was busy now and she could hear various people enquiring about the strange car outside. 'Got a visitor,' she heard Griff say.

'I guess you know Matthew quite well,' said Lydia.

Llinos nodded. 'Oh yes. He's a nice boy. We both like him. You know that my Griff and Matthew are partners – in the sheep, like.'

'Yes, he told me.' Lydia picked up her cup and took a delicate sip. 'I'm taking Matthew home on Saturday. He can't manage here now, so it's the only thing to do. He'll have the best of care and then, I hope, he'll continue his course at college.'

Llinos hid her rising excitement. Did this mean that Matthew's sojourn in Wales was over and that the farm would be up for sale? A wave of deserved triumphalism came over her. This was what she had predicted when she had counselled Griff to be patient. Of course, she hadn't foreseen the accident, but that was incidental. Matthew was never going to stay.

'Oh,' she said, leaning forward and offering Lydia another cup of coffee. 'What a shame, we'll all miss him.' Then, after a pause, she said, 'What about Cariad Elin? What'll he do with the stock?'

Lydia shook her head and smiled her sweet smile. 'I've no idea, but that's one of the things I'm going to talk about with John. I expect he'll have some thoughts.'

Griff came through into the kitchen. He had been keeping an ear on the conversation and had gathered most of what had been said and was now getting excited. This was a perfect time to buy the farm. The market was depressed and with Matthew ready to leave, he could get it for a song.

'I'll take you out there whenever you're ready, Mrs Williams,' he said.

'I'm sure I can find my way, if you'll just give me a little map.' She positively knew she didn't want to sit in the same vehicle as that man.

Griff was equally determined. He wouldn't miss the meeting between Lydia and John for anything. If his suspicions about what was going on at Cariad Elin were correct, then who knew what might happen? He longed to see the exchange between John and Lydia and watch the effect on Lark. It was well past time that she got her comeuppance. *Jesus*, he thought, *the prospect is definitely too good to miss.*

A wolfish smile spread over his face, contrasting oddly with his wobbling jowls. Lydia swallowed nervously. What on earth could Matt see in him? she wondered.

Griff cast a swift glance at Llinos, wondering if she had said anything about the girl. It would seem not, for Lydia, although she was now tapping her manicured nails irritatingly on the deal table, still spoke calmly, talking about her husband as though they were on perfectly aligned wavelengths.

'Shall we go in my car?' Griff picked up the keys from the table. 'The weather has been bloody awful and the road is still flooded in places. I don't think your rented car will make it.'

Lydia sighed. Despite her distaste at the notion of being his passenger, he was right. But she resented the feeling that she was being manoeuvred, and she sensed some undercurrent that she couldn't quite identify. She looked hopefully at Llinos, wondering if there was some way that she could persuade her to be the guide, or at the very least, to accompany them. But Llinos was already clearing away the lunch and going towards the bar to take over from Griff. She preferred to avoid confrontation.

'After you, Mrs Williams.' Griff waved his arm towards the archway which led into the bar. Gathering up her purse and gloves, Lydia walked out past the few drinkers and Llinos, who parted her small mouth in a careful smile and wished her goodbye. Griff couldn't resist looking over his shoulder back at his wife. He grinned foolishly, trying to impart his feeling of the success of their mission, but Llinos didn't look. Her mind was already several steps ahead, preparing for the sale.

The early afternoon was already darkening and scuds of rain dashed through the valley, carried on a clumsy west wind. John had looked anxiously at the sky as he moved the sheep back to the field. If it was going to pour again, then it would be madness to put them back in the same dangerous conditions. He grumbled mentally yet again about the lack of drainage in the fields and worked out a method of doing it. It would have to be completed before next winter or they would be in the same situation again.

The sheep trotted eagerly across the yard now that the water had dispersed, the lambs gambolling alongside, impervious today to the slight rain. They were happy to be out of the barn. John watched them, looking for any problems, but all seemed well and he was pleased with their progress. Next autumn he would buy a quality ram – perhaps he and Lark could go to some of the shows and have a good look round before making a decision. But he was sure that it would be a sensible thing to do.

The invidious section of his brain which kept reminding him that Cariad Elin wasn't his and that he should get back to his proper work, he chose to ignore. He was happy now, and frightened to contemplate moves that might spoil this feeling of pure joy. Dealing with Lydia and Matthew could be difficult but he would put his mind to that, maybe tomorrow, then after they'd gone he and Lark could get back to their life together. 'Yes,' he said to the last, would-be escapee lamb as he pushed it into the field and swung the heavy gate closed behind the flock, 'I'll sort out Lydia tomorrow.'

Lark was in the bath. Steam from the hot water filled the small room and she lay back, luxuriating in the scented bubbles as they washed away the mud and warmed up her body after the climb on the mountain. Her shoulder felt sore and she screwed her head round to look at it. A livid bruise was growing across it and down the side of her arm. Gingerly, she touched it and quickly took her fingers away as pain shot through the muscle and radiated down to her fingers.

'I think I've pulled ligaments or something in

my shoulder,' she said to John when he came into the bathroom with a mug of tea.

He knelt down and took her arm in his hands. 'Whatever have you done to yourself?' he said, kissing her before gently manipulating her arm and shoulder up and down. She winced; it was painful but it appeared that nothing was broken. John stood up and looked in the little mirrored cabinet. He found a bottle of aspirin and put two tablets into her mouth and gave her the tea to wash them down. 'That'll help,' he said, 'and when you get out, it might be a good idea to put it in a sling for a few days.'

Lark smiled and shook her head doubtfully. 'We'll see about that.' She looked up at John. He was standing by the mirror, his face troubled, still remembering the fright he'd had earlier when he thought she'd left him. 'Come in here with me.' She grinned and moved her long legs to one side, leaving room for him to join her in the soapy water.

For a moment John hesitated. It had been years since he'd shared a bath with someone and suddenly he felt shy, remembering the difference in age between them.

'Come on,' she urged, putting on a sexy voice, 'I can show you a nice time, sailor!'

He laughed then and started tearing off his clothes, and within seconds was in the bath with her, shouting excitedly as the water slopped over the side. 'You know that you're a temptress,' he said, leaning forward and drawing his soapy hands across her body, 'you've cast a spell on me.'

She giggled quietly, busy with her own hands under the water where his urgency for her could be felt, engorged and ready to be guided towards her eager body. 'It's a mutual spell,' she murmured, 'we've both been enchanted.'

Their union was clumsy but utterly thrilling, reaching heights neither had realised existed and leaving them once again in a state of exhausted exhilaration.

'Oh, Helen,' John muttered after they had climbed out of the tub and sat, wrapped in towels, on the damp floor, 'you are unbelievable.'

'I'm just a woman,' she said simply. 'Your woman.'

The road to Cariad Elin was indeed flooded in parts and the embankment above the ditch had collapsed in places, allowing rivers of water and mud to cover the road. Lydia, looking at it from the high passenger seat in Griff's Land Rover, admitted to herself that he had been right. She would never have negotiated this road in the little rented car, map or no map. The flurry of rain had passed over the valley but the wind which had brought it in so swiftly was blowing for more. In fact, the wind was fast becoming the most problematic climatic condition of the afternoon. Every now and then, when they emerged round a bend into an area cleared of trees, a gust would make the car wobble and Lydia, casting a swift look at her driver, noticed him folding his lips in concern and pulling nervously on his ridiculous moustache.

'Wind's getting up a bit,' he said unnecessarily,

'can be bad in this valley, this time of year.'

'Why on earth would anyone want to live in this God-awful place?' The words came out of her mouth in a rush of contempt, and for a moment Griff was taken aback and felt almost insulted.

'Oh, it's very beautiful in the summer,' he said defensively. 'Artists paint it all the time.' But even as he defended the valley, the thought struck him that she would be encouraging Matthew to sell, and he should paint it in a worse light. 'Of course, it's very hard to make a living here. The bloody sheep take more money to feed and look after than you ever get from selling them.'

'So why are you doing it?' Lydia asked pointedly.

'Hobby for me, see. I've got the pub, haven't I?'

She nodded, renewing her determination to get Matthew away from North Wales. John could make all the arrangements about selling the place – these were his people, after all, and he should know who to contact. Then, once back in Toronto, they could get their lives back on track. John could get a new project going – there was plenty of work for him if he wanted it – and Matthew could go back to college and start to make a career for himself. It might not be with Fred Eland now that there had been a little falling out, but Matt was so charming and clever, he would make a living anywhere.

'John is good with the sheep,' Griff's high voice suddenly broke into her plans, 'and so is that Lark.'

Lark. There was that girl's name again. Matthew hadn't mentioned her, so neither had Lydia. Actually she'd forgotten all about her. 'Just who is "Lark"?'

A giggle bubbled in Griff's throat. This was wonderful, but he must play it sensibly. 'Don't you know? Well, I am surprised, I thought Matthew would have told you.'

He negotiated the last bend before Cariad Elin and drew up before the entrance gate. 'She is Matthew's girlfriend, or was. Came to the farm with him last summer. A real hippie, she was then. You could smell her a mile off.'

Lydia's mouth opened in astonishment. Matt with a hippie; that certainly wasn't his style. 'Was, you said, was. Isn't she now?'

Griff jumped down from the car and opened the gate. 'None of my business really,' he said, driving through and then getting out again to close the gate behind him. 'But,' he continued as he drove up the rutted lane, 'she hasn't been to visit him in the hospital for weeks. Still at the farm, though.'

The wind was howling now, blocking out the noise of the engine as they pulled up in front of the house. Griff pushed open his door and struggled round to Lydia's side to help her out. 'I'd better hang on,' he said, shouting above the wind, 'you might need a lift back.' And he directed her towards the back door, holding the soft woollen fabric of her coat at her elbow, his pleasure at the prospect of the meeting almost overwhelming him.

The scene that greeted them, when Griff quietly

355

pushed open the scullery door and ushered Lydia in ahead of him, couldn't have been bettered if he had arranged it.

John and Lark were kneeling face to face in front of the great kitchen fireplace, he tenderly rubbing her damp hair with a towel, their now drying bodies covered in warm robes. Lit only by the rosy glow of the disintegrating logs, they appeared to the startled onlookers like figures from a mediaeval painting, magical, alone and secure. Even when the sharp tip-tap of Lydia's boots struck the quarry-tiled floor their reaction seemed to be made in slow motion. Their heads turned and their pupils, enlarged with desire, gazed uncomprehendingly on the intruders.

But then Lydia's explosive 'Christ!', followed by a grunted snigger from Griff Parry, burst into the room and echoed in John's stomach like an executioner's call. He closed his eyes and waited for the end.

Chapter Thirty-Six

Afterwards Griff couldn't decide whether the actuality of being there was better than the relating of the story. He acted out every part with such relish that the tale he told first to Llinos, and then to anyone who asked, became so embellished that eventually it bore little relationship to the facts.

'You should have been there, Llinos, *cariad*,' he

said, still excited at midnight when they lay in bed waiting for sleep. 'It was like something from the telly.'

His wife, who was hearing the story for the third time, was barely listening. She was calculating the market value of the farm and working out the better prospect – straight sale or auction.

'I really thought John Williams would have a heart attack, but that Lark, well, she never turned a hair. Just got up and left the room.'

If Griff had been allowed to stay inside, he would have seen Lark return, dressed, to the kitchen, but John had peremptorily sent Griff out, to wait in his car. At first, he'd told him to go altogether, that he would take Lydia back to her hotel in Bangor, but Lydia had shouted that she wouldn't go anywhere with him.

'He'll take me,' she'd yelled, pointing at the fat publican whose round black eyes darted this way and that following the volcanic melee.

'Do you mind waiting outside?' John had said in a voice that made it clear that refusal was unacceptable. He had stood by the fire, the brown monk-like robe tied securely around his body, bare feet planted firmly on the rug. His hair was still damp, and now that he wore it longer, beginning to curl at the nape of his neck. Griff thought of the picture that had greeted him and Lydia: the two of them kneeling like penitents and John drying Lark's hair. *They've been in the bath together*, he thought, and a spasm of excitement ran through him as he imagined Lark naked. 'Good God Almighty,' he breathed.

He moved slowly towards the door. 'I'll wait in the car, Mrs Williams,' he said, but she wasn't listening and didn't turn as he made his way to the door. Her eyes were fastened on her husband and her mind was whirling with the implications of the scene she'd just witnessed. *No wonder he didn't want to come home,* she thought bitterly, *he was sleeping with this girl.*

'You're sleeping with her.' It was a statement rather than an accusation and John nodded. Griff paused in the scullery to hear the reply, but before John could speak Lydia's voice rose to a shriek which he was sure he would have heard if he had gone through the back door into the yard.

'You're fucking her,' Lydia yelled, 'you're fucking your son's girlfriend.' And she slammed her purse onto the table with such force that the cups and plates on the dresser jumped and rattled in alarm.

'Hang on,' John put out a hand to calm her but she turned and screamed again.

'She's young enough to be your daughter. A girl, Matt's girl, and you've stolen her. You disgusting old fool. Oh God, how could you?'

This last came out in a wail and John swallowed. He had known that this day and this confrontation would come, but not like this. He had hoped for it to be on neutral ground, or at least at a time when the evidence of his 'crime' would not be so explicit.

'She and Matt were finished.' The words came out limply and he knew they sounded pathetic.

'So you got in quick, eh?' She was sneering

358

now. 'Picking up his leavings.'

It sounded awful, put like that, but how else was he to explain it to her? He looked over to the door and saw Griff was still in the room and eagerly following the exchange.

'I told you to get out.' His voice was bone-chillingly cold, and when Griff hesitated momentarily, John started towards him with such a look of hatred that the fat man grabbed the door latch and dashed out of the house.

Lydia felt suddenly faint, and sat down heavily on one of the kitchen chairs. She had never for one moment suspected anything like this. Not John, her husband who had been unable to satisfy her sexually. The cold, unadventurous architect who barely got worked up over a successful drawing, let alone lovemaking. Tears of rage gathered in the corners of her eyes and started to fall like monsoon raindrops down her white face.

Silently John turned and walked over to the sink. He reached underneath and found the new, unopened bottle of whisky and put it on the table in front of her. Still without a word, he took a glass from the dresser and put that beside the bottle.

'I'm going to get dressed.' He spoke quietly. 'Take a drink.'

She was left alone, weeping, in the large, softly lit kitchen. Daylight was almost gone and black night obscured the small square windows, and she was frightened. 'The bastard,' she cried to herself, 'oh, the bastard.' And with trembling hands she opened the bottle and poured herself a large drink. It slithered down her throat, burning and warming her until it reached her stomach. It made her feel a little sick, but that didn't matter, she almost welcomed it.

Draining the glass, she lifted her head and looked around the room, noting the beams and the rough plastered walls. It was a style, natural here, of course, which interior decorators struggled to effect. The lamps and rug, though cheap, were all perfectly chosen and added to the beauty. It was, she thought with a bitter laugh, a perfect setting for a love affair. Suddenly her eyes fastened onto the photograph on the mantelpiece. She, Matthew and John. A younger, happier family.

When he returned a few minutes later, she was calmer and was pouring herself another. 'Still drinking, I see.' She waved her glass towards the bottle.

'As it happens, no.' He came to sit opposite her and she looked at him properly for the first time since she had walked into the house. He looked well, despite the shock of her arrival, which had obviously shaken him. He was stronger and heavier, his face less drawn and his skin, last year so papery white, now weather-beaten and glowing with good health. Despite his greying hair, he looked younger than when he'd gone away. Almost like he'd been when she'd first met him all those years ago.

'Your hair's longer.' It was as if she had worn herself out, shouting, and now could only converse in trivialities.

'Yes.'

There was a movement behind her and she swivelled in her chair to watch Lark come into the room. Even in her jealousy and rage, part of Lydia could see why men wanted her. She was quite lovely. Tall, slim and now in jeans and a dark sweater, looking strong and capable. The firelight caught the bronze in her hair so that it appeared like a cloud around her face, dancing and magical.

The girl glanced at John and Lydia followed her eyes to see what her husband would do. She wished she hadn't. The look of such aching devotion that John bestowed on Lark pierced a hole in Lydia's stomach, through which the confidence she had gained over the years drained suddenly and dizzily away. She felt alone, out of her depth in this strange and uncomfortable place, and unable even to think clearly.

'Lydia,' John's voice was quiet and almost pleading, 'I'm sorry, truly. I didn't want you to find out like this.'

'How the hell were you going to tell me?' The words spat brokenly from her lips, 'With flowers? Over dinner? What difference does it make?'

She got up, pushing the chair away with a rough scrape. Lark looked at her and then flicked her eyes away to look at the photograph on the mantelpiece. Lydia was different now, older and somehow more knowing, as though the few years between that snap and this terrible afternoon had changed her.

Lydia noticed the glance and shrugged. 'We all change, honey; you will too. And him, as well.' Her laugh was cruel. 'He's getting old and by the

361

time I've finished with him he'll be broke. That's when you'll be on your way.'

'Lydia, don't.' John reached out to take her arm but she shook him off.

'Don't touch me! Don't touch me ever again.' Her voice was rising again and John shrank back. He wanted to talk, to apologise or explain, try to tell her what had come over him, but he couldn't. He didn't understand it himself and if he admitted the truth, he was just as frightened as she was.

'I'm going,' Lydia announced. 'I can't talk to you now, here, with this,' she jerked her head towards Lark, 'this person listening. You'll have to come to my hotel tomorrow.'

John nodded dumbly. A new thought had suddenly occurred to him. Lydia would tell Matthew, and how would he ever be able to face him? *Oh Christ,* he thought, *what have I done?*

As if reading his mind, Lark slid her hand into his and gave it a comforting squeeze. Throughout the entire confrontation she had been silent, a ghost in the performance although she was the main player, and seeing her move closer to John, Lydia turned her wrathful face towards her.

'You've got nothing, honey. You're just a port in a storm, someone to have his nervous breakdown with. When he comes to his senses, he'll dump you. Just like my son did.'

If she felt better for saying this the feeling didn't last long, for Lark moved forward from behind John and spoke to Lydia for the first time. 'He'll never leave me, don't you know that? He can't. And he'll never leave Cariad Elin. This is where we belong.'

Her words, spoken in her clear liquid voice, cut icily through the shadows of the room. Lydia felt the hair on the back of her neck prickle and she stared nervously into the girl's face. She was suddenly struck by her eyes, unnoticed before, which glittered like grey-brown pebbles, granite sharp and petrifying.

Lydia took a step back, struggling to move. 'You're crazy, both of you,' she whispered. Whirling round, she picked up her purse and gloves and almost ran to the door. When she looked back, her hand quivering on the latch, they were standing, fingers still linked, enormous figures blocking out the light from the fire.

'She hardly spoke a word all the way home,' Griff continued that evening, remembering that awful drive back to the village, trying to keep the Land Rover steady in the gale, while the passenger beside him trembled and sobbed out expletives of a type he'd never heard from a woman's lips. 'She wouldn't come in, oh dear no. Just got into her car and tore off on the road to Bangor. I quite expected to hear of an accident.'

'You'd better go and see Matthew tomorrow. See what he's going to do about selling.' Llinos took off her glasses and put down the notebook in which she had been jotting down figures. 'We might be able to get it before it goes up for public sale. That Lydia will probably want to keep things quiet.' She settled down in their bed and closed her eyes. 'Though what on earth you want the trouble of an old hill farm for, I can't imagine. A waste of money, I think.'

She switched off the bedside light, leaving Griff to smile to himself in the dark. 'Oh I wouldn't say that, my little love,' he said, as she started to breathe evenly. 'You don't know the half of what old Griff is planning.'

Lydia wasn't as lucky as Llinos. Sleep wouldn't come to her and she felt sick and shivery as the shock penetrated. She paced the thickly carpeted hotel room, going over in her mind the events of the day until the feeling of nausea she had felt in Cariad Elin began to overwhelm her and she had to go into the bathroom to be sick.

The day had started off so well. She had ignored the mild sensation of jet lag and accepted and enjoyed the admiring looks she'd received during her appearance at the hospital in the morning. It was good to feel smart and pretty and although rarely wanting in confidence, she liked to have her ego bolstered now and then. And it had been. The orthopaedic consultant, whom she'd seen after visiting Matthew, had been charming, even going so far as to invite her for lunch or, failing that, for dinner.

'Well, thank you,' she'd said. 'I would love to accept, but my plans are, as yet, fluid.' She smiled at him, allowing her eyes to flatter him so that he stood a little straighter and pressed another cup of coffee on her.

'You see,' she continued, 'I'm going to see my husband this afternoon. I expect well have dinner together. We have a lot to talk about; he's been away from home for several months.'

The consultant nodded. He'd wondered about this marriage and imagined that it was, to all intents and purposes, over. After all, Matthew's father was living in the farmhouse with that girl and the nurses had plenty to say about that. He glanced slyly at Lydia again. She was a stunner, just the sort of woman he liked. Smart, confident and able to converse properly. He couldn't imagine throwing her over for a bit of fluff.

'Well, before you fly home, please let me entertain you. There are several good restaurants in the area. It would be my pleasure.'

'OK.' She nodded her head slowly as though reluctant. 'It seems I can't refuse you. And will your wife be joining us?'

He barked out a laugh. 'I hope not. We've been divorced for three years.'

Lydia laughed too. 'Well in that case, I'll be happy to save you from eating alone. We can discuss Matthew's continuing care.'

He choked a cough. 'But of course, dear lady, of course.' She had answered in the singular, no mention of bringing her spouse.

She had enjoyed that encounter, which had showed her in her best light, and, who knew, it could lead to further enjoyment. But that was this morning, when she had been completely in charge of her life.

Now she scrabbled clumsily through the mini-bar in her room, looking for something alcoholic which might help with the hammering in her head.

'He doesn't want me any more,' she whispered

brokenly as she threw herself miserably onto the bed, clutching a little bottle of vodka. 'What shall I do?' She burst into tears, again – she had been weeping on and off for the last six hours. Eventually, exhausted, she dropped off to sleep but woke less than two hours later, hot and cold and shivering, with her cheeks still damp from the earlier sobbing. Her hand shook as she reached for her travel alarm and she struggled to focus on the luminous dial. 'Oh, Christ,' she whispered; it showed two o'clock in the morning and there were hours to go before sunrise. The banging in her temples was worse than ever and now the three miniature bottles of vodka she had drunk earlier were beginning to force themselves up into her throat. Her bottle of aspirin stood beside the clock and she swung her legs shakily off the bed and stood up. Taking the bottle she went into the en suite bathroom and found a glass.

Her hand was shaking so badly when she opened it that the tablets scattered all over the sink, some dropping onto the floor and some down the plughole. 'Why shouldn't I?' she asked her ravaged face in the mirror as she grabbed unsteadily at the small white pills. 'That would show the bastard.'

At Cariad Elin, John and Lark were fast asleep, lying close, secure in each other's arms. They had been quiet all evening after Lydia had dashed from the house, each thinking about the recent events, but finding it too raw to talk about. Instead, they'd busied themselves with the necessary chores, seeing to the livestock and bringing in wood. At supper they'd sat opposite each other, mostly silent, but now and then one of them would reach out a hand and take the other's and hold it tightly. It was a comfort.

'I won't go back to her,' John said when they got into bed. 'I promise you.'

'I know.'

'I love you.'

Lark turned towards him and put her arm around his body. 'I know that too,' she whispered into his ear, 'and you are the man I have chosen. I love you.' And he turned peacefully onto his side away from her, exulting in the way she curled her body around his as he drifted off to sleep.

Chapter Thirty-Seven

Matthew heard about the shenanigans at Cariad Elin soon after nine o'clock the next morning.

'Early visitor for Matthew,' called Sister as she opened the ward door.

'Hi, Ma.' He looked up with a grin, expecting to see her stepping elegantly into the room, full of life and sardonic fun. But he was disappointed. It wasn't Lydia and his mouth turned down when Griff Parry's balding head peered hesitantly round the door.

'Oh, hello, Griff.' Matthew took another spoonful of the cereal he'd been playing with for the

367

last hour. Ma had promised to bring him something interesting to eat and he was hopeful that she would bring it soon. 'I bet I can find a Danish in this town,' she'd said yesterday. He bet she would too.

'Matthew. How are you today?' Griff came in and sat heavily on the plastic chair beside the bed. It squealed in protest and Matthew noticed with amused distaste that his partner's buttocks hung uncomfortably over the plastic edges. He could imagine the line that would be cutting into the thick white flesh.

'I'm OK. What are you doing here so early?'

'Oh, I just thought I'd come and see what you were going to do with the farm.' He saw Matthew beginning to frown and added hurriedly, 'You know, now you're going back to Canada and your Mam and Dad are splitting up.'

'What the hell are you talking about?' Matthew sat up suddenly and dropped the bowl of cereal onto the bed table, slopping the milk onto the bed and letting the spoon fall to the floor.

Griff's mind worked overtime. Matthew didn't know. His mother hadn't told him, probably hadn't come in to see him last night. That wasn't surprising, considering the state she had been in. He bent down, grunting, and foraged clumsily for the spoon which had tumbled under the bed. He was playing for time as he decided how to tactfully relate the scene of the previous day.

'Griff?' Matthew was getting impatient.

'Yes, yes.' Griff straightened up, breathing hard, and put the spoon into the bowl. 'Your mam came to the pub yesterday; she told us that she was taking you home. No secret, is it?'

'No, of course not. But what about the other thing you said?'

'About them splitting up, is it?'

'Yeah.'

'It's your dad, see. He's got another woman and your mam found out. Yesterday.'

Matthew was confused. How could Dad have another woman? He was there, at the farm, and, according to him, worked off his feet. He had no time to play around.

'You've got that wrong.' Matthew fixed his blue eyes on Griff and for the first time the older man got an inclination of how unpleasant an argument with the junior member of the Williams family might be. The boy might look younger, now that he had been in hospital for three months, but there was something new behind his eyes, something less casual and accommodating.

Griff shifted his pinched buttocks, wincing as the flesh left the edge of the chair. 'No, no,' he insisted painfully, 'I was there. I heard the row. I saw it with my own eyes.'

'You've got another visitor on the way,' Sister announced, looking back over her shoulder as she bustled into the room. She tut-tutted with annoyance, picking up the cereal bowl and noticing the wet patch of spilt milk on the bedcover. 'There's messy you are, Matthew Williams,' she chided as she left the room. 'And don't forget the physio is coming. Ten o'clock sharp.'

John strode quickly down the ward, shrugging off his parka and shoving his father's old cap, which he'd taken to wearing, in its pocket. He brought a welcome breath of fresh air and coun- tryside into the room. Some of the older male patients recognised the unmistakable odour of mountain sheep and sniffed gratefully; it reminded them that there was a world outside the controlled atmosphere in which they found themselves.

John wanted to get this meeting over with. He'd been planning it since early this morning when he had awoken at his normal hour and jumped out of bed, surprisingly refreshed and ready to face the difficult day ahead.

'I'm going to sort it out, now, before things get worse,' he'd told Lark as they spread hay and pellets out for the sheep.

'Good,' she nodded. 'Better sooner than later.'

'Dad?' Matthew said doubtfully, as John reached his bedside. Griff peeled himself off the chair and stood up.

'Morning, son,' John grinned, trying to hide the nervousness he felt. He looked over at Griff and then back at Matthew.

'I guess you've already heard. Parry hasn't wasted any time.' He looked at his son's confused face and added, 'Or maybe your mother told you.'

'I haven't seen her since yesterday morning.'

'Ah.' This was a surprise. He wondered why she hadn't visited or even phoned. That was so unlike Lydia. Getting her version in first had always been her style.

'Dad. Tell me what's going on.'

'I will, but not while he's here.'

The look John gave Griff was unmistakable in its contempt, and the publican, looking from father to son, saw a hint of the same expression in Matthew's face.

'Don't worry,' he said, trying unsuccessfully to make his voice as cold and indifferent as John's. 'I'm off. I'll talk to you again, Matthew, about our business.' He stressed the word 'our', hoping to salvage some of his importance.

'Yeah.' Matthew was dismissive and Griff didn't linger.

He was good at being patient and his day would come.

'Ta-ra, then, Matthew, Mr Williams.' His wobbling jowls spoilt the attempted look of poison which he directed at John, before setting off down the ward. He was aware that they were staring after him, probably with identical expressions.

There was now no excuse for John, but his mood today was so positive that he didn't need any excuses. Compared to last evening, when Lydia's unexpected arrival had thrown him into confusion, he now had things clear in his head and was no longer prepared to obfuscate. If what he was going to say upset Matthew, then so be it. In a way, it was par for the course, and both of them were well used to that.

'I'm leaving your mother,' he plunged in directly. 'I have found someone I want to spend the rest of my life with.' He paused and then continued, 'I'm extraordinarily lucky.'

'Who?' Matthew was very still and didn't look at his father but stared through the window, watching the cottonwool clouds dash recklessly across the sky. A part of him didn't want the answer; he already knew.

'It's Lark. Or, I call her Helen, that's her real name. She wants to be called that now.' He took a deep breath before rushing on. 'Look, I know this is a shock to you, and I'm sorry; but it happened. There's no going back.'

Matthew was silent, still gazing out of the window, and for a moment John wondered if he hadn't heard. But that wasn't possible. Tentatively, he reached out his hand and put it on his son's shoulder. It lay there unrecognised.

'Where's Ma?' The words emerged in a small, childish voice and John shook his head in surprise.

'Your mother? I've no idea. At her hotel, I suppose.' He got up and walked restlessly around the bed. 'I thought she might be here with you.'

The silence hung like a pall as Matthew continued to stare out of the window and John paced quietly on the plastic floor. A cleaner at the other end of the ward was dragging her bucket and mop slowly along the passage between the bed bays and her voice, rising and falling as she chattered to patients and staff, seemed to come from another world. John felt as though he was watching himself in a movie. The situation wasn't real.

'I feel bad for you and your mother, of course,' he tried again, 'but I'm happier than I have ever been. Nothing can change that...' His voice trailed off as his son's white face turned towards him.

'Why don't you just piss off?' Matthew's voice was icy with disgust and contempt, and his eyes burned holes in John's face. 'I don't want to hear this, so don't tell me any more about your happiness or your "extraordinary luck".' He pulled himself up and swung his legs carefully out of the bed, then grabbed the crutches from their place beside the locker. 'As far as I'm concerned,' he continued as he dragged himself upright and stood gaunt and fragile-looking but still a couple of inches taller than his father, 'you're just a sad old man. How long d'you think it will be before she gets sick of you?' He laughed mirthlessly. 'A month? Two, if your "extraordinary luck" lasts. She's a traveller, she moves on. Once the place to stay has gone she'll find somewhere else. And someone else. Don't you know that?

'And I'm selling,' he yelled as John walked quickly away down the ward, conscious of many curious eyes watching him, 'as soon as possible. So you and your girlfriend can get out of my house.'

John sat, shaking, in Matt's Land Rover in the hospital car park, and wished desperately and for the first time in months that he could have a drink. He was so frightened. He knew that everything that his son had said was true; he must have been an idiot to have thought otherwise. She was young, over twenty years younger than he was, and beautiful. There could be no reason for her

373

wanting to stay with him, or even at Cariad Elin. It was only a small hill farm, old and uncomfortable and constant hard work. She could have so much more.

A car drew up beside him and a young man got out and went round to the back seat to unbuckle a small child from its safety seat. 'We're going to see Mammy and the new baby,' he said to the little girl, 'hurry up.' The child stared at John as she was swung out of the car and gathered up into her father's arms. As they walked away the child mouthed bye-bye and made a little wave with her tiny hand. It summed up all John's recent thoughts and he could feel tears pricking again at the corners of his eyes. 'Oh Christ,' he cried out loud, 'what am I going to do?'

He sat for half an hour going over and over the scant conversation he'd had with Matt. He'd planned to say so much more, to explain his feelings and Lark's. To discuss his thoughts on the future for them all, and most of all, to let Matthew know that this new episode in his life would not affect the relationship between them. He would try for an amicable separation from Lydia. After all, he knew full well that she had not been the most faithful of wives. There had never been any hint of scandal in all their years together, but he knew, as husbands and wives always know, that there was something.

But now he had lost the chance to say all that. Matthew's utter rejection of him had been so shocking and so accurate that all he could think to do was flee the ward, leaving the truth of his situation dripping hatefully from his son's lips.

A shower of rain pattered in on the wind and drizzled heavily on the windscreen. He looked at the dashboard clock and saw that it was past eleven o'clock. He should get back to Cariad Elin. He would have to tell Lark that he had failed to control the situation and she would be unhappy and probably think that he was cowardly and incapable. Not much of a man for a woman like her to love. And then there was Lydia.

That brought up a new problem. Where was she? She hadn't been to see Matt since yesterday morning and he'd been in the car park for nearly an hour now, sitting opposite the hospital entrance door, and hadn't seen her go in. As he sat there, a small worm of worry started to chew through the lining of his stomach. She had been dreadfully upset when she'd left the farm last night, but following her style, she wouldn't normally have wasted any time before telling Matt what had happened. All of a sudden it became urgent that he see her, and he turned the key in the car and put it in gear. But he didn't know which hotel she was in. They hadn't got round to discussing that, and he sat with his knee jerking and the engine idling while he thought. After a while he took off the handbrake and drove out of the car park. She would stay at the best place and he knew where it was.

'Mrs Lydia Williams,' he said to the receptionist who stood behind the highly polished counter of the hotel. She looked up from her computer and quickly scanned this person who stood before her. The thick parka, muddied at the hem and torn slightly on one sleeve, did not meet with her approval and she arranged her features in an offputting, superior smile, ready to deny entry. It was a smile that her employers, far away in New York, would have hated. They wanted customers; it didn't matter who they were, as long as they had money.

'Mrs Williams, yes...' The girl paused and glanced again at the computer. 'She's in room two-oh-four. Do you wish to go up?' she said reluctantly.

'Yes.' John was short. 'Of course. Why else would I be here?' He turned towards the lift.

'I haven't seen her today,' the receptionist called after him. 'Perhaps she's out and forgotten to hand in her key card.'

John didn't bother to answer but got into the lift and pressed the button. It was now so urgent that he see Lydia that he wasn't prepared to argue, and when the lift stopped and he emerged into the thickly carpeted corridor, he hurried towards the door marked 204.

There was no reply to his rap on the door and he knocked again and called softly, 'Lydia, open the door, it's me, John.' A couple coming out of the room opposite looked at him curiously as he rapped again at the door and shouted his wife's name. The sinking feeling he'd had since leaving the hospital increased, and he realised that he was playing out several scenarios, all with himself and Lydia as central figures. *What if* ... he thought, *what if she's*... He couldn't even bring himself to put it into words in his mind, and he hammered desperately on the door, shouting his wife's name. The passing couple stopped close to the lift and looked back, concerned that there might be a scene. The woman whispered to her husband, and after a split second's thought, he returned along the corridor until he was standing beside John.

'Is there a problem?' he asked tentatively.

'My wife, she's not answering.' John's voice was shaking. 'I think she might have … er…' His voice trailed away.

'Is she ill?' The stranger looked concerned and raised his finger in a beckoning gesture towards his wife. She hurried to join them, looking as if she was enjoying the excitement. She waited with them as John knocked hopelessly on the door again.

Suddenly there was a sound from behind the door, a rattling as though someone was awkwardly trying to turn the handle.

'Lydia?' John whispered, his face pressed against the door and leaving a smear of sweat against the paint as the door slowly opened.

The three outside craned their heads to look at the scene inside. The room was neat, barely disturbed since the maid had been in the morning before, but the bed was tumbled, the counterpane hanging half on the floor and the pillows awry. Beside the bed on the pale pink carpet, there was a patch of vomit, bile-coloured and beginning to smell, and a spotted trail of a similar nature leading towards the en suite bathroom.

'God, Lydia,' John hurried in and took the limp figure of his wife in his arms. Her face was ghastly, yellowy white, and her swollen eyelids barely opened. He recoiled from the sickly odour that emanated from her parched lips, but picked her up in his arms and carried her easily to the bed.

'What's the matter?' He drew the cover over her before dashing into the bathroom to get a wet flannel to wipe her mouth. She was shivering violently, but her face when he touched it was burning hot.

'I think we should get a doctor,' the man at the door said, staring at the bed and holding his wife back from coming further into the room. 'Your wife looks quite ill.'

'Yes, please. Please call one!' John looked desperately over his shoulder, grateful to see the couple retreat hurriedly. He covered Lydia with another blanket which he found in the wardrobe and forced a sip of water between her lips.

'I've been throwing up all night,' she whispered hoarsely.

'But what is it, honey?' He held her and tenderly kissed her hot forehead.

She didn't answer but closed her eyes and rested her head on his arm.

Chapter Thirty-Eight

He stayed with her in the ambulance, and then waited in the A&E corridor. She was assessed first by the casualty officer and later by a consultant who hurried into the department, white coat tails flying and a trail of junior doctors behind him. John recognised him – he had been in charge of Matthew when he was ill with pneumonia – and when he emerged from Lydia's cubicle, John was pathetically glad to see him.

'Mr Williams, we meet again. Your family seems to be getting its money's worth from the NHS.'

John ignored what might have been slight sarcasm. 'How is she? And do you know what's the matter with her?'

The consultant didn't answer the question but nervously tapped one finger against his lips as he thought, and then countered with one of his own. 'Has your wife been in a tropical country recently?'

'Yes, she went to the Caribbean at Christmas. But that was weeks ago.'

'Could you try to be a little more precise? Which island? A trip to Central or South America involved?' The consultant gazed patiently at the ceiling while his juniors shuffled nervously and examined their shoes.

John cast wildly about in his mind. He didn't

know – he hadn't been listening properly and had only glanced briefly at the picture on the front of the postcard. 'I think she was on Bermuda, but she did fly on to somewhere in Central America for a few days.' John looked at him and then to the three junior doctors, who were shifting from foot to foot, anxiously waiting for their boss to suddenly pose them a difficult question. It was his usual trick.

'I could be wrong,' the consultant said in his usual self-deprecating style which came across as completely false, 'but I think your wife is suffering from some sort of infectious illness. I'm pretty sure it's malaria, but of course we haven't done the tests yet.' He raised a warning hand as John opened his mouth to ask a hundred questions.

'She'll be nursed in isolation to begin with, until we know what's going on. Now before you ask, at the moment her illness isn't life-threatening – we've already put up a drip and will get fluids into her. But there are always secondary infections to combat and we will have to be watchful. These young men,' he glanced at his team, 'these young men will take the utmost interest in her illness. It might be the only time some of them will ever see it.'

John didn't know what to think or even if he should believe the doctor. Surely Lydia couldn't have developed malaria all these weeks after her holiday? He wondered if he should say something about his suspicions that she might have harmed herself, but that would make him look stupid, and from the pitying glances he was getting from the assembled doctors, they obviously didn't regard him with much respect.

'I didn't realise that malaria could take so long to appear,' he said, his voice flat and exhausted. 'That's a new one on me.'

'Well, it's not your line of work, is it?' The consultant produced another of his sneering smiles and turned to the most junior of his team. 'Dr Patel. See if you can tell me which type of malaria it could be.'

'Quartan, sir. Up to six weeks' incubation period.' The young Indian house officer was certain. He had seen far more cases of this disease than his boss could ever imagine.

The senior doctor was momentarily disconcerted. In asking the wrong junior he had lost some of his authority and would need to find more difficult questions for the rest of the afternoon rounds. But he kept his smile in place and said, 'Quite right, well done,' before briefly nodding to John and walking rapidly away down the corridor to continue his tutorial.

'We're moving her into the isolation ward.' A nurse had stuck her head out of Lydia's cubicle, 'You can see her before she goes.'

He peered hesitantly around the curtains, almost afraid of what he might encounter, the memory of her quivering and vomit-stained body still very fresh in his mind. At first he could see nothing of Lydia, for she was obscured by the lumpy body of the nurse who was leaning over the examination couch washing Lydia's face. But when the nurse moved away, he was able to get closer and take his place beside the bed and look down at his wife.

He felt the breath catch in his throat. She looked so small and fragile, her head barely making a dent on the pillow and her body invisible under the mound of red honeycomb blankets. Her eyes were closed and for a moment he thought she was asleep, but as he stood there she whispered, 'John? That you?'

'Yes, Lyddie, how are you feeling?'

She opened her eyes slightly and peered at him. 'Like shit,' she said.

He smiled, that was a bit of the old Lydia. 'Hang in there, honey,' he said, 'you're going to be all right.'

'Mm,' she nodded, then closed her eyes again. She was very tired, but as she heard the noise of John beginning to leave the cubicle she raised her head painfully off the pillow. 'Tell Matt where I am.'

His nodded and muttered agreement satisfied her, and he left her sleeping as he went out of the cubicle.

'I couldn't tell him,' he confessed to Lark later on, as he watched her give the chickens their afternoon corn. 'I got one of the nurses to go up to his ward.'

She listened while she spread the corn, carefully eyeing the birds as they pecked and clucked around her feet. It was very gratifying to see them so healthy with their bright eyes and combs and smooth, glossy feathers. She had fixed up a light in the hen house so that they had continued to lay throughout the worst days of winter and her supply of eggs to the shop and pub had remained fairly constant. Sometimes it seemed that the chickens would do anything for her. 'Perhaps that was for the best. I don't suppose either of you could have coped with another argument.'

'Well, I couldn't, that's for sure.' He sighed and rubbed stiff, callused hands over his face. The whole day had been truly dreadful. His positive mood of the early morning had been squashed, and now he was too tired to even think about the mess his life was in. He looked up to the sky and sniffed the air. A great bank of dark cloud was gathering out to the west where the next front of wet weather was already forming. It hid the dying sun so that night was already coming into the valley, and all John wanted to do was get into the house and close his eyes.

'Why don't you go in and have a rest?' Lark had, yet again, uncannily read his thoughts. He looked up sharply and caught a flicker of pity in her eyes. For a moment he revelled in it, grateful that she understood what he was going through. But then, slowly, a flush suffused his cold face as he realised what he was accepting from her. Pity. He was stunned – what had he become?

'No!' Suddenly he was angry. Everyone was walking over him, telling him what to do, what to think. And worse than that, he was letting them. His expression hardened. 'No, I'm going to take a look at the sheep and then I must shift some of the hay in the barn away from the hole in the roof where the tiles have blown off.' He pulled the old cap firmly over his eyebrows and, not looking at her, set off towards the field. Halfway there, he paused and called over his shoulder, 'You go in and have a rest. You've been carrying this farm on your own for the past few days.'

She watched him walk away and smiled softly to herself. Her instinct had been correct; self-pity was not really his true nature. 'Come on,' she made chucking noises to the compliant chickens and threw a handful of corn into the hen house as she herded them towards their roosts for the night, 'time for bed.'

Lydia made a slow recovery. After the first few days, she wasn't really ill, but she failed to make real progress and lay quietly in the isolation room staring aimlessly at the wall. Matthew came every few hours to see her and, masked and gowned, hobbled to her bedside to sit patiently with her.

'Your mother isn't too good,' the consultant told him one evening after Matthew left the room and paused by the nurses' station for a chat before returning to his own ward. He hadn't needed to be told that. Lydia had barely replied to his bantering remarks but had lain gazing out of the window, and Matthew wasn't even sure that she could hear him.

'We don't seem to be able to get her interested in sitting up and taking notice.' He signed the last of his pile of notes and continued. 'Your father says that it's not really like her. Full of beans normally.'

Matthew shrugged. 'I wouldn't take a lot of notice of his opinion,' he said unpleasantly.

The doctor was entirely used to keeping his

feelings hidden when dealing with patients and their relatives, but this took him by surprise. There was obviously another agenda going on in the Williams household, and that could be the reason for Lydia's apathy. 'Has she a friend, perhaps, who could come and see her, buck her up a bit?'

'Not here.'

'No, I suppose not.' The consultant sighed. 'Oh well, we'll just have to take the slow route. Let her recover in her own time.'

As he heaved himself up onto his crutches and awkwardly made his way to the lift, Matthew thought about what the doctor had said. Ma had plenty of friends back home, but none that she would like to have visit, specially while she was in this state. It was later, when he was lying in his own bed, that he thought of the man she'd met in the Caribbean. He was the doctor who was going to be taking over his own care, and apparently a good friend. Ma wouldn't mind him coming over. It took another several minutes for Matthew to remember the man's name, but then it came to him, suddenly. Joe Bithell, that was it. He sat up in bed and grabbed hold of the bell ringer. 'Janice,' he called to the night nurse, 'Janice, honey, get me the phone.'

Spring was finally coming to the valley. The cold winds continued to blow, but they didn't have that edge, that depth that made one feel that winter would last forever. Now, when the wind whipped between the hillsides, bending the short wild daffodils nearly horizontal and sending the lambs into the shelter of the stone wall, it lasted only for an hour or two before giving up. Then the sun would lighten and warm the pasture and shine through the small windows at Cariad Elin and drive Lark mad with desire to be out of doors.

She was leaning against the field gate one lunchtime, watching her lambs dash around the growing pasture, when a car drew up in the yard. She recognised it and walked across, waving her hand in greeting, to meet Bethan, who was emerging from the driver's seat. 'Hello.' Lark took her visitor's hand and gave it a welcoming squeeze. 'We haven't seen you here for ages.'

'I know, love.' Bethan smiled and shook her head ruefully. 'I'm always so busy. But I have a day off and I thought I'd come and see you. See how you are.' She looked at the girl and noticed at once how she'd changed. The wild, restless look that so alarmed or attracted people had softened. Now she seemed more mature, relaxed, and, Bethan sighed, so lovely. How could anyone resist her, least of all a middle-aged man?

She glanced around the yard and up onto the hillside before saying, 'Where's John today?'

'Oh, he's gone into Bangor. He has to see Lydia and Matthew before they fly home. There are things to sort out, you know.' A small cloud passed over Lark's peaceful face and a line of strain appeared between her eyebrows, but she quickly resumed her cheerful mood. 'Come inside,' she urged. 'Come and have a bite of lunch with me.'

They had bread and cheese and some of Lark's homemade pickle, which Bethan pronounced good enough to win at the WI fête, and washed it down with copious cups of tea. Bethan loved her food and never minded about putting on extra inches around her already ample waist. She tucked in with relish, although noticing, while she ate, that Lark merely nibbled at her cheese and rolled her bread into little balls instead of eating it. It made Bethan feel a little nervous and she wondered if Lark knew that there was an ulterior purpose to the visit. Cup in hand, Bethan looked around the kitchen and noticed the new pine units by the sink and the radiators against the walls.

'I heard you'd been having some work done. Central heating? My word, that's lovely, but a bit extravagant, especially when you're not...' She paused, blushing slightly before struggling to arrange the sentence more tactfully, 'I mean, when you won't be staying here.'

'But we are staying here.' Were the words said defiantly or just stated as a matter of fact? Bethan couldn't decide and put her cup down carefully in the saucer before reaching out and covering Lark's long fingers with her own plump hand.

'Lark, love...' She hesitated before plunging in, bringing the news she'd heard this morning in the village, and now was positive that Lark didn't know. 'Cariad Elin is sold. Beti Rowlands told me not two hours ago, and she'd heard it straight from Llinos Parry. Matthew has sold it to some friend of Griff's. A builder, I think. He's going to put up holiday cottages.'

For a moment, Lark thought she was going to faint. The room spun and Bethan's words spun with it, driving their horrible meaning into her head. She stood up, clumsily knocking over her chair, and walked to the window to gaze helplessly at her mountain.

'I don't believe you.' Even as she said it she knew that it was a fact, and her voice shook with fright.

Bethan came to stand beside her and put an arm round her shoulder. 'I think it's true,' she said quietly. 'We've been aware of this Sean Harper and his plans for a while. He tried to buy some of our land a while back, but of course, this farm is the prize, what with the views and all. Matthew will have made a lot of money.' She bit her lip, wondering what to say next. 'You can be happy somewhere else, *cariad*,' she said to the girl, 'you'll have each other.'

Lark turned then and Bethan saw the utter despair in her curious eyes. 'We can only be happy here,' she whispered and put her hands up to her face and started to sob.

Chapter Thirty-Nine

John heard the news at about the same time. Lydia told him, spelling out the facts slowly, watching the colour leave her husband's face and his mouth slacken and turn down. He looked pitiful, and for a moment she had a fleeting stab of compassion. It soon passed; these days she felt little other than contempt for him.

'You'll have to get out within the month. That crappy little farmhouse is going to be demolished.' Her voice echoed cruelly through the comfortable lounge of the hotel where she was convalescing. Fortunately, they were alone – it was too early in the season for many guests, and the few who were staying had gone out. Lydia relished the space: it allowed her to imagine that this sixteenth-century house was hers and that the attentive hotel staff were her own servants.

Joe had loved the place, too, in the week he'd spent here, revelling in the history and adoring the country-house atmosphere which the hotel successfully purveyed. 'We must come back one day, it's so great here,' he'd said before he left to fly back to his practice.

Lydia shook her head. She enjoyed staying in the hotel, but knew for certain that she would never come back to Wales. 'We could visit another part of the UK,' she'd said, making a concession to his good nature, 'maybe Scotland – lots of golf there.

You'd like that.'

And he'd grinned and dropped a kiss on her head. 'Whatever you say, honey.'

John got up and walked to the window. He stared across the pretty gardens to the Menai Strait, which divided the mainland from the island of Anglesey. The view was stunning: white clouds scudding swiftly across a bright blue sky while the water tossed and rippled, making the few small sailing boats which had ventured out this morning bend and tack as they were driven by the wind. He ached to be outside, away from this warm, overfurnished room, away from Lydia and the terrible words she was saying.

'When was it sold?' He amazed himself at being able to speak so calmly.

'Yesterday.'

He turned away from the window. 'Why didn't you tell me what was going on?'

Lydia shrugged. 'It was Matthew's decision, his property. He can do what he likes with it.'

'But he knows how I feel about Cariad Elin. He should have...' John let the words fade away. He knew why he'd been kept in the dark. Matthew and Lydia were taking their revenge in the most obvious way possible.

'We're flying home on Saturday night.' She spoke matter-of-factly, as though the subject of Cariad Elin had been dealt with and there was no more to say. 'Matthew can't wait – he's like a little kid – and Joe and I are going to take him away for a little holiday. Fatten him up a bit, get him back to normal.'

'I'd say he's pretty normal right now,' John said bitterly, 'as capricious as ever. Christ, it's only months since he announced that he was going to stay in Wales forever!'

'That was before you stole his girlfriend.' Lydia laughed unpleasantly. It didn't matter how many times John had tried to tell her the true facts; she had made up her own version and was sticking to it. He sighed. There was no point in going over it again; she wouldn't listen. Even Matthew preferred Lydia's story – it lent drama to the affair, and somehow he would manage to come out of it looking good. Who would believe that a normal girl could fancy an old drunk, when he, Matthew, was around? She'd gone where the money was. And anyway, now, when he thought about Lark, she had become a different person. In his mind, she was older and plainer and somehow weird in a way he hadn't realised before. Dad was welcome to her.

Lydia got up slowly from her sofa using her thin arms to lever herself upright. John moved to help her but she brushed him away and stood by herself. The closeness that had been temporarily renewed between them at the onset of her illness had gone now. His refusal to give up that girl and Matthew's utter contempt for his father had seen to that. And the sudden arrival of dear old Joe by her bedside had been a timely reminder of how much fun she'd had with him. Compared to John, he exuded all the things she adored: money, confidence and a zest for living. And added to that, he adored her.

'I'm going for divorce,' she said, and watched

391

his face for a reaction. Disappointingly, there was none. 'Fred Eland will draw up the papers for me as soon as I get back, and you know he'll do exactly what I want.' She gave another of her short, mirthless laughs and added, 'Don't think you're coming back to the house, because I'm going to sell it. When you come home you can find yourself a place.' She snorted a laugh again. 'Better find somewhere cheap. Fred will make sure that I'm well taken care of.'

He was still failing to react, simply nodding, and, she realised, only half listening.

'Did you hear what I was saying?' She moved closer to him and stared into his thin face, trying to make his eyes meet hers, but they didn't. He was looking over her shoulder into space as the full impact of the sale of Cariad Eli trickled through to him, and beginning to feel lightheaded. Oh God, how would he tell Lark? It would destroy her.

He looked down vaguely at Lydia and then gave himself a little shake. 'I have to go.' The urgency was patent as he looked round for his cap and scarf and snatched them up from one of the coffee tables.

This sudden change of mood disconcerted her and she scowled as she watched him hurry to the door. 'You brought it on yourself, you know,' she called after him spitefully, but he didn't stop. After a few seconds, looking through the great bay window, she saw the Land Rover going down the hotel drive before turning at the gate onto the mountain road.

Matthew came into the room, hobbling on his

crutches but already looking better for being away from hospital food and boredom. 'Did you tell him?'

'Yeah,' she nodded, still looking out at the drive.

'How did he take it?'

She turned away from the window and looked at her son. He was so handsome – who could fail to love him? – but… 'Maybe you should have been the one to break the news,' she said, a slight note of disapproval in her voice. 'It was your farm, after all.'

He shifted the crutches and balanced carefully on one of them while he put a carefree arm around her shoulders. 'Aw, Ma,' he cajoled, 'you're so much better at that sort of thing.'

He nuzzled his head into her neck until she laughed and gave him a small tap on his cheek. 'Bad boy,' she said lovingly, and then, 'Come on. Let's go and do something about food. If you behave yourself, I'll see if I can persuade someone to go out and get you a burger.'

Chapter Forty

He knew as soon as he drew into the yard that the news had arrived before him. Lark was standing by the field gate gazing up at the mountain, and the expression on her thin face was so inconsolably lost that he knew he would never find the right words of comfort. He climbed slowly out of the car and went over to her. She didn't turn to greet him, and when he wrapped his arms closely around her, she remained stiff and apart as though he wasn't there.

'Helen?' He murmured her name into her neck and rubbed his hands in a comforting gesture up and down her stiff back. 'Helen, *cariad,* it'll be all right. We can work something out.' Part of him prayed that she wouldn't ask how. His brain was weary: too much had happened in the last couple of weeks and he could no longer think logically. Through the tangle of his thoughts, a memory surfaced that he had been going to look into Parry's involvement, but too many things had happened to distract him. Now it was too late.

Lark was silent, her eyes fixed on the mountain and her breathing so shallow as to be barely noticeable.

He put his lips gently on her neck, kissing her cold pink earlobe and nuzzling into her skin for comfort. 'Please don't worry, my love,' he whispered, his voice almost inaudible, exhausted and muffled in her coat collar. The clean, fresh scent of apple wood came from the fabric. She must have been shifting logs earlier in the morning, doing the work around the farm that he, in his obsession with outside problems, had been ignoring. He felt shamed and useless. 'Talk to me,' he begged.

She turned her head and looked at him. 'Can you stop the sale?' Her dull eyes held a little spark of hope and her bronze hair flew carelessly about her face as the wind began to blow in from the west.

'No. I don't think so.' His voice was hollow and suddenly tears came into his eyes, and in order not to upset her further, he had to turn his face away. That was worse. Now he was looking at the gently sloping fields where the ewes were cropping steadily at the growing pasture, and their lambs – his and Lark's lambs – were joyfully clambering over the stone wall and playing chasing games. Daffodils and celandines bobbed in the wind, fresh spring yellow which contrasted so peacefully with the bright green of the sunny meadow grass. Was he seeing it for the first time? Or remembering how he used to feel in those far-off days before Mam died and the world was young?

He closed his eyes, wanting the scene to spoil, become mundane and everyday, but when he opened them and looked up to the mountain top there was another exquisite picture. Clouds were beginning to gather, enormous rolling banks of brilliant white, piling on top of each other and being driven forward by the ominously heavy grey beneath. The peak was still clear and he could pick out individual rocks. He knew them all by heart; it had been his playground long ago. His eyes flicked over to the west. The clear sky wouldn't last for long. Soon it would disappear under heavy mist as the rain blew in, first a few drops flicking in the wind and then a steady drizzle. *Those potholes have to be filled in,* the back part of his brain reminded him. Then reality struck and he remembered that this land, this home, this part of him, had been wrenched away.

'Oh God.' The words burst forth in a desperate groan and he closed his eyes against the view. It was then that he felt a pressure on his body as Lark raised her arms and held him. For the first time that day, he started to relax. She murmured comforting words into his ear, words that at first he didn't properly hear, but he loved her more for saying them. It was only much later that he remembered with astonishment that she had spoken to him in Welsh.

They were still in the yard a few minutes later when Robert's battered Land Rover careered up the muddy lane. Awkwardly they let each other go but stood side by side, waiting for their friend.

'A bad do, this,' Robert said without bothering with the niceties of greeting. 'I told you that Harper was looking for land. *Duw!*' He shook his head in disgust. 'Never thought Matthew would give in.' He looked at the couple, appalled by their ravished faces.

Earlier, Bethan had told him about Lark. 'Thought she would faint, honest!' Bethan had said, shocked still by the girl's reaction. 'Cried her eyes out, she did. Poor love.'

'What about John?' Robert had said over his shoulder as he delved into the engine of his old Ferguson tractor. 'He's got quite attached to the place now. Must be weeks since he's spoken about Canada.'

Bethan nodded. John and Lark had become, in a matter of a few weeks, a settled couple, so much a part of Cariad Elin that it was hard to remember that she had originally come to the valley with Matt.

'Oh dear,' Bethan sighed, 'it will be hard for them setting up in a new place.'

'He'll go back to Canada.' Robert straightened his back and reached for a spanner. 'That's where the money is. They won't starve, that's for sure.'

Bethan clucked her tongue sadly and wagged a plump finger at her oil-smeared husband. 'Not the point, boy *bach*. Not the point.'

Now, as he looked at the distraught couple, Robert could see that Bethan was right.

'I don't know what to do, Rob,' John said miserably as they leant against the field gate. Lark had excused herself and gone inside. 'I'll put the kettle on,' she'd said quietly. 'Come to the house in a minute and have a cup of tea.' The two men watched her go, tall, straight and moving swiftly towards the house in that economical walk which was so attractive.

'You're not old, man. You can still work. Make a fucking good living, I'd say.'

'But not here.'

'No.' Robert didn't try to pretend. He looked up at the hillside and then at the sloping fields. He tried to imagine what they would look like with cabins dotted about and perhaps a restaurant and car park where the farmhouse was now standing. 'Fucking hell,' he said in disgust and spat heavily and deliberately across the gate into the field.

'Beats me,' he said a few moments later as they walked towards the house, 'how Harper ever got planning permission. Greenfield site like this and the council so keen to try and protect rural areas. National Park, isn't it, after all.'

The words didn't sink in for a moment. John's mind was busy formulating a proposal to Lark that they should go to Canada. He could still make a good living there, and if they went to the west and bought a property in the Rockies, or maybe on one of the islands off the coast of British Columbia, then it wouldn't be so different from North Wales. There were mountains, and valleys and acres of empty space. They would be together. That was the main thing. He would build them a house, a wonderful house, one that would complement, not detract from the environment. Lark would be happy there. They could keep animals; in fact, there was nothing to stop them from building up a substantial holding...

'What? What did you just say?' Robert's remark had suddenly filtered through to John's fevered mind and he roughly grabbed his friend by the arm.

'Calm down, boy.' Robert jerked his arm out of John's hand so quickly that his jacket gave slightly at the seams with a little ripping noise.

'Sorry, Rob.' The words tumbled excitedly out of John's mouth. He felt as though he had just been thrown a lifeline. 'What did you say about planning permission?'

Robert repeated what he'd said. 'It's National Park, man, and agricultural land. Normally they take ages to make decisions, fucking enquiries and public meetings. How's he done it?'

John rubbed his face with a cold and shaking

hand and forced his tired brain to think properly. Lydia hadn't said how much Matthew had got for the land, but he was ready to bet that it hadn't been a lot. Griff Parry had arranged it all, probably brought in his own solicitor, and made sure that the sale went ahead quickly, with a big cut for the fat landlord. Harper probably hadn't bothered with the necessary permissions – that would come after he'd carefully greased a few palms in the council offices. He just wanted to get hold of the land. Cheaply.

'Jesus! He hasn't got it. He'll do that in his own time.' John breathed the words out, excited but now able to think in a controlled way. He looked at Robert and slowly began to smile. 'I think I can stop this. The council will never allow it when I've spoken to them, and that bastard Harper isn't going to want this place without the permissions.' He laughed and punched Robert playfully on the arm. 'It's going to be all right.'

Robert pretended to square up but then backed off and just cuffed his boyhood friend around the ear. 'Get off, you mad bugger,' he said, his wide grin exposing his missing teeth. 'You telling me that you can stop this sale going ahead?' He shook his head and kicked at a loose stone in the yard. 'Don't get your hopes up, John.'

'No, listen. You said yourself that this is National Park and agricultural land. Harper would need to have a really good reason for the council to allow change of use. Building a few holiday bungalows can't possibly be a good reason.' He punched his fist angrily into his other hand. 'It would go against everything the Park stands for. And Rob,' John whispered, remembering the scene in the lawyer's office when Matthew had been told of his inheritance, 'Dad wrote in his will that the land had to be farmed in perpetuity.'

'Oh...' Robert sucked in air through his loose teeth and nodded his head slowly, 'Makes a bit of a difference, that. Bit of a fucking difference.' He thought for a moment and then added, 'D'you think Matthew will sell to you, if the Harper deal falls through? Elfed says he's pretty pissed off with you.'

John's face hardened. 'I dunno, I'll have to cross that bridge when I get to it.' He looked towards the house where he could see Lark moving about by the scullery window: 'Rob,' he said slowly, 'do me a favour. Don't say any of this to Lark. I couldn't bear to raise her hopes and risk them being dashed. Let's wait until I've been to the council and then a lawyer.'

His stomach was churning; fright had made him physically ill. He couldn't stand any more emotional turmoil. They must quietly live through the next few days and try not to talk about it. Lark would know that he was going to arrange things, but not how. He could plant the idea of moving to Canada and then, if they had to, she would be prepared. But he mustn't, above all, allow her to believe that they could stay at Cariad Elin. Her disappointment, if he couldn't achieve the miracle, might kill them both.

'Don't say a word, Rob,' he repeated. 'To anyone.'

The rain came in the night, carried on the wind, pattering gently at first and then heavier as the heavy clouds rolled into the valley. John and Lark lay in bed awake, listening to the water running down the gutters, and clattering on the corrugated roof of the machine shed. The noise was strangely comforting, a normal occurrence in the life of the farm.

They had spoken little that evening. John sat in the leather chair after supper, rehearsing his conversation with the planning officer. He tried to guess the opposing arguments and think up ways to counter them; it was something, after all, of which he had experience. And then, if he managed to stop the sale, how could he persuade Matthew and Lydia to let him have Cariad Elin? Oh God, that required more thought and he was exhausted. His eyes closed slowly and in a minute he had escaped his problems and was deeply asleep.

Lark watched him from her rocking chair opposite and smiled a little. That was what he needed, and she didn't resent his shrugging off the responsibility of organising their lives, for a little while. She had her own thoughts, jumbled up hopelessly at the moment, which she would need time to sort out.

Chapter Forty-One

'I'd know you anywhere!' The planning officer came round from behind his desk and thrust out his hand. John was momentarily disconcerted. It had taken him a few days to set up this meeting, and he hadn't realised he already knew the man standing in front of him. The short, bald man who grinned at him so widely was a stranger. But this had been happening on and off since he came home and now he was better prepared. The name block on the desk read 'Evan Price Jones' and John flicked his eye at it and trawled forgotten recesses of his brain. There had been thirty to a class in the grammar school and three classes each year. Ninety boys of his own age. Callow, spotty youths when he'd last seen most of them, but they were men now, altered by time and experience, and he was supposed to remember them all. He looked at the name block again, and from somewhere the recollection of a tough little boy who was the star of the school football team flashed into his head.

'Hello, Evan,' he said in a tone which was as casual as he could muster, 'how's the soccer these days?'

It was pure luck, but it was the first piece that had come to him in many weeks, and he took full advantage of it. By the time he stepped out of the office, Evan Price Jones had put the wheels in motion to block any type of non-agricultural development on Cariad Elin.

'Give me your son's address in Canada and I'll write to him today telling him that he can't sell for housing. And I'll get hold of Harper and tell him likewise. That bastard should know better, anyway. He keeps trying to get land on the sly and we have to move quickly to catch up with him. It will be a pleasure to frustrate him.'

'Evan, do me a favour. Don't let my son know that it was me that brought this to you.'

The planning officer grinned. 'No problem, John. I know all about oversensitive offspring. Mine refuse to take any advice. Think I fell to earth yesterday.' He laughed and punched John on the shoulder in a friendly schoolboyish gesture. 'No. I'll write that it has come to my notice, blah blah blah. That's what we always do.'

As John was walking along the street after-wards, on his way to the solicitor's office, he found that he was whistling a little tune and grinning stupidly. It occurred to him suddenly that the whole conversation had been conducted in Welsh and he hadn't even realised it at the time. It was as if he'd never been away. And the plan, formulated with Robert's help, might work. 'Step one,' he said to himself, 'now for the next one.'

He wished desperately that he could tell Lark, but he was scared. What if it went wrong? They'd begun to talk about Canada and starting a new life. She hadn't said very much but she had listened, nodding her head now and then and

403

smiling when he'd described the beauty of the Rockies. She was calmer now, in control of her emotions and somehow more compliant than she had ever been. He supposed that she was coming to terms with the situation, and he was grateful and loved her for that.

At Cariad Elin, the subject of John's loving thoughts was sitting on the double bed and gazing at her face in the dressing-table mirror. The person who stared back at her, she barely recognised: a pale, flat face with dull eyes and an expression of such despair that she could have burst into tears just looking at herself. She felt strange, uncomfortable, not ill exactly, but different, as though all the certainties that she had known were disappearing. For, despite the front she was putting up for John, she could no longer find the equilibrium that had allowed her to cope for so many years.

'You know I can't leave,' she whispered to the glass, 'this is my home.' The pale face nodded back to her and above the dark red head she could make out the reflection of the sky and hillside showing through the window behind. Clouds were forming on the peak, wisps of grey which floated gently around the rocks, drooping and reforming as the wind took them.

'Oh!' she gasped and turned away from the mirror and got off the bed. She had to look properly out of the window. The frame was hard and left a mark on her forehead where she leant against it. But it didn't matter. Nothing mattered any more. Not herself, and not John. It was happening again. The other person was taking over and she had no way of stopping it. But she could delay it for a little longer.

When John came home, she was in the kitchen, making their supper. He looked at her nervously, as he often did these days, but she seemed calm and almost cheerful.

'Hello love,' she said, putting her face up to his for a kiss.

She looked better than she had for days. There was a little colour in her face and her hair was tousled and springy, allowing the light to catch in her curls. *Thank God,* he thought, holding her close and feeling her warm, lithe body next to his, *she's all right.*

If he could have seen her eyes at that moment he wouldn't have been so sanguine. They were dark and glittering with unshed tears, which he would never see. She had been determined that they would be happy for the last days.

'I've been walking on the hillside,' she said lightly. 'It's wonderfully spring-like now.'

He drew back and looked at her, but she was calm and smiled and pulled herself away in order to attend to her cooking. 'How did you get on in Bangor?' she asked. 'Did you find a buyer for the stock?'

That had been his excuse: selling the stock on Matt's behalf, along with the machinery and the Land Rover. It wasn't true, of course. He hadn't spoken to Matt or Lydia since that awful day when she had told him about the sale. They had gone back to Canada and he presumed that they had given instructions to Griff to get rid of everything. He worried constantly that Lark would hear about it in the village, but she hadn't been there for several days and showed little interest now in activity outside the farm. He put on a rueful face and shook his head.

'Nothing doing, I'm afraid. The market is very depressed. Robert thinks it will be better in a few weeks' time, when the lambs have put on a bit of weight.' He could feel a flush rising in his cheeks and walked quickly over to the fireplace and bent to riddle the ashes. He couldn't bear lying to her.

Lark lifted her head and stared at his back. She felt, rather than knew, that he wasn't telling her the truth. But these days she was never sure. It was as if she had forgotten how to use one of her senses.

'Supper's ready.' The words sounded abrupt as she put a chicken and mushroom pie on the table, crisp golden pastry and a wonderful smell of hot chicken and herbs. John bit his lip as he straightened up. Nothing between them flowed any more; they had become like actors in a little play, with conversation which had become shallow and of the moment. He longed to be able to tell her about this afternoon's meeting – it had gone so well – and later, at the solicitor's office, where he had pointed out the terms of his father's will. But he couldn't. It might raise her hopes too much.

Sitting at the table and sniffing appreciatively at the supper dish was a poor substitute for telling her, but it was the best he could do. 'Mm. Smells great,' he said and grinned at her.

'By the way,' he reached into the pocket of his jacket and withdrew a roll of brochures, 'I picked these up at the travel agent. It'll give you an idea of the sort of places in Canada I've been going on about.'

He didn't notice the slight tremor in Lark's hand as she cut a large piece of pie and put it carefully on his plate. How was he to know that her throat had closed and she had no idea of how she would swallow her helping? 'Oh, OK,' she said with difficulty. 'I'll take a look after supper.'

Robert came over at the end of the week Lark was hoeing the little vegetable garden she'd dug in the days before the farm was sold. It would never be planted, she'd accepted that now, but it gave her something to do. Her imagination had already provided a picture of it in full growth. Robert gave her a quick kiss on the cheek. 'Hello, *cariad*,' he said, 'all right?'

She nodded. 'We're fine,' she said and looked up to the cloudy sky from which small raindrops were falling. 'John's having a go at the wall in the river field, if you want him. And I've got some pickle for Bethan to take to the WI stall. Come in the house and get it after you've seen him.'

The sheep had gathered for shelter under the big trees, some still grazing at the poor grass whilst others settled down to chew mechanically. Robert cast a professional eye over them. They looked fit and healthy and the lambs were growing. John and Lark had done well.

'Hello, boy,' he called to John, who was at the

far end of the field piling fresh stones on top of the wall.

The rain was getting heavier and it required a few yells before John heard him and looked up. He waved an arm, and after a final heave at one of the big round stones, he stood back for a moment to examine his efforts before trudging across the field to join Robert under the tree. 'I'm not much cop at building walls,' John said, looking back at his work.

'Oh, it'll do. Not supposed to be an exhibition piece.'

'Mm.' He remained unconvinced and then asked, 'Anyway, what brings you here?'

'Got news for you.' Robert was grinning, and John began to feel a little thrill of excitement buzzing in his stomach.

'What? Tell me.'

Robert paused, trying for the best effect, but eventually said, 'We heard, well, Elfed heard, in the pub. The sale is off. Griff Parry is fit to be tied – lost his commission, hasn't he, and mad as hell. Serves him fucking right!'

John felt his knees buckling and for a moment thought he might sink to the ground. He couldn't believe that his luck had held and that what Evan Price Jones had promised to do had been accomplished so quickly. 'Oh Jesus,' he said, as a big grin widened his mouth. 'What next? Did Elfed say?'

'Well,' Robert lowered his voice although it was hardly necessary. Apart from Lark, who was in the house, they were totally alone. 'Well,' he continued, 'it looks as if it's going for auction.

Sean Harper has pulled out completely, but Elfed's pal who works in the agent's office says that he thinks the Parrys are interested. They'll go for auction because they think they'll get it cheaper. It seems that it's going to happen quickly as well, before anyone else can get a sniff of the place.'

'That's what you said they'd do!' John paced about in excitement, irritating the ewes who lurched to their feet and trotted away. He was ecstatic. Now he had a chance. 'They've played right into our hands.'

Robert was cautious. 'Slow down, for Christ's sake, you idiot. If what you told me before is true, then you've still got to play it cool. Matthew and your wife are not going to hand the place to you on a fucking silver plate.'

'I know, I know, and I'll be careful. Now, you said that Will Llewellyn was still a pal of yours.'

'Comes to see me every summer when he makes his annual pilgrimage to "the old home town". Of course the wife and snotty kids won't leave New York, but Will still comes. Making a fucking fortune, he is.'

'And you're sure he remembers me?'

'I told you. Often talks about us swimming in the quarry. Must be about the most daring thing he's done in his life.'

'Right. Then I'll get in touch with him.' He looked at Robert. 'Keep your fingers crossed.'

Chapter Forty-Two

April had brought unusually peaceful weather to the valley. Mild south-western winds blew in, bringing on the spring flowers and allowing the cold, wet fields to dry out. Lark opened all the windows at Cariad Elin and, in a flurry of sudden activity, hurried round the rooms, cleaning and setting them straight. She sorted out the drawers and packed the rest of Matthew's clothes into cardboard boxes. John addressed them and took them to Bangor, to the General Post Office. While he was out, she packed all the old clothes that had been his mother's, into another box. It was a difficult task and she held the lilac flowered blouse to her face, breathing in the musky scent of lavender for a moment, before gently laying it with the other well-loved garments.

The month that Lydia had given them was nearly up, and in an odd way, it had seemed longer. Each of the passing days had been precious to Lark and she had savoured them, pressing them into her memory, like wild flowers into a diary. She was at peace with herself now, having come to her decision, and able again to be close and loving with John. Their evenings and nights were spent entirely together, talking, laughing even, sharing their experiences of life.

'I missed Mam so much,' John said one evening, sinking back tiredly into his chair and gazing at the fire. 'But I couldn't tell anyone because Dad wouldn't let me talk about it.'

It was the first time he had ever spoken about her and it was as if a huge weight had rolled away. A flood of other memories followed, suppressed for years, but now he ached to speak of them. And Lark listened, smiling when he spoke fondly and holding his hand when the recollections were obviously painful. He stripped his life naked for her.

She told him about her life as a traveller. 'It was fun at first, so unlike anything I'd ever known, and I thought it was what I'd been looking for.'

'But it wasn't.'

'No. Just another mistake.' She heaved a large sigh and shook her head.

'Cariad Elin was what you were looking for, wasn't it?' John asked.

She was sitting on the rug beside his chair and he reached down and put a tentative hand on her shoulder. Her body felt soft and warm and the muscles seemed to be less firm, as though they were melting in the heat of the fire. 'Yes.' It was said simply and without emotion.

He leant forward and took her face gently between his hands. 'Helen, darling. Why does it matter so much? Is the place more important than the people in it?'

She was silent, and as he waited for her to speak, the urgency to know became vital. 'Tell me, *cariad*, tell me. What is it about this place?'

The wind suddenly rose and muttered restlessly in the chimney. The burning logs cracked

411

and split apart into a myriad of blue and yellow sparks, and the room was suddenly lit with strange colours. His hands burnt on her cheeks and he trembled as she slowly reached up and put her slim hands over his. Her gaze was locked onto his. The firelight had turned her eyes into pools of clear amber, so compelling in their depth that he felt that he was moving forward into the strange but familiar country that was being revealed. He could see brown and purple hills and pale green woods, floating clouds above waving pastures. It was Cariad Elin, but different from how he had ever seen it. Utterly exquisite and peaceful. He thought of paradise and nirvana, places that he was sure didn't exist but should, and envied her. He wished with all his heart that he could see his home through her eyes.

As he watched, the picture dissolved and he was looking into water, where bits of stone and pebble moved restlessly on a murky riverbed.

Lark had taken her hands away from his and was carefully touching the skin beneath her eye to wipe away a tear. 'I'll make some tea and toast,' she said, standing and turning towards the range. She moved slowly, and as he watched he was sure that she was floating in slow motion, like the clouds he'd seen in the picture.

He shook his head stupidly, 'Yeah that'll be good,' and leant back, fighting the exhaustion that had come over him. He'd already forgotten his question.

Later, when they lay in the warm bed where the sheets smelt sweetly of the fresh mountain air, he

412

tried to remember the evening's conversation. It was impossible. His mind was full of plans for the auction and how he was going to arrange it. He turned his head and looked at her. She was sleeping, lying still like a figure on one of those mediaeval tombs in an old church. Only her chest moved up and down and a little sighing breath perfumed the air. Now, he thought, *I could tell her. The saving of Cariad Elin is practically assured and we're in little danger of being turned out. And it would make her so happy.* He turned on his side and put a hand gently on her shoulder. *I'll wake her now.* But still he held back, still cautious, preferring to curl his body around hers and allow sleep to dissipate his indecision.

Lydia telephoned the following day. 'The sale is off,' she said abruptly when he picked up the receiver. Lark was out in the yard and John was glad that she wouldn't overhear any of the conversation.

'I know,' he said. 'I heard about it in the pub.'

'The place will be auctioned on Friday. Matthew wants to get on with it before we go on holiday. And he wants as much as he can get for it.' There was a pause as she waited for John to beg or plead for the farm. She was disappointed. He did think about it, briefly, but something in her peremptory tone brought out all the repressed stubbornness that he had inherited from his father.

'I've told the auctioneer that the sale will be off, if you bid. The solicitor has said that in the event of no buyers, the terms of the will would allow

413

Matthew to put it up for rent.'

He barked a short laugh. 'Don't worry, Lydia, I won't bid. I've got better things to do.'

Her voice was cold when she replied. 'Well, honey, make sure they're cheap things. Fred says I'm entitled to half of everything we've got. Including the business!'

'Christ, Lydia, just help yourself. It's what you've always done.'

The phone was slammed down at the other end and John stood for a moment, staring at the old Bakelite handpiece. He wondered how twenty-three years of marriage could have been wiped away so easily, with no vestiges left of the love and passion with which it had begun. Was it entirely his fault? Had he allowed it to die? He didn't know.

He put back the receiver and went through to the kitchen. He looked through the window and saw Lark in the garden, working with a hoe on the little vegetable patch. He stood and watched her for a moment. It was she, he knew, who had restored him and given him back his manhood. His lovely Helen, who, he smiled to himself at the reference, had cast a spell on him.

He wandered outside, still smiling, and stood in the yard, gazing at the view. Soon all that he could see would be his – the hill, the fields, even the sheep. As soon as the sale had gone through, he would buy the share back from Parry. Then he would start again in earnest. *Oh God*, he thought, *it'll be wonderful.*

Lark watched him from under lowered eyelids and was shocked when she noticed the peaceful smile on his face. He had been behaving so strangely during these last days, as though only pretending to be worried. She couldn't read him any more; her body was changing and things that had once seemed so clear were now misted and viewed only through a fog of confusion. At first, she thought that he was being calm to help her, but now she was sure that wasn't it. Maybe he didn't care about losing Cariad Elin. He wasn't even fighting to hold onto it. A wave of nausea washed over her and she could feel the colour draining out of her face. For a moment, she thought she might faint and gripped desperately onto the hoe, pushing it hard into the ground. Her head dropped and she looked down at the soft black earth at her feet. This was her land and his. They belonged here.

'Helen, *cariad*.' He was standing in front of her. 'That was Robert on the phone. He wants me to go with him to Welshpool on Friday. There might be a buyer for the stock – we could get a better deal than just letting Parry take it over. Matthew could probably use the dough.' She looked up and he quickly turned his face away. He was lying.

Neither of them slept much on Thursday night. During the day, John had wandered about the fields, too restless to settle to any task. Lark had walked with him for part of the time, silent and watchful, wanting him to tell her that everything would be all right, but knowing that he wouldn't. She looked desperately about her, at the hillside which glistened in the spring sunshine. The pasture was growing and she felt as though she could see every tender new blade of grass magnified many times, and feel the leaves on the rowans getting ready to burst into life. It was too much, and with a muttered excuse about getting supper, she turned and ran towards the house.

John watched her, feeling her distress and wanting to go after her and take her in his arms, and promise her that everything would be all right. But he was now too deep in the he to help her. The only way out for him was to make sure he got the farm. She would forgive him then for not being honest, and they could restart their lives together. He knew he could never leave her; they were as bound together as two humans could be.

So they lay, wakeful, each with their own thoughts and not able to read or understand the other.

Lark turned on her side and looked out of the window. A thin crescent moon shone faintly in the inky sky and tiny pinpricks of stars punctured the velvet canopy. She had always loved the night. Edges were blurred then and anything might happen.

She felt John's hand on her hip. He was awake, and restless, as he had been all day. For some reason, he was too worked up to sleep and had been turning from side to side since they had gone to bed. She bit her lip. Had she made a terrible mistake? Perhaps he was upset about Cariad Elin after all. Maybe she had been so wrapped up in her own feelings that she hadn't understood him properly. *Poor, poor John,* she thought. *As soon as he realised how much he loves his home, it's taken away from him.* And she remembered how much she loved him and turned and gathered him into her arms.

By the next morning they had regained their old relaxed happiness and sat on either side of the kitchen table eating their breakfast. Last night's lovemaking was still having its effect and they gazed lovingly at each other over large cups of tea.

'I'll be home before supper,' he said, putting down his cup and reaching his hand out to cover hers.

She looked across the room and out of the window. It was another fine mild morning and she could see the sheep dotted on the hillside, white against the green, spread like cotton grass on moorland. 'I can't bear to lose them.' Her voice caught in her throat and she tore her eyes away from the view.

John squeezed her hand. 'Don't upset yourself, *cariad.* They're only old sheep.' He could hear his mother's voice in his head and knew that he had been speaking in Welsh.

Lark nodded. 'Yes,' she replied.

She stood in the yard beside the Land Rover as he prepared to leave. He was dressed in the smart trousers and jacket that he had worn on the day that they'd met.

'Did he ever see her again?' she said slowly.

John was confused. 'Who? Who are you talking about?'

'The farmer and the fairy Elin. Did she ever come back?'

He smiled and took her in his arms. 'What made you suddenly think of that?' He held her tightly and looked over her shoulder to the mountain where the first clouds of the week were beginning to gather. *There'll be rain tonight,* he thought, *rain on my land!*

'Did she?' Lark insisted and then, changing tense, 'Does she?'

'Oh yes,' his voice was soft. 'She comes. She takes them home.'

They stood for a moment, holding onto each other, the only people in a fresh green world. The sun shone and the wind blew sweetly from the west and on the hillside a curlew whistled.

As he drove away, he turned back to look at her. She was standing, face up towards the mountain, tail and slim with her glorious bronze hair dancing about her face. He smiled to himself as he turned onto the road. He could barely wait until this evening. How happy she would be.

Chapter Forty-Three

'His face was a picture!' Robert yelled again, striving to make himself heard above the rattles and grinds of his old van as he drove them along the road from Bangor. He, Elfed and John were squeezed into the front seats, grinning like fools with the excitement of the day.

'Gone to a telephone bidder,' Elfed announced, imitating the solemn voice of the auctioneer.

'What fucking telephone bidder?' Robert squealed, his voice exactly that of Griff Parry, causing the three of them to collapse again in hysterical laughter.

'I thought he might have a heart attack,' John wiped his eyes, 'his face was as white as a sheet. And Llinos – well, it's the first time I've seen her look even remotely flustered.'

'I heard in the pub afterwards that she had got some MP interested in the place – going to turn it into a heritage museum, a sort of historical farm, for fucking tourists. Big on politics, is our Llinos.' Robert grinned. 'My Bethan says she's after a seat in the Assembly.'

John nodded and took a deep breath. The excitement of the day had just about finished him and the best part was yet to come. Robert had urged him to phone Lark from the sale room, but he'd resisted. How could he miss the look on her lovely face when he told her?

'You paid a lot, mind.' Robert had calmed down now as the rain started to patter on the windscreen. He pulled into the lay-by where John had left the Land Rover. 'Well over the current price.'

'It was Parry,' John sighed, 'he wouldn't stop bidding. Became a matter of pride or something.'

'Will you have to give Llewellyn a cut?' Elfed was curious. The machinations that his father and John had cooked up and sworn him to secrecy about had amazed him.

'Christ, I hope not. He said he'd do it for the

hell of it. When I've paid for Cariad Elin and Lydia's had her way, I'll be cleaned out.'

Robert gave him a punch on the arm. 'Just like the rest of us then, boy. Eh?'

Elfed coughed, a little nervously. 'You'll still want the pup, won't you? She's a bit expensive, but a good dog, mind.'

John smiled and nodded at the anxious young man. 'Don't worry, boy *bach*, I'll come and pick her up tomorrow. It's about time Cariad Elin had another dog.'

They stood, the three of them, in the lay-by, grinning and patting each other on the back until John moved towards his car. 'I've got to get back.' He was suddenly nervous. 'I must confess to Lark what we've been up to.'

Robert put a brotherly hand on his friend's arm. 'She'll be fine, man, don't fret.'

John nodded and went to get into his car aware that the other two were watching him. As he started the engine, Robert's large hand appeared through the window.

'Welcome home, John Williams,' he said softly, 'welcome home.'

The few miles home seemed to take forever. John noted every bend in the road, getting more and more excited until he turned past the road sign and knew that all the land on this side of the road was his. Every stick and every stone was his and Lark's and would be their children's after them. Tears filled his eyes and for a moment he was almost unable to drive. The relief of finally getting Cariad Elin was overwhelming.

The rain was coming down harder now,

streaming across the windscreen in waves, and he switched the wiper blades to a faster rate so that he would be able to get a clear look at the farm buildings. It would be like seeing them for the first time and he craned his neck to look through the gap in the high hedge.

The house and barns were there, nestling in the lee of the hill, old grey granite walls and slate roofs glistening in the rain. His heart gave a great lurch and he felt sick with excitement.

She wasn't in the yard to greet him, but the rain was driving into his face now and he couldn't have expected her to be there. He jumped out of the Land Rover, slammed the door with a crash and hurried in through the scullery door.

'Helen!' he called. 'I'm back.'

The kitchen was empty and his greeting echoed back to him. 'Helen! Where are you, *cariad?*' he called again and swiftly looked over to the fireplace to where she normally sat. Her chair was empty, and as his heart began to beat faster and faster, he saw that the fire was almost out and the grate was gloomy and cool. He turned swiftly and ran to the hall door, throwing it open with such force that the old hinges creaked, and sped up the narrow stairs. The landing was dark and the bedrooms echoed his footsteps noisily as he quickly threw open each door and looked inside.

She's outside, I must have missed her, he thought, and ran down the groaning stairs and out into the yard, calling for her as he peered into the barns and sheds. In the poultry house, the hens clucked indignantly, and the sheep on the hillside looked up expectantly from their grazing as he walked towards the gate. He looked up to the peak but the cloud had come down and he could only see for a few yards. 'Oh God,' he whispered, 'oh my good God.' And he turned and ran back to the house.

He hadn't noticed before that the kitchen table was laid for supper and now he smelt the comforting aroma of cooked meat coming from the range. For the briefest second, hope returned and he was able to tell himself, *She'll be back in a minute*. Then his eyes fell upon a piece of paper resting on the table between the knife and fork, where he normally sat. 'Oh sweet Jesus!' he breathed, as with a sinking heart he recognised Lark's writing.

He slowly reached out his hand to take it, but he couldn't make his fingers go all the way, and he stood looking at the paper while the light in the room began to fade.

'I'd better get the fire going.' He spoke out loud to the empty room and he noticed wearily that his voice sounded exactly like his father's. Ignoring the letter, he went over to the grate and riddled the ashes, before placing a few small sticks onto the remaining bit of fire. It was only after the logs had caught and yellow tongues of flame licked at the fire again, that he picked up the letter and brought it back to his chair beside the hearth.

'John, *cariad anwyl*,' she had written,

Please don't be hurt and angry with me, but I have to leave. I have fallen in love and cannot live peacefully without my passion.

I feel like the fairy woman who thought she could leave the place she loved and settle for second best. The legend tells that she couldn't, and now I know that neither can I.

I love you so much, John, but I also love the farm, which in so many ways is utterly part of you. I tried to show you how I felt, but I don't think you understood. Now, I am frightened that when we leave here, which we must, our love will lose its magic. Second best would not be possible for us.

Think of me sometimes when you are living amongst those high white mountains where you plan to build your new home. I will always be yours and will be waiting for you, when you come home.

Be happy, my love,
Helen.

The letter fluttered to the floor and lay on the rug beside his feet. There was a pain in his head, a throbbing which threatened to explode. His whole body ached and he felt old and tired. The fire burned quietly in the grate and he put a hand down casually to pat the dog's head. But that was what his father had done, and he had no dog. He had no one.

It was then that he cried, 'Oh Elin, my *cariad*, don't leave me. I can't live all the long years without you. Come home to me, Elin.' And as the tears fell unchecked down his cheeks, he sprang up and ran out into the yard.

'Elin,' he howled, his eyes straining to the mountain peak where the mist danced and swirled in dark grey shreds, 'come home, come home, my cariad. I need you.' But his words were stolen by the wind and taken up to the high moorland where only the plovers listened and whistled a sad reply.

Exhaustion overtook him and he turned back to the house and went inside, back to his chair, where he closed his eyes and lay back until the tears dried in silvered streaks on his face.

The wind had died in the chimney when he rose from the chair. The room was dark and he went from lamp to lamp, switching them on and admiring the pools of light which illuminated the old room. He found the oven gloves hanging over the rail on the Rayburn and bent down to open the door and withdraw the casserole that Lark had made for him. It smelt good and he sniffed appreciatively as he put it carefully on the heavy mat on the table. There was a new loaf in the bread bin and he cut himself a large slice. He had a moment's worry about where to find the serving spoon, but it was there, in the drawer where they had always kept it, and he ladled himself a large helping onto one of the blue and white dishes. Before taking his meal to the table, he took off his jacket and pulled the folded newspaper from its pocket. Then he sat in his place at the table, eating his supper and studying the livestock prices.

And far away, safely enclosed, the boy floated in the dark, sucking his tiny thumb and dreaming of green fields and sheep-dotted hills. His time would come.

Epilogue

The pup galloped after him, stopping now and then to sniff and burrow into interesting tussocks of pasture. He made pretend chases at the occasional sheep, but John curbed him with a sharp word and the young dog dropped his head and came back to heel. It was going to take time to train him properly, but Elfed was doing that. The pup darted off again and John watched him running ahead, stumbling over rocks and rolling over. He smiled. Elfed was going to have a job on his hands.

A tiny cloud appeared in the aquamarine sky, white and fluffy and now beginning to shred in the slight breeze which blew in gently from the sea. He could smell the ozone and breathed in deeply, feeling the cold fresh air fill his body and revitalise his tired cells. He reached the stone ledge and, with a welcome sigh, sat down to admire the sun shining over the sea and the blue mound that was Anglesey. The pup jumped up beside him and leant against his side.

John was glad he'd made the climb. The air was different up here, and when he looked back down at Cariad Elin he was entranced by the beauty of the view. The buildings shimmered in the evening light, the stone softening to silver and the windows glinting like jewels. The trees in the river field were at their most lush and afforded generous shelter for the cattle. He could just make out the swish of the bullocks' tails as they flicked the evening insects away. Above him, the little shredded cloud had covered the peak and he looked to the west to see if more were on their way, but the sky was clear and pale. He turned his face back towards the peak, and as he watched, the cloud became a form.

Oh no, his mind cried. *It's too soon. I can't leave, not yet.* But he had been brought up on the legend and now knew it to be true.

His legs felt numb and he knew that he couldn't rise from the rocky slab to greet her. *'Cariad?'* he whispered. 'Have you come for me?' And he strained to see the face of the fairy woman who was walking steadily along the sheep track towards him.

'John?' Lark's thickened figure blotted out the cloud behind her and her voice was muffled in his ears as though he was only hearing it in his mind. 'You stayed… I've just found out.'

He couldn't speak, couldn't answer her or take in what she was saying. He knew he was dying and was relieved that she had come for him – the fairy Elin, who would take him to the summit of existence before he shredded into the mist. There was acceptance, even gratitude, and he waited calmly for her next move.

Should he have been able to feel her hand on his shoulder and see the clear amber lights in her eyes? Why was the hand that she put on his cheek warm, and the smile that parted her perfect lips so joyful? The cloud was dispersing and she stood there, a solid figure, so familiar and so longed for.

'John! It's me. I've come home.'

And then he held her, realising, as he put his arms around her waist, that he was alive and she had changed. She was no longer the solitary girl whom he had loved beyond all sense. She was Elin, who would be his wife. There would be a family at Cariad Elin. His family.

The publishers hope that this book has given you enjoyable reading. Large Print Books are especially designed to be as easy to see and hold as possible. If you wish a complete list of our books please ask at your local library or write directly to:

Magna Large Print Books
Magna House, Long Preston,
Skipton, North Yorkshire.
BD23 4ND

This Large Print Book for the partially sighted, who cannot read normal print, is published under the auspices of

THE ULVERSCROFT FOUNDATION

THE ULVERSCROFT FOUNDATION

... we hope that you have enjoyed this Large Print Book. Please think for a moment about those people who have worse eyesight problems than you ... and are unable to even read or enjoy Large Print, without great difficulty.

You can help them by sending a donation, large or small to:

**The Ulverscroft Foundation,
1, The Green, Bradgate Road,
Anstey, Leicestershire, LE7 7FU,
England.**
or request a copy of our brochure for more details.

The Foundation will use all your help to assist those people who are handicapped by various sight problems and need special attention.

Thank you very much for your help.